MISTRESS

OF

BONES

MISTRESS

OF

BONES

MARIA Z. MEDINA

MAGPIE

Magpie Books
An imprint of
HarperCollins*Publishers* Ltd
1 London Bridge Street
London SE1 9GF

www.harpercollins.co.uk

HarperCollins*Publishers*
Macken House,
39/40 Mayor Street Upper,
Dublin 1, D01 C9W8
Ireland

First published by HarperCollins*Publishers* Ltd 2025

1

Designed by Devan Norman
Sword illustration © Vector_Line/Shutterstock

A catalogue record for this book is available from the British Library.

ISBN: 978-0-00-877419-6 (HB)
ISBN: 978-0-00-877420-2 (TPB)

Set in Perpetua Std

Printed and bound in the UK using 100% renewable electricity by CPI Group (UK) Ltd

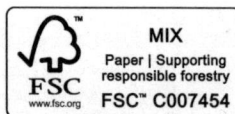

MIX
Paper | Supporting
responsible forestry
FSC
www.fsc.org
FSC™ C007454

TO ADVENTUROUS HEARTS AND
DETERMINED SOULS

The Lord Death and the Lord Life stared down at the barren land.

Their creatures would form and rise; they would wriggle and they would try. And then they would die.

So?

They raised the continents.

And the Lord Life thrived and the Lord Death gained meaning, and so did the other gods keeping vigil. Turning their bones into chains, they anchored the continents and seas in place.

Most agree the gods made the sacrifice willingly.

Some believe they regretted it almost immediately.

I

DEATH

NINE YEARS EARLIER

Azul del Arroyo didn't fully know what would happen when she set out to bring her older sister back to life, but since she was ten, she didn't much care.

It took courage to sneak down to the inn's cellar, even more so to saw off Isadora's cold finger. Azul's dagger was too blunt, Isadora's rapier of no use, but Azul did it, and she rolled the digit in her handkerchief before hiding it inside the pouch hanging from her neck.

She waited and stayed silent, because she knew her gift was strange and that nobody would thank her for using it. And she prayed to all five gods, but especially to the Lord Death, to allow her sister to come back from his domain just as the chicken had when Azul was seven, and her favorite cat when she was nine, and the couple of mice and the little snake at some point in between.

The Lord Death must've listened, because a day after she returned home to the small Sancian town of Agunción, Isadora was at her family's door, her memories after falling sick with the fever completely gone. The doctor at the inn must've made a horrible mistake and sent her straight home, Azul assured everyone as only a ten-year-old could. After all, Isadora was alive and free of illness. And if her sister had walked from the meadow of tall grass behind the house—like the chicken and the cat and the mice and the snake—instead of stepping out of a traveling carriage, well, Azul wasn't about to confess it.

Because there was nothing Azul wouldn't do for Isadora.

THE PRESENT

"There's been a suspicious death, Emissary."

Virel Enjul, Emissary of the Lord Death, looked up from his sketching—bones, of course, free of flesh and tendons and blood. They were meant to become an armor, and sweat was enough of a stench to carry around.

The messenger at the entrance of the room wore all his corresponding flesh and tendons and blood tucked into snug breeches and a long waistcoat. Sancian fashion, come to intrude into Valanje, as if, unable to conquer its neighboring country across the floating sea, Sancia had decided to invade through clothing instead.

Enjul didn't care for these fashions, but they didn't bother him either. They would die, just as this man would, and something else would take their place. The Lord Death was supreme, after all. Nothing escaped his reign.

"Come forth, and speak," Enjul ordered, abandoning the sketch and focusing his attention on the man. Natural decay had already taken hold of the messenger's body, death inevitable for everything that was ever born or grown.

All Emissary Enjul ever saw was the death surrounding him.

The man approached the emissary's desk, a sturdy thing used to the weight of thick, unread volumes and ledgers. He met Enjul's eyes for a heartbeat, then focused on the emissary's chest. "A suspicious death was reported on the docks at Diel."

Diel—Valanje's Pride, Valanje's Treasure. The country's southernmost city built on untouched Anchor—the gods' bones. Another difference with Sancia, where they had no respect for Anchor and wore it on their houses and their persons as if they had the right to own the gods.

But *that* fashion would never take hold in Valanje—Enjul and others like him would make sure of it. "And?"

"Your . . . your presence has been requested by Rudel Serunje, Emissary."

All who entered the Order, the service of the Lord Death, studied death in all its forms—divine, natural, unnatural, premature—but only those with a piece of the Lord Death himself, those blessed to see the decay of death and feel the god's guidance, became emissaries. And emissaries did not investigate petty sailor scuffles, even if they occurred in great Anchor cities.

Enjul's thoughts must have shown on his expression, because the messenger hurried to elaborate on the request: "Serunje, Valanje's Eyes, was in charge of an envoy to Sancia's capital, to Cienpuentes, and had returned home with the Sancian delegates when the death occurred. An emissary was demanded, sir. You are the closest one."

"A Valanjian's death?"

"One of the Sancians, Emissary."

Sancians, Enjul thought in irritation, *bringing their problems and their disrespect of the gods along with their fashions.* He stood, slipping his latest drawing into the leather-bound folder holding the rest of his sketches.

Strange manners of death had always appealed to him, but in his experience, what others considered strange and suspicious only ever amounted to trite and mundane. A *suspicious* stabbing, a *suspicious* poisoning—the death simple enough, the culprit the only thing suspect. Such things were not his purview but a guard's.

Rudel Serunje had purposely made his message vague, either out of a need for secrecy or to incite curiosity. Since nobody would think to toy with an emissary of the Lord Death, Enjul would honor the request.

"Did you witness this death?" he asked.

"No, Emissary, but there are rumors." The messenger swallowed. "I heard strange magic was involved. That the body was there and then not. Reduced to green ashes and dirt, they say."

And just like that, Virel Enjul, Emissary of the Lord Death, found his heart in a tight grip and a growl in his throat.

"A malady?" he demanded, disgust pulling his mouth into a snarl.

The man backed up to the door. "Yes, perhaps, Emissary, sir."

"Have a mount ready. I leave within the hour."

Enjul took his sketches and tore through the hallways toward his quarters. Maladies. Rare, so very rare there had been only whispers of one in his lifetime.

Long had Enjul heard the rumors of the malady taking up residence in Cienpuentes; long had he wished to put an end to it. Sancians didn't seem to care, just like they didn't care about defiling the gods' bones on which they'd built their capital, and he wished to correct their mistake. But his emissary duties belonged with Valanje, the land of the Lord Death, not Sancia, where belief in the Blessed Heart and the Lady Dream reigned supreme. Infuriating that they thought these two lesser gods amounted to more than the Lord Death or the Lord Life. Had Death and Life not created the Blessed Heart, the Lady Dream, and the Lord Nightmare? Had they not plucked the moons from Hope and Despair's remains?

Now this malady might have arrived in Valanje. Now Enjul might have it within his grasp, and he'd see it erased from this world, thrown into the understars and Void beneath the lands. A spark ignited inside him, spreading warmth inside his body and hastening his steps. His god agreed.

The trip to the Anchor city of Diel took two uneventful days, eastward across the low mountains, and no matter how often Enjul traveled here, the sight still dazzled. For how could a city built on the gods' bones fail to impress?

Diel rose from the land, a wide peak of glittering blue Anchor covered by houses of all colors and sizes. It stood, alone and magnificent, the high point of an enormous valley of farmland extending from the mountains and the thick forests in the far north and south to the sea at Diel's eastern footstep.

It was a good thing the sea separated the great island of Valanje from Sancia and the continent of Luciente. The gods' blood limited the reach of Sancia's rotten beliefs, the maelstroms making passage across impossible but for narrow routes south and north.

The closer he got to Diel, the more magnificent the city became, the blue rock of its base almost too bright for the eye to take. For someone like Enjul, who was always aware of the signs of death on every person crossing his path—every flower, every plant—such a display of rock was a welcome respite from the rot. That the Anchor was Lord Death's own bones only made it even more magnificent.

Farmers and travelers walked by the roadsides to make space for riders and carts, their clothing a simple, dustier version of what Diel's citizens wore. No doublets, no cumbersome skirts for them; no velvety plumes attached to their hats and no half capes. No elegant rapiers or long swords.

Soon the dirt path turned into the intricate mosaics of flagstone covering the streets winding up the peak of Diel. Buildings grew in elegance, the glittering blue of the gods' bones peeking here and there, undisturbed.

Enjul dismounted and walked toward the grand building topping Diel, where the slopes were so steep it was dangerous for horses to traverse. Valanjians hid at his approach, and guards stood at attention. No words were needed to grant him access into the Great Council House. Here in Valanje, in the land of the Lord Death, an emissary needed no permission.

Rudel Serunje was waiting for him in one of the parlors, tall and lean. He wore a waistcoat over his traditional long shirt, the lower folds falling all the way to the knee. The rings around his golden-brown irises were a warm gray—narrow, friendly. They didn't clash like Enjul's wide, thick, deep violet ones. They made him approachable. People in Sancia, used as they might be to the differences in Valanjian eyes, wouldn't gawk at Rudel as they might at Enjul. *It must have served him well in Cienpuentes*, Enjul thought, *made him forgettable and easy to underestimate.*

Serunje stood and gave Enjul a slow, respectful bow of his head, belying the sudden tension in his body. "Emissary."

"Valanje's Eyes, explain the situation."

Serunje offered a cup of water. Enjul refused with a sharp move of his hand, and the Eye placed the cup back on the side table.

"First, I must explain how we came to be at Diel's port, Emissary," Serunje said with no little wariness.

"Proceed as you see wise," Enjul conceded, hiding his irritation. His hands itched with the need to find this malady, to have it under his purview. Surely it must be nothing but the shadow of a person, a wraith that had somehow gained flesh and bones. Brittle, like its existence. Easily dispatched under his hands or his sword.

"I was sent to Cienpuentes as one of our . . . emissaries to their court," Serunje began with a dry twist to his tone. "They are appreciative of our—Valanje's—success without the need for Anchor and would love nothing more than to learn our secrets, especially after the Anchor mining ban."

In Enjul's opinion, about the only smart thing Sancians had done since the raising of the lands, and that only after Girende, one of their Anchor cities, had eaten itself into a hole and fallen into the Void. "I heard they might overturn the Anchor mining ban, now that their queen is dead."

How long until they took all the Anchor they could reach and the whole of Luciente caved in on itself? The gods' bones kept the floating continents in place above the Void—without them, they would fall. Why were Sancians so intent on mining their home to its doom?

No wonder a malady had risen there. No wonder the poison of their greed had taken human form and sought to spread.

"Even if they do," Serunje said, "the truth is that they are running out of Anchor. Those with a brain in their head seek other ways to add to their fortune, improve their crops, or discover other ways to streamline their businesses. They have reached out to their east as well as to Valanje. We find this might benefit us, expand our trade in Sancia and beyond."

"Free passage across Sancia to the rest of Luciente?" Enjul asked, though if he was impressed his tone gave no hint of it. There was no going around Sancia, not for Valanje. The sea didn't reach far enough around Sancia for them to access other countries in Luciente, and there was nothing beyond the sea but the free fall of the Void. "You aim high."

"If not free, then at much reduced fees. To this end, Cienpuentes put together a group of representatives to return our visit. One or two with promise, the rest their court's discards. On our way, we stopped at Agunción, where we picked up two additional travelers, and from there we traveled to the coast, where we crossed the sea to Diel."

Enjul hadn't moved from his position by the window. The view of the Sea of Eyes was alluring, but that wasn't the reason he had chosen his spot. Sunlight enhanced the view of his bone breastplate: a reminder of who he was and why he was there, a reminder that one couldn't escape death. "You have explained your arrival. Perhaps it's time we concentrate on the reason I was summoned."

Serunje grasped his hands in front of his waist, the first obvious sign of nerves since Enjul's arrival. "I must remind you, Emissary, this is an extremely delicate matter. The death of a Sancian in Valanje is not a good way to begin a deepening of the relationship between both countries."

"You called me to investigate a suspicious death." *Malady* was on the tip of Enjul's tongue, but he held back. He must not put ideas into the other man's head. Enjul would look at the facts, then decide. His pulse thrummed at the possibility that Cienpuente's malady had truly arrived to his lands. Wishing did not make things true, he warned himself. He had warned himself of this many times since leaving for Diel. "I must know the details."

Serunje gave him a fast look, then focused on one of the paintings on the wall: Diel in all its glory, with the orange and pink farms, the richness of auburn and yellows on the buildings, the deep green of the sea and all the little ships anchored to its docks. And, of course, the brilliant blue of Anchor. "I barely believe it myself, but, Emissary, I would not have requested your help if the matter hadn't been this strange. As part of the envoy alighted from the boats, one of the young women we met in Agunción turned to dirt right there on the docks."

Ah. Enjul inhaled sharply. "You were witness to this?"

"I had already disembarked and was organizing the deckhands to take care of our trunks when the commotion made me look. All that remained of the woman was her clothes and a pile of green-brown dirt."

Enjul took a step forward, and Serunje a matching step back. "Who witnessed this, then?"

"The woman's younger sister was by her side, along with others from the envoy. The sailors from the boats bringing them from the ship were there as well as a few men from our guard."

"May she not have fallen into the water? A trick of the light?"

"Everyone swears the woman was on the dock, then turned green and simply . . . crumbled."

"A lie to push Valanje into a lesser position during these trade talks."

"No, Emissary Enjul. The guards are loyal. Besides, there is no way someone could've orchestrated such a thing, paid all those witnesses."

Enjul dared not hope, but hope rose anyway. "What is your explanation?"

Serunje tugged at his brown hair, gathered at his nape like a horse's tail over his shoulder. "I wish I knew. De Mial has been demanding an explanation, so I requested your presence. I've kept the group here, isolated those I could."

"De Mial?"

"The delegation's leader, an ambassador with some status within Cienpuentes's court. He is the reason we took on the two women. He grew affectionate toward the older sister while we rested and re-stocked in Agunción, and the sisters considered the trip some sort of adventure. From what I can tell, they had never traveled to Valanje before. Our envoy made for an alluring prospect—secure travels and engaging company."

"And you allowed this?"

"I saw no harm to it. They were obvious locals, not spies sent to interfere."

"Is there a suspect?"

"None that I can discern. Everyone was shocked, and the sister, as you can imagine, was beside herself. She's been insisting on returning to Sancia, but I couldn't allow her to leave. She has been restricted to the guest quarters here for the time being."

"Did you secure the dirt and the clothes?"

"They await your inspection."

Enjul gave a curt nod of approval. "Go back to the incident. Describe everything that happened in as much detail as you can."

"We had taken the boats to one of the smaller docks. Myself and three of our escort alighted first. Another boat carrying Isadora del Arroyo—the deceased—and her sister, Azul, along with Ambassador de Mial and his sister as well as Nereida de Guzmán, another member of the envoy, began to disembark behind me. De Guzmán went first, I was told, then the younger Del Arroyo, followed by the elder. That's when it happened. I heard the cries, turned around, and found the pile of dirt and Azul del Arroyo digging into it. I called for order and for the guards to stop her, but . . ." Serunje frowned, as if recalling something unexpected.

"All the details, Rudel Serunje."

"When the guards took ahold of Del Arroyo and brought her away from her sister's . . . remains—no. No," he corrected himself. "She wasn't keen to keep by her sister. She was trying to return to the boat. It was De Guzmán who stopped her. Del Arroyo managed to free herself, but by then I was there. She demanded to return to Sancia, and when I told her she must stay until we investigated the situation, she addressed De Mial and begged for him to do something and allow her to return to Sancia."

"She would leave her sister's remains?"

"Her words were, 'Don't you want to see my sister again? Help me get to her bones.' Or something of the sort."

Enjul took another step forward. "Is that what she said? Are you certain?"

Serunje paled but stood his ground. "Yes, I'm sure of it. She was very distraught."

Sharp satisfaction coursed through Enjul's blood. He smiled, relishing the warmth it brought. "Tell me more about this Azul del Arroyo. How old is she? Is she from Cienpuentes?"

"She is about nineteen years of age. I do not believe the family comes from Cienpuentes, although I was told their mother spends most of the year away. The mother is said to be quite beautiful and earns her money as a surrogate. I asked about them before granting them permission to travel with us, naturally. They own a good house in Agunción, and don't lack for money. The older sister is—was—known to enjoy the tavern and duels at dawn. Good with her rapier, I was told. The younger is never far away, although she doesn't seem to participate in the sport."

Serunje's tone softened when he continued, "I had some talks with Azul del Arroyo on the ship. She's a curious thing, eager to learn and travel but shackled by sisterly loyalty. I believe if it weren't for her sister, she would've adventured into the world already. The older sister isn't keen to travel, apparently. Wasn't."

Nineteen years. Enjul savored the morsel of age in his mind, intrigued and a little awed. Was that all it took to go against your gods in such an outrageous manner? How reckless the woman must be, how disgusted at everything the gods had to offer. Sancians, showing their lack of true faith once again.

"I will meet with her now."

Serunje frowned at the hard edge of Enjul's tone. "Emissary, she's a distraught young woman mourning her sister. Be gentle, if you must talk. It would do us no good if she complains to Ambassador de Mial. Will you not talk to him first instead? Assure him we are doing all we can to investigate the situation?"

"Del Arroyo first."

Serunje pursed his lips into a disapproving line, but spoke no further. Enjul followed him through the hallways and stairs of the building, disregarding the muted signs of comfort and riches surrounding him, until they stood in front of one of the guest quarters. His gaze remained fixed on the door, anticipation rolling his insides. He allowed it, savored it—it did not come often.

First Serunje knocked, of which Enjul didn't approve. He wished to see the malady's reaction at their sudden presence, drink in its shock and surprise and fear.

Then Serunje opened the door, and the young woman—not a wraith or a string of flesh held up by brittle bones, as he'd imagined— stared defiantly back at them, dressed in a shirt and breeches too big for her, brown wavy hair loose over her shoulders and back, a single drop of Anchor hanging from one ear. He watched her brown eyes widen at the sight of him, and forced his not to do the same, forced the shock down his throat to simmer inside his gut.

Virel Enjul, Emissary of the Lord Death, had taken a good look at Azul del Arroyo, and the lands tilted on their Anchor stands.

For she had so much *life*.

II

AZUL

Azul del Arroyo had once as a young child sneaked into the kitchen and stolen a piece of chicken. The wing had been delicious, the resulting bare bones a source of guilt. She had sought to assuage it by burying it in the yard—the bone, not the guilt, but perhaps both—and that's when she had first felt the singing in her heart, the excitement, the *need* to follow this instinct to wherever it led.

So, she had let it happen, curious to see what would come of it. And something had slipped out of Azul—although she wouldn't identify what until much later. The mud around her sunken hands had turned gray, the nearby weeds brown, as the chicken bone had grown other bones under her fingers. Bones and flesh and skin and *life*.

And then the animal had clucked, shocking Azul into releasing it.

But Azul had gone after it, caught this revived chicken, and brought it back to the kitchen. She meant to kill it and put it back in the pantry so nobody would notice her small theft. She had watched their cook prepare chickens plenty of times. She could do it. But the moment she had chopped its head off, the chicken's flesh had turned back into dirt and its blood into mud, with not even the original bone to be found. The life Azul had given back on a whim, taken on another.

Azul had told no one, had rarely touched another bone until her favorite cat had run under a cart, until her pet snake grew hungry and then fell limp and unmoving. Until Isadora had died, aged fourteen.

Until now.

Because now she must go back to Isadora's remains—to Sancia and the ossuary keeping them in the city of Monteverde—steal one of her bones, and bring her sister back to life.

Any other option was unfathomable.

But they had locked Azul in a room in one of the huge buildings on the very top of the Anchor city. The room was big, comfortable, with wide windows opening into the valley, the sprawling city a sharp drop of three or four floors below. A cliff of a building, half carved into the mountain itself, even if there was no hint of Anchor in its bare, whitewashed walls.

A big bed occupied a corner near an empty brazier, and a delicate writing desk and upholstered chair graced the opposite side of the room. A wardrobe and a settee around a low table finished the ensemble. Her trunk had been brought in, but Azul hadn't touched it. Instead, she had chosen to dig into Isadora's, changing her dirty travel clothes for one of her sister's billowing shirts and a pair of breeches a tad too big for her slighter frame. Azul had forced Isadora's earring, saved from the pile of green dirt that had been her sister's body, into her own earlobe, discarding the simple hoop their mother had once gifted her.

"We can't accept their invitation," Isadora had said in an uncharacteristically curt tone.

"It would be a waste not to," Azul had mused, like she didn't quite care—as if, after so many years stuck around Aguncíon, the urge to explore the continents weren't an itch under her skin that had finally blistered open.

"How can we trust them?"

"They come from the Cienpuentes court. How can they not be trusted?" Sensible words. Smooth. Designed to pick at her sister's strange defiance of what was a perfectly sound plan.

"And how will we come back?"

"Diagol told me they'd arrange for guards to come back with us." Azul had kept her irritation under control, willing Isadora to come back to her normal self, to the sister who demanded crossing rapiers outside the tavern if anyone so much as looked at Azul the wrong way. "The route is well traveled. De Guzmán

was once the queen's lover—you've seen her, with her rapier and elegant shoulder plate. Nobody would dare attack her."

Still, Isadora had shaken her head. *"I don't know, Azulita. It doesn't feel right, going to Valanje. Not while Mother is away."*

Azul had smiled. *"Mother said she would take us on trips, and where is she now? Having another baby. We've traveled before, Isadora. What's one more trip?"*

"We've never gone that far."

"It won't be far once we're there."

"I don't want to go, Azul," Isadora had finally said.

And Azul had not listened. She had nagged until Isadora gave in. She had put her curiosity above Isadora's wishes.

She should have listened.

Servants came to bring her food, fill her basin, or empty the chamber pot. They refused to answer her questions or take messages. The guard posted outside would turn the lock after they were done.

How was she to make her way back to Sancia if nobody would talk to her? If she couldn't convince them to hand over the key?

Azul sat facing the door, playing solitaire on the low table and getting ready to shove the next visiting servant aside and try her luck with the guard, when the door opened, and Nereida de Guzmán appeared on the threshold.

Azul dropped her cards at her appearance, too surprised to hide her expression. "Sirese De Guzmán!" she exclaimed. At last, someone to be convinced.

Nereida de Guzmán, part of the Cienpuentes envoy to Valanje, watched her with something hard and cold and calculating gleaming in her eyes. A courtier's usual demeanor, or something else? Nobody had been able to explain exactly why she had joined Sancia's delegation, except perhaps as a sign of goodwill—here was a noble important enough to become the queen's lover, part of a Sancian family powerful enough to make things happen both in Sancia and Valanje.

Why was she here now?

Azul clenched her jaw but held on to hope that she might finally get some help. She had been holding on to too many things the last few days—rage, composure, sanity—and would not fail now. Roughly stacking the playing cards into a pile, she retreated to perch on the chair by the desk and waved toward the settee.

"Please, come in," she said, as if the woman were an honored guest and these Azul's quarters.

Nereida sat on the settee with an innate elegance that spoke of wealth and status. It shone on her finely tailored breeches, the fabric of her white shirt, her exquisitely embroidered green vest, the bejeweled hair combs holding her long, curling midnight-black hair away from her tan face. No Anchor peeked from her hair jewelry—only silver and precious green stones.

Valanjians, they had been warned during the crossing of the Sea of Eyes, did not like overly ostentatious displays of mined Anchor. Being from the countryside, Azul and Isadora had been awed by the many heavy blue necklaces, Anchor-and-pearls bracelets, and ornate brooches adorning their traveling companions on the way over. They all rested in the depths of the nobles' trunks now, as if being hidden under their shirts and linens made their existence any less damning to Valanjians.

What a shock to see De Guzmán now. Everyone else in the envoy had been friendly enough, but Nereida had shown no interest in the trip, her companions, a good talk, or anything beyond the edge of her upturned nose.

"Sirese Del Arroyo," she said in that cool tone of hers. She turned slightly, her hand reaching for something by her hip but finding only empty space. Abandoning the quest, she focused on Azul. "You are being treated well?"

Unwilling to waste time with niceties, Azul leaned forward and asked, "Why won't they allow me outside the room?"

"They are suspicious of the happenings at the dock."

Azul's nails dug into the fabric of her breeches. "My sister has died. They have no right to keep me a prisoner while I mourn."

De Guzmán's assessing gaze seemed to miss no detail, and Azul felt like a strange creature on display, an oddity that had caught someone's attention and must be studied and measured to see if it fit into a certain frame.

"A curious end, your sister's," Nereida said.

Azul had expected comments like this from the moment they brought her to this room and had prepared her answer. "An act of the gods." People were happy enough to blame the gods for all their misfortunes, even those who didn't think them real beyond their bones, so why shouldn't they bear this blame as well?

"Is that so?" Nereida asked, calm as the night sky.

"You were there the same as I was, Sirese De Guzmán. Nothing touched my sister. There was no assailant, no bolt or arrow. She just . . ." Azul squeezed her eyes hard, her voice failing under the weight of the fact. "She just passed on to the Lord Death's embrace."

"If there is anything . . ." A rare trace of hesitation entered Nereida's voice. "Anything you want to confess, I will not share it."

"Confess?" Azul inhaled sharply. Did the woman think she had murdered her own sister? Or . . . Cold sweat gathered on her lower back. Did Nereida suspect her secret? How? She had done nothing for years. How could this woman from the Cienpuentes court, so far removed from her and Isadora's life in Agunción, have any inkling of what she could do? No. De Guzmán was only digging around. "There is nothing to confess, sirese, and I don't want to speak about the matter any longer. I wish to mourn my sister in front of the Lady Dream, in Sancia, where she spent her life."

And if her voice hitched at that last word, she hoped Nereida de Guzmán hadn't noticed.

"They have sent for an Emissary of the Lord Death," the woman said.

Azul recoiled. "No! Why?"

No other god had emissaries; only Valanjians felt the need to represent the Lord Death with such zealousness.

Nereida's gaze drifted around the bland room until it fell to the stack of cards on the low table and the crude design on the front of one. Isadora had drawn it when she first won the deck on a dare. Oh, how they had laughed at Isadora's lack of artistry!

"Why an emissary?" Azul insisted through the lump forming in her throat.

"They want your sister's death explained." The maelstrom of disgust and dread curling Azul's stomach was nowhere to be seen on Nereida's expression. She might as well be a piece of flesh-colored Anchor—cold, beautiful, and above mundane concerns such as death. "They will keep us here for a few more days while the emissary conducts their investigation."

Azul burst out of the chair. "They can't do that!" She paced between the screens separating them from the bed to one of the windows looking onto the fields and the forest and the mountains. To the screen. To the window. Finally, she whirled toward the settee.

"Sirese De Guzmán, can't you do anything?" she pleaded. "I need to get back to Sancia. To Monteverde." To Isadora's bones. To Isadora. To the end of the dread eating her from the inside out that would only be satisfied when her sister was standing in front of her, alive and safe. "Surely they can't simply hold us as long as they please? You're an official envoy, do something."

Nereida held her gaze, unfazed by her desperation. "There are more important matters involved in this visit than your sister's death."

Azul felt slapped. The Del Arroyo name was solid enough, but Isadora and Azul by themselves had not enough value to risk whatever negotiations the envoy had been sent to secure. If one of their half siblings high in Cienpuentes politics had come with them, would her wishes have carried more weight?

Azul lifted her chin. "What is it, then," she asked, "this matter that is so important?"

The door opened, and the outside guard appeared. "Your visit must come to an end now, miss."

Nereida stood, giving the cards a last lingering look. "The Anchor ban."

With those words she exited the room, leaving Azul to punch the mattress until the burning rage had spent itself and dispassionate composure filled its place. Let the emissary come, she dared the city sprawling under her windows. She would deal with him. What could he find but a strange accident of nature? An act of the gods? People did not turn into dirt. Azul would answer his questions, charm him if needed, then talk her way into freedom.

For could she not bring the dead back to life? She could also make this fanatic of death acquiesce to her will.

III

AZUL

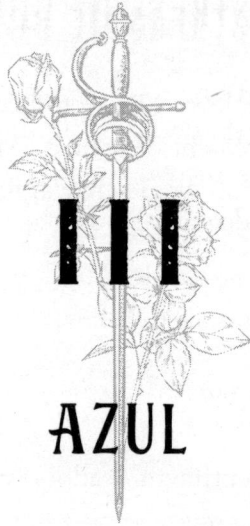

NINE YEARS AND A FEW MONTHS EARLIER

Azul sat on the grass, her back to a tree while Pica, her favorite cat, lay curled up by her side. Her family's whitewashed house rose in the distance, short and square, no windows to be seen. They were all inside, opening into the tiny patio her mother adored so much whenever she deigned to live with them.

Azul hated that patio.

Small, suffocating. Why stay there when there was so much outside?

Carefully, she unfolded Isadora's letter, arrived just the day before but read plenty already. Azul missed her sister like she would miss her heart if she woke one day and found it gone. Her tutor had recently taught her about that organ, guided by her curiosity. To think there was a thing inside your chest that kept you alive. But if you couldn't see it and you couldn't touch it and could only sometimes hear it, did such a thing really exist? It seemed far-fetched. Even if she had seen their cook rip a chicken open and take out its innards plenty of times, it didn't seem possible.

But it was. She had this thing, a heart, inside her chest, and having Isadora away felt like her sister had taken it with her.

Azul flattened the letter on her lap and read greedily. The first attempt was always a little slow—she'd rather listen to stories than read them, and Isadora's writing was tiny and crammed together to save space—but after a dozen rereads, the words flowed easily.

Dearest Azulita,

I wish I were home with you.

Azul snorted at the sentiment. Isadora was lucky to be away at the Temple's school, and she couldn't understand why Isadora would wish to be back instead of wishing Azul would join her.

But Azul could never join Isadora at such a distant school—a whole five towns away!—because the offer was only for Isadora. One of their mother's customers had given the invitation to send her eldest daughter as a reward for another healthy baby delivered. Another child for a couple who could not have one of their own.

Azul knew she should be glad her mother provided such a service, had been told often enough what a great gift to Sancia she was, but what was the point of having so many half siblings if she never got to meet them? And those were just her siblings on her mother's side—what if she also had siblings on her father's side? She'd heard murmurs, as children often did when adults forgot they existed. Comments about another sister or a brother in the court of Cienpuentes.

Once, Azul had been eager to learn all about them, but the fancy had passed quickly. She had Isadora. Why should she wish for anything else?

The lessons here are interminable, and the benches hard under my ass—that is a new word for you, Azulita, and learn it well because you'll find many uses for it in your life. Just don't let anyone else hear you say it. Mayhap when I am back, we shall have a contest, see which of us finds the most ways to put it to use!

Azul looked down at Pica and whispered, "Ass!" somewhat afraid the word might drift all the way into the house and fall into Cook's eager ears.

Pica yawned, showing a row of neat teeth, then snuggled into her paws.

Azul giggled and returned to the letter.

Last weekend, we had another exhibition and I bested everyone in class. You should have seen Mari's face when my rapier touched her vest! You'd think I'd run her straight over with my Maravillosa instead of poking her with the end of my training blade. The horror! The outrage! The queen, brought down by a mere peon!

The dean told me afterward that next time they'll have me fight the girls in the upper year if I want. I think I shall. They're very good, and what joy is there in fighting those you've already defeated? What do you think, Azulita?

Azulita thought her sister would do as she wished, as she always did, so she refrained from forming a true opinion on the matter.

It is most unfair that even though I won the fight, I'm still stuck having to care for the Temple. The statues are old and the pedestals older and someone stole the Anchor from half their eyes. The Blessed Heart has no eyes left, and the Lord Life stumbles around with just one. The Lady Dream still has both of them, because one of the girls' family is part of the court and donated them. I think one day I shall like a piece of Anchor too. Something flashy. I'll flaunt it around Aguncíon, and everyone will be in awe. I think I shall embroider that on a ribbon tonight and tie it around the Lady Dream's leg. Then I'll embroider one letting the Lord Life know Mari once cursed him for allowing me to live. He shan't be happy about that!

I can't wait to see you again, Azulita. There is so much I wish to tell you about. Curse these single sheets of paper! Why can't they give us more to write home? Know that you are in my heart, and I miss you dearly, and once I am done with this place, you and I shall never be apart again!!

Love, Isadora

Azul folded the letter and held it close to her chest. One day they would be free to do as they wished, travel where they wanted, meet the rest of the world. Valanje, with its Anchor peaks, and Bremón with its red lakes. The cities painted inside the frames in the parlor, and the ones her tutor had described to her. Faraway places too scary to visit alone, but the trip of a lifetime with Isadora by her side.

Until then, she'd have to be content with seeing Isadora during her yearly school break.

She couldn't wait.

THE PRESENT

There was a knock on the door, and Azul almost leaped out of her skin at the unfamiliar sound. None of the servants had knocked. Nereida hadn't knocked. And here it came again, the sound, repeating. Whoever was behind the door wanted her to think she was in control. And so, the time had come to face either Serunje or the Valanjian emissary, Azul guessed, tugging at the folds of her plain shirt.

The third knock came, with no change in cadence or strength, and this put her on edge more than the knocking itself.

"Come in," she said.

The door opened, and a large man stepped into the room. Azul couldn't help but take a step back. His height was his own, but the breadth had been aided by a massive dull-white breastplate made of bone, topped on each shoulder by equally bulky shoulder plates. Not the small ornamental ones those like De Guzmán and other nobles wore, but giant things meant to send a message, meant to impress. Meant to frighten.

And frighten they did—she had never seen the like. A man like this would barrel into you, and you would never stand back up. He would unsheathe the long sword hanging from his hip and run you through without a second thought. But it was his face that struck her the most.

A marquetry of animal and human bone pieces had been fitted into the shape of a mask that covered the upper half of his face, long fangs running down his cheeks. Were he to smile wide, they would dig into his flesh. But someone like this did not own that kind of smile. Blond hair hung in long, loose waves around his face and down to his chest, seemingly snagging on the thorns and tiny spikes of the armor only to flow like water instead as he moved deeper into the room.

When she found his eyes through the two holes in the mask, she saw deep violet rings framing golden irises.

Death, here to claim her. This was no shriveled shell of a person too consumed with tasting death to live, as the scary tales described emissaries. This man was *different*. Magnificent. This man took her breath away and sent her heart tumbling inside her chest.

This man was worth serving gods.

His eyes widened the moment they fell on her, and she was glad she had caught the tiny movement in this controlled, self-assured man. He had probably expected something else. A grander presence. Not Azul del Arroyo, a nineteen-year-old countryface who couldn't even fight with a rapier, because all she had been taught was how to use a dagger.

But Azul had met Death before. At the inn, at Agunción, at the docks of Diel. For Isadora, she would gather her courage and face it again.

"So, you've come to kill me," she stated. She didn't know what to focus on: the mask, the eyes, the hair. The spikes on the breastplate.

The emissary stared back, eyes unfathomable, one hand resting on the hilt of his sword. He made no movement, said nothing. He didn't even seem to breathe.

Azul finally settled for looking into his eyes. "If so, go ahead and end this waiting. Leave this room with an innocent soul added to your collection of bones."

His mouth lifted slightly on one side, and Azul knew she had said something wrong.

And still, he wouldn't talk.

And still, she fought not to squirm under his stare.

She reached for the chair. A way to hide the increasing trembling of her limbs.

"Is it 'killing' when you can never escape Death?" the emissary asked. The voice fit the man: deep, not quite smooth; silk snagging on roughness, like his hair. It tumbled inside her head and crawled down her throat.

She turned slowly, dragging the chair between them. "It is when you deal it without reason."

"I am Virel Enjul, Emissary of the Lord Death." He lifted his hands. Big, with long fingers ending in blunt nails blackened at the ends. "My hands are his hands. My reasons, his reasons." The mask's fangs did dig into his skin when he smiled wide, a mocking slash in a pale face surrounded by white bone and golden threads of loose hair. "The gods do not murder, Miss Del Arroyo. They impart divine will."

Azul's hands clenched around the back of the chair. *Courage.* This was only the Lord Death's messenger, and she had fooled Death before. Still, her throat felt like grinding stones as she forced it to work. "Without justification, it will always be murder."

"How human of you to assume the gods need justification."

"They gave us will and morals—they must abide by their own rules."

Enjul didn't move. "Tell me about your gift," he said, the last word catching on his tongue.

Azul shook her head. "I have no gifts."

He looked away, and Azul's knees almost buckled from the sudden lack of pressure.

"Maladies are the stuff of folktales," he said. "The Order has many theories about them, of course, but they're theoretical. Not one has ever been found. On our lands, that is."

He thought her some monstrous creature from a children's tale. Azul slipped around the chair and sat down. "I'm sorry your travel has been for naught, Emissary," she answered in a steady voice—only the merest of trembles, which she hoped he wouldn't notice, although she had a good idea that he would. "I am no malady."

His gaze returned to her, and she stiffened. "Yet credible witnesses heard you ask to return to your sister's bones."

"Seeking prayer, nothing more."

"Is that a Sancian custom? Praying to bones instead of the gods?" He focused on her earring. "I suppose it should come as no surprise, given what you do with Anchor."

The censuring tone irked her, as did his focus on Isadora's earring.

Turning her head, she answered demurely, "Wearing Anchor is respecting the gods."

"If you truly respected them, you'd leave their bones as they chose."

Azul wanted to tell him the gods wouldn't have left them out in the open, in the fields and the mountains, if they hadn't wanted their creations to harvest them. But a Valanjian would never understand. "I want to pay respect to my sister's memories. Since she had no time to make any here, I must go back to Sancia."

His hands clenched, as if he wanted to strike her down. "There have been rumors about a malady resurfacing in Sancia. How lucky that the source has fallen into our hands."

Azul bit her lip to control its trembling. She hadn't done anything with her gift after bringing her sister back all those years earlier, although the temptation had been great. She had been too scared people might find out and think differently of Isadora—too scared Death might decide to take back what she had stolen.

Had someone finally realized what she had done back then?

"You're mistaken," she said. And then, gathering what defiance she could, "Do you call every grieving family member a malady?"

"'Diagol,'" he quoted, "'don't you want to see my sister again? Help me get to her bones.'"

The room turned chilly. "Misguided words, Emissary Enjul, spoken in a moment of grief."

He walked up to her and leaned down. Azul's spine pressed against the back of the chair.

"Don't you want to know why she crumbled? Aren't you curious about why she lasted this long to then suddenly disappear? I could tell you."

It was impossible to hide the widening of her eyes. It wasn't just her lack of will? Her utter failure? Then she remembered—the why didn't matter. She would bring Isadora back and they would never return to this land.

She lowered her gaze, fixed it on the way the fabric of his pants bunched into graceful wrinkles where they crammed into his knee-high boots.

"There is no need to know, Emissary. It wasn't my doing, and I wish to be allowed to return home." She swallowed a lump in her throat. "Please."

He considered her as someone might consider something equal parts morbid and fascinating. "Why?" he said in a deep, smooth voice, "I ask myself. Why would someone who has seen a *most beloved* one crumble to dust in front of their eyes request to see their bones elsewhere? How would they know their bones were not on the dock or fallen into the sea?"

Azul paled, blood gone so fast she felt faint at the enormity of her mistake. "W-words spoken in ha—"

Enjul straightened. "A malady's creation cannot survive in the land of the Lord Death without his permission."

It doesn't feel right, going to Valanje—Isadora's words. Isadora, who didn't really believe in the gods. Azul's insides churned. The emissary did not step back, did not appear to notice how close she was to losing her stomach on his boots. Or did not care.

"The god is here?" she forced herself to ask. It seemed an impossibility. Gods, they existed far away, didn't they? If they existed at all beyond the Anchor that used to be their bones. Happy to take prayers and send nothing in return.

"He is the land; he's in everything we consume. He has no body, but we carry him inside us. And I am his will."

Fear ran a finger down her back. True terror, not the desperation of impotence or annoyance of having to wait. No, this permeated her bones, her flesh. It made her heart increase its tempo until it beat against her ribs, demanding to be released. She saw the truth of his words in the lack of inflection in his tone. This wasn't an inquiry into Isadora's cause of death—had never been.

This was a judgment on whether Azul should live.

He recognized her fear but didn't gloat. Instead, he looked relieved that he could go back to his real self.

He glanced at the sunlight dimming through the window. "We will be traveling to the emissaries' quarters in the morning." He turned toward the door. "Gather your belongings. I will allow you one trunk."

"*No!*" Azul cried, jumping out of the chair. "Allow me to go back to Monteverde."

A laugh escaped him, short, rough, and full of disbelief. "You think I'd allow someone like you to roam the continents? You're an affront to the gods. You meddled with Death. You refused his right and your sister's right to find peace in his bones—and who knows how many others'—and imposed your will over nature and godhood. You are unrepentant. You cannot be trusted with the power you own. No, you shall be studied, so we can stop your kind from causing harm in the future. After that, you will be confined so your rot doesn't spread."

His words shocked her numb. "I won't go."

The massive shoulder plates lifted in a shrug. "You'll come. Dead, alive, it makes no difference." The savagery of his smile returned. "I would take you dead, so you cannot repeat your affronts, but I have been told it'd serve Valanje better if you remain whole. For the time being, at least."

"You cannot prove it," she cried, desperate. "I'm normal!"

"And yet everything is dying except for you."

Azul stared, uncomprehending. "What do you mean?"

He paid her no heed and walked toward the door.

"Wait," she pleaded. His steps halted; his hand stilled on the door's handle. "You are wrong. I am no malady. You are from Valanje; you have no idea of how we mourn our dead." Then it wrenched out of her—all the broken hope, all the bleakness, all the hollow in her heart: "*Please.*"

He opened the door and gave her a last glance, the mask and the violet and golden eyes peeking over his shoulder plate. "This eagerness, this desperation—this is why you cannot be allowed freedom."

The door closed behind him.

IV

AZUL

zul fell back on the chair, hands gripped tight against her mouth. Politics, she had thought when Nereida came to talk to her, games of words and manners that she would win before returning to her land, her sister.

The emissary played no games. The emissary did not care. The emissary knew what she was. He had known from that first widening of his eyes that she had mistaken for surprise at her appearance. The tone of his words, the contempt in those golden irises when he had labeled her an affront to the world. He would take her with him, either moving or as bones.

But she had until morning.

She grabbed the brazier's iron poker and waited by the door, perched on the chair for a better angle than her short frame would allow.

But no servant came. No guard. The door remained closed; the poker too thick to do any lock-picking. She abandoned her position to get some rest and, after a few hours of fitful dozing, was back at the door with the first light of dawn, pressing her ear against the thick wood. When she finally heard footsteps, she hurried back onto the chair, her limbs shaking with the intense rush of blood through her veins.

Azul had doled out violence before—you couldn't be one-half of a sisterhood prone to duels and brawls without meting out some—but there was something so unexpectedly raw and heartbreaking about doing it alone that made her feel like it was the first time. It made her want to cry and rage and shrink with fear.

The door opened, and sweat covered her palms as she tightened her hold on the poker and lifted it over her shoulder.

Nereida de Guzmán entered, black hat low over her head and raven braid falling over her dark blue waistcoat. Her rapier hung low against her hip, and a satchel crossed her chest, resting on her other side.

Azul's mouth opened in shock.

Unfazed, Nereida took ahold of Azul's belt and wrenched her off the chair.

"If you want to leave, tell me the truth," Nereida said, pulling Azul close to study her face. "Is it true you can bring someone back from death?"

Azul recovered and returned Nereida's stare. "Why would you ask?"

"Answer, or stay in this room until the deathling takes you away."

"You stopped me from getting back on the boat and left me to rot in this room. Why should I trust you now?"

Nereida narrowed her eyes in annoyance. "You can't best Death's man in a fight, and that poker won't help you with the guards. What other option do you have?"

The empty hallway behind Nereida beckoned, growing lighter by the second. The building was silent now, but soon it would fill with the everyday noises of a household going about its morning business.

She fought to get the words past her throat. "It's true."

Nereida leaned closer. "How?"

"I'd need a bone," Azul said.

Loosening her hold on Azul's belt, Nereida leaned back to peer into the hallway. "Which?"

"Any will do. A leg, a finger, a tooth—it doesn't matter."

"How does it work, exactly? How does a bone bring a person back?" Tension hastened Nereida's voice, but also cold calculation. She spoke as if she had no feelings about the process—no shock, no curiosity. Whatever her opinion, it remained locked behind her expressionless face. A mask of skin instead of bones.

"I'd need the bone and something organic or alive to grow the new body."

"Such as another person?"

Azul gave her a look of horror. "Such as a tree, or food, or fertile mud."

Nereida nodded to herself. "And what sort of person comes out of it? Must one teach them all they ought to know again?"

"The body will have the memories of the bone, will remember as much as the bone does until its life was shorn, and not beyond."

"So simple," Nereida murmured. "A bone and dirt to make a person."

And a piece of Azul's own soul to give it sentience. This, she didn't mention.

"Can you promise the person comes back just as they were?" Nereida insisted.

"You've met my sister; you've talked to her. You wouldn't have known the difference had we not arrived to Valanje."

Nereida acknowledged this truth with another short nod and extended her left arm. "I will trust you, for now. These are my terms: I will help you out of the city and onto a ship, and in exchange, you will bring back to life someone of my choice."

She could've offered a damp prison cell in Cienpuentes filled with rats, and Azul would not have cared. "Deal." She took Nereida's arm, gripping it tightly and feeling the answering hard grip. They shook once.

Then Nereida was striding across the polished hallway, Azul at her heels. They ignored the guard slumped by a set of winding stone stairs and took them at the same hurried speed, hands trailing the central pillar, heels echoing against the steps.

"Don't hide your face, don't hunch your shoulders. None of them have seen you except for the few servants and the emissary. They have no reason to suspect you."

Nereida didn't wait for an answer. She shoved a curtain aside at the end of the staircase leading to a wider, finer corridor growing brighter under the encroaching daylight. Azul fixed her attention on the back of Nereida's waistcoat. Time, an enemy not even the gods could best. How long did they have until someone noticed her gone?

The building was never-ending, the halls interminable. They passed servants and guards who paid the pair no attention. Nereida's footsteps matched Azul's heartbeats, a steady trot, rising, rising, on the edge of turning into a full-out run. They ate the marble floors one step ahead of the morning light.

The guards at the entrance must've known Nereida, because she did not ask to be allowed outside, and they did not halt them to ask the reason for their hurry.

The taste of salt in the air shocked Azul, increased the prickling on her skin. She was leaving the land as she had entered it—without its owner's permission.

Hurrying, she took her place by Nereida's side. A town sprawling from the top of a mountain was easy to navigate—spiraling streets and steep stairs tumbling toward the azure sea. Seagulls cried overhead, as if they were raising the alarm.

Azul wiped her brow. The lack of food and sleep was catching up to her. Sweat stuck the back of her shirt to her skin, clammy in the chill of dawn. She'd had no time to grab a waistcoat, to grab anything. What she wore was all she owned now: her own boots, her sister's breeches, one pair of well-worn shirtsleeves. One gold-and-Anchor earring.

The town leveled once outside the Anchor tip, the houses becoming wider rather than taller. Daring a peek behind, Azul again marveled at the number of buildings covering the Anchor, their faces forming straight cliffs, their square windows watchful eyes for the god's bones.

Nereida's sharp inhales were the only hint that the trip so far was affecting her in any way. Her features were handsome, her green eyes alluring and so stone-cold. Azul could see why such a beautiful, closed face had found favor with the late queen. This face would give nothing away, no secrets, no distaste. It could spew a lie as much as it could invoke a truth, and one would never be the wiser.

They rounded a corner, and the flagstone turned into mud and horse manure as the main port blossomed in front of them. Azul gaped at the two enormous ships anchored near the harbor and the few farther back—so much bigger than the one that had taken them across. Their sails were tied up, the oars retracted, seemingly ready to slide right into the city.

Carts and donkeys and sailors and farmers filled the space between town and seawater. Shouts, curses, neighs. Nereida herself appeared lost as she surveyed the spread. Azul grew restless, her gaze drifting over her shoulder. Sunlight was firmly in place now, the silver orbs of Luck and Wonder in hiding. Azul missed their reassuring visages. So many things could go wrong when you didn't have the moons watching over you.

At last, Nereida began walking again. Dodging people and beasts of burden, they made their way to a far dock marked by a pole covered in strips of fading blue.

A few workers were unloading one of two small boats moored to the floating deck below the stone of the port itself. Nereida and one of the men standing by the pole exchanged coins, and it was done, the relief intoxicating. Azul turned to give Diel one last view.

And found the mask of bones staring back.

The emissary prowled toward them, the throng of activity parting around his form. He was in simple shirtsleeves, his hair disheveled, his armor gone, the bone mask firmly in place.

Death, here to take her back.

Azul took a step backward. She willed her legs to take another and another. He was almost on top of her. She could see the violet around his irises, nearly black in the shadows of the mask.

She felt Nereida's presence at her side. Azul turned to warn her.

Nereida de Guzmán needed no such warnings. Taking a pistol out of her satchel, she leveled her arm and shot the Emissary of the Lord Death right in the chest.

The sound was deafening; an acrid stench filled the air. Azul flinched and covered her ears, then watched in horror through the resulting gunpowder cloud as Virel Enjul staggered back and crumbled to the ground, the front of his shirt a mass of black and darkening red.

"Move," Nereida said through gritted teeth. She shoved Azul toward the ladder to the floating platform, and Azul stumbled down the rungs. Then Nereida was there again, pushing her until she jumped onto the boat.

Azul scrambled over the benches until she was as far as she could go. The boat rocked under her, a couple of sailors pushing it away from the platform with an oar, away from the growing gathering of people, their shouts, and their pointing.

Nereida sat in front of her, blocking her view of the port. And she, too, was a sight. Her face, a blank canvas of calm except for the tight, pale line of her mouth, her eyes hidden by the hat's brim as she returned the pistol to her satchel.

Azul couldn't look away.

The sailors rowed. The port became distant.

Nereida looked up and met Azul's stare. Cool. Collected.

Azul should be thankful Nereida had dealt with the emissary. Azul was now in a boat, about to board a ship in neutral waters, where nobody could imprison her again.

Where was the relief? The hope? For someone who had never killed a person, Azul was leaving many corpses in her wake.

This is the price, Nereida's dark green eyes seemed to say. This is the price of your wishes. The price for not listening, for venturing into the land of the Lord Death. Isadora. The emissary. Two deaths. How many more would her wishes cost?

Azul turned her focus on the ship that would take them back to Sancia.

The sight kept her insides rolling. The Lord Death would find no joy in losing one of his emissaries. How long until Valanje sent another after her?

And if an emissary caught up with her, Azul acknowledged with grim certainty, she would not be granted the mercy of staying alive long enough to escape again.

V

THE COUNT

The count leaned in to study the masterful brushstrokes, haphazard at close distance, yet inexplicably detailed once the eye took in the whole painting.

Emiré de Anví disliked how something could reshape itself so easily. He enjoyed order in his life, things set in a certain way. At only twenty-six, he was already set in his ways: his black hair, tumbling down in natural curls over his shoulders and upper back; his cheeks, shaved clean every morning without fail; his clothes, always of the same elegant cut, the same materials, the same colors—white and creams and golds. He held a black wide-brimmed hat with a full soft white plume, and he tapped it impatiently against his breeches. This painting in front of him, a portrait of the late Sancian queen, was an abomination of everything he sought in life.

Like the rest of the palace, it was encased in an ornate frame. It hung on a beige wall supporting an ornamental ceiling full of molded waves covered with a dusting of Anchor. This palace, the Heart of Cienpuentes, was the pinnacle of centuries dealing in Anchor.

Fragile, extravagant. Unlivable.

De Anví abandoned his perusal and strode down the long hallway, his dress ankle boots echoing against the polished stone floor with each measured step. The desperate yearning to escape the palace's confining enclosure he kept locked inside, although it resurfaced from time to time, like when he paid his daily visit to His Majesty.

His Majesty, being five years of age, couldn't care less about his daily visits. The feeling was reciprocated.

Emiré de Anví hated the little bastard.

It had been just over two years since the queen's death, and a year and a half since the attempted kidnapping of her child, an affair De Anví had helped unravel and which had earned him his current position in the Royal Guard. A position he hadn't wanted, hadn't hoped for, and quite resented, but which had been granted nonetheless.

The guard standing by the end of the hallway bowed his head when he drew near. A muttered "Your Honor" escaped him.

As second-in-command of the Golden Dogs, the Royal Guard, greetings like this were a given and went unnoticed. His position allowed him free roam of the palace and gave him the kind of life the Heart had created for itself: fragile, extravagant. Unlivable.

He came upon another set of guards, who opened the big, heavy wooden door leading outside. Without breaking his stride, he trotted down the stone steps, fitting his hat on his head and pulling his half cape over his right shoulder. It was too warm to bother with one, but De Anví would wear it all the same.

He kept his pace even, avoiding carts, horses, and their manure. Twilight was upon the dozens of islands that made up the Anchor city of Cienpuentes, shadowing the buildings in contrast with the darkening sky—no longer the pink hue of winter, but the beautiful deep blue of early summer. Houses rose two and three stories in height; narrow bridges connected them over his head, and broader ones connected the islands over the flowing water of the River Espasesmo. The wide streets surrounding the Heart gave way to the meandering flagstone paths of the city as he made his way to his favorite tavern.

Now that the official mourning for the queen was over, the silent halls and rooms of the Heart would soon be filled by summer balls and celebrations given by Regent de Fernán in honor of the child king.

What a bleak handful of months, of years, waiting for him, stuck in the palace like a dog on a leash, waiting to see who died first—the master or the pet.

"Count de Anví."

De Anví, waking from his musings, found himself in a shadowed alleyway running by the river's edge. The sight was familiar—he took this route every other day. Ahead of him, three men in dark clothing blocked his passage, black masks covering the upper halves of their faces.

One stepped forward. "Your Honor, our employer would like a word with ye."

De Anví cocked his head. "And who might that be?"

"You'll find out when you get there."

"I think not, then. Tell them to schedule an appointment—I am on private business."

"We must insist," the man said, adding a small growl.

Did the man think he would be cowed by dogs? "Your wishes are of no matter to me."

The man's hand went to his sword. The two behind him copied his movement. "Then we shall make it your business." He began to unsheathe the rapier.

De Anví's hand gripped his own Valiente, a present from his late father. One foot glided backward, and his body turned sideways. He was isolated, but the narrowness of the alley worked in his favor. Here, they could not surround him. Here, they'd be stuck in line like ducks after their mama. Then it would be a simple matter of pushing their corpses into the water and letting the river's current work its wonders.

He suddenly craved the excitement, the risk of a fight. Pride would not allow him to intentionally fail, but he could always be bested. One missed feint and a rapier between his ribs, and then the Lord Death would be to blame for the promises his death would break, even if De Anví had only made them to himself.

The man's rapier slid out of its sheath. "Come now, Your Honor. Don't make things difficult for yourself."

Things had never appeared simpler, in De Anví's opinion. He brought out Valiente and pushed his half cape aside, allowing for a full range of motion.

His opponent's eyes narrowed. Did he think him a man of words and not swords? If he were brought up in Cienpé, perhaps, but De Anví was bred and raised in the countryside, where fights erupted at a moment's notice and the paths at night weren't always safe.

He pressed forward, the other man raising his rapier in response, waiting to see who would attack first.

De Anví decided he had a liking for it, to start something rather than be dragged into it.

Valiente pierced through the air, its path met by his opponent's rapier, De Anví's mind on the next move, and the next, and the one after that.

After the man parried the count's initial attack, he attempted a strike in return. De Anví blocked it easily, pushing forward and aiming for the man's shoulder. A rapier could sever things besides veins, and De Anví had always preferred the subtle tearing of tendons and muscles to bloody shows of conquest.

His attack was parried again, easily. They were testing each other, figuring out their speed, their accuracy, their reflexes.

The man lunged for De Anví's arm. Valiente met his rapier, the ensuing rasp filling the air over the murmur of the river.

The man's companions remained silent behind him, waiting, bored. *Curious.* De Anví would have expected them to cheer or jeer or try to join in.

But then, these men didn't want him dead. If they killed De Anví, how would their employer talk to him? That explained the half-hearted attacks coming his way—they were not a matter of skill but of necessity. De Anví's opponent sought to maim, not kill.

This fight would not give him the satisfaction he craved, but perhaps he could still find some sport in it.

"What's this?" cried a new voice from behind the men. "My, what luck—a show of underhanded tactics!"

De Anví and his adversary stopped. The two men in the background turned to glare at the newcomer. The front man's attention didn't waver—he trusted his companions to deal with the new danger—and De Anví allowed himself a spark of intrigue. Hired criminals did not usually trust one another this much.

"This is not your concern," one of the men told the newcomer. "Scamper."

"Scamper, you say," the newcomer answered. "What am I, ten?" His rapier was halfway out of its sheath, the glint of the little Anchor left in the river's bottom reflecting on the metal.

Miguel Esparza knew how to make an entrance, De Anví had to admit.

The men's leader, realizing he was stuck between two combatants in a narrow passage, pushed his rapier back into its scabbard.

"Another time, then." Giving his back to the count, he motioned the other two toward the end of the alleyway.

De Anví felt a pang of disappointment at the men's easy capitulation, his heart still beating an eager rhythm.

"Not so fast," Esparza said. "Who are you and what do you want with His Honor?"

"Not your affair," the man in front of him said. Before Esparza could reply, he'd shoved past him, the other two following.

"Hold," Esparza demanded. "On the City Guard's order!"

But the men's steps had hastened into a half run, and in the next breath, they were out of sight.

Esparza cursed before turning to the count. "Where is your shadow?"

De Anví rearranged his half cape and closed the distance between them, gesturing for the other man to walk ahead of him. "Which one?"

"Not the one under your feet."

"I told Tonio not to come with me tonight."

"Tonio should know better than that. A count, a high-ranking member of the Royal Guard walking alone without his personal protection? One day, Death might receive your invitation." Esparza clucked. "And what of your other shadow?"

"The Witch," De Anví answered, his jaw tightening, "I'll meet later."

"Don't mind me if I tag along for now."

De Anví didn't mind, still hungry for something *more* since the masked strangers had given so little.

They emerged from the alleyway and crossed onto the next island. A few minutes later, they took their usual seats in the small hole of Casa Rojita. Ale promptly followed.

De Anví took a sip, then idly studied the tavern. Most of the customers were familiar, although he did not know who they were—unlike the countryside, city dwellers were not free with their names. There was a kind of safety in this room full of known strangers that made De Anví return again and again, mindless of dark alleys and the danger his rich clothing attracted. Besides, he was used to people greeding for what he owned. He had spent a third of his life at court, after all.

"Who were those men?" Esparza asked after sipping his own drink. He grimaced in disgust, then heartened himself and drank some more.

De Anví shrugged.

"You're too cavalier with your safety, De Anví."

The count snorted. "I did not see you calling for help."

It was Esparza's turn to dismiss the words. "They'd have been easy pickings for the both of us."

"Perhaps."

"What did they want?"

"I've not yet the gift of reading minds."

"You are like this, and then I no longer wonder why you aren't married."

De Anví froze until even his eyes were as cold as metal. Forcing himself to relax again, he said conversationally, "You court the Lord Death with your words, Miguel. You will find him one of these days."

Esparza returned the stare with a mocking one of his own. "It's a race, then, to see who meets him first."

Silence settled over the small table, the murmur of other conversations drifting close. "If the god is willing," Esparza finally muttered, tipping his mug against his lips, "I'll find him first."

"Any rumors that should concern me?" De Anví asked, studying the other man. Although he wore nondescript breeches, shirt, and an open doublet, Miguel Esparza was in fact a member of the blue tabards, the City Guard. But what made him valuable to De Anví was his excellence in scurrying where he wasn't wanted. The count took a heartier sip of his drink. Esparza often called himself a rat, and the word carried no insult, because that's what he was—a city rat. Fast, stealthy, with a bite.

"Nothing I've heard."

"The Marquess de Mavén?"

"Quiet as a duck on a pond."

"Then I guess those men weren't his."

"Whoever they belong to—if they belong to anyone beyond their coin—must like you alive, even if slightly broken in the process."

"They said their employer wanted a word with me."

"Court politics?"

"Likely, but nobody has attempted kidnapping before."

"You weren't so high up in the Golden Dogs last time court was in session."

The man wasn't wrong, De Anví conceded. "If it was important business, I'm sure this won't be the last time I hear of it. And the other matter? Is that why you happened to cross my path?"

"What, can't one wish to spend some time with a friend? Ah, don't answer, you are right." Esparza retrieved a small pouch from inside his doublet and handed it over. The count didn't bother examining the contents—he knew what it held, since he'd asked Esparza to procure it for him: a single sliver of pure Anchor. So tiny it could easily fall between his fingers and never be found again.

Cienpuentes had once been as bright and blue as the sky—or so the tales went—but there was barely any glittering Anchor left. It had been mined away except for the bottom of Espasesmo's delta and the lake, places not even the smartest engineers knew how to access without condemning their workers into the strong currents and the maelstrom in the middle of the lake.

Though they had tried.

He pocketed the pouch.

"You won't look inside?" Esparza remarked.

"Why, have you decided to start fleecing me?"

"I was able to acquire two pieces. At a lower price."

De Anví's eyebrows arched. News of the likely Anchor mining vote must be spreading. Someone was going to be either very happy or very sad about making this deal.

He wondered if he should look for full pieces again. He had once entertained the idea of turning the few he already owned into a set of necklace and earrings—the most beautiful of gifts, fit to adorn the most beautiful of women. Different images flicked through his mind, different designs—the yearning in his heart taking shape.

With a sigh, he forced himself to wipe the thoughts from his mind. What good was a gift when you had nobody to gift it to?

At least, not anymore.

"It's true the mining ban is being lifted, then?" Esparza asked before taking a sip of his drink. "Girende's sinking, forgotten so soon." He studied the count. "You are part of the court. What will be your vote? Will you condemn us simple peasants to Girende's fate, or abide by the late queen's wishes?"

"When I decide, I might let you know. Now, go, before the Witch arrives."

"You don't need to order me twice." Esparza finished his drink with one last giant gulp and a bigger shudder, tipped his hat, and left.

De Anví didn't have to wait long for the Witch to appear, wearing her favorite young man. It had been a while since he had seen her using another body, and sometimes he wondered what her victims thought about while the Witch took over. Did they still see and hear and feel, or were they thrown into a dark dream?

The Witch took the seat opposite De Anví, and he could see the eager gleam in her green eyes, not quite concealed by the mask covering the upper half of the face.

The man she was currently inhabiting was in his early twenties, with the same dark hair and lightly tan complexion shared by nearly everyone in the tavern, including the count. The mask, a simple snug affair covered in black fabric, had no ribbons tying it back around the man's head.

He had once asked her about this mask business, early on in their acquaintance—not friendship, for De Anví did not have friends, and, he guessed, neither did the Witch—and she had promised she could only peek through the masks of those who agreed to allow her in.

But then, the count had also sworn to willingly lay his life down for the sake of the king.

So, Emiré de Anví had never touched a mask since.

"You were ambushed," she said.

De Anví stilled. He was surprised . . . but not truly. Amazed at how quickly the Witch had learned of it, certainly, but not that she knew—the Faceless Witch had her fingers in every house's business. Luckily for the Witch, most scoffed at the notion of someone *like* the Witch even existing.

The citizens of Cienpuentes held two very strict beliefs: their prospects and their purses. Anything else might as well not exist. Something like the Witch was a reality they were happy to ignore unless they sought her out. An anomaly they didn't want explained but were happy to use whenever it suited.

To everyone else, this was a young man here for a drink and talk. If the man's friends were to walk in, they would think nothing was amiss.

De Anví knew better.

"Your ambush must have something to do with the late De Gracia," the Witch said eagerly.

"Why do you think it's related to the dead marquess?" he asked, curiosity slipping through. The notion that the encounter had anything to do with De Gracia's death hadn't entered his mind. The Marquess de Gracia had been a brusque widower uninterested in politics, despite belonging to the court. His murder had come as a shock, and rumors ran rampant. An awful debt? A secret mistress? Blackmail? Or, De Anví's favorite—wrong place, wrong time?

He would know, having been caught in a very similar net by the Witch sitting in front of him.

"Him, a ban supporter, three months ago," the Witch said. "Now you. Everyone knows you don't care about the ban or politics; they might want you out of the way."

"You can sound a little less excited at the prospect," De Anví said dryly. "Unlike him, I'm still alive. You don't need three men to kill someone. One with a crossbow and half a decent aim will do. It's more likely De Losa finally got tired of her machinations and decided to buy my vote."

And why shouldn't she? The Countess de Losa had been poised to take the position De Anví now held if it hadn't been for the Witch's interference. He had often hoped De Losa's political schemes would get him ousted, but disappointingly, it had never come to pass.

The Witch dismissed that with a wave of her hand. "De Losa is too busy ingratiating herself to De Fernán, now that the royal mourning is ending."

De Anví mulled that over. "She's aiming to become the regent's spouse?"

He could see it. De Losa wasn't the kind of person to give up on rank and power—ingratiate herself with the regent and his Anchor mining now, become his spouse next. If De Fernán were to be removed, even become regent herself.

"Forget about her," the Witch said. "Someone must be looking to buy your influence."

"Such as it is," De Anví muttered before tasting his drink.

"But," the Witch continued, fingertips drumming against the table, "what do they want? Your support for the ban? Or your opposition?"

"It doesn't matter. Girende's cave-in was too long ago." And people easily forgot the lives lost, the crumbling of a faraway Anchor city into the Void. "The coffers are feeling the strain." Especially the gentry's. The queen had been a staunch supporter of the ban on Anchor mining, but the queen was now dead and De Fernán held the regent's chair.

The fall of a proponent for the ban and the subsequent rise of someone who wasn't hadn't been lost on anyone.

"The law will change," De Anví continued. "De Fernán will make sure of it. He likes his money too much."

"The Temple might complain."

"The Temple will receive new statues, and the gods will need Anchor for their eyes."

The Witch pursed her lips. "It's probably as you say."

"Yet you obviously disagree."

"The Marquess de Gracia was a stern supporter of the ban. Now he's gone, done in by a dagger in his heart, and his heir doesn't seem to care about what happens with Anchor." She pointed at De Anví. "*You* have never cared, and now you're ambushed, but not robbed or killed. The same person who murdered De Gracia might be looking to influence your vote. It's all connected."

De Anví studied the Witch. "Perhaps this interest in De Gracia is wholly your own. Perhaps you seek a new body and have taken a liking to his son." And damn him if hope didn't color his words.

If the Witch switched bodies, then there would be no reason for De Anví to stay around her, in Cienpuentes, in the Heart. There would be no broken promises, no need to keep the Witch's current body safe.

The Witch lifted her chin with an arrogant grin and ran her hands down her waistcoat. "No, this one suits me quite well. I have grown attached to it."

Yes, hope wasn't for the likes of De Anví.

"Still," she added, her features sobering, "something feels amiss. I shall visit the Heart tomorrow. We might find more."

De Anví was brought back to the moment a year and a half ago, when the Faceless Witch had become his constant companion; the moment she had decided to become his shadow, mere months before De Anví was finished with his family's tradition of a stint in the Golden Dogs.

He had found her amusing at first, always speaking as if she were best friends with everybody. Because of this, everybody indulged her, no matter which body she wore—a servant's, a soldier's, a noble house heir's—never realizing they were all the Witch.

And then one day she had come to De Anví with rumors of a plot to abduct the baby king.

Foolishly, he had allowed the Witch to explain further.

Even more foolishly, he had agreed to help end the plot.

If only there were a god of time he could beg to take him back to the moment he'd told the Witch he'd help. Maybe then the child king would be gone, De Anví's tenure in the Royal Guard over, and he wouldn't have to see the Witch and her new face, have a constant reminder that he was stuck.

But even if there were such a god, what did gods care about humankind? As a child, he had often pondered this. Why did they create such feeble beings that they had needed to raise the continents so humanity could thrive? Why not wipe everything and begin anew?

He would have.

"Let us talk of happier things," De Anví said. "Are they ready?"

"That, they are, my friend." She retrieved a pouch from under her waistcoat and put it on the table.

De Anví took the Witch's pouch and tossed Esparza's across. "For the next round."

A playful smirk crossed her face as she secured the slivers of Anchor inside her waistcoat. "If you would only wear a mask, I'd gift you as many dreams as you want."

The count stood and set his hat onto his head. "Once again, I must refuse. These single dreams will do." With a nod, he made his exit.

He was willing to deal with the Faceless Witch, give her Anchor in exchange for dreams, stand her presence for the sake of his promise, but he'd never allow her to look into the deepest recesses of his mind.

He rarely allowed himself.

Later that night, he opened the Witch's pouch and found three marbles, smaller than pearls and ten times—no, a hundred times—more valuable.

De Anví sprawled on his bed and swallowed one of the Faceless Witch's dream pills. The bleakness of the day faded away into eagerness, into this hope he kept locked inside himself.

Because tonight, he would dream of Nereida de Guzmán.

VI

AZUL

Azul huddled in a corner of her and Nereida's cabin, hiding from the gods' blood, from Luck and Wonder, from the stares of sailors and travelers. The seas were neutral zones—to spill human blood on the gods' own blood was unforgivable—so even if the tale of the incident at the port had spread, nobody would bother her. Nereida had vanished somewhere, leaving her alone with the image of Virel Enjul falling to the ground, his mouth half open, the cloud of gray and black gunpowder obscuring the sight of his chest.

So different from her first trip across the sea a few days earlier, when Azul had leaned over the handrail of the *Seven Hearts*, talking with Rudel Serunje in her rusty Valanjian while Isadora disappeared into Diagol's cabin. The seawater had run clear those nights, revealing the handful of understars blinking in and out of view through the thick clouds beneath the sea.

The clouds under the sea were dark at night, but Azul hoped they might be masses of pastel pinks and soft violets under the sun's light, no different from the clouds in the sky. Back on the *Seven Hearts*, she had wished them gone so she'd catch a glimpse of the chains of Anchor keeping the continents attached to the Void below.

Her current ship followed the coast north before turning east and arching around the maelstroms in the middle of the sea. Could the Anchor be seen from this route more easily than the southern one she had taken into Valanje? Azul didn't care to test the idea. She did not want to look at the gods' bones just as she did not want to look at their blood.

Seeing the world without her sister had never been an option—what if something happened to Isadora while Azul was away? And yet it was because of Azul that something had happened to Isadora after all.

The Lord Death had destroyed Isadora, and Azul had caused his emissary's death. A fair trade, she told herself, but she doubted the god saw it as such.

She was about to go peek at the sea anyway when Nereida entered the cabin wearing her usual mix of coldness and haughtiness.

Questions inundated Azul. Whom did she need Azul to bring back to life? A parent? A past lover? She had been the queen's mistress, and the queen was now dead. Was that whom she intended to steal from Death?

Azul felt no qualms about the possibility. As long as Nereida helped her get to Isadora's bones, Azul would bring back Nereida's childhood nanny if that's what it took.

"Stand," Nereida said.

Azul did so, dusting the back of her breeches and turning to face the woman.

And found a rapier aimed at her heart.

She jumped back, startled, her hand going for her dagger.

But she didn't have it. She only had Isadora's clothes on her back and Isadora's earring dangling from her ear.

"Show me proof of what you can do, or you will go no farther," Nereida said with the same cool politeness she had used when firing her pistol.

Gray and black and specks of dark red spattered over a white shirt. Azul tightened her fists. "You can't intentionally cause harm over the gods' blood, they . . ."

Nereida harrumphed. "I have killed Death's emissary. I am already damned in their eyes. Now, demonstrate that you can do what you say you can."

She had expected this, Azul reminded herself. She had a plan.

"I need a bone." She cursed the shakiness in her voice, the sudden onslaught of doubt. It had been so long since she last used her power—what if she could no longer access it? What if the Lord Death had taken more than Isadora from her? The thought made her feel faint. This, she had not accounted for.

"Use one of those you pilfered from the ship."

Of course, Nereida wasn't wrong, and pilfered Azul had. Slowly, she took out a small bone from inside her shirt. She had discovered it hanging from a chime right outside their cabin. She had acquired other bones, too, from the remains of their first repast aboard the ship, and a small flute abandoned in a corner that was now hidden inside her boot. Azul would not allow herself to be powerless again, locked in a room with no choice but to follow someone else's whims.

"I'll need that." Azul gestured toward what should've been her evening meal, abandoned on one of the two cots in the cramped space.

Nereida nodded, and Azul knelt by the meal tray. She put the big untouched chunk of bread into the untouched bowl of stew and pressed the bone into the soft crumb.

Her heartbeat slowed. Life, it felt, halted around her, waiting with bated breath, the magnitude of the moment overwhelming nature itself.

The bone under her fingertips strummed a silent song to her soul, a chord that reminded Azul that bones were the basis of everything. A chord she'd felt every day since the moment she was born, small and angry under a summer's blue sky.

Relaxed by the reminder, she allowed the bone's calling into her flesh, into her blood, into her own bones. Euphoria filled her chest as power ran down her arm and gathered in her palm. It took what life remained out of the food and beyond, leaving behind decaying gray tendrils over the wooden bowl, the wooden tray, even the rough fabric of the thin mattress.

Then life re-formed beneath her hand, the swirl of power on her palm forming the shape of an eye. The Eye of Death, she had always called it in her mind, sucking the life surrounding it to give back what it had once taken.

Bone spread, muscles formed, blood seeped into being, and a piece of her soul, of her essence, made the leap into this new being, leaving an aching hole in her chest that only time would refill. The feeling was nothing compared to when she'd brought back Isadora. Then it had felt as if half her soul had been sucked out of her bones until only a brittle husk of Azul remained.

Feathers caressed the inside of her hand, the bird thrumming with renewed life. When she cradled it, it chirped and attempted flight.

"*Necromancer.*" Nereida backed against the door, free hand covering her mouth, rapier shaking in her loose grip. Her expression contained everything Azul had never seen in it: shock, disbelief, fear.

Elation.

Nereida fought to blank her features. "It's true, then," she said in a wisp of a voice. Then, louder, "And you can do this with people?" A grimace escaped her self-control. "You did this before . . . with your sister?"

Azul nodded, the aftermath of using her gift shaking her arms, clattering her teeth. The gaping ache between her ribs made it hard to breathe.

"Why bone? Why not flesh or hair?"

"I . . . I'm not sure. Maybe hair doesn't remember flesh, and flesh doesn't remember skin, and skin doesn't remember blood. But bone remembers all."

Nereida looked away, hid her frown with the rim of her hat, its single pale plume overly bright in contrast with the black felt. A handful of heartbeats passed. A hundred. Then she glanced back at Azul. "Are you not afraid of the gods' retribution? What stops them from destroying you where you stand, like your sister?"

"It was the land," Azul said. "The . . . the emissary said the Lord Death would not allow her existence in Valanje. Isadora never had trouble in Sancia." The reminder reaffirmed her convictions. If Azul were a malady, as the emissary had insisted, then wouldn't one of the other gods have struck Isadora down as soon as she had been reborn? "Had I known Valanje's god would react like that, I would never have suggested the trip," she added fervently.

"A small price to pay, to stay put in exchange for a second life," Nereida agreed. "But have you no qualms for your soul after you die? Have you no fear the Lord Death will throw it to the understars and the Void?"

"Wouldn't you risk that and more for a sibling?"

Nereida's features hardened, her mask back in place. Her rapier slid into its sheath as she turned to open the door. "Our deal stands. After we disembark, we'll hire horses and go to Cienpuentes, to—"

"No."

"Pardon?"

The bird attempted to flee, but Azul wouldn't let it. It was a reminder, and reminders were always good when betting on one's future. "You are capable," she said, keeping her tone steady. Sneering would never do, and Nereida would see right through any attempts at false adulation. "And I need your help. Take me to my sister's bones first, and I will do as you request."

Nereida touched her rapier again. "You are free and on your way to Sancia, so you shall do as you agreed."

"After my sister's bones."

"I had not taken you for an oath breaker."

That hurt. Azul always kept her promises, no matter their shape. "I'm still willing to help with whomever you want me to bring back."

Nereida's fingers drummed against the grip of her rapier. "Where are these bones?"

Azul watched the other woman closely. Azul had no weapon, but with the element of surprise, she might be able to get within melee range. While she preferred daggers, she also knew how to throw a good punch. One had to, with Isadora as a sister. "Monteverde."

"It's on our way to Cienpuentes," Nereida murmured. Her gaze sharpened. "You mean to bring back your sister and no other?"

"Only Isadora," Azul assured her.

Nereida's gaze fell to the bird, now calmed within Azul's grasp. Figuring her point had been made, Azul opened her hands. The bird hopped over her fingers, then took flight in a burst. It flapped around the room until it found the freedom of the open door.

They watched it go, then Azul spoke: "Do you have siblings?"

Keeping her attention on the hallway, Nereida took her time to answer. "Yes."

"A sister?" Azul asked when no more information was forthcoming.

"An older sister and a brother." Finally, Nereida focused on Azul. "What is your point?"

"Do you love them? Imagine," Azul said harshly, "what it would be to lose one of them."

Nereida's mouth tightened, but she must've found it within herself to imagine Azul's grim scenario because she nodded. "We will travel to Monteverde and seek your sister's bones, then you will fulfill your part of the agreement."

"I give you my word."

Nereida snorted. "Leave your word for duels and tales, Del Arroyo. It will do you no good outside of them."

VII

AZUL

NINE YEARS EARLIER

They hadn't let Azul see Isadora. Not after she'd woken up to find her sister hot to the touch and slurring words. Not after she had told one of the inn workers.

No, they had locked her up in another room and given her trays of food and a chamber pot and looked at her with pitying eyes while telling her to be a good child and stay over by the bed.

Azul didn't like sleeping alone. She did it while Isadora was away, but now that they'd had to share a bed at the inn, it was so nice to stay up at night, talking about Isadora's exploits at the Temple school and her words-and-swordfights with her year mates. If it were up to Azul, they'd travel from inn to inn forever instead of returning home until Isadora had to leave again.

When Azul had said as much aloud, Isadora had agreed wholeheartedly. She had promised that's how they'd spend the days once she was done with the Temple: exploring together to their hearts' content.

But now, Azul stood in her sister's guest room to find the bedframe bare, the mattress gone, the room empty.

"Where is my sister?" She rounded on the inn's owner, who had followed her into the room. The woman had been kind to them, joking during their dinners and assuring them they'd be safe at her inn. "Where is Isadora?"

"Come here, dear." The woman gathered Azul in her arms. "Your sister is with the Lord Death now, and no foulness shall touch her again."

Azul grasped at the woman's shirt, her body such a contrast from Isadora's smaller form. "I want to see Isadora."

"Don't worry, child. We'll take care of her."

"But *where* is she?"

The woman sighed. "Waiting in a safe place. Tomorrow the cart will come to take her remains away to rest with the gods."

Isadora rest with the gods? Not if Azul had anything to do with it.

Swiftly, she made some calculations in her head. Her sister's body must still be here if they were waiting for a cart, and the inn was not so big. She looked up at the woman and allowed the trepidation in her heart to show in her eyes, filling them with tears. "Take her remains away to where?"

"Monteverde, of course."

THE PRESENT

"Ossuary? There is nothing like that here," the man at the Monteverde inn said. Not the same inn where Azul and Nereida had left their hired horses—no need to make the job easier for anyone who might follow—but a run-down place on the edge between those with their fortunes intact and those who could not afford to move.

"Are you sure?" Azul asked. She looked for signs of shrewdness in his haggard face, or any hint of wanting coin for the information.

"Lived here all my life," he answered, narrowing his eyes at Nereida, who stood quiet and impassive behind Azul.

Perhaps, Azul thought, *they called it something else around these parts.* "The place where they keep people's bones."

The man made a face of disgust. "I know what an ossuary is, and there is no such thing in this town. We don't deal with the Lord Death's refuse here. If you're not going to buy a drink, stop wasting my time."

Azul spun on her heel, intent on wasting someone else's time. She strode out of the stuffy, low-ceiling room and considered her surroundings.

The Lord Death's refuse—what a rude but succinct way to put it. Luck willing, a view not widely shared, or this town's ossuary might end up being just a hole in the ground.

Monteverde was a sprawling mantle of buildings surrounding an ancient fortress built on a low hill. The houses were wide and elegant, comprising walls and doors but no other openings—they could afford open patios inside.

The ruins of the fortress peeked between the houses. Calls were often made to tear it down and build something more elegant, but legend claimed its foundations had been laid by a god—which one, no one knew—and superstition died slowly in places like this. Ravaging wars were things of the dark past, and skirmishes inflicted only upon the borders, not towns this far inland. And yet, they thought, might not their safety exist because a god was looking out for them? What would this god say if they were to tear down their gift?

Noticing a woman watching them with curiosity from under a doorway, Azul approached.

"Forgive me," she said in her friendliest tone. "We are new to Monteverde. Could you direct us to the ossuary?"

"The ossuary?"

Azul deepened her smile to the point of hurt. "Where they keep people's bones."

The woman brought out a piece of ribbon from inside the belt holding up her breeches and waved it in front of her, guarding off ill intent. Azul wanted to snatch it from her hands and stamp on it, even if doing so would be stamping on the Lady Dream.

"I have nothing to do with the dead," the woman said, full of distrust. "Don't bring your problems to me."

With another wave of her ribbon, she stepped inside the house and closed the door in Azul's face.

"Friendly bunch," Nereida commented.

She should know, Azul thought, *considering the woman had uttered less than a handful of words since their talk inside the ship.*

Azul turned, looking for more prey. Surely someone in this city must know where they kept Isadora's bones.

Her gaze strayed toward the hill. Perhaps they kept the bones in the fort itself? She directed her steps that way and waited until the housing quality increased, the buildings just a little wider, the flagstone on the ground a little less dusty.

She approached an older man dressed in fine clothing slowly making his way along the street with the help of a beautiful cane.

"Excuse me, sirese," she said politely. "Do you know where they keep people's bones? Is it at the fortress?"

The man spat at her feet, and Azul took a hasty step back.

"Bones?" he said in a rough, unpleasant voice. "Leave me be and take your problems with you."

Something unpleasant crawled up her insides toward her throat, but Azul refused to acknowledge it. If this man wouldn't speak, the next one might.

"Hold," she heard Nereida say, but she paid her no attention. She had spied someone else to ask—a boy of about twelve selling dried flowers out of a cart.

"Hello, there," she told him. "Could you point me to Monteverde's ossuary? The place where they keep people's bones?" she added, because when she was his age, she was too busy learning to spell *damn* to worry about fancier terms.

The boy wrinkled his nose as if Azul's words had the smell of a dozen chamber pots. "We don't have that here."

But they did. She remembered the innkeeper's words as clearly as if she'd heard them five heartbeats ago: *Monteverde, of course.*

"Are you sure?" she insisted. "What do you do with your dead, then?"

"Same thing you do," he answered a little belligerently. "Pay the Temple for a prayer and hope it's enough to win the gods' goodwill. You going to buy flowers or not?"

"I might if I knew where I could offer them to the dead."

"Then you got a long way to go," the boy said. "They're all down in the capital." He looked around, then leaned in, adding in a whisper, "Mom says they eat them for dinner at the court, and that's why the gods struck down Girende."

"They're at the capital?" Azul pressed, her friendly smile forced so deeply into her cheeks she might never carry another expression again.

"That's what I said, isn't it?"

Well, it couldn't be. Abandoning the boy, she focused on another citizen making her way along the street.

"We should—" Nereida began.

"*No.*"

Behind her, the boy's cursing filled the air, damning their souls to Fellman's End for wasting his time and leaving no coin.

"Sirese, if you please," Azul asked of the passerby. "Is it true the bones of the dead go to Cienpuentes?"

"Ah yes. To Cienpé, they go. I was born there, you know."

Azul didn't know, didn't care. With a murmur of thanks, she walked on.

She felt Nereida keep up with her hurried steps and realized her own breath was coming out in uneven gasps. She stopped, biting down on her fist as if gnawing her hand to the bone would somehow make Isadora's own bone appear under her flesh.

Cienpuentes! How could that be?

Ah, if only she had pressed harder back at the inn.

Belatedly, she realized she had come to a stop by a statue of the Lady Dream. The goddess's hands rested on her hips, her legs standing apart, offering plenty of room for the ribbons tied around her limbs.

As children, Azul and Isadora had embroidered such strips themselves. Isadora had wished to slay monsters—the ones that came at night out of caves deep in the earth to steal people's bones—while Azul hadn't known what to wish for. So, she had embroidered some gibberish and tied it to the legs of the statue along with Isadora. She had figured, *I will think of something later, come back, and redo my stitches.* Of course, she had forgotten. But now the memory was a thick ball in her gut. She should've wished for Isadora's safety. What a selfish child she had been; why had she not thought of this?

"Cienpuentes," she said as if it were a curse rather than a destination. She looked at Nereida with sudden hope in her eyes. "Perhaps the local ossuary is kept a secret?"

"What would be the point?" Nereida ignored Azul's crestfallen expression and looked at the darkening sky. "It's too late to travel. We must find an inn to stay the night."

Azul wanted to contradict her, but she knew Nereida was right. She tried to instill reason within herself. Cienpuentes wasn't so far—three days of travel at most. It wouldn't make a difference to Isadora's bones, which had been lying there for near a decade now.

But the emissary's death . . .

Every breath they exhaled outside the ossuary holding Isadora's bones was an opportunity for the emissary's death to catch up to them and stop their plans.

"Not an inn," she thought aloud. "Too easy to track if someone comes after us."

"Where, then?"

"My mother has a friend here. Lina del Valle. She will give us a place to stay and keep our visit secret, I'm sure of it."

"You were also sure of where your sister's bones lie."

The words were cool but not unkind, so Azul decided against planting her fist on Nereida's face. "That was someone else's lie. This woman, I know well."

Nereida thought about this for a moment, then nodded. "We'll stay with your family friend. But, Del Arroyo," she added in an icy tone, "no more delays. No more lies."

Azul nodded. "I am as eager to get this done as you are."

Not long after, they were ushered into a comfortable receiving room with a view into Del Valle's patio. Two settees with artfully bowed legs cornered a low, elegant table. Blue and gold drapes covered one of the walls while a framed landscape covered another.

Nereida placed her hat over the white mantel and inspected the room. She fit in here, with her dark hair, green eyes, and elegant blue waistcoat. The days of travel had left little mark on her except for the dust on her boots.

"Are the houses in Cienpuentes much grander?" Azul asked.

"Some are, some aren't."

"Yours?" Azul walked up to the drapes. Knowing there were no windows to the outside didn't stop her from pushing the fabric aside to check the street and make sure no galloping soldiers from Valanje were thundering their way.

"Of no concern to you."

A servant returned with their hostess in tow. Lina del Valle was a handsome middle-aged woman worthy of the house she owned. Arms covered by embroidered fabric hugged Azul tight against a stiff stomacher, and rose perfume wound around her senses.

"My dearest Azul," she exclaimed, "what a most welcome surprise!"

"Aunt Lina," Azul answered—although they shared no blood link, the woman had always insisted on being called so. "We are in need of a respite, and you've always been so good to us."

Del Valle examined Azul's tired face, the ill-fitting clothes. "What trouble has that wild sister of yours landed you into?" She looked around. "Where is she? Hiding behind the curtain?" The words were meant in jest, Azul reminded herself as she forced another smile.

"Not this time, Aunt. This time it's of my own doing. Isadora is . . ." A hard swallow. "Well, she is occupied elsewhere at the moment." She added a laugh, weak and pitiful.

Del Valle joined her with a much more buoyant sound. "Azana's two girls away from each other? Something I'd never have thought possible. Who is your companion, then?"

Azul hurried to make introductions. "Aunt Lina, this is my dear friend, Mar de Flor," she said, giving the false name Nereida insisted on using. Azul couldn't fault her. If Del Valle hadn't been her mother's friend, she would've used one herself.

"You must both stay, then," Lina del Valle was saying. "I insist. Rest from your travel and tell me of your problems. They won't be so bad once I'm done with them, I assure you. Are your belongings with you or traveling separately?"

"What you see is what we come with, I'm afraid," Azul told her. "We had to leave in a hurry."

Del Valle waved toward the settees. "You are safe here, my love. Your mother would never forgive me—I would never forgive myself—if I didn't help you when you're in such obvious need. Sit, make yourselves comfortable. I shall order refreshments, and some clothes will be found so you can change out of your traveling garb."

Azul touched Del Valle's hand, her eyes pleading. "We must keep our presence a secret. Someone might be following us, and we don't wish to be found. Nobody can know we're here, not even Mother."

"Of course," Del Valle assured her. "Stay. Gather your strength. I will take care of you and your friend."

VIII

AZUL

True to her word, Lina del Valle ordered her cook to prepare a fast dinner and instructed one of her maids to bring a selection of clothes that might suit Azul and Nereida.

It was decided that the two of them would travel to the capital in the morning with a couple of Del Valle's guards as escort—she would not have it any other way.

By the time they were given a guest room to sleep in, the fist gripping Azul's heart since learning Isadora's bones weren't in Monteverde had lessened in strength. Plans had been put in place, so simple they surely couldn't fail.

Unless the emissary's death caught up to them.

Azul shoved the thought away as she tried to get comfortable on the bed she was sharing with Nereida.

De Guzmán slept with a dagger.

Azul wished she had one to do the same.

How many ships crossed the sea every day? How long would it take for someone in a hurry to secure passage? Of course, an emissary wouldn't worry about such mundane things. They could simply demand a spot, and who would say no to Death's own?

Hard to believe the Lord Death still had such control over his land. Did the other gods reign over the rest of the continents like he did?

Were they angry their subjects had never thought to create emissaries for them, or did they laugh at those who lacked faith in them?

She wondered idly how other countries treated the gods. Did they tie up their wishes to the Lord Life's legs in Divinad? What about Bixe, where they favored the Lord Nightmare? Did they spend their days hoping their deity would avoid visiting them at night? Or perhaps they celebrated their god in other ways—wishing them onto others or trying to become a nightmare themselves through fights and words and fearsome acts.

Did they spend their days wondering if the gods were even real or just another tale, or were they fervent believers like the Valanjians and their emissaries?

She had heard stories of traditions beyond Sancia, but they rarely mentioned how they dealt with their gods. Azul had always assumed this lack of information was because their praying wasn't that different, that there wasn't so much difference between tying up your hopes to the Lady Dream's legs and hoping for a loved one's return in front of the Lord Life.

"Why did you believe me so easily at Diel?" she whispered to the ceiling, dark and austere in the early summer night. Her fingers toyed with the fabric of her borrowed nightgown. "Had you heard rumors about me before? The . . . the emissary knew about me."

Nereida, lying on her side and facing the door, took some time to answer, and when she did, Azul was surprised she'd answered at all. "I believe there are grains of truth in every old tale."

"There are tales?" Azul asked, astonished. "About what I can do? You called me something. You know the name of my gift?"

"Necromancer."

"Necromancer," Azul repeated, tasting the word on her lips. It sounded no better than *malady*. "What does it mean?"

"Death riser."

The words sent chills along Azul's spine. Such a bleak choice of words when all she did was bring beings back to life. "Why have I never heard of something like that?" Azul knew all kinds of scary stories, and she had never heard one by that name.

"It's an obscure tale in the North. I doubt many know of it."

"You did," Azul pointed out.

Nereida didn't respond, and Azul felt the silence press on her, forcing her thoughts to meander once again.

"We should've left this evening," she murmured. "Whoever they send after us might catch up if they ride fast."

"They won't. It will take time for them to figure out what happened and decide what to do. We don't know if the emissary knew of our destination."

Azul winced. "I let it slip when he was questioning me."

"It is of no consequence. If they send someone after us, I will take care of them the same way."

"And if it doesn't work?"

"I'll use my rapier."

Azul's head snapped to look at Nereida, then relaxed. There was something comforting about sharing a bed with someone so self-assured; it made her feel at home. Azul and her sister had shared a bed until they moved into the bigger house in Agunción and earned separate bedrooms.

What a terrible feeling, knowing Isadora wasn't a knock away, that if Azul slipped out of bed and made her way to the next room, there would be no sister to welcome her. No late-night talks or wonderful nights lying next to vibrancy and warmth.

Azul closed her eyes and allowed her thoughts to wander. There was a tug now in her mind, and she hadn't noticed how much she missed having a link like that.

Following it, she touched the bird's consciousness, so far away now, and felt its mind acknowledge the nudge and open to her intrusion. With animals, such a link was easy. Azul had tried it with Isadora once, in a fit after a sibling fight, and found that human brains were too complex for the link to be used in such a way. Maybe with time and prodding, such things might be possible, but Azul had had no wish to do it. Azul wanted her sister, not a doll.

The bird was perched on a low tree branch, and the sight of a building sprawling ahead felt familiar enough that the animal must've been looking at it for a while. It had the makings of a Sancian building rather than Valanjian. Lamps shone bright in the night, spilling light from the windows and wide-open door. Sudden neighing startled her, and the bird burst into flight, chirping in alarm. The land fell below, the dark shape of the building took form, the few treetops, the path leading up to the road, the vast blackness of the fields in the distance.

Soothing the bird, she directed it downward, watched the world rush up to her until the bird found footing by the stables. A groom saddled a fresh horse while another mare drank greedily from the trough. Someone shouted by the entrance of the building, the words warping strangely through the bird's hearing. Azul examined the surroundings eagerly, her body and spirit weightless and free. She nudged the bird onto the saddle, testing the material with its claws while the groom brought the horse closer to the entrance. More noises, more sounds. Frantic. Yelling. Someone demanding haste? Movement over the dirt path. Another horse, huffing from exhaustion, its coat dull with the dirt of travel. A hop to get a better view.

The link was suddenly cut.

Azul gasped, choking on her pounding heart. The bird was gone, killed by a well-placed smack from one of the grooms, no doubt. Beside her, Nereida craned her head to study her in the shadows, then returned to face the door. No questions, no further concern. Nereida left Azul alone with her nightmare, and Azul understood. Nightmares shouldn't be shared, even though she hadn't been dreaming, and Azul would not confess that another being she had brought back to life was now, again, dead.

Dead like Isadora.

Lying here, with Nereida by her side where Isadora should have lain, the capital seemed continents away. The empty hole inside her chest felt big enough to eat Monteverde whole.

"Whom do you mean to have me bring back from death?" she asked, grasping for something to keep her afloat.

Rustling noises, movement next to her when Nereida rolled into a different position. "We shall use an inn when we get to Cienpuentes. Think of a name for yourself instead of this questioning."

But thinking was the last thing Azul wanted to do. "Is it true the nobles at court wear so much Anchor they shine like stars?"

"Your sister told me during the trip that your mother birthed one or two heirs of the court," Nereida said. "Did she lie, or do they not acknowledge your existence?"

"My mother's business is private. Aside from Isadora, I have met only two of my half siblings, one of whom sought me out without his sire's knowledge."

"How did you and your sister end up with your mother instead of your natural fathers?"

"Isadora was the first, the one who made Mother realize how much she loved carrying babies. Without Isadora, I would not be here."

"And your father?"

"His wife died while Mother was still pregnant, and so the contract was nulled. He offered to raise me anyway, but Mother decided to keep me. Money was not an issue by then. Mother is beautiful, the children are always healthy. Her services command good money. Sometimes I think she's the Blessed Heart made flesh and bones." *A sort of emissary, perhaps*, Azul thought, *for another god and under another name.*

"And she never sought to marry? To be kept by one of her clients?"

Azul laughed. "Mother does not like romance, except for what is required to produce a child." If Azul were to be honest, she did not think her mother liked children that much once they were out of her. Isadora had been a revelation, Azul a whim, but they had often been left in the hands of family friends and tutors—and in Isadora's case, the Temple's school—while their mother was away bringing another child into being.

"Why do you think they send the bones to Cienpuentes?" Azul asked. "How can they have space for all of them?" And why had the innkeeper told Azul they would be in Monteverde after her sister's death? Was it because they had believed a ten-year-old unworthy of the truth, or had those people at the inn known no better either?

The Lord Death's refuse, the man had called bones. Maybe people around these parts simply didn't care to know.

Nereida offered no answer, and Azul rolled to lie on her side, facing the curtains. They were dark red, simple but of obvious quality. Thick enough to block the sunlight. Thick enough to stop Luck and Wonder from peeking in.

Closing her eyes, Azul tried to link back to the bird only to remember the bird was gone. If she hadn't been so curious about the commotion at the building, if she hadn't forced it . . .

Regrets, Azul reminded herself as she closed her eyes, would take her nowhere.

And, as the night advanced and no one came to demand their presence, Azul finally drifted to sleep.

IX

THE COUNT, AGAIN

A YEAR AND A HALF EARLIER

Count de Anví studied the two toddlers playing on the plush rug. They whined and squealed and made their presence annoyingly obvious in the big white-and-blue room deep inside the Heart. A nurse attended them while two fellow golden tabards stood guard by the double doors: one with a pike, the other with a rapier and a pistol. Another set of guards waited on the other side of the door behind the count and the Faceless Witch.

He spared her a glance. Damn the Witch to the Void. She was wearing Bard Celeste in full visiting regalia: embroidered breeches, embroidered deep red doublet, chestnut hair swept into a beautiful arrangement supported by silver hairpins ending in small blooming flowers. A lace mask matching the doublet covered the upper half of her face, but it didn't hide the twinkle in the honey-brown irises ringed in gray.

"So," said the Witch, "can you tell which child is the king and which one is the decoy?"

"I'm not their nurse, how would I know?"

"They do look awfully alike, don't you think? Looking at them like this, you can understand how someone thought they might be able to swap them long enough to steal the king."

The count returned his attention to the children. "You trust your source?"

"Yes, she enjoys her dreams too much to mislead me."

De Anví wanted to ask what that had to do with anything, but he would rather not know. These dreams the Witch procured left him wary, just as the Witch herself did.

"Should we tell Captain de Aria of this plot unveiling under the root vegetable he calls his nose?" the Witch asked.

De Anví ignored her. The Witch was simply using his dislike for the head of the Royal Guard to provoke him. For all that De Anví didn't know the Witch so well—except for the fact that she *was* a witch—the Witch knew him too well. How? That, he was still trying to figure out. His servants were paid well, he didn't attract undue gossip, and he kept no romantic entanglements.

"Surely, whoever is planning on kidnapping the king can't have that many people willing to help," he whispered. There were no other toddlers residing in the palace. "Taking one of the toddlers outside will be too obvious unless supported by a larger plot."

"It doesn't take that many if you have people on the inside," the Witch agreed in a jovial tone that made him wonder if she'd had a hand in helping come up with this scheme.

It didn't matter. He was nearly done with the Royal Guard; it was not his problem.

"Once the swap is revealed and news gets out that the king is gone, possibly murdered, the court will fall into disarray," the Witch continued. "Regent de Fernán will be a joke—how can a regent be allowed to speak policy when there is no king to regent for? The court will freeze while they search for the king, then search the bloodline when they fail to find him. They will look for another heir. And you can be assured whoever is behind the plot already knows whom they'll find: some wonderful puppet ready to do as they need."

Not unlike the Witch's bodies, De Anví thought wryly. "Will these traitors assassinate the actual king once they have left the decoy behind?"

"No, they will keep the child alive, along with any proof that he is the true king, and raise him to do their bidding. It's useful to have an alternative plan in case things go awry and their puppet decides to grow a will of his own." The Witch licked her lips. "Schemes, so very enjoyable."

And the one thing De Anví wanted no part of. "I assume you paid your informant well enough that this tale will not spread further."

"Of course I did. My dreams aren't cheap."

"We'll need to find out who the leader of the plot is and take them into custody."

"Hmm. I'm not sure that's the correct way to proceed."

De Anví was scared to ask, yet couldn't help himself. "How else?"

"You take out only one person, another will take their place. It's so much better to catch everyone in the act, don't you think?"

"Captain de Aria will never allow the king to be used as bait."

The Witch smiled knowingly. "That's why we're not going to tell him."

"If not him, then who?" De Anví had no real power to speak of, his position too low in the Royal Guard ranks. The only reason he was allowed in the king's presence at all was the strength of his family name. Accusing someone on the basis of hearsay would get him nothing but ridicule, and he had a feeling the Witch would not provide any solid proof unless he played this game according to her rules.

The Witch appeared to ponder his question, although he was certain she'd long settled on someone to spearhead the foiling of this kidnapping. The only thing he didn't know was why she was involving him.

"De Losa, I think," she finally said. "She is hungry for power, and won't mind going behind De Aria's back."

De Anví nodded in agreement. The Countess de Losa was known for having her sights on eventually commanding the Golden Dogs. "The proof of parentage shall need to be secured, so there is no doubt the child being saved from the kidnapping is the true king and not the decoy. There can be no doubt when the traitors fail and are apprehended that we have the correct child. The queen's blood will be needed to ascertain the child is from her lineage."

"No doubt about it."

"Without anyone knowing we're securing it. We must not give the traitors cause for concern and allow them to cover their tracks."

"Indeed." The Witch's gaze switched to his face. "How will you manage that feat? The Royal Crypt is well guarded."

This was the point where he ought to step back, now that he'd given his opinion.

But now De Anví could not pretend he had never heard of a possible plot against the king. He might not want the Witch's dreamy wares, but De Anví had his own dreams for the future. While a kidnapping might cause an uproar, it would be nothing compared with another king appearing later. The scandal would upend all of Sancia—and his life, by association. Cienpuentes had enough troubles as it was.

No, he must see this through or be shackled with the worry about others' incompetence. He had spent nights waking up with his heart in his throat and his skin covered in sweat for less important matters.

As for how to find out things without anyone knowing, he knew just the man: Miguel Esparza, his favorite city rat.

THE PRESENT

Two days after his attempted ambush, De Anví donned darker, simpler clothes than he usually wore. It felt strange not to be swallowed by whites, creams, and gold. He welcomed the change, though, the spark of excitement and adventure that the need to dress this way had awakened inside his soul. Of course, different clothes could only do so much as he strode through the more disreputable streets of Cienpuentes, and since he was unwilling to use a mask, people could tell something was off about him—if they didn't outright recognize him—and it rendered them reluctant to talk.

Ah, how he missed being simply a count. How he longed for his life before his "advancement" into the second-in-command of the Golden Dogs, when not many outside court paid him attention unless he showed some coin.

"Like the old times!" exclaimed the Faceless Witch with what sounded to De Anví like all the delight in the world, still wearing her favorite man. "When we scoured the town looking for stolen royal blood!"

Gods, would there be a time when he could finally be rid of her? When he no longer needed to keep track of her deeds? Every day, the river grew more appealing. Slipping into the Lord Death's embrace would take no great effort—he had long set his affairs in order, just as he had long accepted his path in life was set and would offer no deviations.

Which was why, when he had been confronted by three masked strangers in a dark alleyway and curiosity bloomed in his chest, he'd found himself unable to resist trying to track them down.

"Be silent, Witch," said Esparza. "Your thoughts aren't needed."

No love lost between Miguel Esparza and the Faceless Witch.

The Witch chuckled. "Do not lie, you can feel it too. It's been too long since we last had an outing like this."

And it would never be long enough, Esparza's expression told them. De Anví commiserated. He had considered ending the Witch in the past, but alas, not knowing her real identity or the location of her true body—not for a lack of Esparza and him trying to figure it out— would've meant killing the man being used as her body, while she simply moved on to inhabit someone else.

"Stay," he told them both curtly, stopping any further bickering. He crossed the busy street and approached a woman selling murky drinks by an intersection. Freshly boiled tea, she told him. He very much doubted it, but bought a cup anyway and asked her if she had seen three masked men rushing away two evenings earlier.

He got nothing, just as he had gotten nothing from the other people he had already asked. Turned out, a trio of hurried masked men was not a rare occurrence in Cienpé.

"We should talk with De Gracia," the Witch suggested once De Anví re-joined them. "It's no coincidence, this timing of his sire's murder and your encounter. And he might have discovered something new about his father's death."

The Witch's increasing obsession with De Gracia was unwelcome news. As much as De Anví resented the Witch's fixation on him, to have her fixated on someone outside his oversight would be worse.

"We might as well," he said, and to Esparza, "You will come?"

A roll of eyes. "Indeed."

So, to the Marquess de Gracia's house they went. It was quite a walk, and by the end of it, De Anví was glad to be in simple shirt-sleeves instead of the elaborate doublet and half cape befitting his station. They didn't have to wait for His Grace, since he was already home, and they were soon shown into a beautiful, airy parlor, where Sergado de Gracia welcomed them and introduced his companion, the artist Isile Manzar.

De Gracia was in his mid-twenties, with dark brown hair that defied custom and was shorn short enough to fall in waves around his face rather than to his shoulders or chest. His friend wore his black hair gathered into a tail by his nape, his skin a richer golden tone than the lighter tan common in these parts of Sancia. He was about the same age as De Gracia, and the ease in his movements and conversation spoke of the young man's friendship with His Grace as well as his talent—here was someone whose art had made him equal to a marquess.

Perhaps, De Anví thought fleetingly as they made use of the two settees in the room, he could ask him how a few blurred strokes could change shape so dramatically depending on the distance from a painting.

Esparza chose to remain by the door, too much of a guard and too aware of his station to join them.

"Tell me," the Witch said, angling toward Manzar, "do you ever wear masks?"

Manzar's surprise was evident. "If I must."

"Do you gain inspiration from your dreams?"

This, he mulled for a few moments. "Occasionally, but I prefer to study my subjects with my eyes open."

"A dream will show what sight cannot."

Manzar shook his head. "The Lady Dream tends to steal them as soon as I wake, I'm afraid."

"There are ways around that," the Witch replied. Then, with a secretive smile, "Seek me later, Isile Manzar, and I will help you."

The young man smiled in response, polite but wary.

"Losing your touch," murmured Esparza.

Something flickered in the Witch's eyes, but her face was too hard to read beneath her mask.

"Your Grace," De Anví said, addressing the marquess, "I'm afraid we are here to raise some bad memories."

De Gracia's easy smile faded into a straight line. "Then you are here about my father."

"Yes." De Anví inclined his head toward Manzar. "Perhaps this would be a conversation better kept private."

"Nothing about my father's death was kept a secret. I don't see why we should start now."

"As you wish. I need to ask if you've done any inquiries about his demise."

"Murder, you mean," De Gracia said, steel backing his voice. "And, yes, but why do you ask?"

"Forgive me, Your Honor," Manzar said, "but wouldn't you be in a better position to know about it?"

"It's a matter of the City Guard, not the palace," De Anví answered. "And I'm sure His Grace trusts their usefulness as much as I do." He spared a glance at Esparza and found his mocking salute.

De Gracia nodded again. "Indeed. But again, what is your interest? If I may be blunt, we have barely exchanged words before today, and now you ask?"

De Anví considered how to best approach the matter. Being second-in-command of the Golden Dogs, if only for a year and a half, had accustomed him to awe, respect, and a certain eagerness to please—even if the outward deference was covering disdain. He'd forgotten there were others who didn't share the sentiment.

"I was ambushed two evenings ago by masked men seeking to take me to someone." By the men's expressions, he could tell the tale hadn't yet reached them. "This one," he continued, motioning toward the Witch, "insists my unsuccessful abduction and your sire's successful murder have something in common."

"The summer court is upon us," the Witch said. "It's been two years since it last convened, and we all know what's on everyone's mind."

"Anchor," De Anví stated.

De Gracia frowned at this. Manzar stood and got them each a drink from a nearby decanter.

De Anví enjoyed the hit of fruity fire running down his throat, but partook of no more than one sip. Placing the cup on the low table between them, he avoided looking at the marquetry swirls on its surface lest he feel forced to spend the rest of the day aligning the cup with the pattern.

"My father believed in the ban," the marquess said, looking at his own cup but not drinking. "Our family had some interests in Girende that went down with the rest of the city. It's a well-known fact." He raised his eyes to meet everyone else's. "Was this why he was murdered? Would the mining proponents be so blatant?"

"You are young—your views can be molded, cajoled, or scared into what they want," De Anví said. "But, yes, these have been bold strokes. Desperation, perhaps?" Did De Fernán lack enough support to lift the ban and had turned to extremes to get it? He looked at Esparza for confirmation. The man simply shrugged.

"Sergado doesn't care about politics," Manzar said. "Everyone knows this too."

"What *do* you care about?" the Witch asked, too eagerly for De Anví's taste.

"Art, science, and the like," De Gracia answered.

"Matters that move us forward," Manzar added.

"And the court moves us backward?" De Anví asked dryly.

"No offense meant, Your Honor," Manzar said with haste. "But from what we hear, they do seem to walk in circles."

"Father warned me of the court's pettiness," De Gracia agreed. "And although he had little liking for it, he was raising me to take his place eventually. I have—had—been helping him since I was a child. I don't care if they mine Anchor or not. My interests lie elsewhere. If Girende's cave-in was meant to be a warning, I'll let scientists and philosophers tell me how I should feel."

"And this is a known view?" De Anví asked.

"We all hold similar views in our circle."

"Then your sire's death was certainly about the Anchor ban. A muddled view like yours is easier to direct than a strict one like your father's," De Anví said. And, damn her soul, perhaps the Witch was right and his ambush was about the ban as well—his views on the ban weren't far from De Gracia's. "Hire personal guards, pay them well, and watch your back. Whoever is behind this plot might not be so lenient if you go against their wishes. Esparza over there can help you arrange for it."

"I've had a personal guard since I was a child. I am well aware of the risks in my position, no matter how inconvenient I might find them." De Gracia pointed toward a pistol lying on the windowsill.

De Anví had yet to be impressed by such weapons. "Those are as likely to explode and take your hand than expel the bullet. Your point, however, stands. I can see you are aware of the dangers."

"It would be foolish not to be," De Gracia added with a wry curve of his lips.

Here was someone who thought his own intellect a step above everyone else's, De Anví thought. They might as well take their leave.

"What shall we do now?" the Witch asked with unashamed eagerness once they were outside the marquess's large home.

"Nothing," De Anví said curtly. "We have no leads on the three strangers, and we learned nothing we didn't already suspect from De Gracia."

"We'll have to wait and see if you get corralled again," Esparza said, though De Anví had no doubt he'd nose into both his confrontation and the elder De Gracia's murder. "Until then, I have my City Guard duties to conduct."

With a tip of his hat, Esparza went on his way. The Witch abandoned De Anví's side as well, thank the gods, likely in pursuit of more information about De Gracia's artist friend.

As De Anví returned to his own house, the familiar blanket of bleak tiredness embraced him. The excitement was gone. All the things he must do—must keep doing—now that this escapade was done pressed on his shoulders.

If only he had someone to share in the pointlessness of it all.

But all he had were dreams.

X

AZUL

Horses again. Azul hadn't spent so many hours on one since she'd been forced to learn how to ride as a child, and she rued that her inexperience was slowing them down when all she wanted to do was fly.

Oren and Anané were the two guards lent by the grace of Lina del Valle. They introduced themselves first thing in the morning, after Azul and Nereida donned their new clean garb and broke their fast.

Azul liked them. They wore traveling gear themselves—riding pants, high boots, short cloaks, brown hats—and rapiers hanging low against their hips. Their smiles were wide and their words warm, so unlike Valanje's guards, who had remained impassible and silent during her forced stay.

Oren kept up a chatter about the people they passed, the owners of the buildings, the contents of the fields, and the farms in the distance. Azul welcomed the distraction and threw herself wholeheartedly into it. The sky was clear, the air crisp. Monteverde receded into the distance, and with it went all her tension, all her nightly worries.

The countryside opened ahead of them, fields as far as the eye could see peppered with old trees. Azul's chest eased at their familiarity. For all her wishes to travel beyond Agunción, she now saw this was the land she belonged to—her domain. Sancia belonged to the Blessed Heart and the Lady Dream, not Death and his emissaries.

Shortly before midday, they came by an inn and decided to stop for lunch.

Azul had disagreed—the faster they got to Cienpuentes, the better. Unfortunately, her companions had not listened.

It was too early for the evening countryside crowd, and they had the small hall for themselves. The lack of other guests felt eerie, and Azul was reminded of the devastating silence that had followed the demise of the small bird.

Her companions didn't seem to notice the unnerving lack of noise or care.

They sat around the table, eating in companionable silence. Even Nereida appeared to be enjoying the bread and cold cuts of meat, until the door slammed open and four figures crowded in.

Oren and Anané tensed at once, letting their food fall to their plates.

The newcomers were all wearing the same hues of black. An insignia was embroidered on their tabards, marking them as someone's personal guard. Their gazes surveyed the room, settling on Azul's group. Their leader stepped forward. Azul did not like the look of any of them.

"You are the group from Monteverde?" the man asked.

Azul choked on her food. Coincidence, nothing else. The road was well used, the existence of an inn proof of it. How could their group not be from Monteverde?

Anané stood slowly. "Who wishes to know?"

"It is no concern of yours. We'll be accompanying the sireses from here on."

Oren burst to his feet. "Is that so?"

The man smiled. It wasn't a nice smile. It wasn't a nice face: craggy and somewhat scarred and with a nose that had been broken at least twice.

All at once Nereida was on her feet, and six hands touched their rapiers' hilts. All but Azul, who had none, and the leader of the guards, who had his men lining up behind him instead.

"Who do you belong to?" demanded Anané.

Azul's hand crept toward the heaviest mug on the table. They might've taken her dagger in Valanje, but she was not defenseless.

"For the sireses to know," the man answered.

"Then speak," said Nereida, tall and calm and feathering the grip of her rapier.

The man inclined his head in respect. "Sireses, if you'd step outside without your companions so we can explain."

"The women are under our care," Oren said. "They won't be leaving with you."

Azul slipped out of her chair. Anané extended her free arm and gently pushed her behind her back. The edge of a table dug into her thigh. Nereida and Del Valle's guards would make their stand here with the tables and stools, not outside, where they'd be easily surrounded.

Anané's and Oren's rapiers came free. The men behind their leader responded in kind.

The man lifted a hand. "There is no need to put the sireses in danger. Do you think you can take on all of us? For what? Some vestige of pride? They'll be safe with us."

"And yet you do not answer our questions," Nereida said, her sword still sheathed. "You do not ask for permission. I will not be taken by riffraff and kidnappers."

One of the men hissed loudly. "Do as you're told, woman."

Nereida arched her eyebrows. "Or what? You will try your luck dragging me outside?"

"I don't need luck," the man assured her. "Not for someone like you."

"Watch your tongue," Anané warned, "or we shall cut it out of you."

A couple of the men laughed. "You and how many more?" one of them said.

"We don't need a crowd to win fights, unlike you," Oren returned, sneering.

"Enough," the men's leader snapped. With a swift kick, he sent the stool in front of him flying to the side, clearing the way to Azul's group.

And then Nereida's rapier kissed the air.

"The flower has fangs," commented one of the black tabards. The others tittered.

Nereida appeared unfazed by the laughter, her stance one that spoke of many hours with a rapier in her hand. Azul could recognize familiarity with sword fights when it stood in front of her—she had seen it on Isadora plenty of times.

"Take care of the trash, then." The tabards' leader gestured toward Anané and Oren. "Don't harm the women."

One of the men stalked toward her, an unnatural gleam in his eyes.

Azul recognized this look too. People often had it when they'd spent too long sitting around with nothing exciting to do.

Azul would cure him of that soon.

It didn't matter that she was standing by Nereida instead of Isadora, that this was an inn on the road and not a watering hole at Agunción—the movements came easy because she, too, had been looking for an outlet since stepping on Valanje and having her world come crashing down on her.

She spun the mug in her hand, then threw it at the man's head.

It hit him full in the face, eliciting a shout and a spurt of blood.

The man staggered back, crashing against a table and some stools, one hand going to his nose, his rapier wobbling uselessly in the air.

Anané whistled. Oren laughed loudly. "What an aim!"

Exclaiming in outrage, the other two plain black tabards rushed forward and were met by Oren and Anané. The rasps and clinks of swords meeting filled the air while Azul searched for another weapon, not taking her eyes off the fight.

How many times had she been in this position before? How many times had she stood behind, watching Isadora's back? Exhilaration filled her to the point of bursting.

A sword tip came close to piercing Oren's side, and he was forced back against the tables. His opponent used the advantage, but his sword was diverted by Nereida's rapier.

With the ease of a thousand duels under her belt, De Guzmán stepped in front of Oren and drove the black tabard back.

Oren gave her space and leaped over a table to stand by Azul's side.

"Sirese," he said with a grin.

Azul answered with the flash of a smile that showed too many teeth.

The tabard she'd felled was now back on his feet, a murderous glint replacing the unnatural glee in his eyes. He advanced toward them, shoving one of his companions aside and allowing Anané to claim a hit.

"What are you doing?" the other man demanded, scrambling back with a new tear on his upper arm.

"Shut up," bloody nose replied, striding forward with the single-mindedness of a starved hunter.

Many had thought Azul prey, figuring her weaker than her outspoken sister, and she'd always been happy to prove them wrong.

Oren stood in front of her, ready to meet the tabard's attack. Their swords met, the tabard's motions angry and powerful and missing all finesse, and Azul wasn't surprised when he brought out a dagger with his free hand.

"Dagger," she warned Oren, wishing she had another clear shot at the black tabard's bloodied face. Relieving the man of a tooth or two would only improve his countenance—Azul was sure he'd thank her for it.

A cry brought her attention back to Nereida. Her rapier had found its way deep into her opponent's shoulder, although the lack of expression on her face would have anyone think she had simply threaded a needle rather than pierced flesh.

Nereida pulled the rapier out, then thrust toward his neck.

The man dodged in the nick of time and brought up his own rapier. Nereida retreated, a cool, calculated move that dared the man to press whatever advantage he thought he had left so she could deliver a final blow.

Azul's gut churned in an unwelcome way.

Fights to first blood, fights to unconsciousness, fights to settle debts—all those she was used to. Fights to the death? Those didn't happen often in Agunción.

But this was not Agunción, and the reminder was like a dunk in a river's winter tide.

This was no simple fight to pass the time, just as their rush from Diel hadn't been a mere game of hide-and-seek. This was about life and stealing people from the Lord Death.

This was about the trail of corpses they were leaving behind when they sought only to keep people alive.

About the Emissary of the Lord Death, all magnificence and virility and life, falling dead at their feet because Azul and Nereida had decided his life was worth less than their plans.

This should never become the norm.

"Nereida—"

"De Biel," a new voice said from the open door. "Have your men stand down."

XI

AZUL

The room fell silent but for everyone's strained breathing as a new man entered the hall, followed by another man dressed in the same black tabard as the rest.

Anané and Oren reaffirmed their sweaty grips on their weapons. Azul could tell they would make their stand to the end, and, Luck willing, it would be swift. But not before they took a few black tabards down with them.

Nereida lowered her rapier, shrewd eyes locked on the newcomer. He had long brown hair tied back and wore a traveling cape, breeches, and high boots. Wide light-blue rings surrounded golden irises. Valanjian.

And something more, different from every other person in the room.

Azul almost took a step forward, shocked by the sight. Then the connotations of a Valanjian's presence there hit her. Her stomach rebelled.

The emissary's murder had caught up with them.

"I regret the inconvenience." The newcomer's voice lacked any inflection, as if he had no stake in what came out of his mouth. "I am Silvo Zenjiel, and I've been sent by Valanje's ambassador in Sancia to extend an invitation to one Sirese De Guzmán and one Azul del Arroyo to become her guests."

Anané and Oren didn't relax. Their gazes stayed on Zenjiel, except for a quick look at Nereida.

"Strange way to invite someone," Oren said. "Guests aren't usually found at the end of a rapier."

"My men grew overzealous, nothing more," Zenjiel said.

"Then the sireses are free to go?" Anané asked.

"It would be in their best interest not to."

Oren's mouth tightened with resolve, and Azul knew that he was willing to offer his life if it meant giving them a chance to escape.

"Nereida," Azul whispered, although she wasn't sure what she wanted to ask.

Nereida didn't look at her. Instead, she cleaned and sheathed her rapier. "The invitation would be accepted more eagerly if our guards were allowed to leave uninjured."

"A fair request."

"Sirese, no," said Anané. "Allow us to go with you at least."

"Go," Nereida said, "tell Sirese Del Valle that we are the ambassador's guests and will be taken care of."

"As you wish, sirese," she answered stiffly. "But we shall remain here for a few days. In case you change your mind."

Nereida acknowledged this with a nod, then addressed Silvo Zenjiel. "Take us to our new gracious host, then."

Azul kept her chin up, but on the inside, she was prodding at every window, every entrance of the room, seeking another way of escape.

They were in Valanje's hands once again.

To her surprise, the moment the black tabards turned toward the door, Nereida pressed a dagger into her hand so quickly Azul almost dropped it. Swiftly, she slipped it under her long waistcoat.

The hilt was made of animal bone.

Another two men were waiting outside the inn, holding on to their companions' horses.

"Such an escort," Nereida commented. "Are the roads this unsafe?"

"No one will dare touch you," Zenjiel answered easily.

Azul and Nereida exchanged a look. They were as good as caught and caged.

De Biel opened the door of a covered carriage.

Grimly, Azul stepped inside and made space for Nereida, De Biel, and Zenjiel. She tried to hold Zenjiel's gaze, but he ignored her and grew a faraway look.

His disinterest rattled. She was prepared to barter her way out of being dragged to Valanje, scream and kick if need be. She hadn't counted on being treated like an unimportant package.

And there were so many questions she wanted to ask of him. But she couldn't. Not with an audience.

Instead, she studied him, cataloging his blank features and comparing them to other Valanjian men she'd seen through the years, to Enjul, the Emissary of the Lord Death. The emissary had been easy to read—he hated her. Zenjiel offered no such ease. The world appeared to leave no mark on him, and the observation left a pool of unease deep in her gut.

Would Isadora have looked like this, given enough time?

No, Azul reminded herself. Not Isadora. Isadora would not have gone through life like a cart through a well-trodden path. She'd have broken the wheels and cut across the fields, no matter how difficult, and she'd be laughing her heart out.

The trip to the ambassador's estate took a few hours. Azul had no real experience with the gentry's country homes, and her grim determination gave way to disbelief as she stared at the massive gardens leading up to the main house. All straight lines and right angles, the way Sancians liked their buildings. Two stories tall with high windows looking onto the front, it was a rectangle of beautiful stone, so light gray it was only a few steps away from blinding white.

The inside was just as awe-inspiring. Two black tabards stood at attention by the main door, and a third one preceded the group while Zenjiel led them across a grand entrance hall and down a side corridor. Azul walked carefully, afraid to crack and sully the polished tiled floors.

A slight breeze carried through the corridor, and Azul allowed herself to enjoy the coolness, allowed herself to study the mosaic of Anchor discard filling the upper half of the wall with different hues of blue. It took a big block of Anchor to collect the small pieces used in jewelry and other shows of wealth, and the resulting refuse, while nowhere as valuable, was itself a treasure. Here, displayed along the corridor, elegant and carefully arranged, was Sancia's pride. What a contrast with the bare hallways of the Great Council House in Diel.

Voices rose ahead, and Azul forced the awe out of her face. Nereida's dagger was a reassuring bulk against her lower back. They hadn't searched her for weapons; they hadn't taken away Nereida's rapier.

She wondered if they were being taken to some locked cellar, and had been allowed to keep their blades to end their own lives.

"Sirese Zenjiel," Azul said, choosing to strike now rather than from a dank cell. "May we speak in private, if only for a few minutes?" If she could convince him they had apprehended the wrong people, seed enough doubt and earn enough freedom to attempt an escape . . .

He appeared not to hear, so Azul had no option but to keep walking behind him.

The corridor merged into a longer one. Windows lining one side allowed a view into a beautiful square patio filled with endless geraniums, pomegranates, and queen's blooms.

"Take that one to the blue rooms," Zenjiel said, waving toward Nereida.

And then Nereida and most of the escort were gone, leaving Azul alone with Zenjiel and a single guard.

Leaving Azul with an opportunity to escape.

She glanced at the guard walking behind her. She could take him.

Zenjiel was another matter. Him, she was unwilling to harm— not yet. There was a lot that she needed to ask.

He stopped by an open door and indicated that she should step inside.

She tried to claim his attention again. "Sirese Zenjiel—"

"Miss Del Arroyo," cut a voice from within the room.

Unease crawled under her skin, so strongly she was sure if she looked down, she would see her flesh ripple across her arm. She turned toward the voice.

Her heart halted, then began a merciless pounding.

Virel Enjul stood there, one hand on the hilt of his sword, the other forming a tight fist. Golden-violet eyes fixed on her beneath the puzzle of bones on his face, that cruel mouth of his forming an unforgiving line.

It couldn't be, Azul told herself, taking a few faltering steps into the room. He must be a brother, or a twin. Maybe all emissaries looked the same.

But you're dead, she wanted to say. *I saw you bleed and fall and die.*

"We will wait outside, Emissary," said Zenjiel.

The door closed behind Azul, leaving them alone in the small room.

"You have been a nuisance, Azul del Arroyo," Enjul said without preamble, firm and solid and not part of her imagination. This man who had been dead.

"But you're dead," she did say then. She stumbled back, hitting the door.

He didn't need his bulky chestpiece for Azul to feel the strange weight of his presence pressing down on her. He wore a long cream-colored Valanjian shirt, the folds parting to reveal his long brown pants. His golden hair fell loose over his shoulders and back, caressing the embroidered collar of the shirt, his eyes shadowed beneath the bone mask.

"I am the Emissary of the Lord Death, Miss Del Arroyo. Your weapons hold no sway over me. Death decides who lives and dies."

Shock fading, Azul forced her mind to work. Would the Lord Death also decide who lived and died outside his land? She could use Nereida's dagger and test this theory. Then what? How would she escape the guards?

And if she did end his life, would he simply stand back up, like some creature from the Lord Nightmare? How many times could you kill Death's emissary before Death killed you himself?

Without her, how would Isadora live?

"How did you catch up so fast?" she asked, staying plastered to the door. "Even if you crossed right behind us, how did you know where we would—?" Her words died as she realized the truth. "You knew all along. You knew I'd go to Monteverde and find no bones there. You knew I'd be forced to travel to Cienpuentes."

The last words were a whisper, more awed than she wanted, but some things just couldn't be helped. Like the sweat pooling on the small of her back or the uneven hammering of her pulse.

"Of course I knew," he answered. "The rituals of death are an emissary's purview."

"You mean to drag me back to Valanje?"

Enjul crossed his arms. "I meant what I said in Diel. You may come willingly, or I'll bring your corpse. Which will it be, Miss Del Arroyo?"

"We are no longer in Diel. You have no authority here."

His smile was slow, alluring—a trap. "The Lord Death has authority everywhere. Who will stop me? Not you, not your companion. You already tried. None but your court would dare stop an emissary, and who are you to them? No one—they showed as much back in Diel. Accept your fate. You are young; your life need not end so soon."

Azul suppressed a shiver at the hard glint in his eyes and held her hands tight against her ill-fitting waistcoat. "Once you have me in Valanje, what will become of me?"

"What you become will depend entirely on yourself. Help me understand the nature of your malady or . . ." There was a certain relish in the way he said those last words, the satisfaction of someone looking forward to her failing whatever test he had planned.

Azul welcomed the reminder of her fate. "Capitulation or death, is that it? Like some Divinadian play?"

"If that is how you choose to see it."

"That's quite hypocritical, isn't it?"

Enjul tilted his head. "Is it?"

"I want to speak with Sirese Zenjiel."

"If you hope to plead your case, know that not even the ambassador has authority over me. Zenjiel cannot help you."

Azul fumbled behind her back until she found the handle of the door. "I don't need his help. I just need you to answer for your hypocrisy."

"Miss Del Arroyo—"

She finally got the door open. Zenjiel and the guard still stood outside, turning to stare at her.

Azul looked at Enjul over her shoulder. He waited, clearly amused.

"Explain to me, Emissary, why you direct your disgust at me when you are happy to allow Sirese Zenjiel his freedom," she said with ill-contained anger as she reached for Zenjiel's hand.

Their fingers met.

And Silvo Zenjiel promptly turned into a corpse.

Azul stared in shock as the mass of decayed flesh and bone dropped to the floor. Shouts rose in the air; the stench of rotting meat slammed into her nostrils. Azul gagged, then was wrenched backward.

Enjul loomed over her, his teeth bared in an enraged snarl. He shook her shoulders. "What did you do?!"

Her teeth clattered. She gripped his wrists. "Nothing! It wasn't me!"

Enjul stilled, returned his gaze to the remains of Zenjiel scattered halfway into the room. The bone of Zenjiel's skull peeked through the putrefied flesh; white showed on bony fingertips. The guard bent in half and heaved on the precious tiled floor.

The mask concealed most of Enjul's expression, but his shock was obvious.

Zenjiel's body had been dead awhile, that much was clear. Dead well before Azul had been brought into the house. Dead well before she had touched his hand.

And then the gleam of shrewdness returned to the emissary's eyes as he arrived to the same shocking conclusion she had back when Zenjiel first stepped into the inn:

"There is another one of you."

XII

SECOND CHANGES

DAYS EARLIER

Virel Enjul, Emissary of the Lord Death, opened his eyes, and Azul del Arroyo's face filled his vision.

There would be no forgiving now. No mercy.

"Emissary Enjul," someone said.

He sat up, the muscles in his chest and left shoulder protesting at the sudden movement. His mask was a reassuring weight on his nose as he bared his teeth at the guard standing nearby.

"Fetch my belongings," he snarled. "I will take the next ship."

"Yes, Emissary."

The man scurried out of the room. The dockworkers had brought Enjul to some fisherman's shack. Nets and ropes lined the walls, and a rickety piece of wood trembled under him when he brought his legs off the table. The stench of fish warred with the smell of gunpowder clinging to his clothes. He took off his shirt and tossed it into a corner, then glanced at his chest and shoulder.

Satisfaction coursed through him.

His skin, barely marked.

The ball of metal he had felt enter his body, tear through muscle, and crush his bones nowhere to be seen, nowhere to be felt.

He closed his eyes, one hand over his beating heart, and searched for the spark that made him different from other Valanjians, the otherly piece he had been born with that marked him as belonging to the Lord Death. A piece so small it could be ignored if it hadn't colored every aspect of his life.

Virel Enjul might carry a piece of the Lord Death within himself, but he was no god. There had been moments in the past, stolen moments of frustration, of indecision, of boredom, when he had doubted his faith. He had wondered what use it was to serve on behalf of the Lord Death, to exist in a world that decayed around him, when Death himself never bothered to speak directly to him.

Now his god was rewarding him for staying true.

It wasn't uncommon for emissaries to survive an accident or a fever that would've killed anyone else, but surviving this kind of wound? Enjul couldn't recall such a thing happening before.

The Lord Death had measured his soul, his belief, and concluded his mission was true. That he must go after the malady and keep her under his control. Stop the rot. Stop her.

And if she put up a fight, he thought, licking his lips, *then he'd take great pleasure in teaching her to fear the Lord Death, just as she and her companion had taken pleasure in attempting to end his life.*

Yes, perhaps he would simply kill her and test how much Sancia's beloved gods liked their malady.

Azul del Arroyo would not escape his grasp again.

THE PRESENT

Azul could never tell how long she stood by the door with the rotting corpse of Silvo Zenjiel, Enjul's fingers digging holes into her shoulders, his gaze trying to bore into her soul. It could've been seconds; it could've been eons.

Then the hands fell, his attention shifted to the guard, and the trembling began. Her fingers first, followed by her whole hands. And she prayed to Luck and Wonder it would not reach farther.

Azul dropped to her knees and reached for the arm lying on the tiles next to Zenjiel's head. Bones peeked through the decaying flesh, the stench of rot inescapable, and Azul was certain she would never smell anything else again. Her fingers threaded through the skin and muscle until she touched bone.

She called on the Eye of Death.

It took so much more effort than the bird or the chicken or her own sister that Azul thought she might not be able to do it at all. The thought was scarier than never seeing Isadora again, so she stared hard into Zenjiel's milky-white eyes and called on the instinct wreaking havoc in her veins, the one calling for her to deny death and remake what had been taken.

The muscle around her fingers became tougher, the skin re-forming. A chain of ripping sounds came from his clothing as the bone used the body and fabric to re-form. But it wasn't enough. It sucked greedily at the spots where it touched the doorframe and the door itself—once a beautiful polished walnut brown, now a web of gray roots. The sunken skin tightened; the face no longer drooped. Another piece of Azul's soul gone to fill Zenjiel's eyes with awareness. She felt its loss, the tearing of her insides, a piercing pain in a place deep inside her. This was no simple animal. *Death* demanded more if he was to step aside and relinquish his claim on a human being.

Then Azul was torn away, thrown backward into the wall, where she crashed with a painful thud.

She blinked, trying to clear her vision. Zenjiel was staring at her from where he lay on the tiles, the tendons in his neck straining as he fought to lift his head, his mouth struggling to open.

Virel Enjul arched his sword and separated Silvo Zenjiel's head from his neck.

Azul screamed. A hoarse cry that clawed up her throat and filled her ears. "What did you do?" she cried.

The Emissary of the Lord Death wiped his sword, mouth relaxed, the mask of bone hiding the rest of his features. "Death is death," he said, "and should remain dead."

Azul could barely understand his words. "But he was alive again!"

A hissing inhale came from the guard hovering behind them. Enjul ignored it and reached down for her. "He shouldn't have been."

He pulled her to her feet. Azul flinched at the contact, but his grip was overpowering and as unavoidable as death itself. He made short work of dragging her out of the room and toward a pair of gaping guards, stepping over the remains of Zenjiel like a sack of spilled goods instead of a man dead by his hand.

"The ambassador?" he asked.

One of the guards had enough presence to answer: "On her way, Emissary."

"Clear out, but don't go far. Keep an eye on Miss Del Arroyo."

Neither of the guards showed disgust or wariness as they walked down the hall. To them, Azul realized, she was an innocent bystander. She wasn't the woman who had accidentally ended Zenjiel, then attempted to return his life.

Which explained why they paid her no heed when they stopped to watch another guard trot down the corridor and cover the remains with a sheet.

Azul slipped away on the tip of her boots to avoid the echo of her heels. A couple of black tabards ran past her, paying her no attention.

She took the first corner of the endless corridor, then a second into a narrower hallway.

Would the chaos reach the stables, or would she be better off setting out on foot? She barely remembered how to saddle a horse. She'd have to hope one was ready, somehow, waiting for her. Doubtful.

Besides, Azul had given her word to Nereida.

Where had they taken her?

She resumed her silent walk, trying to form a map of the building inside her head. How such a vast building seemed to be composed of only corridors, she couldn't begin to comprehend. Where would they stash an interloper? Did they have jail cells in this place?

Her steps slowed to a halt as she passed by an opening into one of the patios. The garden outside was drenched in shadows, the silvery moonlight of Luck and Wonder probing here and there, blessing the land with their presence.

It was hard to guess who had been more shocked at Zenjiel's sudden turn into a standing corpse, the emissary or Azul. She had sought to prove Enjul wrong, that bringing her sister back was not the affront to the gods he believed it to be, and he had shown her he was as merciless as death.

The ease with which he had executed Zenjiel made her innards churn. Did she not have a responsibility here beyond her promise to Nereida? Would she really allow the emissary to steal the life she had begun to bring back?

A bone, that was all that she needed. A toe nobody would miss. And later, when she escaped with Nereida and brought Isadora back, she'd complete what Virel Enjul had so cruelly interrupted.

Once away from Enjul, Zenjiel would be given the opportunity to live. Then maybe the hole inside Azul would begin to close.

Turning, she retraced her steps and chose another hallway away from the patio and deeper into the less elegant side of the building. The servants' area would be here, and the guards' quarters. The kitchens had to be nearby or annexed.

The cellars.

They had stowed Isadora in the inn's cool cellar until it was time for her body to be moved. They would do the same with Zenjiel.

At the sound of incoming footsteps, she dipped into a nook formed by one of the pillars and held her breath.

A guard and a servant walked by, speaking in hushed tones and ignoring their surroundings.

No shouts of alarm yet. How long until her disappearance was noticed? She must hurry.

Azul slipped from behind the column, alert to any incoming noise. The deeper she got into the servants' zones, the more populated they'd be. If someone noticed her, what excuse could she give?

She peeked around a corner. A guard stood by an open archway, a lamp by his feet flickering light against the shadows.

Should she walk by, full of bravado, or try to find a way around? Perhaps through one of the patios?

"You will not succeed," said a voice behind her. "You may think of a thousand ways to reach his bones, but you will fail every one of them."

Azul stiffened and looked over her shoulder. Emissary Enjul stood a few paces away, his bone mask and pale shirt bright beacons in the moons' light.

Now she understood the lack of alarm cries. Why invest the manpower when he thought he knew her so well?

"Is that why you didn't search for me?" she asked bitterly.

The Emissary of the Lord Death shrugged. "You are easy to read; your plans lack any finesse or subterfuge. You pose no challenge." He closed the few steps separating them and grasped her wrist.

Azul shook off his hold. Surprisingly, he let go. "You might find my mind lacking, but I can follow," she bit off. "Lead."

He smiled then, a cruel curve of his lips that let her know he was allowing her the last word because that was all she had left.

All Azul could do was grit her teeth, dig her nails in her palms, and follow.

He took her back to another room, its open window bringing in the scents of the queen's blooms.

"You shall cease these attempts to use your foulness," he told her.

"I will," she assured him.

He cocked his head, her lie obvious to them both. "What you do has no place in this world. Why do you insist on doing it?"

Azul walked to the window, putting some space between them. The view into the patio had changed. The bushes and plants looked less dreary, standing strong against the darkness of the night, thanks to Luck and Wonder's moonlight. If that wasn't a sign meant to encourage her, Azul would eat her shirt. "People who needlessly die deserve the chance to be brought back to life."

Enjul drew closer. "And who are you to decide these things? A mere human? A blight on the world nobody would miss if it was gone. Why this life and not another? Why Silvo Zenjiel and not a neighbor done in by their horse?"

She glanced at her hands, tinted golden by the lamp in the room. "Silvo Zenjiel died by my hand, and so it's fair my hand brings him back."

"If I am not mistaken, his death came at someone else's hands a while back. They found a pistol ball among the remains."

"But he was . . ." She waved her hand, frustration threatening to choke her. "He was alive again. And I—"

"How did you know?"

Azul turned enough to peek at Enjul. His proximity was unsettling, his presence close to asphyxiating. He fed her guilt for bringing Isadora to her death with every mocking twist of his mouth and the way he spoke, as if her fate were a done deal. Fear mingled with irritation that this man could take her away and nobody would put up a fight. "What?"

"How did you know he was a walking corpse? The description of your sister's death was different from what happened in that room. This other malady's results are somewhat different from yours, so how did you know?"

Did he think of Isadora and Zenjiel as dead flesh walking, with no soul or thought of their own? "How could you not tell?" she challenged.

"Aren't you Death's emissary? Were Zenjiel simply a walking corpse, shouldn't you have noticed?"

Enjul drew back the chair in the room and sat down. "Death is death. It all feels the same. Except for you." The lamp's position made it impossible to read his eyes under the frame of bone, but she sensed his stare nonetheless. "Answer my question, Del Arroyo. How did you know?"

Azul returned her attention to the patio. What she said next would mean the difference between going freely to Cienpuentes or having to attempt escape again. She didn't need a great mind to know that from now on, it would be nearly impossible to get away. Even if by Luck's grace she managed to escape this grand house, Enjul only had to wait for her at Cienpuentes's ossuary.

"I could sense it. I'm sorry," she added as he opened his mouth, "my mind is too simple to describe it any better."

"And yet I must ask that you find the words."

"No."

He leaned back and linked his fingers on his lap. "I am in no hurry, but you seem to be. This house is comfortable, and I wouldn't mind using it for an extended stay."

It was Azul's time to openly study him, taking care to blank her features and hide the fear, the anxiety. The hope. With relief, she found that none of those emotions made it into her words when she spoke— the emissary would latch on to those like a bloodthirsty hound. "I'm sure it is. And if I were to describe every detail of how I identified him, no doubt you'll leave me to enjoy the house's amenities while you attempt to find others like Sirese Zenjiel. I am obvious, Emissary En-jul, but not thoughtless. If you want to find more 'walking corpses'— and you do, because you relish reminding me that death is all you are about—you will need me."

"You finally show some sense," he agreed. "I wonder how long it will last?"

Ah, the emissary was willing to play. She got her rising triumph under control but allowed a slight curve of her lips. "If Sirese Zenjiel were to be brought back, mayhap he could tell us who killed him, and who brought him back to life. They might be the same person; they might be different. It might be a conspiracy; it might be chance."

Enjul shook his head as if disappointed her good sense had lasted so briefly. "I will never allow it."

She stared straight into his eyes. Golden. Violet. Beautiful. Something told her if she didn't take care, she might get lost in them. "But think about it," she said almost gleefully. "Wouldn't it make your investigation easier?"

He held her gaze, meeting her dare, returning her mocking smile until the thrill of anticipation hitched her breath. But of what? She wasn't sure, and something told her she didn't want to know.

"Explain what you do," he said, ignoring her goading. "Did you control your sister's body as if it were a doll?"

"No!" Azul exclaimed, the game forgotten. It suddenly felt very important that he understood this. That while he might think her a malady, she was no monster. "It's not possible. It can't be done."

"But you had some kind of connection to it?"

"To *her*."

A snort when she elaborated no further. "Miss Del Arroyo, you can answer my questions here, in a holding room, or back in Valanje. It's up to you to decide the ease of your travel and the quality of your living."

For a moment, Azul envisioned taking out Nereida's dagger and plunging it into the side of Enjul's neck. The image was so heartwarming she took another step toward him, her fear forgotten long enough for words to slip out of her throat. "But we're not going to Valanje, are we? Not yet, anyway."

Enjul stood, so slowly, so gracefully, fear ran up her spine like icy fingers. A predator reminding its prey of who was in charge.

But he was not completely in charge, was he? Azul had something he lacked.

"And where are we going?" he asked, his tone so dark and smooth it threatened to make a mess of her heartbeat. And not because of fear.

"Cienpuentes," she answered, locking her knees when he took a step closer. His scent filled her lungs. Not the kind of rotting smell that ought to follow a man like this, but rich like soil under her hands ready for the blossoms of spring.

"Is that so?" he said, leaning even closer until his mask filled her vision, and that strange mix of thrill and anticipation coursed through her veins again. She fought the urge to meet him halfway until something broke—his mask, her forehead, or their gazes. "Do you happen to know who the other malady is, then?"

Sense returned, and she took a step back. His scent followed. "No. Until today I thought I was the only one with my gift."

He cocked his head. "Why do you insist on calling it that?"

"Because it is a gift. I'm no scary monster from old tales." *I'm not you*, she wanted to say.

"If you truly thought of it that way, wouldn't you be using it more?" He must've noticed her flinch, because his tone became persuasive. "Yes?"

As if such a thing would work on her. "As you said, I am no god. I have no right to judge."

"Ah yes, you will only use it on those who die by your hand. Is that how your sister died to begin with? Were you curious to see if you could use your *gift* on a person and killed her?"

"No," she bit out.

"How selfish of you, then, to use it only on your sister. I think, Miss Del Arroyo, that you well know it's no benign gift but a foulness. It gives me some hope that you are merely misguided instead of simply reprehensible."

"Reprehensible or misguided as I might be," she answered through clenched teeth, angry at herself for allowing him to rile her, "perhaps it'd be good for you to lower yourself to my level, if you wish to apprehend this other malady." She took a few calming breaths, short and shallow, while he mulled her words. He still was too close; she didn't want to be overwhelmed by his scent and presence all over again. To be tempted into doing something unwise.

"I will travel—me and De Guzmán will travel—with you to Cien-puentes and help you find whoever brought Sirese Zenjiel to life after his death." Cienpuentes, where she would find her sister's bones and hide her away with Nereida's help. "And then, when our business in the capital is done, I will go with you to Valanje."

Enjul allowed the silence to settle and fray her nerves before speaking, "Why should this other malady be in Cienpuentes and not Aviene or Rozas?"

"Why would anyone care to kill and bring back one of the Valan-je's ambassador's trusted men but for political reasons? And politics means Cienpuentes."

A gleam of triumph flashed in his eyes, and Azul knew she had given away more than she meant to.

"Why kill and bring back a man unless there is a way to manipulate them and learn what they know? There *is* a connection between you and the corpses."

"There is," she admitted reluctantly.

"Does it exist with everything you bring back?"

"Yes." She swallowed hard. "I could sense Isadora was alive, and now I can tell she is no longer here."

"What about animals? Surely you must have practiced your foul-ness on them. Does the link exist as well?"

"Yes."

"As I thought."

Irked by his knowing tone, she spoke again: "But Sirese Zenjiel felt different from my sister." As if he were a simple animal, not a person. This she kept to herself—why give the emissary more information?

"If this other malady has no control over the corpses, as you have said, then why kill and bring him back at all?"

"That's for you to figure out."

He turned his back to her, and she was disconcerted anew by the softness of his hair against the width of his shoulders. Murderers ought to be all harsh, vicious angles, with no beauty to recommend them. He had known Zenjiel was alive again and killed him all the same.

Her gift was a good thing, not a foul malady—new life was a celebration, not a curse. He had no right to dispute that, wouldn't judge her so much if he understood what it took out of her soul to use it. The reminder turned her mouth dry. She must not use her gift on another person if at all possible—if she gave all her soul away, how would Isadora live? Who would look over her and make sure she got to experience a full life?

"Silvo Zenjiel's death could have been an accident," Enjul said. "Perhaps his killer felt guilty, like you, and decided to repair their fumble."

Azul winced. "He's—was—high enough to have his own guards, wasn't he? You'd have to go out of your way to accidentally cause such a person's death without anyone knowing. Could it be one of your ilk? Another emissary? You make death your domain, after all."

Enjul turned slightly, enough for Azul to fear that he would loom over her again and she would find her wits scattered on the floor. "Such a creature wouldn't have been born in Valanje without the Lord Death's knowledge or permission."

"Then you need me," she said. "Sirese Zenjiel can't be the only person this malady has brought back, if their aim is political power. It could be anyone in Cienpuentes. They don't lack for court members, I've heard. Your emissary status will not help you there. The people will cower and hide from you, and the malady might run. Without me to point out the signs, you may spend years walking around the city, not realizing half its citizens used to be dead."

He said nothing, so she added, "Whoever it is, they'd need to be in close contact to bring people back to life, I'm sure."

"Not to mention murder them," Enjul muttered.

And Azul knew he meant to re-murder all of them. An unexpected weight sat in her stomach. Heavy, but not quite dense enough to stop her quest for Isadora's bones. "Knowing who this malady brought back will narrow who has access to all those people."

"And you will return with me to Valanje after this deed is done in Cienpuentes? No other ploys?"

She looked at him solemnly. "I give you my word."

"Honor is a cheap quality when confronted with the choice between integrity and our heart's want. And you want too much, Azul del Arroyo."

Azul couldn't deny this. For Isadora, she'd do anything, break any promise. But this was between her and Enjul, and she did mean it. Once Isadora was alive and safe and hidden, Azul would happily go wherever Emissary Enjul told her to.

Azul was starting to learn she could be quite ruthless.

Hadn't she felt relief over this emissary's apparent death at the port? Was she not happy to take Death to Cienpuentes as long as it put Isadora within her reach?

"Take me to Cienpuentes," Azul said, "and I'll do whatever you want." She couldn't outright barter for her sister's life, of course—Enjul would never accept that—but it wasn't as if she could hide her intentions. In this, the emissary was right: she was too easy to read. It would be on her to figure out how to access her sister's bones without his knowledge.

And she would have to do it fast, for he would give her only so much time before he sent her to Valanje.

Enjul stared at her for a long time, no doubt considering how the trip might pan out, weighing Azul's worth while he had her trapped versus this other necromancer doing what they wanted.

Then he leaned forward, close and close and close until his bone mask was resting against her temple, and everything in Azul screamed to open the Eye of Death and feed off his body.

"Remember, Miss Del Arroyo: What you do affects others." Chilling words breathed hotly into her ear, sending shivers down her back. "They affect your mother, they affect your other siblings, they affect Nereida de Guzmán, they affect all who have aided you. Do not allow your obsession over your sister to ruin those surrounding you. You may attempt to run, but I will find you again. I will not stop until you're accounted for, your transgressions against the Lord Death answered for. Do not believe that just because you hold this one piece of knowledge over me, I am in your hands. You shall make my search easier, but I will not think twice of ending your life if you become a nuisance, nor will I hesitate in ruining those who have become part of your plans."

He left her side and went to the door, opening it to the empty darkness of the hallway outside. He paused, offering his arm as if they were polite acquaintances instead of people with completely opposite views on life.

"Shall we?" he asked.

Azul forced herself to close the distance separating them and gingerly hooked her fingers around the inside of his elbow. His shirt was as soft as it looked, the arm underneath as firm as any other's. She had expected something to happen at the contact, a similar feeling of wrongness to the one she'd had when first stepping onto Valanje, but he simply felt human. The parts of her Enjul had unsettled with his words and threats anchored back into place.

The gods were no fools.

But the emissary was human, and people could always be fooled.

XIII

THE CITY OF
A HUNDRED BRIDGES

Cienpuentes spread below Azul, Nereida, and the emissary, the dozens of islands so saturated with buildings there was no original rock left to see. The city overflowed, like the river whose delta it had invaded, to crawl around the big round bowl of the lake, as if attempting to join on the opposite side.

From their perch on the hill on the outskirts of the city, Azul had never seen something so intimidating or impressive. The city's Heart rose in the middle of the islands, a solid stack of gray and white stone, its multitude of windows blinking in the noon light. The Heart's height was far superior to the surrounding houses—and those houses were already two and three stories higher than the single-floor houses Azul was familiar with. No space for patios in this city, although the streets did seem to form plazas here and there, and tops of trees dotted some of the paths and riverbanks. West of the Heart lay the exception to the lack of open space: a big plaza and another big structure. Another similar house, inspiring and intimidating at the same time, rose north of the palace. Other buildings claimed the eye to a lesser degree, thrown across the city, places of importance.

One of them would be the ossuary.

An invisible sundial formed in her mind's eye, except it counted days, not hours. Now that they had arrived at Cienpuentes, this agreement between herself and the emissary would turn into a game between a resourceful mouse and a rat who thought himself a cat. A race for her to find her sister's bones before he realized she had no intention of helping him find the other necromancer as long as her sister remained gone.

She glanced at Enjul, riding by her side. He was close enough that it had taken some effort to get used to the feeling, far enough to be an itch at the edge of her senses. He had dispensed with his mask, since his presence as an emissary in Cienpuentes would demand too many explanations—and to this, she wished him good luck, because a lack of mask could not change his arrogant demeanor.

His nose was too long for his face, his cheeks too high, his mouth too wide, his lips too thin. It wasn't a handsome face. It was a harsh face. A face that made no sense without one half covered by his bone mask.

And yet, why couldn't she stop looking up to catch another glimpse of it? What about it made it so fascinating she felt compelled to check if her memory measured up to the original? Was it simply her wish for life in awe at the presence of death? Or did it have something to do with the strange thrills of anticipation that ran along her nerves by simply being nearby?

"You've spent some days in Valanje," Enjul said mockingly, catching her glance. "Surely you've seen other faces like mine."

"None that matched my bleak mood so much," she assured him, and returned her attention to the path ahead.

Keeping Enjul's position as Emissary of the Lord Death a secret meant they would not be using Valanje's official quarters in the city. They wouldn't be using Nereida's residence either, the one gifted to her by the late queen. Too public—her return ahead of the delegation would make people curious.

Nereida had suggested an inn, but Azul had had a better idea. One that would keep them away from curious innkeepers and wagging local tongues: Azul had family in Cienpuentes, and she'd had an open invitation to visit since she was twelve and one of her half siblings had defied their father to seek her out.

Still, they had been forced to wait over a week for a response. A week spent confined to a room much as she had been back at Diel, with not even Nereida to play cards with. Azul was fairly certain it took fewer days to bring a message back and forth to the capital, so Enjul must've used the time to find out everything he could about her family. Just as she had used one of the tiny bones she had lifted from Nereida's supper in the ship to raise a rat and spy on the household.

This was a promise she had broken, but with herself. After the chicken and the cat and her sister, Azul had promised herself no more. No more of her soul given away. She wouldn't chance not having enough to bring Isadora back. Then Nereida had come, demanding to see what she could do. And then Enjul had cornered her, forcing her hand with Zenjiel. And after the bird and Zenjiel, a rat had not seemed so bad. *What a slippery slope*, Azul thought as they took the path toward the city.

Cienpuentes drew nearer, and soon they passed the exterior settlements to enter the city itself. Buildings and overhead bridges caged them in, the streets full of people and carts and donkeys and shouts and smells and curses. They crossed bridges made of wood, bridges made of stone, bridges that looked like they would fall under their horses' hooves, and bridges that looked like they had been built while the gods were still pondering whether to raise the lands or not.

They passed pairs of City Guards, lounging here and there as if they had nothing better to do, their distinct blue tabards easy to notice among the crowd. They crossed a market, the carts and stalls dwindled to nothing at the late hour. They went by small shrines with statues of the Blessed Heart, all with flat chests and a pregnant belly, some with the juncture of their thighs covered, others proudly showing a male's member. All with colorful strips of cloth tied around their legs and neck, each piece of fabric indicating someone's wish.

Azul was forced to ask directions to their destination a few times, since nobody would make eye contact with Enjul, and Nereida had retreated so far beneath her wide-brimmed hat they might need to send a search party to find her again.

At last, they arrived at Almanueva. Her half family's house, elegant and white, rose two stories high and took up a block of its own, like some genteel houses in Cienpuentes liked to do—the gentry demanded their solitude, even in such a cramped city. The bottom floor had no openings aside from the grand main door and a side entrance for horses and carts, but the upper floor was filled with glass panels. Azul doubted they could be opened—who would invite the city smells into their home?

A footman appeared in the side entrance, and soon they were entering a small receiving area with horse stalls. The animals would be sent back after they had rested—a city like this was not made for idle mounts, and Azul had no doubt Enjul would rather Azul waste her time by walking on foot.

Another ornamental entrance greeted them. Another show of power. A house on a cramped island, with open space to receive riders and, Azul soon found out, a small patio of its own. These things did not come cheap. These things were passed from parent to heir along with hefty sums of money to keep them there.

And the inside! Tall ceilings; long, wide windows; walls painted in creams and whites; and floors covered in earthy patchwork tiles. The patio, small but open, full of bushes and flowers and a tiny pond hosting a handful of lilies. *This was not Cienpuentes*, Azul thought in wonder, *this was home*. Bright and airy, the harsh sounds and smells of the streets were a thing of the past. She didn't need to close her eyes to feel herself back in Agunción, even if the riches on display were far superior to anything she would ever find in her town.

The trip had drained her, but she felt her strength returning all at once.

"Is my brother in residence?" she asked of the footman leading them.

"Not at this time, sirese. But he will be back shortly. He asked that you make yourselves comfortable. Your rooms are ready, and refreshments have been ordered to one of the parlors."

They were led to the second floor, where three rooms had been prepared. They were tiny, barely big enough to contain the beds inside, but full of light. Azul never wanted to leave.

Her traveling satchel was brought up, along with a jug of water for the basin. She changed into a fresh shirt and washed the dirt from her face and arms. Her hair was rebraided carefully, Isadora's earring polished with the cuff of her sleeve. She felt invigorated. It was too light outside to see her reflection in the window looking onto the patio, but she felt the huge grin spreading across her face. Soon Isadora would be back. Soon Isadora would feel like this.

The grin faded.

Azul knew better than to allow her eagerness to take control. She needed to be cunning. Her half family's power would help her only so much, and Enjul was too good at guessing her movements. She would get only one chance. She must think further ahead than the next immediate move.

Nereida was waiting outside her door, still wearing her traveling clothes. She had dispensed with the hat, but the reluctance to show her face was obvious. What had Nereida left behind in Cienpuentes, Azul wondered, that made her so unwilling to be recognized now that she was back? Surely it couldn't be her attempt to kill the emissary—she had not been arrested at the ambassador's estate, and Enjul showed no ill feelings.

Azul didn't ask, because she knew Nereida would not answer.

Together they made their way along the hallway and down the marble stairs, passing graceful side tables and beautiful landscapes hanging on the walls.

The same footman was waiting for them. Silently, he ushered them into the parlor, where plates filled with delicate bits of pastry filled the marquetry surface of a low gilded table. Two matching settees framed it, almost toylike in size. Nothing big and gaudy for this house; everything was ethereal, like the soft curtains framing the windows, the gliding vine-like legs supporting the tables, and the delicate vase full of fresh flowers.

Nereida made use of the settee, unafraid its thin legs might break under her strength.

"If this is all . . ."

Azul turned to the footman. "Sirese Enjul?"

"He's gone on private matters, sirese. He informed us he will return in time for supper."

Gone, was he? Azul nodded and the footman stepped outside through a curtain of wooden beads.

"Do you wish to go now as well?" Nereida asked while serving herself some of the cold drink provided with the food.

Azul sat on the other settee. "He will expect that. One of the men who followed us from the ambassador's estate is likely standing guard outside the entrance." She met Nereida's speculative glance. "I've been helpless, not completely witless."

Nereida smiled faintly and picked one of the pastries. It crumbled into flakes at her bite, but she managed not to get any of them on her person or the tiled floor. She had eaten these before, probably many, many times, while Azul had learned of their existence only minutes ago.

Azul grabbed one, then another, then a third. They overflowed her hand, and they would never fit into her mouth.

But then, she did not mean to eat them.

Retrieving another tiny bone from the sea voyage, she pressed the cakes together into a flaking, messy ball and allowed the singing in her veins to overcome the reluctance she had built over the years. The Eye of Death flared, and the bone sucked greedily at what Azul was offering. How easy now to allow the power to flow, how natural to feel the pinch in her soul, how simple to ignore the bite of pain in her chest, and the knowledge that she must make sure there was something left to give Isadora. But animals pulled only a fraction, and what they took would eventually regrow.

The tiny mouse squeaked between her hands, and she allowed it free. It leaped to her thigh, the settee, and then the floor before scurrying away. Having the emissary return from death had been shocking enough—Azul did not want to experience such surprises again, and a mouse, small, insignificant, and unseen, would make an excellent second set of eyes where the emissary was concerned. And unlike the bird, she'd not allow it to die from her carelessness.

Nereida watched with morbid curiosity, still and silent. Fleetingly,

Azul wondered if Nereida planned on killing her once she brought back whomever she wanted returned. If, at their base, she and the emissary weren't so different, and Nereida also thought her an affront to gods and nature. But in Nereida's case, whomever she wanted back weighed more than a fear of divine retribution.

"Do you think me a monster?" Azul asked.

Nereida's expression darkened. "I have met monsters," she said. "And you have a long way to go."

The footman gathered the curtain of beads to the side, the clacking noise bringing the women's attention to the entrance. A young man wearing brown breeches and an open waistcoat stood there with a grin so wide it overtook his handsome face. Azul fished for any resemblance, in the dark brown color of his hair and the slight wave it carried, in the twinkling of his brown eyes, darker than hers but holding such a similar shape.

Sergado de Gracia opened his arms. "Sister!"

XIV

AZUL

SEVEN YEARS EARLIER

The lad, sixteen years of age, stared down at Azul del Arroyo, herself a mere twelve years old. Azul's eyes were as round as boiled eggs; her mouth hung ajar at the sight of the boy, at all the finery perched on him, at the sword hanging from his belt, at the smugness on his face.

"I am Sergado de Gracia, and I am your half brother," he said. "I have come to take you home."

Azul closed her mouth and glanced around them, seemingly unimpressed by the notion of having a half sibling.

Of course, De Gracia knew about her mother's occupation and knew this girl had a lot of half siblings. He knew a lot of things—coaxed out of his father's study late at night, when curiosity was best satisfied. That's where he'd learned about his half sister. A sister! Left behind when his mother had died, when his father no longer needed another baby to make her happy.

But what about *his* happiness? Did he not deserve a sister to dote upon, to tease, to keep him company in the dull hours of the day?

The slip of a girl with her too-long breeches and too-long shirt—made so to save on clothes down the road, he assumed with a snicker.

Something she wouldn't need in Almanueva—finally her attention returned to him.

"I can't go," she whispered.

"Why?" he asked in surprise. Did the girl not realize who their father was? What position the Marquess de Gracia held, what advantages it would bring her?

Her small face became quite solemn. "I must look out for my sister."

THE PRESENT

The memories had gone hazy with time, but Azul recognized that boy in the young man sitting in front of her. Less arrogant, more joyful, but with the same determined lift of his chin.

Sergado was doing his own study of her person, the satisfied smile never dropping from his face. As an afterthought, he dipped his head respectfully toward Nereida.

"Forgive me, Sirese De Guzmán, I wasn't aware you'd be one of my sister's companions."

Nereida watched him carefully. "I wish to keep my presence in Cienpé unknown for the time being."

Sergado showed no surprise at the request, either because it hadn't been one or because he was used to his guests' eccentricities. Or, more likely, he simply didn't care. He sat next to Azul, perching on the edge of the settee.

"If that is your wish, I will keep quiet. But it won't last long," he warned. "Servants eventually talk, no matter how well they're paid. In fact, I received a visit from Sío de Guzmán a few days ago."

Nereida cocked her head, her expression smooth like silk. "Is that so?"

"Indeed, your brother accompanied the Count de Anví."

"What a coincidence."

Sergado smiled slightly. "Isn't it? Worry not; your name did not come up." His attention returned, eager and unabashed, to Azul. "And your other companion? I am told he chose to visit the city until supper."

Azul's smile twisted into a grimace. Nereida sipped from her glass of juice to hide her reaction.

"Is there something amiss?" Sergado asked with sharp interest. "I assume that he, too, is of some importance. Or is the guard outside the house one of yours?" he asked Nereida.

Nereida put the glass down. "No. As I said, I do not wish to call attention on my person."

"A feat, I assure you," De Gracia told her, the words pretty but cold. His voice warmed when he faced Azul again. "Should I do something about it, Sister?"

Azul blinked. *Sister.* She had always been Azulita, never Sister. She wasn't sure she wanted the role. Sergado didn't need her protection, and what did she have to offer as a *sister* without that? The thought sat like an ill-fitting vest, too tight across her chest.

"It's not needed, thank you," she finally said.

Sergado agreed, "Better to see the vermin than hear it scurrying."

A startled laugh escaped Azul. "Yes, indeed."

"But if anything changes," Sergado said, his tone still light, "let me know, and I'll be glad to deal with it."

"You are very generous. I must thank you and our father for giving us such a wonderful welcome and allowing us the use of your house."

Nereida stilled at this. Sergado bit his lower lip.

Azul watched them with suspicion. "Did I say something wrong?"

"No, Sister dearest." Sergado reached to cover her hand with his. "I thought you were aware. You see . . . our father passed away a few months ago."

"Oh." Azul thought this over. It came as a shock, and a slight pang of regret did rise in her. The man had sired her. Once upon a time, he had agreed to raise her if her mother didn't want to be responsible for her. Once upon a time, the opportunity had appeared for her to meet him. But it hadn't come to pass. If it had, maybe she'd feel more than a fleeting sting of pity.

"I am sorry to hear," Azul said truthfully, and grabbed another small cake. The action seemed to relax her brother, who drew back his hand.

"One day I will tell you about him," he told her, allowing the words to trail into silence.

Azul smiled. "But not today."

"But not today."

XV

PLANS PUT IN MOTION

HOURS EARLIER

The darkness of night filled the small sitting room. One of the footmen had asked Enjul if he'd like a lamp, but he had refused the offer. Virel Enjul had often found that darkness brought its own kind of clarity.

What a shock his first view of Cienpuentes had been. He couldn't comprehend how greed could grip a heart with so much strength. How people could find it in themselves to carve such a gift out of the world, to turn blue peaks into a mass of flat, barren gray. No wonder they treated the gods as curiosities rather than divine beings, why they tied up wishes to the Lady Dream's legs and expected her to grant them as if they hadn't stolen her bones—their guilt would be too crushing if they were to admit the truth.

It spoke to the lows they were willing to achieve in order to keep their coin bags full.

Azul del Arroyo had acted docile as a newborn lamb during their trip to Cienpuentes, but like her countrymen and Anchor, he had no doubts she was simply biding her time to strike.

Ambassador Enzare had recommended a man who could act like a shadow, and after meeting this shadow, Enjul still couldn't decide if he was as astute as the intelligence in his eyes showed, or as careless as his demeanor implied. This had surprised him, as he prided himself on being an excellent judge of character.

Had he made a mistake by trusting this stranger to shadow Del Arroyo? The fact that he couldn't himself was meddlesome, but he must conduct his own inquiries on the second malady, and Del Arroyo must be given some appearance of freedom to hang herself with.

Closing his eyes, he brought his hand to his chest and searched deep within himself. When you carried a piece of the Lord Death with you, you needed no statues or temples to aid in your prayers.

A welcoming peace settled over him.

Have I erred in trusting this shadow to follow the malady?

Enjul didn't often ask his god directly—the god had more important things to do than answer his questions—but there was something about De Gracia's house that made him fanciful. Perhaps it was the way moonlight played with the shadows, the smell of blossoming Sancian flowers drifting through the open window. Queen's blooms. Such a delicate, resilient fragrance. They called them jiren avels in Valanje—little moons—for they appeared as white as the two ladies when in full bloom.

Back in the ambassador's estate, he had learned the details of Azul's half brother's wealth and position at court. De Gracia's home lived up to his expectations. Such a grand building, yet understated. It had been a reprieve to see the marquess's family hadn't succumbed to the need to plaster Anchor all over the walls, unlike the ambassador's residence. It said a lot about Azul del Arroyo's loyalty to her half sister that she'd rather live in the countryside than among so much wealth.

Loyalty—such a tricky emotion. It was driven by honor, which could be broken by temptation, and love, which could easily fall into obsession. Enjul had no doubt of which side Azul del Arroyo's loyalty fell. Her zealousness to bring her sister back with no regard to her sister's or the god's wishes spoke for itself.

What made someone develop such warped views? Perhaps it was the fact that she had so many half siblings but had only been able to hold on to one. Here was another bizarre Sancian custom—the need to pass one's blood on to your children. If you desired a child so much, why not welcome one without a family? Perhaps this was how the Blessed Heart manifested among their subjects—the need for creation rather than acceptance.

As a child, he had found it hard to leave his parents to join the Order, and at one point in the following years, he had even gone back to visit them, guided by an instinct that told him he would never fully accept the Lord Death until he had seen them again.

He found them happy and settled, glad Enjul was making a name for himself in the Order. He had nothing but fading memories of their time together and, after that one meeting, no real reason to visit again.

He now had the Lord Death.

A tingling sensation spread from his heart, easing a sort of homesickness he hadn't realized was there. Sancia was strange and disturbing, a maze he must carefully navigate, but he had the Lord Death's blessing, and that was enough.

Soft clacking had him open his eyes. Azul del Arroyo pushed the wooden bead curtain aside and entered the room, a small smile playing with her lips as another breeze fluttered the curls escaping from her braid.

Enjul stilled, wondering how long it'd take her to notice him. Something urged him to make some small noise. He craved the sight of her shock, the way her eyes narrowed when she tried to figure out how to outmaneuver him.

Azul let out a sigh as she approached the window. She placed her hands on the windowsill and inhaled deeply, her face sharpening under the moonlight.

Who would've thought a malady could contain much *life*? He had wondered if he might not find the other malady by simply walking around and looking for a burst of life, but something told him Azul was unique.

He draped an arm over the back of the settee, impatient now to see her reaction at his presence. She did not disappoint.

She turned with a gasp at the rustling of fabric, then scowled. "I didn't know you were here," she said.

"That much is obvious," he couldn't help but answer.

Her chin lifted, and she turned toward the entrance of the room. "I'll leave."

"Why?"

His question surprised her as much as it surprised him.

"I wouldn't wish to bother you," she answered curtly. Then her voice became somewhat amused. "Wouldn't want to infect you with my rot."

"I survived the trip here by your side, I think I'll survive another hour or two," he answered dryly.

She stiffened at this, her eyes darting from him to the entryway. Did she expect him to want to play cards with her or something like that? He snorted with amusement. "What do you think of your half brother's house, Miss Del Arroyo?"

Azul's gaze returned to the view of the patio. "It's very grand. Beautiful. It . . ."

"It?" he prodded when she didn't continue. If the woman was in a sharing mood, he would not stop her. The more he knew about her, the more he'd know how to control her. It was a dangerous game, for he had a feeling that the more he knew about her, the more he wouldn't be able to step away.

"It reminds me of home." There was a soft, wistful quality to her words that touched something inside Enjul this malady had no right to touch. He didn't have time to dwell on this as she arched a brow and asked, "Do you have a home, Emissary? Or do you simply go from death to death?"

He relaxed against the back of the settee and wondered if she'd take a seat or remain at arm's length. He hoped she'd stay where she was—much easier to read—but part of him missed being toe-to-toe, eye-to-eye, as they'd been back at the ambassador's house. "My home is with my god."

Her mouth twitched, and a wicked gleam entered her eyes. "It must be nice to carry your home along with you. Like a snail."

Being in her half brother's house had given Azul del Arroyo a good dose of confidence.

Slowly, he unwrapped himself from the settee and took one step toward her. She didn't move. Perhaps the moonlight and darkened room had wrapped her in the same fanciful mood that had taken him. And perhaps, for one night, that was acceptable.

Tonight was a reprieve. Tomorrow, they'd take up arms again.

"Why did they name you Azul?"

Del Arroyo blinked at him, clearly surprised by the question. "What does it matter?"

"Names are part of who we are, are they not? If I must study you, why not start there?" His gaze flickered to the small piece of Anchor dangling from her ear. She wore it as an act of defiance and rebellion, and while the sight of the gods' bones being used in such a way disgusted him, it'd take a lot more to rile him. "Is it a homage to the gods?"

She let out a startled laugh. "I'm named after the summer sky."

It fit her. She thrummed with a sort of vibrancy that was hard to find in the winter months. He leaned closer, peering into her eyes. In the dim light, they were small dark pools, with no rim to speak of. If there was Valanjian blood in her, it had been in generations past.

"And you?" she dared. "Why did they name you——?" She hesitated, as if she wasn't sure speaking his name aloud would smite her where she stood.

Enjul smiled wide. "Why did they name me Emissary of the Lord Death? Isn't it obvious?"

He expected her to glare at him and leave. Instead, he found an answering hint of a wicked smile. "Not obvious at all. If I were the Order, I would've chosen a very different name."

One more step, and he was breathing in her scent. Rain over a grassy field, he decided. Fresh and full with the thrill of the storm to come. "Such as?"

She opened her mouth, then bit her lip. "I prefer not to say."

"If we are to . . . What shall we call it? 'Help each other'? We must be truthful with one another."

She grew serious. "The truth is that you will never give as much as you want to take from me. Keep the reasons for your name, Emissary; I do not need them. Good night."

A pang of disappointment hit his chest as she walked out of the room. He'd hoped this strange moonlight interlude would've lasted a few minutes longer.

It didn't matter. There would be plenty of time going forward to instigate, observe. And catch.

THE PRESENT

Azul woke to the early songs of birds. After meeting her personal needs, she rushed down to the same cozy dining room they had used for supper. Bathed in the morning light, it appeared twice as big as it had under candlelight. A few trays had been placed in the middle of the table, and to her relief, the only one occupying a seat was Nereida.

Fresh bread, boiled eggs, sausage, jam, butter, fruit. No porridge, no honey, no fried cake. Ah, well.

Grabbing a seat opposite Nereida, Azul chose her morsels. "Will you accompany me?"

"Where you are going, I don't need to accompany you."

"What will you do, then? Will you visit your brother?"

In the ensuing silence, Azul glanced over her shoulder at the open door and swallowed a half-gnawed piece of bread and jam. Badly chosen seat, badly chosen question.

"He's still upstairs," Nereida told her.

Enjul? Sergado? The latter, she assumed, for she had seen a few candles' worth of light pouring from his window across the patio when she had woken in the middle of the night. As for Enjul . . .

Their strange encounter last night felt like a dream. There had been no mention of foulness, maladies, and sisters. It had felt . . . cozy. Strange. Like coarse fabric on the verge of turning malleable by the familiarity of use.

"You could ask the servants," said Nereida.

Azul shook her head. "I can curb my curiosity if it means not awakening theirs."

A snort. "Because they aren't curious already," Nereida murmured before eating half an egg.

"'Tis true," Azul admitted. "But I'll allow their imaginations some freedom." She gulped down some of the minty drink offered with the food and considered one of the spoons. Solid, expensive. Pretty. It could fetch some coin.

A few coins landed by her plate.

"You might need those," Nereida said. "Don't worry, there are more."

With one less concern, Azul stood with resolve, retrieved the coins, and made her way outside.

The sky was turning the beautiful azure of summer, not a cloud in sight, carrying with it the promise of a heated day. But for now, the night's chill lingered in the air. The street spread on either side of Azul, sleepy and empty, which made the man leaning against the opposite building all the more conspicuous.

She hadn't been stopped from leaving the house; and why should she when she was earning a shadow? Azul approached the man, a smile on her face. If Enjul insisted on having her followed, she might as well find a use for her follower. Her brother's words came to mind: *Better to see the vermin than hear it scurrying.*

"Excuse me, sirese," she greeted him. "Are you here for the house or my person?"

The man tipped his hat respectfully. No ostentatious feathers caressed the wide brim, no signs of riches in the dirt clinging stubbornly to its black fabric. He looked to be around his late twenties, with dark hair gathered at the back of his neck and a jaw that hadn't met a razor in a few days. He flashed a smile at her perusal.

"You must be a local," she guessed, "so you might as well lead the way to the ossuary and save me the time of asking others for directions."

It wasn't as if she could lose the man in a city she didn't know or as if Enjul were unaware of her plans. The thought worried her. Getting out of the house unaccompanied *had* been easy, shadow or not. Had Enjul changed the rules of their game without her realizing it?

With another quick show of his teeth, the man dislodged himself from the wall and led the way down the street. The buildings were taller than she was used to; the bridges threatened to cave under or above them. It didn't take long for the streets to lose their relative quiet as they widened and narrowed at whim, the pounding of hooves

and rattling of carts echoing from wall to wall. The people of Cienpuentes were waking up and apparently enjoyed shouting at both each
other and the morning light. A rider galloped past, making no allowance for what or who stood in their way. The excitement was palpa-
ble, and Azul drank it in. In the distance, she thought she heard the
cluck of chickens.

"Are those chickens on the roofs?"

Her shadow did not answer, so she asked instead, "Did the emissary send you to watch over me, or was it the ambassador?"

He nodded, almost imperceptibly.

"Is Cienpuentes always this busy?"

A shrug of the shoulders.

"I hope they're paying you well. I can't afford a tip."

A disgruntled harrumph.

"And your name," Azul insisted, "may I know it?"

Unsurprised by the lack of answer, Azul smiled for him. "Then
pick one and give it to me, so that when I find your employer, I may
praise your work and arrange an increase in your wages."

A low, rumbling laugh came from her companion, and while no
name was forthcoming, Azul did not mind it. There was courage to
be found in walking through a strange place with someone by her
side, even if he was little more communicative than a shadow.

Her attention was drawn back to the river and the buildings rising
to cage it, old and sharp at the same time. Two statues adorned the
ends of one overhead passageway, stone horses reared on opposite
sides of someone's entrance, and all the flowers perched in their iron
grids outside the windows brightened the dull color of gray stone,
weathered brick, and white bird droppings.

Azul savored all these sights, all the sounds, and even all the
smells. Soon she'd share them with Isadora, and then she'd be sent
back to Valanje. Who knew when she'd see all these things again?
Things so Sancian and yet so strange. Monteverde was a good-sized
city, but it had been allowed to expand. No such thing could be
said for Cienpuentes. Life had been crammed in here, dropped like

dice on drunken, late-night games. Isadora would like it here, Azul decided, content with the thought that although they might have to part ways again, at least her sister would be left with plenty of things to enjoy.

Having somewhat satisfied her heart, Azul's mind returned to the task at hand. The number of bones kept at Cienpuentes's ossuary must be enormous. The city was huge, its dead inhabitants too many to count. The sheer size of the collection of bones defied her imagination. She prayed that those in charge had kept some semblance of order and records instead of dumping them into piles as a cook might with chicken bones after the broth was done.

The ossuary itself was a boring square structure with an elevated entrance and a narrow set of steps. Windows peppered the outside, high enough to be out of reach for a man on his tiptoes, never mind someone of Azul's height.

All this, she observed over the increased pounding in her pulse. Isadora, kept in such a place. Cold and drab and leeched of all joy. It broke her heart to think about it.

She bid her shadowing guard to wait outside, then took the steps and entered the building. Azul had an inkling Enjul assumed she needed the whole body to bring someone back to life, concluding that a single visit in plain daylight wouldn't be enough, and nothing would be lost if he allowed her that much.

He had only seen her use her gift on Zenjiel. He had no way of knowing she could simply pocket a piece of a bone and bring the person back later unless Nereida had told him, and Nereida wouldn't risk their agreement. She and Nereida had escaped Enjul before, and Nereida must know Cienpuentes well. Together, they would get rid of Azul's shadow and escape Enjul, as they had done before. And after Isadora was back, she'd return to face his rage, as she had promised.

Unfortunately, it took no time to realize the ossuary kept no bones. It was a shell of a building, full of cramped rooms and faded rugs and ugly fern-green walls.

Azul turned to the man assigned to deal with her inquiries. "This is the ossuary?"

A suffering sigh escaped him. "Yes, sirese. Again, this is where your loved ones' remains are dealt with."

If that was true, how come the building didn't feel any different from her brother's house? Her fingers ran across the rim of her hat. "Are you sure?"

"Yes, sirese."

"So, why won't you allow me to see them?"

"As I explained, for that you will have to go to the Temple and make an appointment with the dean. There is a procedure for these things. We are not an exhibition you can enter at whim to satisfy your morbidness. A deceased's remains aren't something to be gawked at."

"But the bones are here? Where?" Far underneath, she suspected. There was no other explanation. With how many bones the ossuary must contain, she would've been aware of them if they were nearby.

"This is the entrance, yes."

"It doesn't seem big enough," she pressed.

The man would not relax. "I am certain. Between us and the Temple, we host from the poorest of citizens to the late queen."

"The Temple is another ossuary?"

"Go and ask them," the man snapped.

Azul studied her surroundings once more, stuffy, green, and smelling of old age. "Thank you, I think I will."

Once outside, she recalled what she had seen of Cienpuentes on her way in, and where she guessed herself to be—on the wrong side of town. She grimaced in annoyance. She could still taste the old dried herbs and stale air from the ossuary. The sun was now in full display—so much wasted time. Ignoring her following shadow, she guessed her way.

She had taken a handful of steps when she spied a woman on a horse in conversation with someone else.

"Good morning, sirese," Azul greeted her. "May I give you coin for a ride?"

The conversation halted as the rider inspected Azul curiously. "Where do you wish to go?"

"The Temple."

The woman rubbed her chin, her eyes distant for a few moments. "I will do it, countryface," she finally answered, offering a hand.

Azul took it and hoisted herself behind her. The woman smelled of horses and freshly baked bread, reminding Azul of Agunción. She held on to the woman's waist and jolted when the woman clicked at her mount and urged it on. With a last look behind, Azul tipped her hat toward her guard. She felt no guilt and no illusions at leaving him behind—she was sure the man knew her destination, just as Enjul must've known she'd find no easy access to her sister's bones.

As they made their way through the crowded city, Azul closed her eyes and tried to find the link she shared with the beings she brought back, and found that the mouse had done in its instinct what Azul had hoped deep in her heart.

To no one's surprise, the Emissary of the Lord Death was no longer in her brother's house but busy traversing the streets, the mouse in pursuit. Virel Enjul meant to know where she went, but didn't wish for her to know where he visited.

She opened her eyes, and the sight of Enjul's quickly dirtying heels disappeared. Azul tightened her grip on the woman and hoped the emissary didn't notice the mouse, and that the Temple proved to be more helpful than the ossuary.

Azul might have some freedom while Enjul conducted his own business, but the reprieve wouldn't last long.

XVI

THE COUNT

THREE YEARS EARLIER

De Anví found Nereida de Guzmán in one of the Heart's grand ballrooms, dressed in her usual colors of deep blue and gold, with her glorious midnight-black hair gathered at the back of her head and adorned with pearls as beautiful as the stars. She was watching the couples twirling on the floor under the candlelight as if they were strange specimens she wished to study but couldn't quite bother to understand.

Having not much use for dancing, he could commiserate. And yet . . .

"Care for a dance?" he asked before thinking twice.

When she accepted and put her hand on his arm, his chest tightened with surprise.

Perhaps it had shown on his face, because her eyes gained a twinkle of mischief.

"Why ask if you didn't expect me to accept?" she asked as he led her among the couples and joined their twirling. It was a simple routine that allowed the dancers to remain close, their hands in constant contact as they went through the steps.

"I do not know myself," he found himself confessing.

Nereida laughed softly. "I had given up on you ever approaching me."

"Why is that?"

"I have known people like you before. They wait for the perfect moment, but the moment never comes, for perfection is beyond our control."

Yet her existence belied her words. "Or perhaps there is something in all of us that doesn't believe we've earned the right to perfection, and so the moment is gone without us noticing what we have lost."

"Does that mean you recognized perfection in me, or is your ego so big that you feel you are owed it?"

He thought about the question, and his lack of a flirtatious, glib answer appeared to warm Nereida's gaze.

"I think to some extent, we all feel we are owed something in life—but, no, I did not approach you because I thought you were owed to me. Rather, the Lady Dream must've been at work, for I cannot explain it myself."

All he could explain was that when he had first seen Nereida de Guzmán not a month before, standing tall in a small plaza behind one of the taverns in Cienpuentes with a rapier in hand and ready to fight, he suddenly understood why there were stars in the sky. A thought so strange, so outlandish, and so intriguing it had tightened his gut and hastened his heart.

She had stood, tall and defiant, a newcomer to the court, bringing the freshness of the countryside with her. A pure kind of energy hard to find in places like Cienpuentes, where its jaded gray buildings and cumbersome politics eventually wore everyone down. De Anví had thought himself impervious to them—after all, he was here only for the duration of his stay in the Royal Guard—but even he was starting to feel the strain.

"*To first blood!*" De Guzmán's opponent had shouted, anger turning his face red.

He had already worn a bloody tear on his sleeve, another on his pants, and a red line across his cheek. By the end of the next bout, the man would be wearing a fresh tear on his shirt, and De Anví, Nereida's name carved on his heart.

"I do enjoy honesty," Nereida said with another laugh, bringing him back to the present.

"It's hard to find in places like this," he agreed.

"Too much glitter. Too much scheming." A note of disgust edged her words.

He couldn't disagree. The ballroom was full of elegantly embroidered waistcoats and finely adorned skirts and Anchor, so much Anchor. Wrapped around throats, dangling from ears, peeking between strands of hair, and winking under the candlelight as if the gods themselves had decided to build a whole new Anchor city and set it inside the Heart of Cienpuentes. "Why are you here, then?"

Her smile was rather wicked. "Why, because I love to play games."

"Not duels?"

She made a tut-tutting sound. "They are one and the same."

"Be careful, sirese. I haven't been at court long, but long enough to know that some games are too dangerous to play."

"Fear not, De Anví," she answered in a light but self-assured tone. "For all that I am fresh from the countryside, I know when the lake grows too deep for me to wade."

De Anví didn't doubt it and offered no more advice.

By their third dance, he knew he would never tire of conversing with her.

Not a month later, he found himself looking at her on another night, at another ball, thinking of the right words, choosing how much of himself he must lay bare to entice her to stay with him and never leave. She must've sensed something had changed in their usual camaraderie, because she had grown serious and somewhat pensive. But a tap on his arm had stopped him from uttering the words. A simple touch from a short woman with Anchor sprinkled into her hair and a lace mask hiding her identity, even though everyone was aware of who she was.

"Who is your companion, De Anví?" asked the queen. "Can I steal her for the next dance?"

And stolen, she had been.

THE PRESENT

The Count de Anví held Nereida de Guzmán in his arms as they twirled around the splendidly tiled floor. His hands were on her waist, her hands on his arms, and he held her a lot closer than the dance allowed. Nobody seemed to mind. The other couples were nothing but swatches of colors, blurs that tugged at the edges of De Anví's mind, but he wouldn't allow the unease to permeate his feelings. Not here, not now.

Above him, a thousand chandeliers illuminated Nereida's beautiful face, the sparkle in her eyes as she smiled up at him. Not a wide smile or one full of coquetry, but the one she reserved for those closest to her. And in his dreams, for just him.

De Anví woke up slowly, the lingering colors and sounds of the dream fading away. He clenched his fists, finding both the dream and Nereida well outside his reach, then rubbed his eyes and sat up on his bed.

That had been the last of the Witch's dreams, damn her soul.

Damn her for tempting him, over and over, and damn him for accepting.

Another day spread in front of him. Another day full of nothing but the longing to be anywhere else clashing with his certainty that one day, he'd be needed. Not by the king or the Witch or even Miguel but by Nereida de Guzmán.

Soon the count was on his way to his daily rituals—washing, shaving, eating—then on to serve his master at the Heart. On the way, he stopped by a small statue of the Lady Dream, her legs and arms covered by hundreds of strings and ribbons, some so old their color had completely faded.

Back home, statues of the Blessed Heart were preferred instead of the Lady Dream shrines usually found in Sancia's countryside. Farmers in his area had more need for a good harvest than dreams that might never come to pass. Being the practical sort, De Anví had agreed with the sentiment. But Cienpé had a way of muddling your thoughts and upending your life, and now De Anví saw the use of dreaming. What else did a fellow have at the end of a day containing nothing but disappointment?

And still, De Anví resented being beholden to anyone else, so he tried to walk right past the goddess's stony face and stop this control she had over his life.

And, like the day before, and all the others before that, sweat pooled under his shirt and on his temples the moment he took one step past. His heart began an uneven thumping in his chest, and he couldn't quite get enough air. He could see all his hopes—the small ones that he didn't allow himself to think about and the big ones that helped him sleep at night—wither and go up in smoke, and, cursing, took one step back and nodded at the Lady Dream, as he had the day before and all the others before that.

A sudden calm washed over him the moment he finished giving his respects. The sweat dried on his skin, his heartbeat evened. And while he hated his lack of will, he welcomed the freeing sensation.

It disappeared once he arrived at the palace and met the guards' bows at his arrival. Nothing like the imposing building to remind him he wasn't free at all. With a sigh, he took off his hat and walked the corridors tiled with pretty geometric designs that felt more like butcher knives under his soles.

He wondered if the three masked men would attempt another ambush later that evening when he was to meet Esparza again. The thought that they might brought a spring to his step. He hadn't gotten anywhere with his investigation into whom the men belonged to, and at this point, he would willingly go with them to their master just to satiate his curiosity.

"De Anví," called a voice behind him.

The count turned to see a tall, thin man standing outside one of the open doors in the corridor. He was dressed all in blue, Anchor glittering on a brooch on his waistcoat. More Anchor adorned his ears and the rings on his fingers.

"The Marquess de Mavén," De Anví answered with a polite nod. This was the head of the City Guard, and though the animosity between the Blue Bastards and the Golden Dogs was a thing of legend, they both ultimately worked for the same child.

De Mavén walked up to him. "Escort me to the back gate, will you, De Anví? I do not wish to end with a golden dagger in my blue back."

"Of course, Your Grace."

Because, truly, what else was he to say?

De Mavén kept a pace verging on the slowest of strolls, and De Anví's curiosity perked up again. Whatever the head of the blue tabards meant to say would take some time.

"The king is doing well, I assume?" De Mavén asked.

De Anví grunted.

"You know," the Blue Bastards leader continued, "there are better things to do than to stand at the beck and call of a child."

So many things, De Anví could spend days counting them.

"There is an opening in the blue ranks."

The words were dropped easily, so easily De Anví wasn't certain he had heard them correctly. He didn't betray his surprise, choosing to keep a mask of indifference on his face, but his thoughts were a maelstrom. Was De Mavén trying to lure him out of the palace?

The man had made no effort to befriend him in the last year and a half, and for a while, had done nothing but sneer at his position and try to get him supplanted by one of his spies. Those schemes had been foiled—by the Witch, De Anví guessed—so De Mavén had been happy to accept that while De Anví might not work for him, neither did he care for Regent de Fernán and the king. Had something changed?

He wondered once more if De Mavén had been the one to send the three masked men after him, but discarded the idea. De Mavén had no need for such subterfuge.

Once that thought was gone, De Anví entertained another one: accepting the offer, switching to the headquarters in the city, and watching the uproar among the Royal Guard. De Fernán would bellow at the lack of loyalty, and the Witch's expression would be one to behold. After so much scheming and maneuvering to get him into this position, that he'd trash all her efforts.

He tasted the image like the best of wines.

Alas, that was what it could only be—an image in his mind. He could not trust the Witch wouldn't do something dangerous with Sío de Guzmán's body were he to abandon his post, or enact some other plan that would make his life even worse.

"I hope you can fill the post soon," he said easily. "Perhaps gift it to the winner of the next exhibition?"

"There's a thought. A hothead in charge of other hotheads. Nothing would ever get done. No." De Mavén shook his head. "This post requires maturity, experience."

"Some say I have neither."

"You might be young, but nothing rattles you."

Nothing used to, in any case. "You waste your time, Your Grace. I am content to remain where I am." Adding that he was loyal to the king would've been too big a lie.

The head of the blue tabards didn't insist. Such things were probably too low beneath his boots. Instead, he gestured toward one of the landscapes adorning the walls of the wide corridor. This one in particular pictured Girende as it must've looked before it sank into the Void—a cluster of brown and gray buildings by a winding river against a background of yellow and green fields. Not a hint of Anchor to be seen, except on the frame itself. *And wouldn't that be something*, De Anví thought, *if the city and its inhabitants had given up their lives for the pieces of Anchor embedded in that frame?*

Surely, not even the Lord Death must have such a dark sense of humor.

"Do you believe Cienpuentes will one day go the way of Girende?" De Mavén asked.

"No."

All the Anchor that could be mined out of Cienpuentes had already been extracted. If the city hadn't gone into the Void yet, there was little hope it might in the future.

"Of course not," De Mavén agreed. "De Fernán wouldn't risk his house, only others'."

De Mavén was a ban proponent, then, although De Anví wasn't completely sure if this was due to true belief or the need to be contrary to the regent at all times and all costs.

"What about you, De Anví. Do you believe we should resume the mining of Anchor as your master does?"

Ah, what a dangerous question in the current political climate. A climate De Anví had no wish to join. "I believe the court will come to a decision with or without my input."

De Mavén chuckled. "Possibly. I suppose as someone whose fortunes aren't based in Anchor, it doesn't affect you either way."

Unlike many other members of the court, whose families had long counted on mining and selling their blue wares across Sancia and to the east. Bremón and the other countries beyond might not dare touch the Anchor under their feet, but unlike Valanje, they had no trouble wearing it on their persons.

"Do you think the gods resent us?"

De Mavén's question took him by surprise. "Why should they?"

"We mine their bones and expect them to make our prayers true for no return." His gaze sharpened, and De Anví shifted his attention to the doors at the end of the corridor, wishing them closer—at their current speed, they might not reach them until a week from now. "Why shouldn't they resent us?"

De Anví had often thought they probably did, but that if there was any mercy in the world, they could no longer see what humanity thought of their existence. Not a sentiment worth sharing at the moment, though. With Esparza after a few tankards? Yes. With the head of the Blue Bastards? Perhaps another day.

"If the gods hadn't wanted us to use their bones, they wouldn't have placed them in such obvious places," he answered noncommittally. "Why ought they resent us when they gave us free range?"

"And yet, some think Girende was a warning that we have gone too far."

A belief commonly held.

"Some think that since we aren't listening, perhaps there is worse to come."

A chill settled in De Anví's gut, but he refused to look at De Mavén. "Forgive me, Your Grace, but I cannot tell if you're trying to warn me or if you're trying to entice a response."

"What would you say if I said I was trying to do both?"

The numbers against the ban must be dwindling fast if those like De Mavén were doing away with subtlety and accosting their rivals at their base. De Anví wondered if he was being tested in some way, if De Mavén was gauging his reactions toward something beyond the Anchor ban.

The unease in the pit of his stomach increased. Whatever plans De Mavén had in mind, whatever role he aimed to fill beyond the one in the blue tabards, De Anví wanted no part of it. The Witch's schemes were more than enough to fill his plate.

And if the Witch became aware someone else wanted to play with her toy? The idea was almost enough to make him lose his breakfast on the palace's floors.

"Think about what I've said, De Anví," De Mavén said in a friendly tone, "and let us talk again after Noche Verde."

De Anví hoped not.

XVII

AZUL

The Temple rose three stories high, but only because it needed to accommodate the tall statues of the gods inside. High openings pierced the stone walls, lacking any type of glass or covering so the gods could see everything that happened outside. And with such big windows in such a big building, Azul had no doubt they must see into everyone's hearts.

Isadora would laugh at this, at the existence of actual gods past tales of old, even though Isadora had spent years studying abroad at a Temple school. But then, Isadora hadn't met the Emissary of the Lord Death. Hadn't learned that at least one of the gods still had power over his lands.

A wide plaza opened on the Temple's side flanked by three-story stone buildings. People, carts, and their wares filled the plaza itself, adding to the heat that was already making Azul sweat under her shirt and waistcoat. She was unaccustomed to such concentrated bustling. Such sudden wide space in the crowded city made the structures seem grander, and her smaller. Insignificant. Azul paid the woman who had brought her here and slipped into the house of the gods.

Inside, silence reigned—a cold and prickly sort that wasn't much better than the heat outside. Five statues commanded the visitor's attention, two on each side, and one featured prominently at the back.

Wisely, she advanced by the wall farthest from the source of all her current problems, the Lord Death.

He and the Lord Life began the two lines of statues, since they had begun all that was. The twins—the Lady Dream and the Lord Nightmare—and the Blessed Heart had come from the Lord Death and the Lord Life's need for company. (Azul made a small arch around the Lord Nightmare, who stood next in line to the Lord Life.) The Blessed Heart then gave the twins a son and a daughter—Hope and Despair—but the children were so similar to dreams and nightmares that the twins grew jealous and killed them.

No statues for those lost gods. Only songs and tales to remember them and the two moons in the sky, made from their remains.

Azul stood in front of the Blessed Heart's statue at the end of the cavernous hall, with their flat chest and their round belly and the wisp of a loincloth hiding the juncture of their thighs, their only accessories the wreath on their head and the Anchor filling their eyes.

Cienpuentes liked her riches too much, so of course the Blessed Heart was her main patron. Nothing better than plentiful harvests and plentiful deals to fill her coffers. Gods like the Lady Dream belonged to country dwellers like those living in Agunción, who spent their lives hoping for more.

A girl sat on a small bench by the Blessed Heart, curious gaze trained on Azul. Isadora came to mind again, and Isadora would look like that once she was back. She would be fourteen again, the age of her bones. She would have to finish her studies again, get to fall in love with a sword anew, learn about heartbreak and learn how to break hearts. And this time, Azul would be there to guide her because Azulita, Isadora's younger sister, hadn't known anything about life. But Azul, a senior by several years, had learned plenty since.

"I'd like to speak with the dean," Azul told the girl. There was always one student left to watch the prayer hall of the Temple—Isadora had often complained about the boredom of this particular task in her letters.

"She's not in," the girl answered.

"Well," Azul said, "then I guess I'll have to wait."

The girl bit her lip. "She won't be back for a while, sirese."

"Where has she gone? I could meet her there."

An instant scowl, and the girl touched the hilt of her rapier, put aside next to her on the bench. "I'm not allowed to say."

The girl's reaction surprised Azul. City dwellers, apparently, were more ready to start fights than even Isadora, something she'd never thought possible. "I mean no trouble. I shall wait for her return."

"She won't be back."

"I will wait, just in case," Azul insisted, stepping back.

The line of benches in the center of the hall faced the Blessed Heart, so Azul went to the smaller side benches facing the other gods and chose a seat in front of the Lady Dream. Flanked by the Lord Death, it made for an unsettling placement. But such was life, Azul told herself pragmatically: a series of dreams that always ended with Death.

None of the statues in the Temple sported strings of cloth. This was a place for reflection, not wishes. Here you were supposed to listen to the gods, not expect the gods to listen to you. And now that she knew the Lord Death was as real as the soil Isadora had turned into on the docks of Diel, she was loath to listen.

Closing her eyes, Azul allowed her mind to wander back to the mouse. The rumbling of voices and wheels and hooves filled her mind along with the sight of boots and mud and pebbles and dirt. Enjul leaned against a wall in a shadowed nook created by the joining of two mismatched buildings, a cup in his hand. He was waiting, and from the looks of it had been waiting awhile. Azul proceeded to wait with him for the major part of an hour until he roused and began moving.

Not far, just a few steps to a narrow strip of a path by the rushing waters of one of Espasesmo's many fingers.

A woman waited there, dressed simply in breeches and a shirt, not unlike Azul's shadow. Commoners in Cienpuentes seemed to enjoy the same nondescript clothing favored in the countryside. The woman's face was bare, but Azul did not recognize her. Enjul, on the other hand, had donned a hat and a mask—still not the bone one— and wore his hair gathered in a loose braid down his back.

They stood at ease with each other, as friends might, but it didn't fool Azul. This was a transaction, not an exchange of pleasantries. The woman's demeanor was too respectful, her visage too serious. Azul couldn't see Enjul well, or hear their conversation, but she didn't dare get any closer. Enjul must be doing inquiries about the other necromancer, and she hoped it would lead him nowhere.

"Sirese. *Sirese*."

Azul gasped, wrenched back into the Temple. The girl had brought reinforcements.

"Young woman," a woman intoned, wearing a dress too simple and too well cut to be anything but a uniform, "this is a place for prayers, not naps."

Azul fought to clear her head. "I'm sorry. Prayer does tend to make one doze off, doesn't it? But it won't happen again. I'm waiting for the dean."

The woman studied her with distrust until she caught sight of the glimmering blue of Isadora's Anchor earring, then her tone softened. "I am sorry, but Dean Eneres won't be back for the day. Do leave your name and address with us, and we will send notice when she is available for a meeting."

She ought to have shown the Anchor from the first, Azul admonished herself. This was Cienpuentes, after all. "Thank you. My name is Azul del Arroyo, and my address, the Marquess de Gracia's house. The matter is of some urgency, so the sooner I speak with the dean, the better."

The woman's mouth slackened at the mention of her brother. Yes, Azul would get her appointment eventually. Of this, she was sure. But would it be in time? A last look at the Lady Dream before she turned toward the exit. One could always hope.

Setting her hat back on her head, she directed her steps toward Almanueva, her shadow appearing next to her the moment she stepped outside. The heat was close to unendurable, magnified by the afternoon sun and the enclosed spaces of Cienpuentes's streets. The buildings held no charm now, the noises loud and deafening. *What an insufferable city*, Azul thought. *What a waste of space.*

✵ ✵ ✵

Enjul was back in time for supper. He spoke little, but his attention kept returning to Azul, as if wondering what she would do next.

With that in mind, Azul waited until late at night to knock on her brother's door.

The floor tiles were cool against her bare feet; her candle, she had left back in her room.

A slight creak a few steps away made her jump. Startled, she watched the next door open and her brother peek out. He was all surprise, his face half-lit by a lamp inside his room.

"Sister?" he whispered.

Still so unused to that term, Azul stifled the urge to look behind her shoulder and see whom he was talking to.

"May we speak?" she asked in the same low tone.

"Of course," he answered, clearing the way into his room. Azul entered, curious. She was certain the door she had knocked on corresponded to the light she had seen across the patio last night. A second door in her brother's chamber answered the unspoken question—an adjacent room. A study?

Her brother pointed to a small chair by a tiny desk near one of the two windows while he sat on a trunk at the foot of the bed. His room was twice the length of hers, with white and golden walls decorated by a few paintings, their browns and beiges wavering under the flickering candlelight. Human studies, all of them. A woman sitting by a well, her diaphanous gown accentuating the slope of her shoulders and the graceful arch of her neck. A man, bared to the waist, arms resting on an axe, a tower of lumber by his side. A person's stretched arms and upper back—and only their back—fading from healthy nails on the left to bony fingertips on the right. Gruesome. Alluring.

Tearing her gaze from the painting, Azul found her brother watching her, clad in his nightshirt and a robe. Was he looking for a reaction to the decor? No, he was waiting to see why she was in his room this late at night, still in her shirt and breeches but otherwise prepared for stealth. She went back to the door and closed it carefully.

"Gruesome, isn't it?" he said with a conspiratorial smile, nodding toward the flesh-to-bone painting. "Unfit for a gentleman's chamber."

Azul shook her head. "It's what we are inside. Flesh and bones. It's good to keep a reminder so we don't believe ourselves indestructible."

"I wish I had hidden it, then. It's my duty as older brother to appear indestructible, isn't it?"

She smiled at this. "I wouldn't know. It seems my fate to remain the younger one."

He crossed his arms and studied Azul from amused, half-lidded eyes. "I've had time to grow into my role, willingly and eagerly, even if I wasn't able to lure you back home. So, tell me, Sister, what is it that you need my help with? Does it have something to do with this sudden urge to come visit me?"

Azul was relieved at the direct question. Sitting by his side on the long trunk, she met his stare. "I need help getting into the ossuary. The rooms where they keep the bones. I tried to gain access today but was unsuccessful in securing an appointment. You're a marquess now; I'd hoped you'd have some influence over these kinds of matters."

He didn't seem shocked or surprised by the request. *Perhaps*, Azul thought, *he was used to people asking his help to enter otherwise inaccessible buildings*.

"The Temple . . . ?"

"Dean Eneres was not available."

He nodded solemnly. "Too many people with strange requests, no doubt." Then, so cautiously Azul grew nervous for the first time, "Why the ossuary?"

She fidgeted with her hands, hoping to appear young and lost and in need of a hero's help. "I wish to pray to my sister's bones—one of my sisters' bones. She was brought here years ago after her demise near Monteverde." She suddenly feared his next question—why not pray in the Temple, since the deceased's soul now belonged to the gods?—so she rushed her next words: "It's something we promised each other, that if we happened to die before the other, even if the Lord Death claimed our souls, we'd leave a part of us behind in our bones for the times when we'd need the other's love and comfort. I know it's strange and against the Temple's teachings, and it might seem silly that the Lord Death would allow such a thing to happen . . . but it's so important to me. It would bring me so much peace to see her remains one more time in case part of her is still somehow there. I must do it without Sirese Enjul or his shadow knowing."

"So, the shadow *is* his," Sergado said. "Why the secrecy? Are you sure you don't want me to do something about this shadow or Enjul?"

The no-nonsense edge to those last words reaffirmed his need to protect her as she had meant to protect Isadora. *Hopefully*, she thought wryly, *with better results*. "I'm helping Sirese Enjul with some matters, but I know he won't return the favor. You know how strict Valanjians are about the Lord Death. Sirese Enjul doesn't approve of my plans. He doesn't think I ought to visit my sister."

"Then allow me to kick him out," Sergado said earnestly. "I can deal with whatever keeps you beholden to him. Stay here at Almanueva with me. It's your right to live here as much as it is mine. I meant to settle an allowance for you, but I've been busy taking care of Father's position."

"An allowance?"

"As is your due as his daughter. I'm not sure why he didn't do it while he was alive. He has always been strict about these sorts of things." A wince. "Was."

"He offered to take charge of me," Azul told him, "but my mother refused."

"Still, strange he didn't do it anyway and kept it secret until you were of age. There might still be such an account, hidden among all his others."

Azul would be lying if the thought of free-given money wasn't a welcome relief. Newly fourteen-year-old Isadora would need to be hidden from their mother. She would need food, clothes, another start in life. To have the matter settled, so speedily and easily, was nothing short of an answered prayer. "How did he die?" she asked. "Our father."

"A matter of the heart, I'm told," Sergado answered, focusing on the empty fireplace across the room. "It was sudden and without warning. He was a good man. Strict in his ways, but with a sense of duty. I wish you had met him."

Azul caught the wishful edge to his voice and felt the bond of true kinship, for she, too, was starting to wish he had met Isadora. "I wish I had."

They sat in contemplative silence for a few minutes. Then, snapping out of it, Sergado smiled and patted Azul's hand. "I will help you gain entry to the ossuary, of course. But it might take a few days."

"A few days . . . ," she said, crestfallen—this she didn't have to fake.

"Things move slow in Cienpuentes. Slower sometimes for me. I am new and unproven. My position opens doors, but others are in no hurry to unlock them." He winked. "For now."

This elicited a burst of laughter from her. He would do this for her, she was sure of it. The look in his eyes, the honesty in his open face. She had asked, so he would try his best. Wouldn't she if Isadora had asked it of her?

Some guilt surfaced at her attempts at manipulating him, but they were easily dismissed—she hadn't asked him to risk anything but a few minutes of his time. She took her brother's hand and squeezed it tightly. "Thank you, Brother."

He smiled, brought her hand to his mouth for a fast press of his lips. "Stay, Sister. I mean my offer. You will enjoy Cienpuentes. You will make new friends, new conquests. You will lack for nothing and you will become whatever you want to be. You can visit your mother and your other sister at will, stay with them for a little while, and they will be welcome to travel here as well. This is too big of a house. It needs a family to feel content."

Would he be so obliging if she asked him to take care of Isadora in her stead? Azul wondered. She might be bound by duty to return to Valanje after this affair was over, but it did not mean Sergado must be left without a younger sister to look after, even if not of the same blood.

He said no more, and there was nothing else she could say, not until she had her hands on Isadora's bones, except for her thanks and a good night.

Enjul was waiting in the far corner of the hallway.

Heart in her throat from the shock of his presence, Azul finished closing her brother's door and made her way to the emissary, feet silent on the cool tiles. He loomed against the wall, also barefoot, also in shirtsleeves and breeches, his hair also tumbling free over his shoulders and back. They weren't so different, Azul thought, she and he in the soft shadows created by the stray silvery light of the moons. A sense of familiarity unfurled in her chest, as if some part of her recognized this moment of strange symmetry.

As if in another time, another life, they might be well matched, soul to soul and heart to heart.

Then, of course, he had to speak:

"Did you have a good talk?"

"Did you hear enough from your man?" she countered in a whisper. "Enjoyed his report, made notes on how to improve his efficiency for tomorrow?"

"He earned his coin and he is glad to have the job."

"It must have been easy," she said dryly. "You knew I wouldn't be allowed into the ossuary, didn't you? You knew I would waste my time there."

His smile was slight, but it was there, strange in the shadows of the corner. "You were so endearing in your pursuit, going around town wasting my man's time. Now, tell me, did you warn your brother about what you are?"

She glanced over her shoulder. Her brother's door remained closed. "Why should I? I mean him no harm."

"I wonder about that."

His certainty rankled. "What do you mean?"

"Did you ever ask your sister if she wanted to be brought back?"

The question took her aback. "She was already dead. How could I ask?"

He took a step forward, and she took a step backward, until they were around the bend in the corridor.

"Not the first time, but after." A pause while she couldn't find anything to say. "No, you never asked. Because you are selfish and were scared of her answer. Scared that there was a chance she would say no, that she didn't want to become an affront in the eyes of the gods."

Azul kept ahold of her anger, but it seeped through in her harsh whisper. "Isadora would never think that. She didn't believe in the gods and—"

"Ah, but you must. Otherwise, why come to Valanje? Was it not because you were curious about the Lord Death, about what you could do? Did it never occur to you that others might not want to blemish their souls under his eyes?"

"*I don't want to go, Azul.*" Isadora's reticence, such a contrast with her usual carefree self, back to haunt her. "Isadora was all that is life," she told Enjul, hands fisted tightly, nails digging into her palms. "She would never accept death."

"How are you to know, when you never bothered to ask?"

She gave him a small mocking bow. "You are right. I shall do that next time." Turning on her heel, she stalked toward her room.

"Miss Del Arroyo."

She paused, well aware that she had gone too far.

His words betrayed no emotion when they came: "I gave you a day. Tomorrow, you shall do as I say."

XVIII

AZUL

The huge plaza by the Temple turned into exhibitions of swords-manship every other week during the summer months. Azul was well versed in these sorts of things from Isadora's love of everything to do with rapiers and duels and winning. Isadora had loved exhibitions, a staple of each summer she had spent away at the Temple school.

When Enjul told her he, Azul, and Nereida would attend that day's match, Azul guessed the visit was all about the necromancer search rather than fake duels among schoolgirls. What better opportunity to find a wide congregation of Cienpuentes's citizens?

Azul put special care into her clothing, as did Nereida, even if they didn't have much clothing to choose from. Sergado had insisted in opening an account for her at a local seamstress once he had learned there were no trunks full of belongings following their arrival, but Azul hadn't had the time to visit the shop yet, what with arriving, being denied at the ossuary, and then kicked out of the Temple just to have Enjul commandeer her presence for the exhibition.

As for the Emissary of the Lord Death, Azul was confident he was still unaware of her mousy spy, and thus had no way of knowing she had witnessed his meeting with the woman.

"You didn't find what you were looking for," Nereida said, having invaded Azul's bedroom while she finished getting ready. It was the first time they had been alone since breaking their fast the day before.

"The ossuary they show the public is a husk." Azul spoke with disgust, combing her hair with her fingers. "The real one is somewhere else, or perhaps underneath, and they are not happy to allow visitors. Sergado promised to help me get inside, but he said it will take him some time to obtain access," she added, not without frustration. "He didn't say how long, but I worry. The emissary is already pressuring me, and once he's done with whatever secret questioning he's doing, I won't be able to shake him easily. His shadow is already a problem. Is there nobody you know who might help us? With whom you might share your arrival in town?"

Whatever Nereida thought of Azul's request, or her involving her brother in this quest of theirs, remained hidden behind the slight hauteur that had become Nereida's permanent expression since arriving to town. Although, if Azul were to guess, for a moment she had looked thoughtful.

With firm hands, she turned Azul around and took ahold of her hair. To Azul's surprise, she began braiding it.

"Do you no longer want me to raise someone?" Azul asked.

Nereida's hands tightened, and Azul yelped in pain. "Our deal stays as is. What I do with my time is of no concern of yours." A few moments of silence while Nereida worked on Azul's hair. "Your sister, how did she die?"

Azul couldn't believe she would ask this. "You were there," she snapped. "You saw how."

Another sharp tug of her hair, then the feeling of Nereida tying a length of leather at the end of the braid. "The first time. That was her second death, wasn't it?"

When Azul's words came, they came slowly. "She caught a fever during a trip. We were on our way back from visiting family friends."

"How did you manage to hide her death from your mother?"

"We were traveling alone. Isadora was old enough to take charge, so a friend took us to the inn before continuing on her way, and we were waiting for someone from Agunción to come pick us up."

"How old was your sister?"

Azul smiled in spite of herself, remembering the cheeky teen her sister had been. "Fourteen. Had already spent two years at the Temple school by then."

"And nobody was the wiser?"

"Why would they be?"

Nereida hesitated. "What if the person were to have died by violent means? Would traces of such violence remain? Cuts? Holes?"

"I told you: Isadora was whole in body and spirit. All her memories, all her essence is—was—still her. The same person, their body rebuilt. No fever, no scarring."

She reached for a half mask Enjul had given her.

With a shocking economy of motion, Nereida ripped the mask out of her hand. Her eyes were bright, her voice hard as she crumpled the scrap of hard fabric in her fist. "Never wear masks in Cienpuentes, Del Arroyo. Never cover your face while you're here."

Azul was too startled to do anything but agree. Then, "But why?"

Unsurprisingly, Nereida did not answer. Azul wondered who could. Her brother? Her shadow outside? Not Enjul—he obviously had no issue with wearing masks around town.

The question nagged her all the way to the Temple, but once they arrived, she forgot all about it. Gentry and nobility mixed with merchants and laborers, and pleasure-seekers filled every walkway, every street, every building with a view into the plaza by the Temple's side. No wonder Enjul wanted them here!

Children ran around in half capes and skirts, selling dried fruit and small cakes to spectators. Banners hung from the buildings, some too faded to tell colors or crests. Caught in the cloying excitement, Azul elbowed her way to the parapet of the second floor's open walkway and took in the view, drank in the sounds.

The Temple school pupils stood in pairs in their uniformed breeches and vests and skirts, most of their shirtsleeves rolled up their arms, waiting under a tent by the Temple walls for their turn to fight. Joining them was a large contingent of guards of two different kinds—the ones with the palace's yellow colors, and the ones with the City Guard's blue tabards.

Nereida carved a spot by Azul's side, hiding beneath her hat and holding a square of lace to her nose and mouth. An upside-down mask, as it were, since she hated the normal ones so much. And in this, she was almost alone, for well over half the crowd wore masks: white, brown, black; felt, silk, and other things; plain, embroidered, lined with small beads sparkling with summer sunlight, holding feathers like exotic birds. Held by ribbons, part of hats, or threaded into side braids with pearl-ended pins.

No wonder nobody had glanced twice at Enjul wearing a mask a day earlier. City of bridges, city of masks. Wealth and secrets all at once.

Below the masks, below the opening mouths, below the grins and the grimaces, was a show of daylight fashion. Elegant, light summer dresses with tight bodices that left the shoulders bare. Embroidered white shirt sleeves—Azul had never seen such before, but they appeared common here—covered by waistcoats of all kinds of colors that made her wish she could fit into one of Nereida's beautiful creations.

But those beautiful waistcoats she had seen on the way over the sea lay in trunks back in Valanje. Nereida wore as simple of a waistcoat as Azul did. No shoulder plates here to indicate houses and parentage, though—the illusion of anonymity created by the masks too big an allure to pass.

It was overwhelming. The colors, the ever-moving duelists in the plaza, the ripples of the crowd, the insults and the curses and the bets thrown in the air. Perfume wafted from the spectators' fans in an attempt to keep the heat and the odor of sweat at bay, adding to the assault on her senses.

After a few minutes of taking in the view, Nereida murmured her excuses and left Azul's side, not to be seen again until later, back at Almanueva in time for supper.

Enjul filled the space, the same mask he had worn yesterday failing to hide his violet-and-golden eyes, and spoke for the first time since their encounter last night. "You've been here already, I gather?"

"Yesterday," she answered. The emissary was too close, and she fought with the person by her other side to gain some ground. "I'm sure my shadow already told you." She leaned against the stone parapet, watching the school pupils retreat under their tent and the guards dominate the space. They took turns, using practice swords with blunted ends dipped in paint. The different-colored groups jeered and cheered and demanded a rematch whenever their fighter lost a point to the other one.

"I was told your sister enjoyed duels with her rapier. I have yet to see one on you."

"Duels aren't easy to wear, Emissary. They dust and break with too much ease."

Fingers landed on her braid, right over her nape. A shiver at the warm contact ran down her back, and she feared it might be excitement. "Fragile, like human lives. May I remind you how I know?"

"I spoke out of order," she admitted easily, if a little breathlessly. The crowd's enthusiasm made for a buoyant mood, even if his touch somehow anchored her in place. "I did not study at the Temple like my sister. Rapiers and swords are not my weapons of choice."

"Ah."

He couldn't possibly think any lesser of her for her lack of godly education, Azul reasoned, since there were no Temple schools in Valanje.

"Why aren't you wearing your mask?" Enjul asked.

"Is my being here a secret? If so, who would know who I am?"

Excited whispers rose around them. Whoever was next must be a bit of an event. Azul chose to ignore it, along with the searing heat of Enjul's lingering touch, and studied the people by the front of the building across the plaza. They were too far for her to see their features clearly, but they must be of some importance, sitting on chairs dragged from inside the building to its wide front steps. Some had decided to remain standing, perhaps not to wrinkle their clothing, but this group had also drifted into halves, like the tabards.

Enjul leaned closer. Her heartbeat sped up, the strange pull she had felt when he first walked into her room in Diel returning in full force. Warmth met her back.

"Are there any?" he whispered close to her ear, so close he might as well be breathing the words into her soul.

Azul made to move away, but he held on to her waist with his hand, his touch all but a brand.

"Answer, Miss Del Arroyo. Do you see any creature who oughtn't be alive?"

She did. One of the blue tabards standing by the tents, outwardly uninterested in the revelry happening around her like a stone in the middle of a stream. A bored guard, anyone else might surmise, but the strangeness of her presence sent a note of alarm into Azul's gut. And another, some woman ambling through the crowd like a lost fish.

"None so far."

Lies had never tasted better on her mouth. Let Virel Enjul think he held all the power, that she was meek and willing to obey.

The pressure of his hand against her torso increased, bringing an unexpected thrill. "Are you certain?"

She kept her attention on the nobles standing outside the building, on the whites and yellows and greens and blues of their clothing. On breathing in and breathing out. His nearness invaded her senses. The warmth of his hand, of his body, his scent of queen's blooms and fresh soil, the force of his vitality. "I am."

"On your honor?" he asked, even closer and full of mockery.

"Why ask when you doubt its existence so much?"

"I must make sure you don't lie to me. And you wouldn't be lying to me, would you?"

The pressure from his hand disappeared, but she had no wishes to move beyond turning to him. His eyes were as beautiful and hard as jewels up close. "What would be the point, since you know everything?"

"Flattery, while appreciated, is wasted on someone like me."

"What do you wish for instead," she asked, "a room full of corpses—a playroom for your god?"

He leaned down until his nose all but touched hers. And the hand was back, too, blocking her escape. "Be careful with your tone, Azul del Arroyo, for when you speak to me, you are speaking to the Lord Death. When you make an oath to me, you are promising your worth to a higher being, to him, who began it all and would have no problem ending you, in this life or after you attempt to claim a spot for your soul in his bones.

"Now use your eyes or your ears or whatever it is that allows you to sense the walking corpses. Have you forgotten the reason you are here and not in chains on your way back to Valanje? I haven't, and you should make sure you don't."

How did one respond to such a speech?

Azul didn't know. Words escaped her, blood fled from her face and her chest and anywhere that was close to him. Nobody was here to rescue her, and truly she had never thought herself as someone who needed to be rescued. But someone must've been looking out for her—another god, perhaps, jealous of the emissary's words—because the crowd broke into shouts and claps, and the sudden jostling jarred them apart.

Inhaling sharply, Azul avoided looking at the emissary. She would act like nothing had happened. Like her heart wasn't inhabiting her throat and her stomach all at once.

"Do you know those people?" she asked Enjul, pointing toward the steps on the opposite side of the plaza. And if her voice had shaken a little, she hoped it had escaped his notice.

"Why, yes. I sure do!" answered the Faceless Witch.

XIX

THE FACELESS WITCH

The young woman's face was a map, and the Faceless Witch took immense pleasure in studying it. Shock and awareness edged with just enough reserve to make anyone curious about what it hid. Well, not all. Many could not see beyond the surface, but the Witch could, and did.

"What a morsel of curiosity you are," murmured the Faceless Witch through the young man carrying her. Still the same man. Still her favorite. Sío de Guzmán, with his raven locks and handsome features enhanced by a simple dark green mask. "What a pity you wear no mask."

The little plaything looked lost. "Excuse me?"

The Witch offered a guileless smile. "Masks are so alluring, don't you think?"

"Who are you?" the woman asked, bluntly as only someone unaccustomed to Cienpuentes's coquetry would.

Hmm-hmm. Delicious, indeed. "An interested citizen."

"And what is your name?"

"One of great charm and beauty."

A spurt of laughter escaped the woman. The Witch congratulated herself—she had been right to approach this one instead of restraining her curiosity and subjecting herself to the torture of waiting.

"Very well, masked stranger," she said. "Will you——?" She stopped, looked around, as if she had suddenly realized what she was missing.

The Witch stepped closer. "Don't worry about your zealous companion, countryface. He was called elsewhere." And then, in a conspiratorial whisper, "I don't think he'll be gone long, little songbird, so we must do the best we can with what time we have."

"Your doing?"

The speculation in the woman's tone was more alluring than beauty or money could ever be to the Faceless Witch—she so loved secrets. Loved to find them, untangle them, savor their content, and then, only then, use them.

"I will admit to it," the Witch said, "if you admit to your name."

"Seems hardly fair, since you won't tell me yours."

The Witch put her hand to her chest, today clad in a dark crimson waistcoat with golden leaves vining the neckline and hem. "Ah, but I need to retain some secrecy so you're tempted to seek me tomorrow."

Another smile, a calculating gleam in her eyes. The morsel might be from the countryside but knew better than to fall headfirst into the Witch's charm. It only made her more intriguing. "Azul del Arroyo."

"Like the summer sky. How fitting. How lucky. Now, tell me, what did you wish to know? I must reward this honesty of yours."

Del Arroyo returned her focus to the plaza. "Will you tell me about those people over there? Those dignified ones."

The Witch leaned against the parapet bricks, her half cape draping over her left shoulder and arm, curtaining them into a private nook away from prying ears.

"Are you certain, Azul del Arroyo, that you want to waste your time learning about others instead of me? About those"—she waved toward the plaza—"you can ask anyone. Their names are well known. About me, though, you can only ask me."

Another round of jeers and cheers filled the air while Del Arroyo paused to rethink her query.

"No," she told the Witch, shaking her head. "I'm fresh from the countryside, and I have to begin somewhere. Tell me."

A deep sigh preceded the Witch's next words: "If you wish. The man over there, in the blue-and-silver waistcoat and stiff cravat is none other than Dío de Mavén, head of the City Guard. Although if he doesn't get rid of that thing around his neck, we might be looking for a replacement. How can he breathe in this heat? The woman sitting by his side is his niece, Maril de Mavén. By their right, that one with the ruddy cheeks is De Pío, one of the captains of the Guard. See how nobody stands near him? He probably still reeks from last night's drunken feast. The opposite from him is De Aria, the head of the Golden Dogs, His Majesty's Guards, and that one, the one standing like he'd rather be anywhere else, is the Count de Anví, his second-in-command."

"The regent doesn't attend?"

"Hah!" the Witch exclaimed. "Does this look like the sort of gathering a regent or a queen would attend?"

Del Arroyo shrugged. If she was hurt by her laughter, she didn't show it. "Seems like everyone is enjoying it well enough."

"No, countryface. Those you see here are nothing to those who own the Heart. Haven't you noticed your host isn't here?"

The Witch grinned at the sharp glance thrown her way.

"My host?"

"The Marquess de Gracia, of course."

"Is he the reason you sought me out?"

"Hmm-hmm," the Witch answered. "I'm quite a curious person, you see. I aim to learn all I can, but De Gracia's servants are too well paid to talk."

"I appreciate your honesty, but there is nothing to learn. I'm a temporary guest, and soon I'll be gone. You ought to ask De Gracia directly, if you wish to know more."

"How formal, how priggish. It doesn't suit you."

"Nothing here suits me," Del Arroyo muttered.

"Ah, but I think it could if you wanted it to."

Del Arroyo didn't bother responding to this. Instead, she asked, "Why do people like masks so much in this city?"

"They find it coy; they like to flirt. A game." A wicked smile— Sío de Guzmán produced the best ones, just short of rakish, yet too obvious to be anything else. "And idle people do love entertaining themselves."

"So do you," Del Arroyo pointed out.

"Only with those worth my efforts."

Del Arroyo ran her fingers across the parapet's top, put a drop of whine in her voice. "Am I not worth the effort of knowing your name, then? If I'm worthy of your curiosity, surely I'm worthy to know more of you."

"A good attempt, but you need to work on your tone if you wish to charm such things out of jaded old souls like mine."

She studied the Witch, taking note of the youthful looks of her face and obviously wishing to ask. Truly, she was so easy to read on the outside. But the inside—ah, the inside—that's where the Witch truly wished to delve.

"What do you dream of, little bird?" she asked, crowding Del Arroyo against the stone barrier. "Do you dream of the pigs and sheep back home? Do you dream of men, or do you dream of women? Perhaps both? Perhaps neither. Do you dream of riches within your grasp or of the things you no longer have?" She lifted a hand to hover it by Del Arroyo's temple. "Ah, the things I could do with your dreams."

Del Arroyo blinked, maybe hoping the action would clear the sight in front of her. Adorable. "You confound me."

"Such is my intention."

"Why?"

"My day would be awfully boring otherwise."

Del Arroyo gestured toward the duelists in the plaza. "Is this not enough? What do you do to fill your days, that they're so boring?"

A hand landed on the woman's arm, startling her. "Miss Del Arroyo."

The deathling was back.

"Ah," said the Witch, "here's De Gracia's other mysterious guest. Also from out of town, I assume?"

The man didn't answer, because of course he wouldn't. The Faceless Witch was well versed in men like him—walls of flesh and bone with no windows to peek through. They stirred another kind of curiosity in her, but she didn't think this one would agree to allow her into his mind. Others enjoyed the hunt, the steady, eventual weakening of their opponents. Not her. The Witch wanted to *know*, and while she did enjoy her games, there were too many minds out there to get stuck wishing for any particular one.

"Are you enjoying your stay in Cienpuentes so far?" she asked with an open smile. Another benefit of this body—gods, she loved this body; if only she could retain it forever!—was the ability to appear young and unabashed and too honest for subterfuge.

"It is a beautiful city," he answered, to the Witch's surprise. Truly, she hadn't expected him to. "But we must be on our way."

Accustomed to giving orders, this one was. It exuded from him: authority, power. The Witch recognized the posture of someone used to eliciting respect and fear. Unfortunately for him, the Witch was not easily cowed.

"So soon? Stay, enjoy the exhibition. Who knows which of the duelists won't be back next time to grace us with their skill?"

He gave her no reaction. But his hand hadn't moved from Del Arroyo's arm. Anyone else might've mistaken this for a sign of passionate possession in the face of an unwanted rival, but again, she was the Witch, and humans were so easily read. Del Arroyo's features had rearranged into pure blandness, and she did not resist the hold. She had expected, if not this, something of the same sort. She was in his debt, that was obvious. And still, something seemed to crackle in the air between them, the tension of two people unwilling to admit their inner desires. Nothing more interesting than secret deals and hidden feelings, was there?

"You will stay long enough to enjoy Noche Verde, I hope," she said smoothly. "It's been two years since the last one; I can only imagine how magnificent it will be this summer."

Not a blink from the man, not even a tightening of fingers or a spark of curiosity. The Witch cursed herself. She had meant to find out about De Gracia's mysterious guests, and now all she wanted was to see what was inside this man's mind. It was tempting. He wore a mask; he might be convinced.

He was looking at Azul del Arroyo now, as if expecting her to answer. What a thoughtful keeper.

"I would love to see it," she said meekly. Slyness suited her as badly as her attempt at charming an answer earlier. A woman like this could never be anything but direct. Underhanded, yes, but direct.

"Ask the Marquess de Gracia," the Witch said. "He should have entrance to the grandest parties. It would be a shame to miss them."

"Will you be there?" Del Arroyo asked.

"Who knows?" The Witch pressed her small wooden fan into Del Arroyo's hand. "A small token of welcome, to remember me by," she whispered. Then, after a small bow, she retreated into the crowd.

The Witch had been half-honest with Del Arroyo—she was a native of the city, after all—and some of Cienpé's higher echelons did come to the exhibition, hiding behind their masks to conduct secret talks. A perfect opportunity for her to peddle some dreams.

She had often wondered in her younger years why she could do what she did, why she was allowed to turn Anchor into dreams, but had eventually concluded that it must've been life's way to compensate her for her lack. A lack of eyes, of ears, of nose—a lack of a face. Every hour, every minute, every second, she felt the weight of the tether linking her consciousness to her actual body hidden in Cienpuentes.

A wasted body—useless, weak, and rotting of old age. Too close to death.

XX

THE ROGUE

ALMOST TWO YEARS EARLIER

Miguel Esparza had fallen in love many times. With brunettes, with blondes, with coin, with liquor, and with more than a few cloaks. So, he was fairly acquainted with the feeling when it rose, unencumbered and glowing, at the sight of the young woman mounted on a fine horse carefully parting the busy street.

"Are you listening, Esparza?" asked his companion in their guarding duty.

"Not in the least," answered Esparza, leaving their spot by the corner and making his way toward the newcomer. He readjusted his rapier, tugged on his gloves, and made sure his hat sat at the perfect angle.

The woman had stopped her mount while she looked around, her expression part apprehensive, part lost, but mostly excitement. Her midnight hair had been braided away from her face, and her tanned cheeks held the sun's warmth as she bent to pat the horse's neck. A straw hat hung forgotten from a ribbon around her neck.

A countryface, no doubt. Dressed in expensive breeches and a traveling brown cloak bearing De Guzmán's family crest, but a countryface nonetheless.

"Hello there," Esparza said, pausing by her side and offering his best smile.

Her gaze snapped to him. Wary at first, then relieved when she recognized the blue color of his tabard and the insignia sewn on to it. Esparza might hate the outfit, but he sure thanked it in times like this.

"Your first visit to Cienpuentes?" he asked, stepping closer and running a reassuring hand down the horse's neck.

"Sá."

When she said no more, he took off his hat and gifted her a bow. "I'm Miguel Esparza, proud member of the City Guard. May I ask what brings you to the capital?"

Her answering grin was nothing but magnificent. "I've come to make my fortune."

He chuckled at the enthusiasm in her words. "A lofty cause, I see. If I may be of assistance? I couldn't help but notice you seem lost. Are you in need of directions? I know the city well, as you can imagine. May I guide you to your destination? Is there anyone looking out for you and your future fortune?"

Her merry laugh filled the air, and Esparza's heart picked up its pace. "Sá, there is. You've seen the crest on my cloak, you must know of my brother and my sisters—I am told they are quite popular. I am Edine, the youngest."

He let out a laugh of his own. "Which of your siblings will you be staying with, then? Perhaps I can be of further assistance during your stay."

"I'm staying on my own. Otherwise, it wouldn't be my fortune, would it?" A hint of regret entered her voice. "I can't imagine we'll be meeting again. I know how busy the Guard keeps my brother. Although I'd be thankful for a general direction, and I do appreciate the offer."

Esparza winked. "Don't worry on account of my duties. I think we'll see each other again, Edine de Guzmán."

And they did.

THE PRESENT

Esparza studied his drink. Murky as usual in the low light of Casa Rojita. The only sign of the earliness in the day came from the fact it was less crowded than usual. His hat lay abandoned on the bench by his side, and he was wearing his blue tabard instead of simply his shirtsleeves or a doublet.

"Drinking already," said Nereida de Guzmán, sliding onto his other side.

Esparza shrugged to cover his surprise. "'Happy is the life of a drunken fool.'"

"'For he knows not the Lord Death is upon him,'" De Guzmán finished for him. "So, it's come down to the cups?"

"Brawls aren't helping, and nobody will cross swords with me anymore." Really, Esparza mused dryly, must he do the Lord Death's job all the way through?

"Don't try so hard for a couple of days. I'm in need of your services."

"We didn't expect you back for a while."

"Plans change."

"So they do, if you seek my help." Esparza sent her a sly look. "I've never known you to be so desperate."

De Guzmán smiled, and for a heartbeat she looked so much like Edine, his heart lodged in his throat. Same nose, same brow shape, same cheeks. Esparza sipped his drink to give his mouth something to do rather than cursing De Guzmán for intruding into his solitude.

"A year and a half ago," De Guzmán said, "you got into the Royal Crypt to make sure the vials of the queen's blood hadn't been stolen, so they could be used to identify the child king."

Esparza remained silent while one of the servers placed a cup of ale in front of Nereida. She eyed it, not with distaste or with curiosity.

She was too good at hiding the former and had long lost any wish to feel the latter.

To save her the effort of summoning any sort of response, Esparza traded his empty cup for hers.

"I need you to do it again," she told him.

"We ended that business back then." Esparza drank deeply, as if trying to drown the disgust in his voice.

"I don't need the crypt this time. I need the ossuary."

"No." He shook his head sharply. "I'm done with the dead."

"You aren't," she answered placidly, "or you wouldn't be here so often."

Esparza threw his cup against the wall, sending the room still. When no punches followed, it went back to hushed conversations and loud slurping.

"Esparza!" shouted someone from the counter. "You owe me for that."

De Guzmán ignored both the demand and Esparza's outburst, her voice calm as she said, "I need you to take someone into the ossuary."

"Why?" Esparza asked with rancor. "What's in it for you?"

"'Don't ask, reap your reward'—your motto, isn't it?"

A smile flitted across his face. "The words don't suit you."

Her fingers tapped on the hilt of her rapier, offering no rebuke.

"Why can't they ask to get in?" he asked.

"Time is of the essence, and people are too slow. If I had any Anchor to offer, it'd go faster, alas . . ."

"You would in spades, if you accepted De Anví's courtship."

"Is he still keeping the Witch in check?"

"Inseparable."

"Is she still wearing Sío?"

"You've been gone mere weeks."

"Feels longer," De Guzmán murmured to herself.

Esparza forced himself to study her carefully. "You don't sound like yourself. What's changed?"

De Guzmán hesitated before answering, "I've met someone."

Arching his brows in question, Esparza waited for her to continue.
"She reminds me of Edine."

Inhaling deeply, Esparza stopped himself from upturning the table and thrashing everything else in the room. Then, viciously, "So, you've decided to help her like you should've helped Edine? How magnanimous of you."

De Guzmán shrugged. "I will pay, of course."

"Of course," he said, his tone dripping with mockery.

"I will also need an audience with the Witch."

"If you pay well enough, I'll get you an audience with the Blessed Heart themselves."

A tightening of De Guzmán's jaw was the only reaction to his insolent tone. "Don't tell her it's me, and make it somewhere private." She fixed him with her gaze. "Will you do it?"

Esparza met her eyes. "It'll be the last thing I do for you, and only because your sister loved you."

De Guzmán stood, put some coins on the table. "I count on your discretion. It must remain unknown I'm back in Cienpé. Surprise is . . . everything."

Esparza called for more ale. "You have my word."

✴ ✴ ✴

"De Guzmán is back in town," Esparza told De Anví as they strode along a busy street. Evening was falling, and the rushing of people hurrying home for supper hid their conversation.

De Anví's steps didn't slow, but his sharp inhale was audible. "How did you learn of this?"

"She asked for my help, on behalf of someone she's met. A young woman, from the sounds of it."

"Anyone we know?"

"I'm not sure yet. I couldn't follow her."

"You're losing your touch," De Anví admonished.

Esparza readjusted his rapier. "She must have new friends in town.

She hasn't touched her house or those closest to her, or been at the inns."

"Something to do with the envoy to Valanje?"

"It's too coincidental, but I don't think so. Her business seems private."

"Care to share?"

Esparza glanced De Anví's way. He wore a dark waistcoat instead of his usual whites and golds—a concession he occasionally did when he didn't care to be recognized—but his confident stride, his posture, was hard to hide. "Why not, I'm already damned to the Void. She seeks an audience with the Witch."

De Anví frowned. "That cannot be good."

"Wanted to make sure the Witch is still wearing Sío."

"Not good at all. Have you contacted her?"

"Not yet."

"Good."

Esparza had never been able to tell what kind of thoughts ran behind De Anví's severe countenance—like De Guzmán, he had spent too long in court, had become too adept at making a mask out of his face—but he admired De Anví's guts for worrying about Nereida in the face of her coldness. But then, at least Nereida de Guzmán was alive. At least De Anví had hope.

She reminds me of Edine.

Damn De Guzmán and her attempts to assuage her guilt.

"Was that all?" De Anví asked.

"No."

"Do I have to wring it out of you?"

"I'd hoped you'd allow me to retain some shred of professional integrity."

"Integrity is for young lads aiming to be tabards. You and I lost ours long ago."

Since it was well known Esparza shared this wisdom, he changed topics instead: "Do you ever wish we hadn't found the king's kidnappers?"

De Anví's voice was heavy with sarcasm when he answered, "What do you think?"

"You could always murder His Majesty in his sleep and blame me."

"I am not so far gone I wish to harm a child, tempting as it might sometimes be. Nay, someone will eventually find a way to supplant me, and the Witch won't be able to do a thing about it."

The thoughtful tone didn't match his glib words. "It really worries you," Esparza said, "De Guzmán asking to speak with the Witch."

"It troubles me that she is back without a word. What a time to make her reappearance, right before court goes into session. What does she want of the Witch? She's avoided her since she took over Sío. What has changed?"

Esparza didn't answer. He had been running through the same questions since that morning.

"I will make the appointment on your behalf," De Anví said. "Don't go near the Witch."

"De Guzmán won't like it."

"Well, she doesn't like me anyway. What's one more opportunity to disappoint her?"

XXI

AZUL, NOT FORGOTTEN

Two days had passed since the exhibition. Two days spent playing games with those around her.

With Nereida, games of cards. With Sergado, games of waiting for ossuary entry. With Enjul, games of sneaking into each other's rooms to rile the other.

The emissary had searched Azul's room right after the exhibition, and Azul had used his absence the following day to search for his mask. What would be more fitting than using its bone to raise an army of spies? Instead, all she had found were sketches tucked away on a table. Sketches made with paper and ink meant for letters. Sketches of plants and birds and bone masks meant for a rounder face—something a youth might wear, or a woman—forming pleasing patterns instead of a broken, scary visage.

The art gave her pause. She would never have expected such a zealot to do anything that wasn't related to his god, and she wondered what else he might keep hidden away, secret from the world. A love for plays? A penchant for collecting pretty stones?

A lover?

No, it didn't fit him, Azul decided, and if the unpleasant twisting in her gut lessened at the thought, who would know?

She had followed him the next day, wanting to bother him as much as he was bothering her. He had led her through a web of streets filled with high-end artisan shops and houses, and Azul, well aware of her shadow, had been careful to keep her expression blank while allowing her attention to snag on a few random passersby for a little too long. Let the emissary and her shadow spend their evening figuring out if she had singled them out because they might be the other necromancer's victims, or because she had taken a liking to their shirtsleeves.

It was a dangerous game, but Azul couldn't stop herself from trying to prod him. Virel Enjul exuded arrogance, so sure in his power, so certain she'd eventually acquiesce and help him find this other necromancer. But Azul wouldn't truly help unless she risked meeting Death—it was the only thing that kept her within Isadora's reach.

Isadora. She was failing her sister. Four days had passed since arriving at Cienpuentes, and they felt like a year. No news from the dean. No news from her brother. No way to know whom else to ask without arousing suspicion.

She hadn't seen the masked stranger from the exhibition again, although she had half expected to, since he had been so interested in her brother. Asking about his identity would take her nowhere: young, dark haired, average looks, wearing a mask. She had snorted at the thought. *Welcome to Cienpuentes*, would've been the answer. No, no point in waiting for him, as much as she could use someone completely unrelated to her family, her captor, or Nereida.

And on the fifth day, finally an opportunity to find more allies without Enjul or his shadow being present: an invitation from Sergado to a private gathering with his circle of friends. He was tired of her long face, he had told her.

In the afternoon, they got into her brother's open carriage—more of a cart with plush leather seats—leaving Nereida and Enjul behind. But not Azul's shadow, elegant on his saddle a few paces behind the carriage.

Azul settled on her seat, arranging her skirts. She had chosen these and a short waistcoat instead of her usual breeches because they had appeared, along with some other clothes, in her room by her brother's grace. Today she aimed to please.

"Brother," she asked as the cart advanced through the cobbled streets, "where is your personal guard?" Lina del Valle had one, and even Azul did in the form of the shadow riding right behind them. She looked around once again, and found no one except the young man sitting by the driver.

"I don't have one."

She was surprised. "But you're a marquess now. You must take care."

Sergado smiled. "I haven't gotten around to hiring someone. One of the footmen will suffice for now. Who would dare attack me out in the open?"

Azul eyed the footman's back and wondered about that. The exhibition had proved there were plenty of people in Cienpuentes with more than passable skill at sword fighting, and who could say no to a good amount of coin?

The carriage moved on, and Azul returned her attention to her brother.

"Tell me more about your friends. You said these gatherings can be large."

"Well, I must collect as many friends as I can. It's the only way to survive here and not die of boredom," Sergado said dryly. "As for my closest friends, you will meet them soon enough. No point in spoiling the surprise, is there?"

Azul scrunched her nose, eliciting a laugh out of him. "Brother," she said, "will any of your friends be able to help us gain entry into the ossuary?"

He dismissed her question with a slight shake of his head. "Don't worry about these matters today, Sister. I am working on it. Enjoy the afternoon, make connections. Things will look better soon, I promise you."

And with that, the carriage stopped and he hopped out, then turned to help her down. She accepted his help, missing her breeches something fierce, and wondered if wearing the skirts in her aim to please had made a difference at all—he appeared no more concerned about the ossuary than he did the last time she had asked. Did he consider it a mere whim?

Entering his friend's house, she let her gaze explore the inside avidly: the beautiful patterns of the floor tiles, the abundance of tall vases and potted plants, the framed paintings.

The high ceilings with golden moldings helped alleviate the oppression of the entrance hall, and so did the wide stairs curving into the second floor. There, a hallway free of potted plants led them to a series of three interconnected rooms. No space for a patio in this long house.

A miscellaneous assortment of people filled the rooms, chatting in small groups or sitting on the settees and chairs strewn around. Refreshments and food had been set on tall tables, while more potted plants made their home in corners, their leaves long and impossibly green.

Azul found herself enthralled by the contrast between the muted shades of the walls and the garish colors of the guests' clothing—not at all like the gatherings in Aguncion.

This was a gathering meant to offer a haven of friendship, and Azul's worries softened as her brother introduced her to name after name: artists, scientists, writers, socialites, from her age to over forty. She was surprised to see that even in this more intimate setting, some of her brother's friends wore masks. Cienpuentes certainly loved her masks.

What was it about them Nereida hated so much? She had tried to fish the secret out of her during one of their card games, but Nereida excelled at not speaking when there was nothing she wished to say.

Perhaps, Azul thought, the woman had simply grown to hate them during her life in the court.

"Azul." Her brother tugged her elbow. "Allow me to introduce you to my closest friend."

She was introduced to a young man slightly taller than her and with a friendly face—Isile Manzar. Simply Isile, he told her, for they were all friends there.

"Do you remember the painting that caught your attention in my room?" her brother asked, a twinkle in his eye.

"I do."

"Well, here's the artist." Sergado clapped his friend's shoulder.

Azul's surprise did not escape their attention.

"You are shocked," her brother said with relish.

"I thought it an old master's painting," confessed Azul, "not a young painter's."

"Thank you," Isile said. "But I'm afraid I'm not sure which painting Sergado is speaking of."

Azul waited for Sergado to clarify, but he was already walking away, leaving her with this new stranger. The best friend and the sister—a connection Sergado was obviously eager to make happen.

"The painting of a subject's back," Azul said, "with the flesh stripped down to the bone."

Isile swallowed. "That's ah . . ."

"What was your inspiration?" she asked. "I have never seen a painting like that before." What in that kind of painting drew the interest of someone like this, young and fresh and far from death? Her breath caught and she fought not to step away. Could this be the other necromancer? As a close friend of her brother, he might have access to the type of places where an ambassador's second-in-command would be.

But, no, she corrected herself, allowing her lungs to work again. What would he gain by killing Zenjiel and bringing him back to life? He already had a protector in her brother. Why would he need the other bodies she had seen at the exhibition, the ones proving Zenjiel hadn't been an isolated incident?

"I'm sorry, Sirese Del Arroyo," Isile said. "That piece wasn't meant for public viewing. It must have shocked you, yes?"

"At first, but it's so beautifully done."

He bowed. "Thank you, again. As for my inspiration, well, you can blame that on Norel."

"Who?"

Isile fixed his stare on her, then grinned. "Yes, of course, you're new in town. Come, let me introduce you to one of our more nefarious members," he said with good humor. He led the way across the room into the next. The conversations there were livelier, louder. *Fights of ideas*, Azul thought as she caught errant phrases.

"Norel!" Isile exclaimed, making himself heard above the noise. A strong voice. Isile was surprisingly sturdy.

A man turned from a group and smiled widely. He was older than Isile and Sergado by several years, maturity starting to line his eyes and touch his temples.

"Isile," he returned in an eager voice. "I haven't seen you in a while. And who might this be?"

Isile made the introductions, and Azul found her hand gripped between Norel's big ones.

"Ah, the famous sister! You are all De Gracia has been talking about for the last fortnight. I've been dying out of curiosity to finally meet you."

Azul wasn't sure what to think. "I'm sorry, you must be somewhat disappointed, then."

"Nonsense. Look at you, so pretty, so prim, worthy of every expectation!"

"I . . . uh . . . thank you, sirese."

"You're scaring her," Isile admonished. "Norel here has made it his life's work to study humanity at its most basic level."

Azul frowned at the turn of phrase. "You study morality?"

Norel chuckled. "Not quite, child, although I do believe there is a strong connection between what we do with our bodies and how we evolve inside."

Azul's expression cleared. "Oh, you study the body. Like a doctor?"

"A doctor who isn't interested in healing," he agreed. "I simply study the connections. I leave the healing to others." He looked at Isile. "You are usually not so eager to introduce me to newcomers. What brought this change?"

"She was curious about the inspiration for that painting I did for De Gracia. The one of the man's back."

"Ah, you're blaming me again for turning you into bloody business."

Isile tut-tutted, amused. "You know you are."

Norel's heavy hand landed on Isile's shoulder, squeezing tightly. Azul winced in sympathy.

"You might be right, but I refuse to accept full responsibility," Norel answered jovially. Focusing again on Azul, he said, "It was my idea, indeed, to bring an artist with me to the mortuary."

"The mortuary?" Azul asked, suddenly keen.

"Yes! It's imperative to keep a good record of the different shapes of muscle and bone. What we are underneath our skin"—he drew a circle over his chest with his finger—"is our foundation. Knowing how it forms, how it grows, will teach us how we affect it and how, in turn, it affects us."

This gave Azul pause. "You believe we have a choice on how our bodies work? You think we can redo our foundations?"

"Of course. Bone is hard, but it grows as we do. It re-forms after it breaks, doesn't it? Bones have no thoughts of their own; they must follow our mind. By changing how we think, may we not change how our bodies respond?"

Azul was speechless. He sounded so sure, and what did she know about bones? Only the instinct calling her to bring their owners back to life. By following her instinct, was she . . . tainting these animals? Isadora? Making them as she wished them to be instead of how they ought to be? But there had been no change in Isadora's personality, nothing odd to indicate she wasn't fully herself. Had there?

"Are you a member of the College, then?" she asked, because Norel was all hope as he waited to see how she took his theories, and Isile looked worried she might run screaming, and she wanted to ignore these new doubts suddenly crowding her mind and her heart.

"Gods, no," Norel said. "I despise their methods. Keeping all their findings for themselves. No. This is why I take Isile with me. We need an artist to keep good records, not badly done sketches by people unused to drawing."

"Why the mortuary, though?" Azul asked. "Couldn't you visit the ossuary and record the bones there?"

"Ah," Isile said, "now we're done for."

"The ossuary?" Norel scoffed. "The ossuary is useless."

"But wouldn't such a collection of bones be great for your studies?"

"The truth of humanity resides in what's left behind right at death, Sirese Del Arroyo. What use do I have of old decomposing bones?"

"Decomposing?" she asked, baffled. "Bones don't decompose."

"Ah, but they do!"

Isile leaned toward her and whispered theatrically, "Beware, sirese, the topic is a difficult one."

"Bah," Norel said dismissively. "The topic is not difficult, it's people's minds that refuse to bend."

"Explain, please," Azul said. *With all haste.* She didn't like the new-found dread squeezing her chest.

Norel stepped closer, making a tight triangle out of the three of them and turning them into cohorts, conspirators. "I have concluded, my dear girl, that bones eventually decompose just as flesh does. It is our insistence in using animals and liquids to strip the bodies to the bones that blinds us to the fact that bones, like muscles and skin, fade too. The flesh returns to the soil, and the bones—our essence—return to our gods."

"But how do our bones return to the gods, when the gods are said to be the Anchor chains?"

"Prepare yourself," Isile warned.

"Be silent, Manzar, or go draw something," Norel said, irritated.

"I must stay and make sure you don't corrupt Del Arroyo's mind," he answered amiably.

"Here is the thing, Sirese Del Arroyo." Norel became eager again. "I don't believe Anchor is the gods' bones."

Azul's eyes widened. "You don't?"

"What kind of god would allow the desecration of their body in such a way?" he asked. His eyes followed Azul's fingers as she touched her earring. "Why would they allow themselves to be mined and sold and traded? Allow their essence to be turned into pretty pieces of glamour?"

Azul was at a loss for words. What a most reasonable point he made. She felt unclean by acknowledging it. It was one thing to believe the gods were no longer around, another to doubt their very bones. Wearing Anchor—well, that was a way to honor the gods, wasn't it? A way to have their protection at all times, in case they weren't completely gone. If the gods hadn't wanted their bones broken down and used, they would've made them unbreakable, wouldn't they?

"What about animal bones?" she asked. "Those last very long— forever?"

"Animals are animals, a single step above flora. We are human— our bodies are infused with souls, not simply instinct. We are completely different species."

"Then bones, our bones, how long do you believe them to last? Before they . . . decompose?" With sudden clarity, Azul realized this would explain how they managed to keep so many bones in Cienpuentes's ossuary.

Norel's face lit up. "An excellent question. You are, indeed, De Gracia's sister. I theorize it should only take about five to ten years to see the first signs of decay, depending on the strength of the person's essence and how attuned they are to the gods. Then at least another twenty or twenty-five years for significant loss of mass."

"And how do you measure this attuning? Do you mean to say those who don't believe take longer to decay?" Azul asked with sharp hope.

"Belief is irrelevant in this case."

"How can it be? Wouldn't the person's essence resist being joined to something they didn't believe in?"

"Ah, but see here, belief is simply a turn of the rational mind. A thought. Essence, however, is tied to our impulses, our morality. Neither the gods nor your essence care about what your mind believes. It doesn't matter if you think the gods don't exist—they care only about the burden of your actions. What do gods care if you have utter faith in them but then go on to commit heinous acts? The gods don't need you to believe in them. They exist beyond our rational mind."

"So, a wrongdoer's essence is tainted? It needs more time to be diluted into something the gods can accept as opposed to someone who lived a good, moral life?"

"Just so!" exclaimed Norel.

Azul did not share his delight. Isadora hadn't had faith in the gods, but her actions, her morality, had always been well intentioned. According to Norel's theories, this virtue would make her bones disappear faster.

"You are looking pale, Azul," interrupted Isile. "Would you like to sit?"

"No, thank you. But maybe something to drink?"

"Of course," said Norel, now worried. "Let me fetch you a glass."

Azul gave him an encouraging smile and used the time it took him to bring her a drink to compose her thoughts. Time, the eternal enemy. There she'd been, chatting and socializing, assuming it was simply a question of days to get to her sister's bones.

But what if she had been running late all this while? If Norel were correct and bones started disappearing in five years, would there be anything left of Isadora by now?

Norel handed her a glass of golden liquor. She sipped it cautiously, her fingers shaking, cold sweat gathering on her nape.

She'd renew her search for the emissary's mask as soon as she returned to her brother's home. She could disguise herself as an emissary and gain entrance to the ossuary. Her Valanjian wasn't so bad as it used to be, and who was to say one had to have a full iris ring to become a servant of the Lord Death? Those in charge here, all the way in Cienpuentes, wouldn't know any better.

"Your coloring is better, I'm glad to see," said Norel. "Have I offended you? Forgive me," he added ruefully. "My friends keep reminding me that my theories are too shocking and a tad hard to swallow. But I assure you, I have spent years studying human flesh and bones."

Azul smiled, a sad, wan excuse of an upward curve that made the two men worry. "I'm not shocked. Surprised, to be sure, but I appreciate your taking the time to explain your theories to me."

"Of course, of course," Norel said.

"But for now," Isile suggested, "let us have some food and drink and talk of less philosophical things, yes? Norel, go find us some seats."

Norel turned at once and cut through the groups of people.

"I apologize," Isile said. "Norel can be too much when he gets enamored of his theories."

"There is no need to——" Azul became aware of a servant politely waiting by their side. "Yes?"

The servant gave them a small bow of his head. "Sirese Del Arroyo?"

"Indeed."

"There is a woman asking to speak with you. She is not a guest, so we put her in one of the other parlors."

Could it be Nereida? Azul's heart began its loud drumming again. There was only one reason Nereida would risk being recognized: access to the ossuary.

With a mere whisper of a goodbye, she returned the glass and followed the servant outside the lively rooms, down the hallway into a smaller parlor. The door closed, and at first, she thought the room empty.

Then someone stepped behind her and placed a cloth against her mouth and nose.

And she thought no more.

XXII

AZUL

Azul regained consciousness as she was being carried over someone's shoulder. She could barely breathe, the constant jostling making her head swirl and her stomach roll. Escaped tendrils from her braid did their best to obscure her vision, but she still spotted the high boots of her captor, caked with mud—dry, unfortunately, and leaving no trace on the mosaic of beige floor tiles.

Pushing against her captor's back, she managed to lift her head and saw a second kidnapper. Lo and behold! The woman wore a mask hiding the upper half of her face.

"She's awake," the woman said.

"I know," the one carrying her answered between huffs.

The position she had taken was too straining and not all that useful, so Azul allowed her head to droop again and closed her eyes against the nausea. Her hands fisted onto the man's waistcoat. She sensed a breeze and heard street noises below—they must be going through one of the high bridges connecting buildings—then it was back into a closed hallway.

Time to bring in reinforcements, she decided. Hadn't she already planned for this very contingency? Concentrating on one of her two remaining tethers, she followed the tugging sensation all the way to the small mouse. It could sneak into any building and gnaw her free of any ropes they might use to bind her, as well as provide a good distraction for her to break away.

But the mouse was looking at the woman Enjul had contacted, so Azul hesitated to call it back. Had the small rodent kept track of the woman, instinctively following Azul's wishes to know more about Enjul's business with her? She was dipping bread in a bowl of soup at a bare-bones kitchen, the scents waking a hunger in the animal. Azul got the feeling that the place was familiar to the mouse already, so it must be the woman's residence.

A sudden halt had Azul bounce hard against her captor and snap her attention back to her body. She peered around. They had stopped in an unfamiliar corridor. She heard a door open.

She was lowered to the floor and helped toward a chair. Azul dropped onto it, hands covering her stomach and her mouth as she waited for the room to stop spinning.

"What's this business?" she managed.

The other captor, the one who hadn't been carrying her and thus wasn't panting and wiping sweat off her own face, flicked Azul's earring.

Azul reeled back, too shocked to swat the woman's hand away.

"We must ask you to stay put," she said politely but with plenty of amusement, for, really, where would she go? "while our employer requests an audience with the Marquess de Gracia."

"Couldn't they simply ask?" Azul retorted.

"Oh, they've tried, believe me. My employer is regretful that such measures must be taken to secure your brother's cooperation, but there was no other way."

Azul narrowed her eyes. "And if my brother refuses?" They hadn't taken her dagger, though they could've. They hadn't harmed her, other than by the nature of jostling her over a shoulder.

"Then I guess you'll grow to enjoy these quarters."

With that sentiment, they exited the room. The *snick* of the lock was loud in the following silence, and she had no doubt at least one of them would remain behind to guard the door.

Sancia, a land where who you were, what you could achieve, was nothing compared to what you could do for others. Azul massaged her forehead. She had no qualms in using others, but it was wearing thin that what Azul could do for others far outweighed what anyone was doing for *her*.

Once her head cleared and her stomach settled, she leaned back against the chair and closed her eyes again.

The woman had finished her repast and was now out of her house. The mouse followed, hungry and fearful of possible predators but stubborn in its pursuit, and Azul felt a pang of guilt. She hadn't meant to impress her will quite so forcefully on the small animal. She had assumed it'd be fully its own after she had withdrawn from its mind. Something to be watchful for, and something she was grateful hadn't happened with Isadora.

Isadora's will was indomitable, her zest for life and adventure unparalleled. No one could control her mind.

Azul followed the mystery woman for as long as she dared, noting the streets she passed, distorted through the mouse's sight, trying to memorize any recognizable spot.

Then, returning to her present predicament, she abandoned the chair and approached the window. She was on a second floor, facing a shadowed alleyway. Climbing down would be a tricky endeavor.

But no need for such extremes.

Taking out Nereida's dagger, she went to the door and banged on it. "Open up!"

"Be silent, you screech," was the response.

She kept up the banging, then stepped to the side. "Open up unless you want the whole town to hear!"

She heard the bolt sliding back. The door opened inward to reveal the man who had carried her, his expression irate. "Shut up, or I'll make you."

Azul slid into the opening and slammed into the man with her shoulder. He grunted in surprise and stumbled back. She used the opportunity to twist and bring the pommel of the dagger right into his groin. And when he doubled over in pain, she brought it down on the back of his head.

The man dropped to the floor. She considered dragging him into the room not to arouse suspicion, but then, if this hallway had any visitors, they wouldn't have chosen it for keeping her prisoner.

Hiding Nereida's dagger, she stepped over the man and hurried down the corridor until she found a set of stairs that led into the streets.

It had begun to dawn on Azul that it wasn't such a good idea that only her brother, Nereida, Enjul, and a mouse had any sort of vested interest in her existence.

Truthfully, Azul wasn't sure how much her brother would give up for her safety, for all that he appeared happy to have her around. He wasn't trying very hard to grant her wish to visit the ossuary. And although she was fairly certain Nereida would give finding her a try if Azul were to disappear, how long would that last?

And the emissary? Enjul would likely thank his god for saving him the effort of having to do away with her.

That knowledge somehow smarted the most.

No, better to have one more person, someone unrelated to her small group, who might find it curious if Azul were never to be heard from again.

Once she had put some distance between herself and the house, Azul picked one of the girls peddling wares and asked her to deliver a message.

"You'll know he's the correct one because he won't answer you, no matter how much you ask, but he might look alarmed once you tell him who the message is from," she told the girl. "And tell him to bring his boss along."

✦ ✦ ✦

The headquarters of the blue tabards was an elegant building forming an L around a small plaza. Situated on the west side of town, not too far from the Temple, it was two stories tall and reminded her of the ambassador's sprawling estate, only smaller and more concentrated. A handful of trees, such a rare sight in this crowded place, shadowed some tables on one side of the plaza. Blue tabards were making good use of them, while others lounged in what few other shadows they could find. Azul supposed most guards were inside with the cooler air, or performing their duties around the city.

Dusting the front of her skirts, she walked up to one of the tabards guarding the wide main entrance.

"What do you want?" he asked, not very politely.

Making sure her head was tilted just so, Isadora's earring on full display, she answered with, "I am the Marquess de Gracia's sister, Azul del Arroyo, and I seek an audience with Captain de Macia."

The piece of Anchor did the trick, and she was ushered into the great entrance, where a few wooden benches had been provided for waiting visitors. She sat, tucked away against a wall, and studied the magnificent staircase leading up to the second floor, its faded rug silencing the noise of blue tabards' boots as they hurried up and down the steps. A few other civilians milled around with worried visages, their mouths set in tight lines. Soon, she focused on the hardwood of the floor under her ankle boots. Such a strange thing for it not to be tile or marble or some other polished stone. It was beautiful, even if scratched and scuffed with use, but so odd. And Azul, so cowardly.

She didn't want to know if the necromancer's victim wearing a blue tabard she had spied during the exhibition was around. She didn't want to know if she was in the building or what she looked like up close. She didn't want to unintentionally run into her, chance a bump of their skins, and then . . .

Then another corpse due to her.

The thought gave Azul pause. Zenjiel and the two people at the exhibition . . . If there were three victims, there were likely more. How powerful was the other necromancer, to raise all these people? Did this person have any soul left?

And more important, if the necromancer were to see Isadora once returned and recognize her for what she was, would they end her life in retribution for Azul ending Zenjiel's?

Azul swore to herself she would not allow this. She would hide Isadora from Enjul and from the other necromancer, have her smuggled out in the middle of the night so nobody would see.

But Enjul's search might be for nothing. The other necromancer might already be dead, soul spent, and those they had brought back gone on without them. What a relief to imagine that Isadora could remain were Azul to meet her end.

A blue tabard came for Azul and guided her up the staircase to a room with a sturdy desk and Captain de Macia standing behind it. Instead of a tabard, she wore a blue waistcoat with silver embroidery and silver buttons down the front, and the same type of breeches and boots as the guards. Draped over another chair was her half cape, dark blue with more silver accents.

De Macia nodded at the guard, who retreated into the hallway. After a warm greeting, she indicated another free chair, which Azul made use of.

"So," De Macia said, occupying her own seat behind the desk, "how is your mother?"

"Very well, thank you," Azul replied. "How is my little sister?"

De Macia gave her a rueful smile. "Keeping my household busy. How long have you been in Cienpuentes?"

"A few days now."

"And you must stay a few more and come to supper with us. Now, tell me, how can I help?"

Captain de Macia hadn't advanced in the ranks for lack of a sharp mind.

"I was subject to an attempted kidnapping earlier today," Azul said matter-of-factly, "so for the sake of my well-being, I thought I should let someone I trust know I am currently staying with one of my half brothers, the Marquess de Gracia."

"Were you harmed?" De Macia asked, all business now.

"No, they were very polite." At the captain's answering snort, Azul added, "Yes, my thoughts too. They intended to use me as a lure to arrange a meeting with my brother."

"'Attempted kidnapping,' you said."

"I escaped."

"Is the Marquess de Gracia aware of all of this?" Then, in a loud voice, "You came alone, yes?"

Azul glanced over her shoulder to catch the blue tabard peek in and nod.

"Should we send word to His Grace that you're here?" De Macia asked.

"No need. I already sent a message with my destination." To the detriment of Azul's purse. Nereida had assured her they had more coin, while Sergado alluded to a stipend—but where was all this money supposed to be? Nowhere within her reach.

After a curt, dismissive nod of the captain's head, the blue tabard returned to his previous position somewhere down the corridor, and she focused again on Azul. "Give me the details."

Azul was glad to comply: "There were two masked captors and the servant who lured me from the gathering. Although it's possible that the servant was simply asked to deliver a message and wasn't aware of the implications."

"What gathering?"

"My brother's friends were having one. He must've sent word that he meant to introduce me, because nobody was surprised by my attendance." Azul studied De Macia's expression—serious but not shocked. "Are kidnappings in Cienpuentes common?"

"While all kinds of crimes happen in the city, yours is not the first kidnapping for the sake of simple talks in the last couple of weeks." Seeing Azul's disbelief, she elaborated, "Three men cornered the Count de Anví not long ago, seeking a similar result."

Azul remembered the count, standing stiff and looking miserable at the exhibition. "He came to you for help?"

"Hah. No, of course not. He's a Golden Dog and we're the Blue Bastards. He would rather choke on his guts, I'd imagine, before coming to De Mavén for any sort of help."

"Then how do you know——? Oh, he thought you, the City Guard, had a hand in it?"

"Not quite," De Macia said, "but close enough. It's hard to keep such things a secret. Knowledge tends to get around."

"Should I be worried they'll attempt to kidnap me again?" Azul didn't want to be confined at Almanueva or gain more guards.

De Macia studied her closely. "You should be, I think." After waiting for the words to sink in, she added, "Coming so close after your father's murder . . . De Gracia is a dangerous name to be associated with nowadays. I know you aren't used to these kinds of——"

"Murder?" Azul exclaimed. "I thought he died from an issue with his heart."

It was now time for Captain de Macia to be surprised, then hesitant.

"Tell me," Azul demanded.

"He was stabbed in the . . ."

An eloquent pause ensued, and Azul finished for her, dryness in her voice: "In the heart. Why did my brother lie?"

"He might not have wanted to frighten you. And to be frank, I shouldn't have told you, if you weren't already told. It wasn't my news to share. But given the current situation, it's better for you to be aware of the danger you face."

Troubled, Azul mulled the captain's words. "Thank you. And his bones? In the ossuary?"

"I imagine De Gracia took care of it all."

"I've been trying to visit the ossuary to pray to my sister's—another sister's—bones. A family tradition. Perhaps I could see both her and my father? But nobody will grant me entrance."

"I am sorry to hear that."

Azul didn't doubt Captain de Macia's sincerity and shook her head when she was offered some water. "I'm fine, thank you." Then, allowing some frustration to seep through, "I wish I could see my sister's bones and be assured that she rests with the gods."

"Have you talked with the dean?"

"Yes. Well, no. She wasn't there when I went to the Temple, and I don't think she'll grant me a meeting, judging by those who took my request in her stead."

"And your brother? What did your brother have to say?"

"He said it might take some time to grant me entrance."

De Macia grimaced. "The bigger the city, the slower time crawls. It's bad timing. With the royal mourning lifted, things are going back to normal and everyone is busy. Celebrations, balls, politics . . . The court will be back in season proper, and there are a lot of dealings that need to be finished before that happens."

Which explained, Azul thought, *why it wasn't so outlandish that people in Cienpuentes kept getting kidnapped.* "I was told Noche Verde this year will be popular."

"Yes, there will be street celebrations and plenty of balls." De Macia sounded pained at the thought, possibly because the blue tabards would be the ones to answer for it if the events got out of control. "De Gracia should've received invitations, of course, but I'll make sure you are included."

"Could you make them for two, or is it too late?"

"That shouldn't be a problem." She glanced behind Azul, and her frown deepened. "What is it?"

Azul turned in her seat to find a new guard at the door.

"Someone has come for the sirese, Captain."

De Macia looked at Azul, brows arching. "Shall we go see if you know them or if my guards must take care of some trash?"

With a grin, Azul agreed. They went down to the entrance, recruiting another couple of men on the way, the sum of their heels thudding loudly on the wooden floors. Her shadow stood outside, hat in his hands, at ease even with the two tabards flanking him. Azul had expected this, but she hadn't anticipated the anger the sight brought out in her.

"I know him," she told Captain de Macia. Curt words the woman didn't deserve but didn't seem to mind.

She squeezed Azul's arm. "I will make sure the invitations are delivered to *your* hands." And she'd make sure Azul was there to receive them.

"Thank you," Azul said, knowing she should be relieved, but unable to shake the fury razing her veins.

Her shadow. Alone.

The emissary couldn't be bothered to check on her himself, so certain Azul was incapable of anything more than being an annoyance.

Sharply, she crossed the entrance and exited into the plaza. Stopping right beyond reach of the guards outside, she glared at her shadow. "I see you come alone. Is he so sure I'll do as he commands every time I slip your reach?"

The shadow nodded in one direction. Azul followed it to find Virel Enjul standing on the opposite side of the plaza, his expression unreadable, but his posture bored enough as he turned and walked away.

He had come, after all. Perhaps he wasn't so sure of what Azul could do. Perhaps he was frustrated that he had made no inroads into figuring out who the other necromancer was, and it was dawning on him that Azul was not so fearful of his status as Emissary of the Lord Death. Or perhaps it was the fact that he could no longer steal her from Cienpuentes on a whim.

She could use this.

Bringing two fingers to her mouth, Azul let a loud whistle go, commanding the attention of everyone in the vicinity. But it was only Enjul's attention she kept for more than those few moments of stillness when she lifted her hand and showed him the small bone in her palm.

XXIII

SEEKING DANGER

FORTY-FIVE MINUTES EARLIER

Nereida de Guzmán had left the house, gone to a tavern, spoken to the woman behind the counter, then returned to De Gracia's to spend her time doing nothing but stare into the patio. Virel Enjul had followed her himself, content with leaving Azul in her brother's hands, accompanied by her shadow.

Content was perhaps not the most fitting term. If Emissary Enjul could separate his soul from his flesh, he'd be happy to follow Del Arroyo wherever she went. Azul—the malady, he corrected himself—hadn't put a step out of place, didn't do as he had expected after she lied to him at the exhibition. The lie had been obvious. He had expected her to search for the other malady's victim and warn them to stay away.

But she hadn't.

Enjul enjoyed puzzles, so every night he went to his room, thinking about what Azul del Arroyo might be planning in that obstinate head of hers and following each possible path to its inevitable ending: this other malady dead, Azul del Arroyo locked away for study at his Valanjian headquarters of choice. And every morning he woke exhilarated, wondering if that would be the day Azul guided him to the proof of the other malady's identity.

He had the vague thought that the woman might be of further use once he was done studying her. What better way to reconcile her affronts to the Lord Death than by helping him search for other possible maladies and eliminating them?

The idea was too enticing, so he had shoved it to the back of his mind and concentrated on Nereida de Guzmán instead. Whatever plan was being spun, she was good at keeping it secret. De Guzmán was not as easy to read as Del Arroyo.

So, why did he find himself waiting a couple of blocks away from the gathering De Gracia and Azul had chosen to attend instead of following De Guzmán?

Ultimately, it didn't matter whom he followed, he told himself. If there was a plan, it would require Azul's presence, and Enjul doubted Azul would set anything in motion before getting to her sister's bones.

He would need another threat to keep her from using her foulness once she agreed to help find other maladies. He was quite looking forward to eroding her erroneous beliefs, to see what kind of convoluted philosophical games she spun to plead her case.

Not many dared contradict his words. Even now, without his bone armor and dressed like any other Sancian, there was a void surrounding him as he leaned against a building. No peddlers approached him; children gave him a wide berth. A boy selling flowers had moved a street away a few minutes after Enjul had chosen this spot, as if worried his floral wares would blacken with decay should he stay nearby.

He considered this aura a gift, one he enjoyed using on those who thought themselves better than their gods. Enjul's disgust rose again at the way Cienpuentes's citizens did nothing but pray for riches. What a deplorable city. Gray and drab, its Anchor almost gone. If the Blessed Heart had a voice, it was drowned in all this greed.

A man gained his attention, inconspicuous, easily ignored—if you weren't the one who had hired him. Enjul left his spot and went to meet him, wariness and fury rising. Why was he here and not guarding Azul? A young girl walked by the man's side, grinning cheekily until she noticed Enjul stalking their way.

Azul's shadow was fast to take ahold of the girl's arm before she could turn tail and flee.

"Why are you here?" he asked of the man.

The man nudged the girl's arm.

"I have a message," the girl muttered, avoiding looking at Enjul. "A woman—Del Rollo or something—said to tell you she's gone to visit a friend at the Blue Bastards, since she got kid-kidnapped and neither of you noticed."

The man fished for a thin coin in his pocket and gave it to the girl before setting her free.

"Kidnapped?" Enjul demanded.

The man simply shrugged.

"I ought to kill you," Enjul said, walking toward the City Guard's headquarters. Ambassador Enzare had shared her maps of Cienpuentes with him, and he had been careful to insist Azul saw none of them, no matter how many times she asked.

Her shadow followed easily, unfazed by the threat but perhaps not quite so relaxed as usual.

The thought that Azul had been taken from their hands was appalling. Although it had certainly been due to her status as De Gracia's sister, if someone else were to discover what she could do . . . the damage could be enormous. Del Arroyo was obstinate and would refuse to use her foulness without her sister's bones, but everyone had a breaking point. And the woman cared too much. She would break.

If anyone were to break her, it would be him, not some stranger out for personal gain.

This game they had chosen to play must come to an end. Enjul would give her one more chance to lead him to the malady, and then he would drag her to Valanje, where no one else would have access to her.

THE PRESENT

Right before Enjul got to her, Azul threw the bone to the floor. It didn't stop him—of course it didn't—and with a firm hold on her wrist, he dragged her into one of the smaller alleys flowing into the plaza. She kept a smile on her face, both for the benefit of the guards watching them and because she had no fear. The moment they were alone—him, her, and the shadow—Enjul pushed her against a wall and took a tight hold of her throat with one hand.

"You dare goad me?" he snarled, his face so close, the violet-and-golden eyes blurred against her attempt to focus.

She grabbed his wrist when the pressure grew, digging her nails into the cuff of his sleeve, the skin of his wrist.

Enjul, his point made, loosened his grip. "Do you wish to die by my hand, is that it? Only way you'll ever get to see your sister again, I suppose."

A handful of times in the middle of the night through the years, she had wondered: if bones called to her, demanded her attention, might she be able to call them back? She had never tested it, though—there had been no need. Until now.

The Eye of Death opened on her palm, right against his skin.

Enjul yelped and threw her to the side, shaking his hand, then bringing it to the hilt of his sword.

Azul stumbled, then faced him and eyed his pose warily, her own hand inching toward Nereida's dagger. Well, she had tested it now, and found she could do no more than provoke a sting of pain. The effort had drained her, even with a simple strip of flesh separating her from his wristbone. Living bones had a will of their own, and his had most emphatically refused her.

The emissary did not need to know that.

"I am no child," she told him grimly, "for you to leave behind to be at your beck and call. You can kill me, this is true, or tie me to a chair until you finish your business here. But as you have probably guessed, I lied. You know I saw more of the necromancer's victims at the exhibition."

"Necromancer. What a whimsical name."

"It must be frustrating, to see that a nobody, a countryface from Agunción, has acquired this gift from the gods without trying, without hours of praying, without whatever it is you've sacrificed to get where you are."

A snarl curled his lips. "You understand nothing of sacrifice, of what it means to have a god touch you with his grace."

"Bah! You may have survived death through your god's grace, but surviving pales compared to creating, doesn't it?"

"If your hope is to *survive* this trip, you are not endearing yourself to the cause. Why should I keep you around when you mock me and my god? When you are of no use to me?"

"Why should I help when you see me as nothing but a tool tucked away as a last resort while you attempt to find the malady on your own? I suppose it's vexing to fail so spectacularly."

"As you've failed to find your sister's bones? Don't protest my treatment of you when it's afforded you so many opportunities to attempt your goal."

Even the most stonehearted individual would have trouble not flinching at that. Virel Enjul knew where to strike best. "It seems we both seek something we can't achieve without the other's help."

He relaxed his stance. "What do you propose?"

If he meant to encourage her to relax, too, she refused to follow suit. "Let us talk in an open area, where anger won't get the best of us."

"You will not attempt that again," he said curtly, motioning toward her hand, "on me or my subordinates."

"I won't if you or your shadows—by the way, thank you for your help—" she sniped to the man by the alley's entrance, who took off his hat and bowed with a smile, "or your Order will never harm me or my siblings."

He hesitated, but only briefly. "Agreeable."

"That's not a promise."

"It isn't."

She nodded in understanding. "I asked for too much. Neither you nor your shadows nor your Order will harm me as long as I don't use my gift. And my siblings, not ever."

"That I can promise, and your siblings I have no reason to seek."

They both knew the first part of the promise was moot—she'd have to use her gift again to raise Isadora—but Azul recognized the truth in the rest of his words. Surprising that he had agreed not to harm her family, as Enjul knew she meant to bring Isadora back and he had shown no compunction in killing Zenjiel, but he must be confident he could stop her before she got the chance.

Azul was happy to let him believe that. "We'll talk, then."

They retreated back into the plaza and found some seats at the shaded tables. Blue tabards were still lolling around, talking, drinking, and playing some kind of marbles game. Someone offered them cold drinks, and Azul realized the tables belonged to a nearby tavern.

Azul and Enjul faced each other, drinks and cold meats and cheese on a platter between them. Nobody paid them attention; her shadow lounged close by.

"Tell me what you truly saw at the exhibition," Enjul asked.

Azul arched her brows. "I see now. Your plan was to wait for me to identify these people for you. You imagined yourself sweeping in after me, interrogating them, then ending their lives to correct the malady's wrongs. A coup for you and your god."

Enjul pierced her with a hard stare. "He's your god too. You owe him for simply stopping your foulness and not your heart."

Azul wondered if that was true. If she were such an offense, if the Lord Death were so powerful, wouldn't he have taken her down with Isadora?

"Show your respect and help as you promised," he continued. "Or is your word worth nothing?"

"If you won't immediately kill the necromancer's victims," Azul said.

Enjul smiled coldly and sipped his drink. "You forget your place,

Azul del Arroyo. You've had your freedom but become a liability, and I will have you sent back to Valanje whole or in pieces. Keep changing the terms of our deal, and you will make me wonder why we have a deal at all."

"Very well," Azul said. "Go around killing random people. Show yourself as the Emissary of the Lord Death and force my fellow malady into hiding. You think you will catch them unaware if all you do is produce a massacre and cause the Guard to investigate the bloodshed? You may have rights as an emissary, but the Lord Death is not the only god of these lands. Those speaking for the Lord Life and the Blessed Heart might have a problem with your bloodthirst."

Enjul blinked. "How many walking corpses have you seen?"

"Three, so far." Azul saw no harm in telling him this much, since he couldn't find them on his own. "One belongs to the blue tabards, the others I don't know. But who knows how many more there might be?"

"The malady *is* getting ears in every building," he muttered, followed by another sip.

Azul wasn't fooled by the apparent ease of his posture. He was trying to hide his thoughts from her, even if the mask already did a good job. "I think so too." After a slight hesitation, she added, "I have a proposal."

"Another deal?" he asked wryly.

"Indeed, I grow them in my garden. But think of it as a refinement rather than a new weed. You might be able to recognize this other necromancer like you recognized me, but your choice to shed your emissary status makes it impossible to access the upper echelons of Cienpuentes."

"It has its drawbacks," he conceded.

"You can hire people to look for you, like you hired my shadow to follow me around, but without my help, you're stuck at hoping someone will cross your path. The necromancer wasn't at the exhibition, since you still haven't found them, but not all the court was there, and they must belong to it. Otherwise, why the need for these spies so conveniently located? How else would they have access to an ambassador's second-in-command long enough to see them dead and brought back to life? I'd bet a fair coin a lot of the nobles probably watched the exhibition from the cooling shadows of the rooms surrounding the plaza, not out in the open with the sweat and the heat."

"An easy assumption."

Her smile was as glacial as his. "Noche Verde is coming up. The court is out of mourning and will put on splendid balls. All the court will be in attendance—easy pickings for you."

"The thought has occurred to me."

"I have secured invitations on my own. You could accompany me and my brother, and nobody would think it weird he brought his guests along. He's a marquess; he will be allowed at all the balls." She had meant the second invitation for Nereida, guessing if they were to make a desperate move, that would be the time, but this could work as well. Easier to slip his reach in the coming days if he had something to look forward to.

"You assume I cannot gain entrance on my own."

Azul took a bite of one of the chunks of cheese. "You would have to announce yourself as the emissary. News that one of you is in town would spread like free-flowing wine, and the necromancer will hide until you're gone. But as of now," she pointed out, "because you haven't gone on a rampage, the victims remain where they are. The necromancer is unaware of your presence."

"I could simply procure the invitations under my name, and only those involved would know of my status."

"Your people have already been compromised—the necromancer killed your ambassador's second-in-command, and you don't know who else might be under their control or we would be staying at Valanje's official house in Cienpuentes instead of my brother's."

"And in return for this invitation, what is it that you expect of me?"

Such easy acquiescence. He was playing with her. What did the emissary know that she didn't?

"I wish for your goodwill," she said. "For us to truly work together instead of this thing we do now where you call for me and I rebel, and then you drop me into the toy box until the next time you are in need. You know what I seek, and you are so sure you will stop me from achieving it. You probably wish to send me away in a cage but you can't risk it—you might need my ability to seek the necromancer's victims. And so, we remain at a standstill. I won't go back on my word, and you promised you won't hurt my siblings. Working together will stop me from raising my sister. Isn't that what you want? Unless, of course, you are worried two necromancers might be too much for a single emissary."

A contemplative silence followed.

"How many people have you raised?" Enjul finally asked.

"Why did you become an emissary?" she countered.

They stared at each other.

He smiled faintly. "It wasn't a choice. I was born a servant of the Lord Death."

"Isadora and Sirese Zenjiel are the only people I've brought back. If you were born what you are, how does it make you different from me?"

"And before them, animals?" He paused, then narrowed his eyes as he considered her question. "Don't pretend to liken your sort to me. I do not assume to know better than the god; he is my guide in life, for my life is his."

"A few animals, yes. Isn't it disappointing being unable to do as one wishes, always following someone else's orders?"

"Does stealing someone from the Lord Death come with ease?" He looked at the plate of food, wrinkled his nose at the cheese, and chose a rolled slice of ham. "I know no other way of life, so I am unable to compare. I am not a mere puppet, Miss Del Arroyo, I have thoughts and a will of my own, and I am glad to have the Lord Death inside me to be a guide, a comfort in life. Looking at those around me, I find myself glad to have a goal, to have strong enough character to see it through."

Azul decided to be truthful to his first question. "Animals come with ease. A person, no. You and I are more similar than you want to admit. I have my own goals, as you know. Would you say I don't fight to see them through?"

"A person doesn't come with ease, you say, and yet this other necromancer has raised three people that we know of, and who knows how many else."

"Their gift might be different from mine. It might come more naturally to them. I see you refuse to acknowledge my question."

"More powerful than you, with lesser conscience."

Azul was surprised at the defense of her morals, even if annoyed at the mention of the disparity between her and the other necromancer's power. "I'm not interested in power." She studied Enjul. "This other necromancer scares you more than I do, don't they?" His mouth tightened, and she waved her hand impatiently. "Yes, yes, the Emissary of the Lord Death is scared of no one. But all this use of otherworldly gifts . . . If there are two of us, there could be more. The possibility unsettles you."

His fists clenched on the table. "Of course it does."

"Has it occurred to you that these gifts are the gods' will?"

Enjul stared at her as if her brain had escaped her head.

She lowered her gaze and then her voice. "If we—people—are a product of the gods, wouldn't our gifts be too?"

"If that were so," Enjul answered, "your sister would still be on her feet. Your gift might appear god-given at first glance, but the god clearly refused it."

"But the Lord Death is not the only god."

"He is the only one who deals with death."

Azul flinched. His words had been cold, and held all the truth.

"Is being chosen by the god the only way to join the Order?" she asked in a subdued tone. "Does . . . does he talk to you, in your head? Tell you what to do? Or is he a shadow hovering over your shoulder, watching your every move?" She pointed at the man waiting nearby. "Like mine."

Enjul let out a small snort. "The Lord Death guides my instincts. He has better things to do than to whisper in my ears all day long like some lazy fool. As for joining the Order, there are many ways and reasons to do so. Some join because they feel it's a calling, some join because it's a job, many attempt to join in the hopes their misdeeds will be forgiven."

"I'll say," she murmured, picking another chunk of cheese. She had seen them, too, people in their old age who saw the end coming and wished to atone before meeting their gods. "And those like you?"

"We, the emissaries, were born with the blessing of the god inside us."

Azul wanted to ask again how that differed from her, but was unwilling to break this unexpected sense of camaraderie growing between them. The sudden ease of sitting opposite each other without the urge to cross swords. He was an imposing man, his total focus on her intense. And yet . . .

This strange kinship, this ease . . . It was dangerous. She had no doubt he didn't share the feeling.

"How did the Order find you?" she asked. "Do they test every newborn baby for the god's blessing?"

Enjul's gaze took on a faraway, almost fond, quality. "No, I looked for them when I realized what dwelled within me."

"So, the god chose you, and you had no choice," she said.

"None of us has any choice," Enjul answered.

"You imply people are set in stone, when it's obvious people can change."

"You can chip away certain parts, if you insist on that analogy, and you can certainly break them, but they'll always be the same type of stone, won't they?"

"I should've used another example."

An actual laugh. "It doesn't matter what you use, all things created remain what they are. You can bend them, mold them, attempt to turn them into something else, but that won't transmute them. A sword will always be the metal it was forged from." He lifted his cup. "Wine will always be the grape it was squeezed from."

"Unlike those things," Azul pointed out, "we have souls. We have the ability to think, grow, change."

"A seed will only grow into a certain tree. It won't change, no matter how much we care for it. It will be sickly if it doesn't get enough water, or lush and fruitful if it grows by a stream—but it will still be the same tree."

Azul read the amusement in his eyes but did not mind it. He had his belief, and she had hers. He lifted his cup, not to hide his features this time but to drink. Azul had grown accustomed to meeting his direct stares, even though he seemed to see right into her soul.

"Had I never raised anyone from death," she said, "would you still think me a foul malady?"

His gaze became pensive. It feathered over her face, her arms, the hands busy with the edge of the plate. "Yes," he said reluctantly. "But perhaps I would have thought better of you."

And Azul couldn't understand why his words hurt.

XXIV

SERGADO DE GRACIA

De Gracia had a reputation for being congenial, for his witty remarks, for his interest in anything from music to nature to philosophy. Any other time, he might've lamented not earning a more dangerous edge to his fame, but for now, all he lamented was the lack of a mace to shatter every bone in the man in front of him.

The man wore a mask, because of course. De Gracia hated those things. There was something suffocating in using them, and something extremely vexing in being unable to read the expressions of those wearing them.

They stood, he and the mask-wearing fool, alone in one of De Zoilo's small parlors. The same one, he had been assured, where Azul should be waiting.

Instead, this.

"I'll need proof that you have her," De Gracia said nonchalantly, "before I go anywhere with you."

"Of course," agreed the man. "Would you like a finger or an ear?"

"Her earring will suffice," replied De Gracia smoothly. By the end of the week, he would make sure the man had no fingers and no ears.

The man sneered, as if De Gracia had proved to be the gutless fool he believed him to be. "Wait here for my return."

"And before you go," De Gracia added, "know that your employer has made an enemy today."

A shrug, because it didn't concern him, and then the man left the room.

De Gracia sat on the single settee, every movement cautious, every muscle tight.

The masked man took his time in returning, and when he did, he carried a simple golden hoop in his hand.

De Gracia wanted to laugh. How much of an idiot did they think him? Judging by the fast flicker of the man's eyes toward the rapier hanging by De Gracia's hip, not *that* much. The sneer had deserted the man, his back grown stiff.

Gone. Azul was gone from wherever they had stashed her. She was his sister, after all, a woman who didn't recoil from sneaking around at night or looking at paintings of stripped flesh and bones.

"Right." De Gracia took the hoop and ran it up and down his finger like a ring. "Take me to your employer."

A masked woman flanked them after they left the building. They took no horses, no carriage. They didn't go far.

The Countess de Losa awaited in one of Cienpé's innumerable parlors, this one resembling a prison cell rather than the airy rooms De Gracia was accustomed to. It didn't bother him, since he spent many of his days underground at the ossuary anyway.

The woman stood by the grated window in a gray stone wall bereft of paintings or tapestries. The old, heavy furniture in the room added to the effect—that of De Losa seeking to treat him like a fortress owner might have treated their peasants a few hundred years before.

She waited for the heavy door to close.

Then sputtered when De Gracia ran her through with his rapier.

The problem with rooms made to look like cells, he mused, wiping the blade with a cloth before returning it to its sheath, was that there was nobody to hear you die.

He knelt by the woman. De Losa lay in a pool of skirts, a trickle of blood running from her gaping mouth and another from the puncture below her breast.

De Gracia scowled. That might be a problem. The wound was too low, the dress too light a color. He cleaned the blood with the same wipe, then placed a hand against her collarbone.

Power thrummed from his chest, down his arm, into the bones under his palm. Like lightning arching from cloud to cloud, it spread from bone to bone.

And the Countess de Losa opened her eyes.

XXV

THE OTHER NECROMANCER

De Gracia sat back on his ankles and watched the woman stand slowly with the help of a nearby chair.

The situation wasn't optimal, and he would have to keep her away from the emissary as he had done with the others, but he couldn't risk Azul being used as a pawn again—next time, he might receive a bloody ear instead of an inept attempt at covering her escape.

He watched De Losa stumble around, her eyes filled with a familiar vacancy. It greatly entertained him, how nobody had noticed the lack of real thought in his studies yet.

How annoying, to have to keep up with yet another one of these. Back in his early teenage years, it had seemed like a grand idea to make a game out of the court, learn everything about everyone. Soon, he had discovered that he had a greater calling than simply playing with puppets, and had deeply regretted the idea. He had kept them around, though, since they *had* come in handy a time or two, and he wasn't above watching for sport. Still, an annoyance.

But he needed De Losa to convince her group to leave him and Azul alone. Her kidnapping plot most certainly had something to do with the Anchor mining ban. Such a nuisance—what need did he have of Anchor? Frustrating, that his father's title meant belonging to the court. He'd rather spend his days choosing bones to build his great project.

Unbecoming of him, possibly, to abandon his sire to permanent death, but it wasn't as if they had shared any real bond. The previous Marquess de Gracia had done his duty by his son—fed him, clothed him, allowed him to learn the ropes of the title—and little more. Still, Sergado de Gracia hadn't jumped overeager into a new study as he had in his teens. He had carefully considered every angle and concluded that it was time for his father to retire from life.

So, His Grace had ceased to be. And then a year later, someone had come around and killed him again.

It had helped in a way, this ironic turn of events, even if De Gracia had hoped for one or two more years to complete the transition into his sire's official role. It alleviated the small, sorrowful part of his conscience—it had obviously been his father's destiny to end prematurely dead, and for Sergado to take his place.

De Gracia stood and searched the desk and its drawers. He found a vow supporting the mining cause waiting for his signature, no doubt the price for Azul's freedom. Very well, he would grant it.

After signing his name with the ink and quill ready on the table, he met De Losa's unfocused gaze. It became somewhat sharper when he allowed her instincts to return. Much better. It was lucky that his studies kept their memories, their bodies going through the motions, unaware that there was no depth to them. No, it was simply the regurgitation of things they already knew how to do.

Lucky, and still something he fought to correct. For in his great project, there must be nothing left of the original owners. His great project must be hollow, his, and wholly his.

For a moment he saw himself through De Losa's eyes: young, tall, handsome, a slight smile teasing a dimple out of his cheek.

"Go now," he told her, although he didn't need to.

And De Losa went—to her home, to her room, to stitch closed the small hole between her ribs with a thread from her embroidery basket. To clean the smear of blood and order her ruined dress be cut into rags. To send a message to those in her circle that De Gracia and his family were no longer a threat and should be left alone.

For his part, Sergado took his time to return home to Alma-nueva. Now, here was a fitting name for his house, full with the hopes of rebirth. Perhaps that's what he'd call his creation once it was complete.

As soon as he'd stepped inside, he sensed the presence of the deathling.

The emissary stood in the shadows by the stairs, his pale hair set free around his shoulders and chest rather than in its usual tail, his gold-and-violet eyes fixed on him.

The temptation to kill him was nearly overwhelming.

Damn Virel Enjul. Damn him to the depths of the Void, where there were no gods and no salvation. Where Luck didn't reach and Death wouldn't save him.

It was his fault that De Gracia was keeping his personal guard away. Someone had ended Zenjiel, and then an emissary had appeared on his doorstep. Sergado had known what the man was from the beginning. He had seen the eyes, had sensed the bone mask, hidden beneath his clothing. He had opted for caution and kept his studies away until he figured out his game.

The man was trouble, but De Gracia had trusted him and the hired shadow to keep Azul safe, had believed there must be a reason he needed her whole. What an utter failure in judgment. He would not make this mistake again.

But he wouldn't kill him here, while he carried his long sword and Sergado had none of his studies at hand to help. Later, perhaps, with poison. Maybe while he slept, with a pillow or a well-placed blow.

Since Valanjians believed in their Lord Death so much, surely this emissary wouldn't mind joining him sooner rather than later. And did they not say the god seeded himself in his believers' bones?

With the Valanjian ambassador's aide gone, here was another chance at getting his hands on some godly bones.

"De Gracia," the deathling said in a cool tone.

Sergado regarded him with his usual cordial expression. "Enjul! How good to see you. Are you enjoying your stay?"

The man didn't return the warm greeting. "You allowed your sister to come to harm."

"What?" He made his eyes widen with innocence rather than narrow in irritation. "She is enjoying a party with my best friends."

"Is she? Then why did I find her by the blue tabards after escaping a pair of kidnappers?"

Sergado allowed the mask to slip away, his voice to harden. "I have taken care of it. It will not happen again."

"I trust it doesn't. Where was your personal guard to keep her safe?"

"Where was your shadow?"

The deathling's mouth firmed, the corners of his eyes tightening. Sergado might not be as proficient with a rapier as others, but he knew how to aim nonetheless.

"Since your man cannot be trusted," Sergado said, "I shall make sure she earns one of my own."

"Was it your doing?"

"Your shadow's incompetence? I hardly think so."

"The kidnapping attempt."

"Why would I do that?" he asked with honest curiosity. "I hold Azul dear in my heart. She is my sister, and I won't see her come to harm."

"Yet you did."

"Is this some kind of Valanjian pastime? Talking in circles?" He allowed a sneer to curve his lips. "It grows tiresome."

A snort of disgust was the deathling's response. "It does indeed." He walked past Sergado, stopping for a heartbeat as they drew close. "Azul del Arroyo might be your sister, but she's under my protection. If anything happens to her, you shall have to answer to me."

Sergado turned to watch him go. "And who are you?"

"Your end, if she goes missing again."

Yes, Sergado thought to himself as he watched the deathling stride away, perhaps poison while he slept.

XXVI

THE DREAMER

A YEAR AND A HALF EARLIER

"What exactly is the problem?" Sío asked Edine de Guzmán, the youngest of his sisters. Irritation laced his voice like it laced the way he tapped his fingers against his thigh. He sat on a stool at his usual spot inside one of the blue tabards' posts throughout the city. His partner had left to do some rounds—of the taverns, Sío assumed—the moment Edine arrived.

"Iriana has me delivering messages in secrecy."

A heavy sigh escaped Sío. Why had the gods shackled him with not two but three sisters in the city, always complaining, always squawking about one thing or the other? "You came to Cienpé to help Iriana and get away from Mother, so what did you expect?"

Edine hesitated. "That's not . . . I didn't think I was to act as some sort of furtive messenger."

"There is nothing furtive about it. You are not a fool, Didín. Some business must be dealt through back doors. You thought you would come and take charge like you do back home, and now you're a simple errand girl. Well, that is the way things work here in the outside world. It's not like in your odes of adventure."

"As with you?" she asked, looking pointedly at the blue tabard Sío wore. It was of better quality than the ones other guards owned, but a tabard nonetheless.

Sío didn't care for her look of pity. "Yes, I, too, must work my way up the ranks. Or you can go back to Alemar and find your fortune some other way."

"No," she said obstinately. "I *will* find it here. But hear me, Brother, that's not why I've come to you."

"Is it Esparza?" Sío tensed. He had seen them together when Edine came to the blue tabards' headquarters. He had done his best to squelch the rumors stirred up that day, but everyone knew of Esparza's reputation. "I told you he would break your heart." A bitter taste filled Sío's mouth. Now he'd have to call the man out for discarding his sister. His heart began to beat wildly and his fingers trembled against his thigh. He could sometimes hold his own against Nereida with a rapier, but Esparza had a lot of experience and—

"No!" Edine said, offended. "Why would you think that? He's a good friend. I'm not here to fall in love, Si-so."

The darkening of her cheeks belied her words, but Sío was happy to accept them at face value. Stopping a smile of relief, he forced his features into a severe expression. "Keep it that way, Edine. I meant what I said. He has a reputation for—"

"He's not like that."

Sío arched his brows. "You will allow me to finish."

Edine rolled her eyes but nodded.

"He has a reputation for liking shiny things and discarding them the second another comes around. And I don't only mean women, so do not look at me that way. His loyalties shift easily, Edine. You must take care around him."

A sudden grin broke her pouting. "One cannot find one's fortune without taking some risks."

Perhaps it was he who should go back to Alemar, Sío thought with no little gloom. He ran his hand over the stiff fabric of his tabard. It wasn't as if he was getting anywhere anyway, even with the commission his family had bought for him.

Edine approached and put a reassuring hand on his shoulder. After a soft squeeze, she stepped back and paced the small space inside the booth. "This is not about Esparza. I haven't gone to him yet, because even though I enjoy his company, I am well aware of his faults." She stopped to wink at Sío. "This is a family thing and I need your help."

Sío nodded, shifting in his seat to better track her movements.

"Iriana has me working as her delivery donkey, going back and forth with her contacts. I have looked into some of them, Si-so, and they have a bad reputation."

"Edine—"

She lifted a hand to stop his words. "I know that's how a city like Cienpuentes works. I'm not so innocent, for all that you'd like to think so. But while investigating one of these deals Iriana has going, I stumbled onto something suspicious." She grimaced. "More suspicious than all the other secret things she has me delivering."

"Does someone mean her harm? You should tell her immediately." The cold sweat was back to dampen Sío's nape. "Let her deal with it."

"No. At least not immediately. But I think she might have involved herself by mistake in some sort of court ploy."

"Most of the business in Cienpé is some sort of court ploy, Edine."

"This one . . . well, I think it involves someone in the Heart."

"The Heart is the court."

Edine huffed in frustration. "The Heart is the king."

He stared at her in disbelief. "You think Iriana is involved in a plot against the king? No. She's not that greedy."

"She does like her Anchor."

"And she can well afford it without the need to risk her life by plotting treason."

"You are not listening, Si-so. I don't think she knows what she's involved with."

"And what is your proof? Show it to me." He extended his hand, palm up.

Edine hesitated. "I cannot. It's a feeling I have from what I've over-heard while delivering her messages."

"If you're that worried, talk to her, explain the situation."

Edine shook her head. "She won't believe me. She will assume I read everything wrong."

"It will give her an excuse to revisit the loyalties of those she does business with."

"It's only a suspicion. If I go to her and I'm wrong, it will follow me."

Sío crossed his arms in irritation. "You came to me for advice, and that's the advice I'm giving you."

Her easy grin came again. "You are wrong, Brother. I came to you to see if you'd like to accompany me in some late-night spying."

Unease grew at the dare in her words. "What do you mean?"

"I think something is going to happen in a week, and I mean to be there to see what it is. Cienpuentes can be dangerous at night, and I could use another rapier to go with mine."

"No," he said, resolute. "Tell Iriana and step aside. This is not your fight. And," he added, pointing at her, "do *not* go to Esparza for help."

"Bah!" she exclaimed. "If you don't want to go with me, I will go myself."

"Don't!"

"We must both do as we see fit," she said haughtily before whirling on her heel and leaving the room.

"Didín," he called after her. "Don't do anything foolish."

Edine didn't hear or didn't care to answer.

Once more, Sío asked the Blessed Heart why they had given his mother four children instead of simply his person. He resigned him-self to having to follow his younger sister late at night in a week to make sure she didn't come to harm. He returned to his stool, in-tent on catching some sleep while leaning against the windowsill, the safety of Cienpé's citizens be damned.

THE PRESENT

Sío woke up to a scream—his own—and a sensation of having been thrown into a lake—his sweat. Cold, it stuck his shirt to his flesh like a second skin. Unnerved, he tore the shirt off his back, balling it into a bundle and throwing it to the corner of the room.

The action didn't make anything better. Trembling, he brought his fingers to his face. The mask was still there, as soaked as his shirt had been. Where was the Witch?

He tore off that piece of fabric, too, and went to splash some water from the basin onto his face.

It didn't help either.

Sunlight shone outside, although he could not tell the exact time. All he could tell was the vague reflection of his face on the glass pane. It was the face he had seen in his nightmares.

Heart pounding, he retied the mask and sat on the edge of the bed, praying for the Lady Dream to come save his mind before he remembered anything more.

"Witch," he let out in a savage growl. "We had a deal. Take me."

Not a moment later, she did, and Sío de Guzmán was free to lose himself in his dreams instead of his nightmares.

XXVII

DEATH

Enjul's pencil moved leisurely across the sheaf of paper, leaving lazy lines behind. *Leisurely* and *lazy*, two concepts that ought never apply to him, yet there were no other words to describe the way his hand moved whenever his mind was elsewhere and his body craved the outlet of action. Some took up fights to relieve the urge, some took lovers, some delved into the flow of gossip.

Enjul took pen and ink and surfaces to leave his mark upon the world.

Because in his art, nothing ever died.

He was in his room on the second floor of De Gracia's impressive house, half sitting on the windowsill with one leg propped up to balance his folder and the sheet of paper, leaning his back against the frame. The itch to put on his emissary mask was almost overpowering.

The need to hide his nature chafed him. The need to stake his claim as the Emissary of the Lord Death among the souls in Cienpuentes at times choked him. He yearned to remind these people who gave their prayers to the Lady Dream and the Blessed Heart that the Lord Death reigned beyond dreams and abundance.

He needed to be a constant reminder to Azul del Arroyo that her fate was sealed.

Even now she sat on a rock in the patio below, brown hair tumbling over her shoulders and knee-high boots kicking back and forth.

Planning her little schemes, no doubt, thinking she had bested him after their talk when he already predicted what moves she would make from now until she was back in Valanje by his side.

His hand paused its trip across the sheet.

By his side. The arrangement of the words felt companionable, friendly, as if two people had freely agreed to travel somewhere rather than one forcing the other. Yet, *until he brought her back to Valanje, in chains if needed* no longer had the same satisfying ring to it as it had mere days ago. It lacked something. Subtlety, perhaps. It carried the grim sense of duty rather than the satisfaction of Azul del Arroyo seeing the truth of her ways, admitting that her gift must be contained, that going against the Lord Death was a grave affront.

The drawing resumed.

After their conversation by the blue tabards' headquarters, he had an inkling of hope that she might come around. After all, while her gift was foul, her brain was not. Her thoughts were shaped by grief, a feeling Virel Enjul was familiar with. He had experienced it himself and had seen it often enough in others to know how it warped reason and belief.

Azul del Arroyo's urge to defy the Lord Death by bringing back her sister would pass once her bone-seeking schemes came to an end, just as the grief he felt for leaving his family to join the Order had, and she'd see that the Lord Death existed, that the god welcomed everyone's souls and offered a refuge after the storm that was life. That her sister was safe and taken care of in ways a cage of flesh and bones could never hope to achieve.

That life was nothing but a short trip between the Lord Life and the Lord Death.

Once she understood this reality, there would be no need to drag her to Valanje. Then she'd truly be by his side, for what better way to be reminded of her sister than standing by the Lord Death's emissary?

With a scowl, Enjul added a few precise strokes, then licked his finger and lightly smudged a few lines. Still unhappy with the result, he moved the sheet to access a clear spot and began anew.

Azul del Arroyo's mask should not have the same fangs his did. He didn't often smile, but the young woman downstairs did. If she must stand by his side, if they must hunt maladies and serve the Lord Death together, he must design a mask worthy of her, not an unfitting thing she would resent day after day.

Being an Emissary of the Lord Death was a solitary job. It had never bothered him—Virel Enjul needed nothing of the path of life save his god, his drawings, and himself—but now he wondered if he had erred by not acquiring a pupil. There were few emissaries, and the head of the Order had once or twice attempted to force some child to his side, but Enjul wasn't a teacher. Yet here he found himself trying to teach Azul del Arroyo the wrongness of her ways.

The wrongness that, in a world where everything was on the way to the Lord Death, she alone stood defiant, a beacon of life among the dead stones in the patio, the dying bushes, and the dying flowers.

Unique. Marvelous.

The sight of her scared him as much as it locked his gaze to her as he began sketching again: the smooth line of her jaw, the roundness of her eyes, the way her nose upturned just so. Features already imprinted into his memory, but that he couldn't help seeking out again and again.

They were . . . fascinating. They made the itch to take up pencil and paper an undeniable urge, and since his god didn't seem to mind, he didn't see why he ought to stop himself.

Some kind of noise drew Azul's attention away from her silent scheming, and she stood up from the rock, her face filling with satisfaction bordering on smugness.

Ah, Enjul thought, *one of her plans must have come to fruition.*

He abandoned folder, paper, and pencil on his bed and strode out of the room, heedless of making noise with his boots on the expensive tiled floors. By the time he made it downstairs and to the front door of the house, a small delegation had gathered.

"Sirese Del Arroyo," a tall woman dressed in full City Guard blue finery was saying. She held two small, thin metal sheets. Behind her, four guards stood at attention, rapier hilts and pike spikes gleaming in the afternoon sun. Across the street, Azul's shadow lounged against the opposite building's wall, expression insolent. As much as Enjul disliked the look, he'd take it over boredom. Insolence meant interest; boredom meant losing Azul again.

The thought made him want to snarl.

Azul was his to watch over, to contain, to keep—not part of some petty court game, the Lord Death lose her brother's soul.

"This is Captain de Macia of the City Guard," Azul said, defiant. Even her chin lifted with the emotion, as if she were a head taller than he and was attempting to look at him down her nose. Her gumption, her obstinate need to stick to her beliefs frustrated him to no end. Frustrated and kept him on alert. Excited him.

And perhaps this was why he was contemplating the idea of her standing by his side. Perhaps it was the thought of having someone who would raise his spirits that brought out that longing in him. Someone who would never tire of challenging him.

Nobody ever dared challenge an Emissary of the Lord Death.

De Macia studied him with narrowed eyes. Enjul knew what she saw—the height, the breadth of his shoulders, the light hair, rare in Sancia. His golden-and-violet eyes, even rarer.

She showed no shock at being in the presence of a man from the land of the Lord Death. Would she, if she knew who he really was? Would her tan skin turn sickly at the knowledge that the Lord Death's own stood in front of her?

Somehow, he thought not. She would show due respect, he knew, but she would not hide behind her guards.

"This is Virel Enjul," Azul continued. "He agreed to accompany me from my trip to Valanje."

De Macia gave him a short nod, still taking the measure of him. "A pleasure, sirese. My family and the Del Arroyos go back a long time."

There was a note of warning in her voice that Enjul registered, then discarded. He didn't care for games, and if he were to reveal his true self, not even a captain could stop him from doing as he wished. Sancians might look toward the Lady Dream and the Blessed Heart, but they were aware of which gods held the true power.

"De Macia," he responded curtly.

The captain's gaze returned to Azul, her expression warm. "Would you rather not stay with us, Azul?"

Azul took her proffered hand and the sheets of metal. Enjul saw the glint of bright blue, and his lips curled. Part of him hoped Sancia followed through with the lift on Anchor mining. Let it fall into the Void when it ran out of the gods' bones while he watched from Valanje.

"Thank you, Captain, but I'll stay here with my brother," Azul said. "You have my gratitude for providing these for me."

"I will look for you at the balls."

"And I for you."

A few more niceties followed, then the captain and her guards were gone, the front door closed by one of the servants. Azul thought to evade him by scurrying into one of the parlors.

He followed, somewhat surprised when she didn't slam the door in his face. But the doors in this building were thick and heavy, and she must have realized it would take more effort than it was worth.

"Are these the invitations for Noche Verde?" he asked, coming to stand by her side.

She seemed to recoil slightly, but he thought more from surprise than disgust. He wasn't sure if the knowledge pleased or disappointed him.

"Yes." Azul handed one over to him. "As we agreed."

He examined the small piece of white ladine metal, hammered down and polished into a smooth surface. A tiny square of true Anchor had been encrusted by the engraved names of the regent and the king.

"I suppose they do it so it's not easy to fake entrance," Azul murmured, almost to herself. She rubbed the Anchor in her invitation, then touched the one dangling from her ear.

When they were back in Valanje, Enjul would make sure they disposed of it properly.

After he was done with the other malady. That one, he would not allow to survive his visit. Azul would get an opportunity because he understood her grief. And now that the idea of her being by his side had entered his mind, he found it hard to give up. But the other? His smile was instinctive, nearly unnatural in its greed.

His god had struck down Isadora del Arroyo but hadn't touched Azul. Perhaps this was why the Lord Death had kept him alive at the docks of Diel: not to go after her and treat her like something to be studied but to form an unstoppable pair. He who made death his life, and she who lived to defy death. After all, hadn't Death and Life started all?

The other malady, however, would soon join the Lord Death.

His hands tightened around the invitation.

"What will you do once you find the other necromancer?" Azul asked as if she held the power to read minds.

"I will make sure they cease to exist."

She flinched at that. "If they are high up in the court, as we suspect they are, you won't get away with their murder."

"That is for me to worry about, isn't it?"

She abandoned his side to stare at the patio. When she looked back at him a few seconds later, there was venom in her words. "I hope they catch you and throw you into a hole with no door."

"Of course you do. That way you'll be free to steal your sister from the Lord Death. But perhaps this time you won't be allowed to call on her soul. Now that the god knows about you, he might not part with her as easily as you think."

Her sharp inhale told him Azul had not thought of this. "Perhaps the Lord Death can't do anything about it," she said through gritted teeth. "Perhaps it is time we take control over our lives. Over our souls."

He laughed at that. "The gods gifted us life, and so our lives belong to them."

"Does a child belong to their parents forever?" she retorted. "Do they need to follow directions for the whole of their lives? No. There is respect, but a person gets a choice outside their parents' opinions."

"Children get no choice. They get told where to go, what to do until they mature." He walked up to her, and her soft floral scent all but overwhelmed his senses. "And once the children age, they realize that the paths taken lead to a destination, and the destination will always be the Lord Death. And in their last moment, with their last breath, they will ask for their gods' forgiveness, because any paths they walked only existed because of the gods' grace. What people think is a choice is nothing but a misunderstood idea about the way the world works."

Azul straightened. "Then perhaps it's time we break this cage and show the gods why they gave us reasoning." She lifted a hand and pressed it against his chest, against the linen of his shirt and the flesh and muscle underneath, and he had to fight to hide his reaction to the sudden touch.

People did not ever willingly touch death.

"This god of yours. Perhaps he wants you to think this way about the world. Perhaps it is his way to remain among us because he knows we will soon choose paths he and the other gods hadn't thought to draw for us. That we will be truly our own, our souls to do with as we wish."

She dropped her hand, and Enjul felt as if she'd just carved away a chunk of his chest and taken it with her. Foolish—the feeling and her words. How someone so cunning, so smart, could arrive at such conclusions astounded him.

"If that were the gods' aim, then everyone would be able to guard their souls against death, not just you and this other malady. You would be one of a thousand, not one of two."

"That you know of."

The insistence in her voice, her conviction, made him want to smile. Yes, he did enjoy these little talks. Why wouldn't he? After all, the Lord Death had put her in his path for a reason, and perhaps the reason was this feeling.

"If there were many of you, the world would be overtaken by those snatched back from the Lord Death. Do you think yourself alone in your grief? Do you think death is not there for a reason?"

"And what reason would that be?"

"For you to appreciate the Lord Life's gift. For you to shape your soul, make it a thing of beauty before you join the Lord Death."

Azul's mouth flattened into a straight line, her brown eyes glittering in a way that made him think that perhaps the beauty of Anchor might one day take another color, another shape.

"Then the Lord Life will approve of giving someone another chance to enjoy his gift." She turned toward the window and closed her eyes, as if taking in the sounds and scents drifting from the lush patio. "Tell me, Emissary, do you ever find joy in anything but the Lord Death, or did they steal all whims and wishes at the Order?"

He joined her. Standing next to her rather than across fit him better. *By his side*, yes. This is how it would be, wouldn't it? The warmth, the companionship, the strange beating of his heart. "I find joy in my work, but my work is not my only joy."

"What do you enjoy, then?"

His drawings, his thoughts, reading through past emissaries' accounts. Watching the sky and knowing it was through the gods that he had a land from which to observe the stars. Music, sometimes, when he was a child.

"I like daggers," Azul continued, as if she hadn't expected an answer from the start. "I like dipping cake in my breakfast, and music when it comes from an artist's hand. I like plays on words, and words that make me curious. I like looking at paintings of places far away but dislike how they make me feel—small and left behind." Her gaze moved toward the square of blue sky. "I like looking at the sky and wondering if one day we shall leave these lands and travel to the stars, and I like wondering what we might find there."

Enjul let out a sound of amusement, rough and strange and odd to his ears. Travel to the stars? As if. "A traveler's curiosity never ends well."

Yet wasn't that what his heart wanted now? To travel with her? The thought unsettled him.

"I wish the Order had never gotten their hands on you," Azul said, sounding wistful. "Then perhaps you'd have grown to enjoy these things too."

"There are many things I enjoy, Miss Del Arroyo, and just because you don't know what they are it does not make them any less valuable."

"Azul." Her mouth kicked up at one corner. "If you insist on having all these talks about gods and duty and fate, it will save your breath if you simply use my name." Her brow arched in a dare. "Even maladies have them."

Azul, like the summer sky. Perhaps that was what was missing from his sketches—color. Bone white suited him, but it didn't suit her. A painted blue mask? No, too close to Anchor, to wearing the gods' bones on her face as if she had their sanction. He'd have to think of something else.

"Miss Del Arroyo will do for now," he said firmly.

"I suppose we'll have plenty of time together for you to grow tired of saying three words when one will do."

Exultation began thrumming along his pulse. "You accept your—" He caught himself before *spot by my side* left his mouth. "Position, then?"

She grew serious. "I promised to go with you, didn't I? You might not believe in my word, but I do."

"Then promise you will cease this plan of yours." He tapped his invitation against his other hand. That the woman had plans for Noche Verde was as obvious as the sky.

Azul smiled slyly. "What plan?"

He smiled back, leaned in, and caught the flicker of surprise in her eyes, the sharp intake of her breath, the parting of her lips, almost inviting.

"What plan, indeed."

Yes, it appeared they both enjoyed games.

Enjul was looking forward to playing them, together, for as long as the Lord Death allowed their souls to remain on the continents.

They held each other's gaze in a rare moment filled with both expectation and calm. A thing of beauty he could never catch with his art.

In the next moment, Azul stepped back, turned away, and walked out of the parlor. He followed a few minutes later and returned to his room. Once inside, door closed securely behind him, he raised the invitation to examine it closer. No mark of Azul's fingers, no scent of her touch, the ladine an impersonal piece of metal that carried no memories of its previous handler.

He tossed it onto the bed and, on an impulse, knelt by his trunk. There he retrieved a handkerchief from under a layer of shirts and pants. He had found it while searching her room.

He brought the piece of fabric to his nose and inhaled deeply, archiving the notes, the sensation, the memories it brought up, and told himself he was simply studying Azul del Arroyo as an emissary ought to study a malady, and nothing more.

XXVIII

AZUL

zul was still thinking about her conversation with the emissary a few hours later, when Nereida knocked on her bedroom door and suggested they go out for a stroll.

Azul accepted immediately, glad to have an excuse to get out of the house and away from Virel Enjul. She had meant to infuriate him in the parlor downstairs, to rattle the invisible emissary mask he hid behind, but all she had gained was the disturbing knowledge that he *was* human after all.

What kind of man would the Emissary of the Lord Death be if the god and his Order hadn't gotten their claws into him?

Azul yearned to know.

Ever since their talk outside the City Guard's headquarters, a part of Azul had been looking forward to another encounter. No, even before that—ever since they had struck their bargain at the ambassador's house. It had been exhilarating, the rapid exchange of words, of ideas. It was a game—or a contest—to see who could put a chink in the other's belief. And, oh, how Azul had missed someone to play games with, a constant, dependable companion in life as well as her heart.

And constant the emissary would be; of that, she was certain. From now until the end of her days, the man would chain himself to her side.

It might not be so bad.

Admittedly, it would be much better than ending up chained in the Order's dank cellars.

Azul hastened her steps to match Nereida's, whose idea of a stroll was all but a jog. But then, Nereida wasn't here for leisure, was she? So, neither was this walk leisurely.

They crossed a bridge, then turned into an alleyway that spat them onto a rare patch of greenery by the riverbank—a space no bigger than the guest bedrooms at Almanueva, filled with soil and grass, with a lone tree growing at its center, its foliage still sporting the green lushness of spring. To their right, another bridge crossed the narrow stretch of water, and the opposite bank was nothing but houses made of gray stone walls.

Someone had painted a mural of the Lady Dream on one, golden yellows and pastel browns a contrast with the gray of the stone. The goddess's blue eyes appeared fixed on Azul no matter how much she shifted position, casting judgment upon her. And for the first time, the thought occurred to her that she did not want to pray to such a judgmental god, so she turned her back to the mural and the river, with its soothing murmur, its dank smell, and the remains of bright blue Anchor blinking from its bottom.

Several paces away, from inside a passageway, her shadow tipped his hat in salute.

Nereida gave him her back. "I have found you a way inside the ossuary."

Azul fought not to gasp. After a smile to her shadow, she also averted her face. "Just me?"

"I have no need to go inside."

"But the person you wish me to bring back?"

"Do not concern yourself with that, Del Arroyo."

"Wouldn't dream of it." Azul's gaze drifted to the goddess's mural, and she cursed herself for the turn of phrase. "How will I get inside, then?"

She daren't believe that the time to bring Isadora back to her side was at hand. She had grown complacent, focusing so much on these

games of cat and mouse with Enjul, the reason for her being in Cienpuentes had faded into memory.

No longer.

"Someone will come to you during Noche Verde and get you inside," Nereida said.

"You trust this person?"

"Yes."

"Who are they?" Azul pressed.

Nereida's eyes grew a faraway look. "Miguel Esparza, an old friend
of my sister's."

Azul recalled their conversation back in Del Valle's guest bedroom
in Monteverde. "You have a sister and a brother."

"I do." Nereida's voice had become strange, but Azul couldn't tell
if that was because she missed her siblings or because she did not.

"Are they in Cienpuentes?"

"One moved away a year ago, the other remains here in Cienpuentes."

The words were stilted now, and Azul was surprised they were
coming out at all. Nereida was a book with multiple locks.

"I am glad you have them with you," she said. "Losing a sister . . .
I would not wish it on anyone."

"But you have so many to choose from," came the reply, sharp and
meant to sting, although Azul couldn't fathom why.

Surprised, she studied Nereida's expression. It gave nothing away.
Those cool green eyes met hers, and Azul lowered her head.

"Forgive me . . . Azul. I shouldn't have spoken so." Nereida's attention drifted toward the river again. "My siblings and I haven't always
gotten along. It's hard when you grow up with so many of them. I sometimes envy your position—having one sibling by your side, but with so
many available should the need arise."

Azul could barely swallow a bitter laugh. "That's not how it works,
is it? A sibling you have never met might as well be a stranger. What
bond is there? They're not interchangeable dolls."

"De Gracia seems to hold you in high esteem."

"He has known about my existence for years."

"Do your other half siblings not know of you?"

Azul gave in to a sudden impulse and crouched to run her hands through the patch of grass by her boots, sinking her fingers into damp soil. Someone must come to water the grass regularly, she realized, for it hadn't rained since they got to town.

"In truth, I do not know whether they do or not," she answered. "I know about them because it's hard not to know where one's mother disappears to for months at a time." Not when your tutor tells you to write letters to her and shows you how to address them. Not when that tutor gossips with the cook or other temporary help over the latest rich family in need of a child but unable to bring one to term. "But my half siblings? I assume most of them are raised to believe they're fully their parents' children."

She stood and fixed a wicked smiled on Nereida. "*You* could be my half sister, and you might never know it."

"The gods wouldn't be that mean."

"Are you sure? I bet you have been remiss in your prayers."

Nereida barked a laugh. "You might be correct on that. It has been a while since I thought they looked after me at all."

Azul couldn't help but look at the mural. "I often wonder the same. I often wonder if they ever looked after us."

After all, didn't some tales say they regretted giving up their bones? Hadn't the Lord Death stolen her sister—twice?

"The gods look after each other," Nereida agreed, "so we must look out for our own. Will you be able to get away from your escort on Noche Verde?"

"Yes," Azul said.

Nereida did not appear to doubt her. Having siblings of her own, she must know Azul would do whatever it took to see Isadora again.

"You never told me who you want me to bring back," she said.

"And I don't mean to."

"I will find out when it's time to raise them."

"Something for you to look forward to."

Azul half expected Nereida to turn on her heel at those words and stride away, but she stayed put. Perhaps this little nook of greenery reminded her of home, as it did Azul.

"Your family isn't from Cienpuentes, is it?" Azul asked.

"I grew up in the northern countryside."

"Temple school?"

"For three years."

"Isadora went to one too," Azul murmured. For the first time since Diel, memories of her sister didn't induce a pang of grief. Just the bittersweet aftertaste of things once held dear. "One of Mother's clients' gift."

"Not you?"

"I was left behind in Aguncíon."

"I wish I had been left behind at home too."

The words were sour and full of regret, and Azul found them surprising. Isadora had been sorry to be away from Azul, but she enjoyed her time at the Temple immensely. Nereida looked like the kind of person who would have enjoyed her time there—hadn't she been a star at court? The queen's very mistress? "Is it because of the queen?"

Nereida frowned in confusion. "The queen?"

"Her death . . ."

A short laugh. "The queen and I did not last that long." The words didn't have any bite to them or any resentment. However their parting had come to pass, it wasn't the drama Azul had expected given the rumors.

"I was looking for excitement," Nereida continued, her gaze growing distant, "and she offered me a world as bright as all the Anchor in the continents. I thought I was prepared for the court, but the fever of being chosen caught me off guard." Nereida shook her head. "We burned like the strongest of flames, but there was no real depth to it. It was never meant to endure. We both knew it, I think, but decided to enjoy ourselves nonetheless."

"Were you with her when she died?" Azul couldn't resist asking.

"No. Our affair had been over by then."

Something in Nereida's tone told Azul she was done talking about that matter, so she returned to their previous subject. "Then why do you wish you had stayed home?"

"It would've given me more time with my family," she said simply.

"You are young—there is still time to find them. Go visit your sister, go talk to your brother."

At least you still have them.

"I might."

"Is your brother still here? Does he belong to the court?"

Nereida's countenance grew dark, and Azul guessed the two hadn't parted on good terms, as happened with siblings sometimes. "Is he younger than you?"

"Older by a year."

"Being a younger sister can be hard," Azul said. "Sometimes it's like you are the older one, for they refuse to look after themselves."

Nereida nodded, her voice strange and wistful as she responded, "You grow tired of checking in with them, so you look away, and when you next glance back, there is nothing to find but razed ground."

"Yes. A heartbeat away from your attention, and everything you know is gone." Azul blinked away the sudden burning in her eyes, wondering what had happened to Nereida and her siblings that she could speak Azul's feelings with so much precision. But she knew Nereida would not share, so she asked instead, "Do you miss being at court?"

"No."

"You won't return after we're done?"

"No."

"What will you do?"

"Not be in the court."

It was Azul's turn to laugh. "Will your contact come to me before we arrive at the first ball?"

"Yes. While you're on the way." Nereida gave her a sidelong glance, her gaze resting on Isadora's Anchor earring. "The court is bright like the stars, like Anchor itself, but it has mined anything good it ever had to offer. There is little joy to be found there."

"Then why did you stay after the queen's death?" Azul asked, full of curiosity.

"I wasn't done with the court then."

Nereida's tone spoke of harsh satisfaction, and a shiver of apprehension ran down Azul's back. "And you are now?"

Nereida's smile was all teeth and full of dark promise. "Yes."

XXIX

NIGHT OF HOPE

The night sky of Noche Verde arched above Cienpuentes, a deep blue green as if Azul were standing among the understars, looking up at the sea. These infrequent green nights of summer—when the Lady Dream forgot she once killed her child and Hope dared to rise—would they bring her good luck?

It had been a week since the failed kidnapping, and four days since her talk with Nereida.

Sergado was still unaware of the kidnapping incident. Azul had tried to warn him about keeping a personal guard, but it was hard to do so without revealing the exact reason, and she didn't want additional guards on top of her shadow. Her brother was protective of her—he would put them on her if he ever found out.

Now, as they left Almanueva on foot and slowly approached the center of Cienpuentes on their way to the Noche Verde balls, Azul realized her plan to lose her escorts would be even easier than she'd expected. The crowds made traveling by horse or carriage impossible. They clogged the way, carrying torches and lamps, filling the air with songs, sloshing the ground with wine and ale. Excitement had turned Cienpuentes's streets and alleyways into living veins of thrumming humanity, cloaked humanity, masked humanity. Azul could barely distinguish Enjul and her brother ahead—the gods must be smiling upon her, envious of the Lord Death.

She took hold of Enjul's arm. He wore a mask today, too—still not the bone one—green and golden and sparkling with beads. It softened the rough angles of his face, matched the blond tresses that appeared dark under the flickering torchlights. "There is one here," she told him, worrying her lip and looking toward one of the alleys. "A necromancer's victim."

Enjul's attention snapped to the alleyway.

"Tall, dark hair, pale skin, wearing a blue hat and no cloak," she added. "Should we follow?"

He disentangled his arm from her grasp. "No, stay with De Gracia and proceed as we planned. I shall catch up later."

Enjul merged into the crowd, making his way toward the alley, and Azul was shocked by how easily he had left her side. It ought to concern her, but the relief was too overwhelming.

Her brother had stopped a few paces ahead, looking at her with curiosity. To him, she said, "I must follow Sirese Enjul, Brother, but I will meet you at the Heart later. If Sirese Enjul and I get separated, and he returns ahead, will you tell him this?"

"Of course, Sister, but what happened? Can I help?"

Azul shook her head with a smile and made for another street. Swerving around a corner, she discarded her cloak and unhooked her earring. She tied a simple mask around her head and unbraided her hair, then approached the other side of the alleyway. She hoped the change was enough to distract her shadow, and was rewarded when, after rounding a few short blocks, she saw him walking ahead of her, his eyes darting everywhere, searching.

She slipped back into a narrow space between two houses and waited for him to walk farther away. Azul felt bad. He would likely be discharged after losing her now and the kidnapping failure, but—

"Please return to De Gracia for safety's sake, sirese."

Azul whirled to face a man lurking behind her, bareheaded and with clothes matching her shadow's. Her heart sank and she cursed her daftness. Why hadn't she considered the possibility that Enjul might put a second shadow on her?

Her mind was racing for a way to get out when the man grunted. His eyes rolled back, and he crumpled to the ground. A stranger stood behind him, mask-free, dark brown hair loose around his shoulders beneath a black hat bearing a small plume. He was sheathing a dagger. She fought to find words.

"Don't worry, he's just unconscious," the man said. "I'm Miguel Esparza, here to help you."

"You're a blue tabard!" Azul exclaimed. Nereida hadn't told her that.

But then, Nereida hadn't told her much.

"On my bad days." His eyes narrowed, focusing on her ears covered by her hair. "You *are* Del Arroyo?"

Azul hurried to take off the mask and retrieved Isadora's earring from her pocket, rehooking it after a few fumbling tries. "De Guzmán sent you?"

Esparza began walking. "Indeed. Come now. We are in a hurry, yes?"

"Yes." Azul followed, shoulders hunched as if they could hide her from curious onlookers. "And Nereida?" she asked, fighting to advance through the crowd.

"Don't worry about De Guzmán. She has her own appointment to meet."

Nereida had mentioned she wouldn't come with her, but it still didn't feel right.

Sensing her reluctance, Esparza gave her a pointed look over his shoulder. "Come, don't come. I don't care, but I won't offer again."

"Sorry. I've grown to be suspicious since my arrival in Cienpuentes."

He accepted her apology by slowing his strides. As the crowds thinned, it was easier to walk. The freedom made her realize how nervous she was.

"Can you truly give me access to the ossuary?" she asked.

"We will soon find out, won't we?"

His tone was jovial, and when Azul glanced up, she found his mouth widening with a smile and his eyes bright in the warm light.

He reminded Azul of Isadora. Of when she did what she enjoyed best—card games, sword fighting, looking for trouble.

When the streets emptied of revelers and Azul was better able to gauge her surroundings, the memories of Isadora receded to give way to renewed suspicions. They had come to a part of the city she didn't recognize. A part that held neither the ossuary nor the Temple.

Her hand touched her dagger, the bone hilt a reassuring presence. "Where are you taking me? The ossuary is not near."

"The ossuary is a useful building for people who work aboveground. The real one is here." Esparza pointed at a square structure illuminated by the two moons. Old—no, ancient—it reminded Azul of the old fortress on top of Monteverde, with its big chipped boulders that seemed capable of carrying the weight of the continents as much as the Anchor did.

They approached through the empty street. After the overwhelming energy of the crowds, the contrast was eerie. Azul was unsettled by it, and the stranger must have been, too, because he motioned for her to be silent and hastened to a side entrance.

He had a key, a giant old thing for the big lock on the door. No lights came from inside once he unlocked and opened the door, no windows allowed Luck and Wonder's shine. With a muttered curse, the man pulled a sheaf from under his tabard and studied it in the moonlight outside.

Azul peeked at it, too—a rough map of corridors and rooms.

"I hope your memory for these things is better than mine," Esparza murmured, folding the page and returning it to his pocket.

They went inside. With the door closed behind them and their eyes not yet accustomed to the lack of light, they advanced in utter darkness.

"Is this a room or a corridor?" Esparza asked by an opening in the wall.

"A room."

He stopped anyway.

"It's a room," Azul insisted. "Two rooms on the right, then the corridor."

"Not a room, the corridor, and two rooms?"

Azul waited. Esparza crossed the doorway and crashed against something.

"It's a room," he agreed.

Slowly, they went deeper into the building, almost falling down sets of steps here and there until they found a room with a few embers still smouldering under a brazier's cover. Esparza was able to bring a flame to life and lit a lamp, and she heard him thank the gods as he passed the lamp to her and retrieved the map.

It was easy work then to backtrack and gain access to a cavernous hall that made her shiver and look longingly toward the dark maw they had emerged from. The light didn't reach the ceilings here, even though the building was only two stories tall. The hall must've been carved into the ground, she surmised. The walls sucked the light from their lamp, refusing to mirror it back. For the first time in recent memory, Azul felt no urge to step closer and figure out how something like that was possible.

A formidable iron gate blocked a set of wide steps leading down into a tunnel. Esparza ran his hands against the thick bars and the intricately wrought middle mechanism locking them in place.

"This wasn't on the map," he murmured. He pushed, pulled, and nothing happened. The old key was of no use.

"There might be another entrance?" she asked. Despite speaking in low tones, their words still echoed in the cavernous space.

"Not on the map either."

"Doesn't mean it doesn't exist."

"Bring the lamp closer," he said, taking out some small metal tools.

Azul watched in fascination as he tried to pick the lock. Did Captain de Macia know her men boasted these kinds of skills? "Will you teach me how to do this?"

"He will not."

Azul jumped with a scream, her free hand slamming against her chest as if to stop her heart from galloping away.

The tools clattered to the floor. Esparza unsheathed his rapier and brought its tip perilously close to Virel Enjul's stomach.

Azul couldn't look away. Blood rushed in her ears, her mind gone blank. Caught red-handed, and so easily. Enjul must've followed to see who was helping her. She had overstepped, as Enjul knew she would. He would now drag her to Almanueva and then to Valanje, and who knows when she would get another opportunity like this? It might never happen. It *would* never happen—this, she knew with certainty.

He must be stopped.

But how? Render him unconscious? Tie him up? How long until he awoke, or someone came across him and freed him? It was two against one, but he seemed so tall and wide and overwhelming she found it hard to believe they could best him in a fight. They were at a disadvantage, for this man wouldn't hesitate to end their lives.

And so, he must die.

No more talks. No more contests of words. No more standing by his side, wondering what truly lay beneath the mask.

Slowly, Azul turned her wide-eyed stare to Esparza. He had a calculating look on his face. He must be thinking the same thing.

A knot formed in her throat, the pressure in her chest becoming unbearable.

If she was to see her sister alive, Virel Enjul, Emissary of the Lord Death, must die.

The certainty made her mouth dry up and her heart pound and her hands sweat.

Nereida had tried to do away with him back in Diel, and it didn't work. Would he stay dead this time, this far from the Lord Death's land? It seemed impossible that he might disappear from her life with such ease.

"You plan to kill me," he said with that arrogant lift of his mouth Azul knew so well, hated so much.

Esparza shrugged, his sword still pointed at Enjul's chest. "No one saw us come, no one will see us leave. Someone else's mess to clean. Or you could leave."

"No need for such extremes. As it happens, I'm quite curious about this place myself. I suggest we join forces and get on with it."

A hiss of disbelief escaped Azul at the same time Esparza tensed and said, "Somehow, I don't believe this good fortune."

The emissary ignored him and held Azul's gaze—a tether he was daring her to snap. "Do not test my patience." His voice reverberated in that strange way sounds travel in the cavern of a hall. It made him sound otherworldly.

It made her feel glad.

Oh-so glad.

Esparza cursed and lowered his rapier. Enjul pushed him aside to inspect the old lock.

Azul's knees wobbled and she leaned against the cold bars of the gate, holding on to the lamp with both hands. He truly meant to help? Her stomach turned, part surprise, part hope.

Between Enjul and Esparza, they got the lock open. The gate moved soundlessly, well oiled and well used, the spikes and swirls in the iron forming bizarre shadows against the ground. The tunnel beyond was built out of the same dark stone as the hall, making her feel as if they were walking straight into the Void.

A series of octagonal rooms blossomed from the end of the tunnel, their surfaces hoarding the lamplight. Bones covered every open space and every carefully carved niche, artfully arranged in bizarre mosaics of skulls and limbs.

"Well?" Esparza asked from his spot at the end of the tunnel. His eyes flickered from room to room, his hand tight around his rapier's grip. Enjul stood by his side, saying nothing, waiting, hands loose by his sides, long sword hanging by his thigh.

"Well?" she repeated.

Esparza gestured toward the closest room. "Ossuary. Do whatever it is you need done."

Azul looked at them in confusion. "These aren't real bones. They're carved stone and wood."

Esparza jolted. "What?" He entered the room and leaned in to inspect the nearby bones. He did not touch them, though.

"Go deeper," was Enjul's response.

Esparza and Azul looked at each other. She saw her thoughts reflected on his face: *A trap?*

With a slight grimace, Esparza motioned for her to run the lamp around the walls. They found a small wooden door, which Enjul and Esparza forced open, leading to a narrow spiral of stairs.

They began the descent, the unevenness of the steps making the trip treacherous. An archway marked the foot of the stairs, and they walked into a wide tunnel. A few rooms lined its length. One had a manual lift going back up to the surface, the rest contained slabs of stone, buckets, and carts. Pale dust marred the floor inside the rooms and trailed into the tunnel. And if Azul hadn't been so distracted by the blue light coming from a hole at the end, she would've recognized the dirt for what it was.

She passed the lamp to Esparza so her fingers could grip the iron railing separating her from the hole. Precious blue stone began a distance below her, no end to the hollow space in sight. This hole had been drilled straight into the Anchor chain keeping Cienpuentes in place.

"Gods," Esparza whispered, leaning over the railing. "What is this place?"

The railing, Azul realized belatedly, didn't reach across the tunnel, leaving an open spot. The floor there, old and uneven, dipped ever so slightly, showing the passage of wheel after wheel, foot after foot. Someone had attempted to wash it not long ago, managing instead to smear the pale dust on the floor.

"There is no ossuary," she said, perplexed. "They throw the bones into the hole."

They had thrown Isadora away.

XXX

THE COUNT, ONCE MORE

A YEAR AND A HALF EARLIER

The shutters were open to the night air, the curtains drawn. De Anví and Esparza peered through the curtains, watching the building across the street and the second-floor passageway linking it to the next house. Underneath another bridge, a trio of men huddled around a shabby brazier—the only light in the street aside from Luck and Wonder, which were currently hiding behind a cluster of clouds.

Esparza, wearing an old blue doublet, rubbed his arms. "Tell me again, De Anví, why we must suffer not only in the dark but in the cold."

De Anví didn't bother to answer, his attention returning to the door of the building opposite. The Countess de Losa and part of the King's Guard were waiting in another building up the street, ready to strike the main house, where the conspirators against the king hid. He and Esparza and a few City Guards had been pushed to the side to watch over this annex—a glorified servant's door attached by the walkway—in case someone managed to escape.

He didn't mind. He welcomed it, in fact. Let De Losa earn all the glory—he had no use for it. Once he was done with this mess, he'd go back to his family's homestead in the countryside, where people meant what they said, and he would be left alone and at peace.

"You're sure you found the queen's blood? You're sure it was there, in the crypt?" he asked, not for the first time. Asking settled the part of him that would not stop prodding his ribs. It worked for a few minutes, at least. "Did you take care to take one vial? We might need it to prove the child's identity."

"Two vials, resting there inside her stone casket, one now under lock and key. Did you know they put the old twin princes side by side? It's amazing their caskets haven't fallen off their ledge to get away from each other." A shiver ran down his frame. "Come to think of it, perhaps the stories are true and their essences remain behind to keep torturing each other. And they put King Harea in his own niche. I suppose getting away with murdering all four of your older siblings ought to be rewarded in some way."

"If you would like to ever collect your own reward," De Anví told him in a cold voice befitting the chilly space, "perhaps you could be of help and pay attention to the outside."

At the lack of response, he fixed his attention on Esparza. A small smile tugged on the man's lips, and his hand toyed with the edge of the curtain.

Realization hit him. "Gods, you're in love again."

Esparza grinned wide. "You know me too well."

"Put her out of your mind if only for a night, will you?"

The other man remained silent for a few moments, staring into the street without really seeing what was in front of him. "This time it might be fated."

"Our saving the king?"

"Ná. True love, De Anví. True love!"

"You've claimed such before," De Anví pointed out.

"Not like this, my friend. A kindred spirit at last."

Or at least for the next few weeks, De Anví thought dryly.

"I finally understand what you find so compelling about De Guzmán," Esparza said. De Anví gave him a sharp look, which Esparza met with a laugh. "I'm only interested in the younger sister, don't worry. Although, perhaps you should. The queen has been dead for over six months. Make your move before someone else catches Nereida's whim."

De Anví's heart made that strange leap it always did when he thought of Nereida. It sent heat through his veins and stabs of anxiety across his nerves. The worry, forever present in the back of his mind: that their courtship might never come to pass. "After the mourning," he said. "It wouldn't look right otherwise. You know some still think she's behind Her Majesty's death."

"You worry too much about what others might think. She was her lover for a few months, not her spouse. Everyone knows she had nothing to gain by her death. Think of Countess Leonés. She didn't care what others said when she took a new spouse three weeks after the old one ended up in the gutters."

"It is not your place to question me," De Anví reminded him. Esparza shrugged in a way that said he didn't care about the warning but he did care about enraging those who gave him coin.

Esparza had it partly right. While De Anví did not care what others said of him, he would not put Nereida in such a position. She deserved his best, and for her sake, he would wait.

Esparza leaned closer into the window, his whisper urgent and sharp. "Someone comes."

De Anví shook off the memories of his and Nereida's last dance together, although he could not get rid of the lingering bitterness. How different things might've been if only he had spoken up. He rubbed his chest, but the searing regret did not abate.

"A carriage," Esparza added in a lower voice.

De Anví heard it now, too, horses clopping on the flagstone. A simple covered cart appeared on the street, coming to a stop in front of the building. De Anví and Esparza tensed when two people alighted from the back and went to the door. It opened for them immediately, as if someone had also been keeping vigil.

The cart moved away, leaving the newcomers inside the house and the street deserted again.

"One of them carried a big bundle," Esparza said.

"A toddler. The king?"

Esparza gave him a sidelong glance. "Are you sure?"

De Anví flexed his hands. "That was the plan, according to the Witch."

"She also told us they would take him to the main house."

De Anví tapped the wall with his boot, attempting to find the perfect combination of speed and solidity with each *thunk* and cursing himself for beginning its search. Tearing himself away from the encroaching fixation and hardening his will against the anxiety stopping would produce, he shoved the curtain open and stepped over the windowsill. "We've been played," he snarled.

Alarmed, Esparza followed him through the opening. "The Witch lied to us?"

De Anví raised his hand and made a sign. One of the men huddled by the brazier under the bridge slipped away up the street. Trotting, Esparza and De Anví crossed the street and reached the narrow alleyway cornering the building.

"She's playing one of her games," De Anví whispered roughly.

"To what end?"

"To give me a present I do not want. She must've figured out De Losa is set to lead the charge on the main house and claim ownership of the plan's success, so she maneuvered the traitors to make the king end up here, or gave us the wrong information so De Losa would be at the wrong spot instead of us."

"Why not stop the ploy altogether? Why risk the king's life?" Esparza snorted. "No, never mind. I already know the answer."

Because the Witch didn't care about who resided in the Heart. She only cared about schemes and how much joy they brought her.

Esparza's hand landed on De Anví's cloaked arm. "There's someone else."

De Anví followed his gaze. A man was darting out of another alleyway, looking around before crossing the street.

"Not one of mine," Esparza added.

"Go deal with him," De Anví ordered curtly.

"No need, he comes to us," Esparza answered, going deeper into the alleyway and stopping by the far corner. He only had to wait a few moments before the newcomer hastened by the backstreet.

Esparza grabbed him and slammed him against the wall, twisting one arm behind his back.

"Wait," De Anví said. He walked closer to the struggling pair. The darkness was nearly complete, but something about the man's features felt familiar.

"Release me," the man seethed. "On the order of the City Guard."

"De Guzmán," De Anví said in surprise, his hand stilling around the grip of Valiente.

Esparza stepped back instantly. De Guzmán spun and glared at them. "How dare you?"

"Mind your words with His Honor, the Count de Anví," Esparza barked.

De Guzmán stiffened and lowered his head. "Your Honor." His gaze flickered to the other man. "Esparza?"

"Why are you sneaking around?" Esparza asked, his tone low but menacing.

"I . . . Oh, you're the reason, isn't it?" De Guzmán turned angry. "She lied to me about Iriana, and she came to meet you, didn't she? What have you dragged Edine into this time? Curse you—"

"Lower your voice," De Anví snapped.

"Sorry, Your Honor," De Guzmán said, immediately contrite.

Esparza took hold of De Guzmán's doublet and pushed him against the wall again. "What do you mean about Edine?"

"She's somewhere around here," De Guzmán hissed. "Looking for you in the middle of the night, I bet. How dare you drag her into one of your schemes?"

Esparza's hold loosened. "I have no meeting with Edine, De Guzmán. I am here with the count today. Where is she? What is she doing around here?"

De Guzmán's shoulders crumpled, his anger vanishing. "Oh, damn, she was telling the truth."

"Explain."

"She's convinced some dirty ploy is being done behind our sister's back."

De Anví was suddenly alert. "Your middle sister?"

"No, Iriana. Edine wanted to investigate some rumors. I've been trying to find her in this maze." He hesitated. "Will you help me look for her?"

Esparza opened his mouth, but De Anví made a sound of warning.

More sounds came, different ones, from a distance: faraway shouts and the rumble of running.

Esparza cursed and pushed De Guzmán away. He glared at De Anví, as if seeking permission, but De Anví could not give it. Saving the king was more important than following his latest conquest.

"Go," Esparza barked to De Guzmán. "Find Edine and take her away. I will find her later and we'll sort this out."

De Anví didn't wait to see if De Guzmán did as he was told. He strode back to the main street and turned the corner. A second later, Esparza joined him, rapier in hand. Figures ran through the passageway above.

Ahead of them, the door of the house started to open. Esparza took two fast steps and kicked it the rest of the way. Cries rose, a scramble. Esparza produced a dagger in his free hand and went in.

"By the gods' Anchor bones!" he exclaimed with savage relish, "I will make short work of you lot, for I've got someone waiting for me."

Opening his cloak and unsheathing Valiente, De Anví followed.

THE PRESENT

No smile, no mischief, graced Nereida de Guzmán's features when she appeared at the entrance of the small storage room. De Anví drank in the sight—the black hair artfully gathered in a braid around her head, the dark blue waistcoat, the embroidered cream-colored breeches, the polished ankle boots. She was the hardest, most bitter liquor he had ever tasted: burning all the way down to his chest, grabbing an instant hold of his mind. He didn't move from his place by the lamp, his back against the wall, and he watched her gaze take in the room, take in the Witch sitting on a crate, then widen as it found him.

Nereida despised surprises as much as he did, and the tightening of her mouth told De Anví he would pay for this at some point. A price he was eager to pay for catching her fleeting, unguarded shock.

She had worn her expressions in the form of a mask for too long, and he was desperate to see it gone.

"My heart!" exclaimed the Faceless Witch, still wearing Sío de Guzmán. "What a surprise! Nereida de Guzmán, back in Cienpé."

De Anví dragged his gaze to the Witch. Her expression—what he could see of it under the mask—appeared fascinated.

Nereida entered the room properly, stopping a few paces away. She wore no mask, her green eyes hard and cold in the lamplight. "Blessed night, Witch." A slight nod toward De Anví. "Count de Anví."

Call me Emiré, De Anví had wanted to ask in their last dance, before the queen interrupted it. He had never gotten his wish. Uncrossing his arms, he took a side step to stand by the Witch's left shoulder. The move did not go unnoticed, and Nereida's chin rose ever so slightly at the display.

"Last I heard," said the Witch in a good-humored voice, "you were well on your way to Valanje. Did the envoy get turned around in the sea?"

"The envoy had no trouble getting passage across," Nereida answered in clipped tones.

"Ah, Valanjian food, then. Was it not to your liking and you had no choice but to return?"

"The food was not a problem."

The Witch let out a short laugh. "You missed me, then, is that it?"

De Anví felt a muscle in his jaw jump at the same time Nereida furrowed her nose with distaste. She recovered fast, smoothing her expression.

The Witch hopped off the crate and stretched her arms. "Or perhaps," she said cunningly, "you've come back out of concern for De Anví's attempted kidnapping?"

She gave De Anví a fast glance. "Kidnapping?"

Damn the Void if he wasn't shocked at the hint of concern in her voice. Words left his throat before he could stop them. "It was nothing of concern."

She remained silent, so the Witch spoke instead: "Did you at least gather what I need?"

De Anví had suspected that Nereida wasn't in the envoy for the sake of the court's interest in Valanjian dealings. Now he had his proof.

"I didn't have the time, no." Nereida took a step closer. Something morphed in her expression, in her posture. Her hatred for the Witch shone through.

The Witch huffed. "If concern for His Honor did not force your hand, and you didn't bother with my inquiries, why are you here? We had a deal, did we not, Nereida de Guzmán?" She patted her chest. "Do you not care about your brother's body any longer? I'd have thought you still did, having lost one sister already."

Nereida smiled, a slow curving of her lips that sent De Anví's heart pounding. This was his Nereida. The Nereida of the dances, the fearless sword fighter, the one whose eyes kindled and sparkled with all kinds of mischief.

He was back in the ballrooms, back in his dreams, back in his hopes. He was undone.

"I've changed my mind," Nereida said, full of mockery. Her mask was gone, her feelings out in the world.

The Witch cocked her head. "Changed your mind? Well, you are young enough to think things can go as easily as that."

Nereida looked at De Anví. "Will you stop me?"

Unnecessary question, for he would never. He thought of Esparza and his desperate wait for the Lord Death. Well, De Anví had always known he would win that race. "No."

"Hold her for me, then."

He grabbed the Witch's arms, immobilizing them.

Stilling after an initial struggle, the Witch asked, "What's this? A betrayal by my closest allies? I am impressed, it must be said." She craned her neck to glance at De Anví. "You are aware of the consequences of this, yes?"

De Anví allowed nothing to show on his face. "Yes."

Then Nereida brought out a dagger, and the Witch pressed into his chest. The renewed struggle didn't last long, and her body relaxed. De Anví had no doubt that her infuriatingly smug smile was back on her face.

"Now, put that away, child," the Witch said. "You want me to believe you'll hurt your own brother?"

Nereida came closer, the smile broadening, the Witch stiffening. "Ah," she said, "but you are not my brother, are you?"

She plunged the blade into the Witch's gut, and De Anví felt the body jerk in his arms, felt his own limbs stiffen in response and sweat gather at the back of his neck. Disbelief and relief warred inside him—that she had dared, and that it was over.

"I wonder what happens now," Nereida said smoothly, her hand pushing the dagger farther in. "Will you die along with your host, Witch?"

The Witch hissed, and her body went lax in De Anví's arms. He grunted and lowered her to the floor, propping her back against the crate.

Blood pooled from the wound when Nereida yanked the blade out. She made no move to stop the flow, and neither did De Anví. He simply looked at her, waiting for a cue. Would she turn the dagger on him now? He almost welcomed it. A much better way to die than what lay in wait for him—one did not cross the Witch, and one did not get rid of the Witch quite so easily.

"Nereida?" The rough words came out of the injured body, laced with pain, with shock, with regret—and warmth. Feelings the Witch was incapable of.

The Witch was gone.

Nereida knelt by the man's side and grasped his hand. "Si-so."

Sío de Guzmán looked down, blinked, then looked back at her, at the bloody dagger abandoned to the side. "Someone stabbed me?"

"It's only temporary," she assured him, and for the first time, De Anví wondered if he had done right in helping her. There was no coming back from this type of wound.

"No," De Guzmán pleaded. He coughed and blood spattered on the beautiful white cravat, the cream-and-gold waistcoat, chosen by the Witch, no doubt, to mock the count. "No, Nida, let me die here."

Nereida's grip tightened. "It sounds impossible, but I promise you, you will come back to me soon enough."

"I don't doubt you," De Guzmán answered after another bloody cough. He grimaced in pain when he tried to sit straighter, his free hand pressing against the wound. "You and Edine—you always got what you went after. But not this time, Nida. Let me die, finally."

"Don't be a fool," Nereida told him roughly. "The Witch won't have the opportunity to get her claws into you again. We'll leave, and she will never force you into being her toy again."

"I wasn't a toy."

"Of course you were. She stole your conscience and your body just to play one of her games."

"I was willing."

"What?"

Her brother's pained gaze sought hers. "I entered the contract willingly, Nida. The Witch didn't force me."

Nereida dropped his hand like it was a red-hot coal. Sío tried to take hers back, but she wouldn't let him.

"Explain," she demanded, her face taking on a deathly pallor.

"Understand me, Sister, I beg of you. I had to find a way to forget."

"Forget? Forget Edine?" she asked in disbelief. "Why would you want that?"

"No!" he exclaimed, and spat more blood onto his waistcoat. "I would never want to forget Edine." He straightened, his eyes bright with urgency. "Don't you see? She died because of me. It was my fault. I knew where she was going that night, Nereida. She came to me, worried Iriana was involved in treason against the king. I stood by, too scared to act. I chose to believe she was imagining things, and then I was too late to find her. They cut her down not three streets from me, and I could've stopped them! I could've stopped them but . . ." He slumped back, the sudden burst of energy gone. "I did nothing, Nida. Nothing. I stood there, a coward. I did nothing. I didn't even have the guts to face her body. I let Iriana deal with it all."

"No." Nereida wiped tears from her cheeks, leaving a smear of blood across her skin. "Be quiet!" she cried when Sío tried to speak again. "It was not your hand that killed her. You were being used yourself. It's what you like doing best, isn't it?" she asked with fury. "Being used by others? Iriana, the Guard, the Witch?" Her mouth compressed into a thin line. Then, "It ends now. Now you get to live and undo your wrongs. Not by being someone's toy and forgetting, but by living on."

She raised her dagger and stabbed him in the chest. A slight miscalculation, a crack of a rib. De Anví slapped a panicked hand on Sío's mouth, muffling his scream. Then Nereida leaned into the hilt and slid the blade all the way into her brother's heart.

Sío went limp, head lolling to the side. De Anví removed his hand and wiped the red palm on Sío's shirtsleeve.

"Why?" Nereida said in a shaky voice. "Why are you here?"

De Anví looked at her bowed head, yearned to take her face in his hands and tilt it upward—the position did not suit her.

"Why?" she demanded again, this time looking at him. "Why would you help me like this? Do you enjoy being a murderer too?"

De Anví sat back on his heels. "I trust your judgment. Of all of Sancia, of all of Luciente, you're the one I trust."

"Why?" she shouted. "If you trust me so much, why wouldn't you help me before I was forced to do all this?"

"I did help you," he pointed out. "I kept an eye on him, did I not?"

"That's not . . . Why? We have barely talked in over a year, and now . . . what? What would make you trust me like that? Are you so daft you cannot trust yourself and you need someone else to guide you through life on a leash? Do you think you know me so well from some worthless conversation and a few dances? How weak you are! You had no trouble letting me go to the queen; you had no trouble staying away. Is that what you enjoy? Watching, knowing you'll never be good enough to partake?"

De Anví leaned over her brother's body and took her shaking hands in his. His gaze held hers, his voice steady. "Do not doubt, Nereida. Whatever it is you came here to do, whatever it is that made you scare the Witch away and end your brother's life, see it through."

Her eyes were a kind of witchery in themselves, a raging storm one moment, a calm sea the next. The agitation in her face ebbed; her breathing eased. With her hands still within his grip, she took a few deep breaths.

The familiar sharpness returned an instant later.

"What did the Witch mean," she asked, freeing her hands and standing, "by asking if you were aware of the consequences?"

De Anví straightened up along with her. "It has been in my mind for a while now, the possibility that she might use her dreams to gain the ability to harm her clients. The possibility for blackmail is too high to pass up."

"You mean something like poison?" Nereida asked, taken aback. "You think using her dreams gives her the chance to poison you?"

"Careful, De Guzmán," he chided her, "your worry for my person is showing."

"Not worry, De Anví, only shock that you would be fool enough to take her dreams."

De Anví went to the door and peered outside the room. "It was the only way I had to reach you."

"Even after suspecting she might poison you?"

A shrug was his answer.

"But even then, why help me tonight," she insisted, "if you suspected this might happen?"

He gave her a small half smile. "I wished to be of real help, for once." Opening the door wider, he stepped outside into the corridor connecting the room with a high bridge between buildings. "Grab the lamp. It's time for us to leave."

Nereida didn't move. "How long do you think you have?"

"I do not know, so we better go ahead with the rest of your plan before I am forced to pay my due."

"If you insist," she said, kneeling again by her brother and pulling her dagger out of his body. "But I can only hope your willingness to help will remain after what must be done."

Then, to De Anví's shock, she proceeded to dig the dagger into one of Sío de Guzmán's fingers and make an awful mess of cutting it off.

XXXI

THE OSSUARY

"What?" Esparza asked sharply.

Azul loosened her grip on the railing and looked at the pale dust crossing her palms. "They throw the bones into the pit," she repeated to herself. "They don't keep them."

Esparza peered over the railing. "Makes sense," he murmured.

"Makes sense?" Stepping away from the hole, she shouted, "How does it make sense?" And damn the gods if it didn't feel like each word was starting to shred her throat.

"Well, they do tell us over and over, don't they? That our bones return in death to the gods." Esparza's voice held a note of fascination. "I just assumed it was more metaphorical."

"Returned to the gods," Azul repeated. With her mind still blank, that was all she could manage. But now she began to see it, too, the sense in it—their bones into the gods' bones. Thrown into the Anchor, into a pit with no bottom. She looked down. The dust on her palms offered no answer. If the bones went into the Anchor, then . . .

Then Isadora . . .

She should've taken two fingers. Three fingers. She should've known. She should've prepared. She should've . . . She . . .

"But it can't be," she said in a small voice, her gaze fluttering everywhere. "There are still bones nearby."

Enjul gripped her arms, turned her to face him. "Where? Take me to them."

"Why?" Azul asked, shaken by the ill-concealed eagerness in his voice, the excitement cracking what was usually a stoic or mocking expression.

Comprehension dawned, a horrific kind of understanding. A sense of betrayal so deep if her heart wasn't already breaking, it would have cleaved in half. "You knew. You knew Isadora . . . You knew about the bones."

Arrogance claimed what she could see of his features outside the mask. "You keep forgetting I am the Emissary of the Lord Death, no matter how many times I tell you. I know all there is to know about death. You would, too, if only you listened, if only you bothered to ask. How many times have you been told that the living return to the gods? It is only you who is at fault for not knowing, not I. Now take me to the bones."

Azul wrenched her arms out of his grasp. "Why?" she yelled. Then another scream, inside her mind, for Isadora. Then a third, when she answered herself, "The bones . . . The other necromancer?"

"Necromancer?" Esparza asked, suddenly wary.

"You think the other necromancer is here," Azul accused.

"What better place for one who deals with death than among the remains of the dead?"

"But I hate bodies."

"Yet you are attracted to bones, aren't you?" Enjul advanced on her. "You are attracted to death. You are curious to figure out what you are, although you won't admit it. It corrodes your insides, that need to know. That's why you were so eager to visit the land of the Lord Death when the opportunity arose."

"Why wait until now? Why . . ." The answer presented itself once again: because he couldn't gain entrance to the ossuary either. Not without making his presence as the emissary known. So, he had waited for her to find access for him.

Azul laughed, a short, rough sound. "How disappointed you must have been! Leaving me alone so much, allowing me so much freedom." She laughed again. This back-and-forth she thought they had been playing as equals hadn't been a duel at all. It had been a children's game where he moved the toys, and she made for a pretty doll. "How frustrating it must have been for you to see me fumble over and over, getting no closer to the ossuary."

"Until now."

Her fist came up, but Esparza caught her arm.

"I don't know what's going on," Esparza said, letting Azul's arm go, "but rather than brawl, we should leave if we're done."

Enjul took her wrist. He wore gloves tonight. *How smart*, Azul thought viciously. How well planned it all had been. "We are not done," he said. "Where are the bones?"

Azul fought to free her wrist, saw Esparza reach for his rapier. "I'm done," she told Enjul. "The Void take you."

The emissary pulled her closer, and Azul was tempted to spit in his face. What a contrast to the last time they had been this close! "But what if she's there, with those other bones? Your Isadora."

Her heart sank, then jumped with a furious beat. "You godsdamned asshole. Why do you hate me so much?"

"I do not hate you," he snarled.

"Liar. It reeks out of you!" she shouted. "We're the same—"

"We are *not* the same. I am dying. We are all dying, except for you. *You* are not dying."

"I don't understand!"

He took a deep breath. "It doesn't matter. Go to the bones," he added, pushing her.

And Azul went, because he was right. It was grasping at unraveling threads, but it was a chance: Isadora, simply forgotten in one of these rooms instead of resting somewhere in the bottomless hole. Isadora, not lost at all. *Isadora*—a litany in Azul's head stopping her from punching the walls, from screaming until her words were made of blood, from tearing her ribs apart so air could get into her lungs. From wrenching her heart out so it stopped hurting so much.

Esparza stepped up to her side, still skimming the sheath of his rapier. He did not like the situation—that much was obvious—but he had no stake in it. Maybe he would help her kill Enjul. Maybe he would stand aside and watch.

But he would not stop her.

And she had Nereida's dagger, with its beautiful bone hilt.

Virel Enjul deserved to die. For his games. For Zenjiel's death and the deaths he meant to cause when he caught the other necromancer's victims.

The certainty of this conclusion calmed the rage in her veins. Azul would check these bones, then she would end the Emissary of the Lord Death.

And after . . . Ah yes, why not? Afterward, she would simply step into the pit to join Isadora and the gods.

It'd be easier than trying to figure out who Azul del Arroyo was without Isadora by her side, why she existed, and why her heart didn't seem to do anything but break.

The first corridor led nowhere interesting. Her sense of bones was stronger this deep, away from the city, and so close to the Anchor, but not focused enough. The second corridor proved to be of more use, forking deeper into a web of tunnels and rooms. These were blocked by doors that looked like they hadn't been opened in years. Ahead, they could see the warm glow of lamplight across a bend in the tunnel. Carefully, Esparza placed their own lamp on the floor and waited to see Enjul's next move.

Enjul addressed Azul in a low voice: "Can you tell how many?"

She glared, disgusted. "No. That's not how it works."

"Chance a look."

Why her? She didn't ask, for it mattered little, so she simply did. And after she did, a hiss escaped her.

"Two men guarding a door," she whispered. "Living corpses. Necromancer's victims," she corrected herself.

"Excuse me?" asked Esparza.

Enjul ignored him. "We need to get inside, then."

"Is that some sort of secret order?" Esparza asked. "The living corpses?"

Enjul assessed him, then said, "Get us inside, guard. Use your blue tabard to send them away. It's best if they don't see us."

Esparza hesitated, clearly torn between giving in to his curiosity and bristling at the emissary's tone. In the end, he simply shrugged and muttered, "Ah well, this—my lot in life."

Sauntering, he rounded the corner. "Blessed Noche Verde, folks."

"Stop," said a voice. "These are restricted quarters."

"I'm under official City Guard orders. I need you to step away while I conduct my business."

"Stop," another repeated, "upon penalty of death."

Esparza snorted, plenty familiar with the threat. "You're not going to make this easy, are you?"

"You have no power here, Blue Bastard. Go back outside."

A pause, then the noise of scuffling. Enjul, mouth tight in a grim line, rounded the corner to join him, Azul right behind. Esparza had twisted one guard's arm around his back so the man couldn't reach his rapier, and was using him as a shield against the other guard, who had produced a pistol.

"Couldn't have warned me about that?" Esparza asked of Azul.

"I didn't see—" Azul winced as Enjul landed a blow on the second guard's arm, forcing him to drop the pistol.

The first guard twisted his free arm to try to rake Esparza's face. Grunting, Esparza leaned backward. The guard finished the turn and jerked his arm free, then reached for his rapier. Esparza landed a fist on his jaw, sending him staggering to the wall. A punch to his stomach followed, and then another finishing blow to his temple. The guard fell to the floor, unconscious.

Esparza turned to help Enjul with the other guard, but there was no need—the emissary had dealt with his foe by impaling his guts with his sword, then twisting it home.

The guard fell, gurgling and convulsing, specks of blood splattering the ground.

"Gods!" Esparza had gone pale. "There was no need for death."

"They were already dead," Enjul said simply, sinking his sword into the other guard's chest.

Esparza jumped away. "Well, *now* you've made sure."

The emissary cleaned his sword on the guard's clothing and returned it to its sheath. Kneeling by the door, he started to work on the lock. Esparza eyed him warily, moving until he was between him and Azul.

Azul understood the fast glances Esparza sent over his shoulder to the corridor beyond. She wanted to leave, too, but where was she to go? If there were bones in that room, she had to know. And she wasn't eager to be alone with Enjul.

So, she didn't encourage him to run, and his stance relaxed. Maybe he had convinced himself there had been no other option but to kill the guards. Maybe it wasn't such an outlandish occurrence in his daily life. Whatever his thoughts, Esparza eventually approached the door, Azul following him as if tethered by a rope.

"Smaller lock," he surmised. "Newer. Harder to pick."

Azul studied the mechanism in question and found that he was right. The whole door appeared new compared with the ones they had seen along the way.

Enjul stepped aside to allow Esparza to try his hand at the lock and glanced at Azul.

In the warm light of the lamp ensconced into the nearby wall, his golden-violet eyes showed no remorse, only determination verging on stubbornness. Such human emotion for such inhuman acts—killing like it meant nothing and not asking for forgiveness in return. This logic, Azul could never understand.

But had she not done the same? Had she not stood by as Nereida had attempted to kill Enjul because he stood in their way? Had she not sworn to kill him herself minutes earlier? She had said it before so many times—at their core, she and Enjul were not so different.

These unsettling thoughts were stopped by Esparza's exclamation of triumph. The door opened. Azul rushed forward, pushing him out of the way, and stumbled into the room.

Inside were two tables, and shelves lining a wall. Papers, parchment, and sheafs of vellum lay spread over the tables or rolled into scrolls. Azul walked to a collection of small wooden coffers neatly stacked on a shelf, their lids unlocked for her to lift. Pieces of bones filled their insides. Old, new. None felt like Isadora's.

"What is all this?" Esparza asked, disgusted.

Azul drifted to where he stood, searching for more boxes that might contain bones. He was looking at some of the papers piled on one of the tables, lifting one here and there with the tips of his fingers to see them under the light spilling from the doorway. Most of them featured inked drawings of bones, the rest of the space filled with annotations.

"Studies of human bones," she told him, herself inspecting some of the pages.

Her words brought Enjul closer.

"A leech's studies," Esparza said. "Why keep them behind lock and key and armed guards?" He made a disagreeable sound. "Upon penalty of death, my ass."

"Can you read?" she asked him.

Esparza narrowed his eyes. "Enough to pass by."

"I meant no insult," Azul said. "But try these."

He did as she asked with the page she was showing him. "I can't make any sense of this." Glancing at Enjul, he added, "Valanjian?"

Enjul shook his head. "It looks like an abbreviated version of Sancian."

"A sort of code?" Azul asked. "Meant to be read only by its author."

"Some of these look normal," Esparza said, disturbing more of the parchment.

"Borrowed studies?"

"Why keep them behind locked doors?" Esparza insisted, then looked thunderstruck and snatched his hand back from the table. "Living corpses, you called them? Void arts? No. It's not possible."

Azul turned so he couldn't read her face. The stark denial in his voice did not settle well, nor did his disgust. Her gaze fell on sketches of much better quality. Bringing them into a better light, she openly admired them. Arms, legs, torsos, heads, all in various stages of being stripped of their fleshy layers. Then a series of drawings she recognized well. A human back in different poses, some with arms extended, others with arms close to the sides. Studies that had resulted in a masterpiece.

The masterpiece that hung in her brother's bedroom.

Alarmed, Azul went through the other pages. The strokes were easily recognizable, with the occasional signature leaping out. Shock left her speechless. Was Isile Manzar the other necromancer, after all? His fascination for the human body was obvious. He could've gained entrance here like he had gained entrance to the mortuary—by using his friends. But again, what care would Manzar have for infiltrating the City Guard, the court? For taking over Zenjiel?

No, Manzar must've made these sketches for the other necromancer as some sort of commission . . .

Ah.

She saw it now. On the crest of some of the papers, on the dried rose petals in a vase in the corner. In the handwriting, the same as the letter she'd received at the ambassador's residence agreeing and delighted to host her and her party at Almanueva.

"It's my brother, isn't it? He's the other necromancer," she said as if waking from a dream. She faced Enjul. He showed no surprise or interest in the discovery. "You knew this too."

She thought he might mock her, laugh at the lack of awareness on her part. Instead, he kept his voice measured: "A conjecture so far. The ossuary falls under the marquess's purview"—Azul jerked back as if slapped—"and he is your half brother. Knowing I am from Valanje, he probably grew cautious and hid his living corpses from my sight and thus from yours as well. That made it harder to confirm."

Azul's mind was a moving puzzle, trying to make all the pieces fit.

"I thought . . . You said you could recognize the other necromancer."

"His foulness is different, undetectable, unlike you. It could be he's already lost what makes you unique, from using it too much."

"A necromancer?" Esparza exclaimed. He ran a hand through his hair. "Do such things truly exist?"

Enjul's attention remained fixed on Azul. "If we kill him, will it end his creations?"

Azul sputtered at this. "You can't. He's my brother!"

"He's *murdered*, don't you understand? One or two: accidents, perhaps, as with your sister. But this many? He must be stopped."

"Not by death! How would you be any different from him, then? Take him to your Order, lock him somewhere like you planned to do to me. Allow these people he's brought back to fulfill their lives. It is their right."

"Their right is to rest with the Lord Death."

"How do you know?"

"Because I carry his will within me!"

"And why is your god's will more important than theirs? That's what makes you so enraged, isn't it, Enjul?" She spat the words. "You've seen death all your life and resigned yourself to it, and now you're scared to hope there's an alternative, that your faith has been for nothing. Prove to me I'm wrong."

"You mean to say that they are still people?" Esparza said, his nervous hand roaming over his stubble, over his neck.

Azul glared at Enjul. "Of course they are."

To her surprise, instead of sneering, Enjul's eyes widened at her words. She didn't quite understand why until she looked down and saw the tip of a rapier sticking out of his chest.

XXXII

HEARTS

ONE YEAR EARLIER

"Have you ever been in love, Azulita?"

Azul looked up from a lovely spread of daggers on sale at the local market. The seller was on her way to Valanje, so none of the hilts sported any Anchor. This suited Azul fine—to have a hilt adorned with Anchor only attracted thieves and trouble.

"Solis Monte, two years ago. You bet my heart in a game of cards, then chased him out of Agunción with Maravillosa after you lost."

Isadora laughed. "If he had truly returned the depth of your feelings, he would've stayed put." She bumped Azul's shoulder with her own, uncaring of the wonders spread on the linen cloth in front of them. Daggers were nothing to Isadora but rapiers cut short. "But, then, I don't think your feelings went that deep, did they?"

Azul remembered the nights spent with Solis's letters under her pillow, the afternoons looking inside the patio and imagining their future house. The Lady Dream had cast a spell on her, and it had disappeared when Solis did, leaving nothing but a small feeling of loss and a lot of bafflement.

But Azul had too much pride to admit as much. "What was he to do? Meet you in a duel at dawn and risk harming my older sister?"

"Ah, Azulita. Love makes you risk everything!"

Azul would agree, remembering how she had sneaked into the inn's pantry to cut Isadora's finger. But her sister was talking about another kind of love. A kind of love Isadora had experienced over and over—sudden, bright, and powerful like the hottest of fires, then ashes after a few days.

To risk everything for such a love seemed inconvenient at best and unwise at worst.

"Perhaps one day I will meet a person like that," Azul said, unconvinced.

"I think you will. Someone who makes you want to be close even if you don't understand why. Someone you want to meet again and again, to exchange swords with, to place bets, to goad into submission. Sometimes you will hate them for it, and you won't understand why you cannot think of anyone but them. And sometimes you'll think you'd be nothing without them."

Isadora's gaze grew distant, and Azul followed it to the pink sky of winter.

"And if you're lucky," Isadora continued, "you will recognize the feeling for what it is before it's too late and they slip out of your reach."

Miss something so obvious? Azul asked herself. *Doubtful.*

THE PRESENT

Esparza cursed and charged the man behind Enjul—one of the two guards left for dead outside. Lightning-fast, he ran a dagger across his throat.

Azul caught Enjul as his legs buckled. Grunting, she dropped to the floor, hard on her knees. With growing horror, she looked over his shoulder to see the guard stumble back, throat gaping open, then steady himself, rapier raised, ready to strike again.

"Fuck!" Esparza exclaimed, hitting the guard's face with the hilt of his dagger. The man crashed against one of the tables, then tried to right himself. Esparza fell on him, smashing his dagger on the guard's head, over and over until all the body did was twitch, and then again and again until that, too, finally stopped.

Breathing hard, Esparza stepped away, his face and the front of his tabard spattered with blood. "Gods!" he yelled. "*Gods!*"

"The other!" shouted Azul.

Esparza jerked back. The second guard filled the doorway, a hole in his waistcoat marking the spot where Enjul had twisted his sword. Losing no time, the guard lifted his pistol and fired.

The explosion tore into their ears. Azul hunched and wrapped her arms around Enjul, squeezing her eyes tight, then blinking away tears. Esparza looked shocked but unhurt and, recovering much faster than her, tackled the second guard.

Azul loosened her grip on Enjul and let him slide to the floor. Stumbling forward, she reached for the living corpse as he grabbed Esparza's throat, grasping the guard's sleeve, pulling the fabric until she found skin.

The guard's hold slackened immediately. The muscle under his clothes shrank until he crumpled to the floor in a mass of cloth and fetid flesh.

Esparza retched. "Fuck," he said in a broken whisper, then wiped his mouth with the back of his hand. He dared a look at the remains of the guard and shuddered. Bringing two crossed fingers to his chest, he muttered, "Blessed Heart have mercy on me, keep me safe from those who'll drag me into the Void."

Azul knelt by Enjul. Coughs shook his body. He lifted a hand and tried to rake at his mask, so Azul removed it for him. His eyes were naked in their shock. Terror stiffened every line of his face.

Trembling, she opened his waistcoat and shirt. An ugly puncture wound was seeping blood down his chest. She pressed her hands against it, trying to stem the bleeding. His skin had lost all color; sweat had plastered his hair to his temples and neck. She pressed harder.

"But at Diel . . ." She faltered, caught by the strange brightness in his eyes.

He opened his mouth, coughed more blood, then wrinkled his brows. He tried again, and she leaned down.

His hand sneaked up to touch her face, trembling and clammy against her skin.

"Go, Azul," he managed. "He cannot know what you are."

"No," she said, hands firm on his chest. "He must already guess I killed his guard and Zenjiel."

"Might still . . . doubt which of us . . . Go. You're a . . . liability . . . for him."

Still Azul refused. "We'll get help."

A smile curved his lips, small and genuine and the most unguarded thing she had ever witnessed from him. "Too late, Azul. The god . . ."

"But you can't die," she said, voice hitching. "You're not supposed to be able to die. Ask your god to save you!"

"Not here. Not . . . this time."

Then she understood. How could the Lord Death do that in Sancia? This was not his domain. Unlike in Valanje, Sancians had killed all connection between the gods and the land by ransacking their bones.

Enjul's eyes widened, and his mouth suddenly twisted in horror, his body attempting to recoil from her.

"Don't bring me back," he begged in such a frightened voice it raised the hairs of her arms. "I want to stay with him."

Tears sprang to her eyes. She saw herself then as he saw her: a monster, something worse than death.

"Stop," she begged. "I promise. Save your breath."

Enjul stopped moving. And still, she pressed against the wound.

And pressed.

Until Esparza grabbed her arm and jerked her to her feet. "He's dead," he said grimly. "We have to go."

"No." She reached for Enjul, her vision blurry. "We can't leave him."

Unrelenting, Esparza dragged her along with him. "We can't be seen here. We must leave before the change of guard." He stepped over the remains of the guard, and Azul stumbled on the man's bones, squelching through the putrid flesh.

Esparza winced but didn't stop. He took her back to their abandoned lamp, to the main tunnel, up the stairs, through the open door and the iron gate and the maze of a building upstairs. Her free hand left a trail of bloody smears as she used the walls to steady her faltering limbs.

Outside, he forced her to face him. "With Luck's help, they'll think they killed each other," he said, his tone low, hurried, and quite serious. "Tell no one of what happened here, not even De Guzmán. Make your excuses to whomever you have to and leave town. Leave tomorrow, if you can. Make something up—a missive from your family or some such. It doesn't matter."

And then he was gone and Azul was alone.

Alone.

No Isadora. No Enjul.

Dazed, she made her way back to the crowded streets, walking aimlessly. Captain de Macia's name came to mind, but her head was spinning, the smells and the sounds and the heat from the crowd so overwhelming, Azul couldn't pin down her thoughts.

She stumbled into someone, murmured some apology, bumped somebody else, apologized again. Then someone ran into her, patted her back, and kept going. Invitations were shouted her way; songs drifted in and out of her ears. A hand checked for a purse, alas she kept her few coins inside her breeches.

No Esparza to keep people at bay. No shadow to ask for directions. No emissary to keep track of.

What was this despair carving a hole inside her? Shouldn't she be glad Virel Enjul was dead? Hadn't she wished for him to get lost, leaving her all the time in the world to find Isadora's bones?

Now she was free of him—free of their deal, free of her promises. It had only cost another rip in her heart. Another death she couldn't undo.

And Azul hated death.

She hated death almost as much as she hated her brother.

How she had begged to gain access to the ossuary! How she had trusted him! How he must have delighted in seeing her fumbling to achieve nothing.

How enraging.

Azul found a few citizens able to give her directions and headed toward Almanueva. A footman opened the main door for her and tried to tell her something. She ignored him, crossed the tiled floors with fast strides, and stomped up the stairs. A musty smell assaulted her nose, like wet plants left in a closed room for too long. It permeated the long dark corridor. She knew her way by now and lost no time in flinging open her brother's door.

The woman on the painting sneered at her under Luck and Wonder's brightness, the man with the axe was suddenly leery. She couldn't face the flesh-stripped back on the wall.

The door to her brother's private study was locked. She slammed her shoulder against it, but the lock held.

Rubbing her shoulder, she approached the closest window. Leaning across the sill, she confirmed the study had its own window, but although the exterior wall had a ridge she could use to cross between the rooms, she wasn't sure she could open the other window from the outside. She was only a floor up, but the drop was significant, and Azul did not possess the gift of mending bones.

She started with the drawers in the desk, then the trunk at the foot of the bed. She didn't hide her intentions; she emptied every nook with no care for their contents. Nobody came to stop her, and she welcomed the sense of accomplishment as she threw thing after thing to the rug or the wall. She laid waste to the room until she found a key for the locked door.

Her brother's study was a simple continuation of his bedroom: same white and gold walls, same elegant furniture. A bigger desk was set flush below the window, with a tall-backed chair abandoned at an angle. Another shelf lined the far wall, an ornate creation of golden lines and blond wood with grates of thin, painted metal protecting the heavy tomes inside. A chest of drawers stood alone in a corner, and when she opened them, she found another collection of bones.

The problem with being aware of bones, she realized, was that there were *always* bones. Dead bones, living bones—they were all the same, a constant surrounding her.

To anyone else, these might look like animal bones, but she knew better. Some looked new, others yellowed with age. How young had her brother been when he began his collection?

On top of the desk, she found more sketches, and in a locked drawer she managed to wrench open, a few bundles. She carefully unwrapped the bundles on the desk. They all held bone pieces that had been glued together to make fully formed fingers. She didn't dare touch them directly.

Another drawer contained jars filled with clear viscous liquid, while another had a box filled with brushes and small, delicate metal tools.

She wished to look away from the bone fingers, but couldn't. They were mesmerizing.

Her brother was an artist. A sculptor of bone. *And an artist must practice*, she thought. But not in such a small room. The ossuary was his place of study; this was his home away from the ossuary, a place to test things when inspiration struck in the middle of the night. He must keep his main collection—a collection that might include her sister's bones—elsewhere. *And why not?* Azul raged to herself, fighting against the crushing despair. He was old enough, he might've seen Isadora's bones in his first forays into the ossuary; he might've taken a liking to them. Was she not Isadora, after all?

Don't bring me back.

The terrified look in Enjul's eyes haunted her from the edges of her mind.

Now that she had proof of her brother being the other necromancer, now that she couldn't ignore the truth, it chilled her to the core.

Would Isadora ask for the same fate, given the choice?

"Breaking into your brother's rooms, Sirese Del Arroyo? How unsisterly."

Azul spun toward the door.

XXXIII

AZUL

Isile Manzar stood unmasked on the threshold of her brother's study, ignoring Azul's shock while he surveyed the room with open and obvious curiosity.

Voice unsteady, Azul asked, "What are you doing here?"

His attention went to the desk. "What are those?"

Azul glanced down at her brother's art. "Fingers."

Joining her at the desk, Isile picked one up. "A sculpture? Painted clay?"

Azul had enough of her brother's rooms, so she answered as she left, "Bone," and heard a gasp of dismay and the dull thud of the finger hitting the desk's surface.

She went to the guest rooms next. Nereida's door opened easily, her room a haven of tidiness compared to the rooms she had just left. Kneeling by Nereida's trunk, she began to search its contents.

Isile loitered by the door. "It's not on me to judge De Gracia's interests," he said, shuddering, "but are you sure it's bone?"

"What are you doing here?" she asked again, pulling a few shirts out of the trunk.

"Is this your room?" he asked, then inhaled sharply. "Have you been wounded? Your hands . . ."

The concern in his voice stopped Azul. Dried blood still crusted her fingers, and dark smears tinted her breeches where she must've unconsciously rubbed her palms against them. "It's nothing," she told him, returning to the trunk and taking out a dagger. Azul doubted Nereida had any more weapons left in the room, so she slipped it into one of her boots and went back into the hallway.

Isile allowed her through, then followed. "I was waiting for De Gracia when I heard you come in."

"Do you know where he is?"

"I wouldn't be waiting here if I knew where he was, yes?"

Azul nodded, then took the stairs to the first floor and stopped abruptly, a muscle working her jaw. Two footmen waited at the bottom of the steps. The one who had opened the entrance door for her, and one of her brother's victims.

"Sireses, please come back to the parlor," the former said. "The Marquess de Gracia will return shortly."

So, Azul and Isile were herded into said parlor and left alone with the other footman, but not for long.

"Sister, stay put until I return, I beg you," said De Gracia through the footman, the living corpse. "I will explain everything—you have nothing to fear. Isile, I will talk to you later as well," he added before leaving and locking the door behind him.

Isile was speechless, but also, not for long. "Did the footman lock us in? Why did he call you sister? Why would I want to talk to him?"

Azul went to the window facing the patio, opening it with ease. Insect calls and the scented heat of a summer night drifted in.

"Have you no concern about all of this?" Isile demanded, coming to her side.

Azul boosted herself onto the windowsill, slipping a leg across. "My brother is a necromancer." She slid into the patio with a small hop. "And he spoke through the footman."

Dolls. Puppets. That was all her brother's creations were. That was why they stood by, allowing life to pass them, why they attacked over and over again, and why her brother could speak through them with so much ease.

Their souls were gone, not reborn.

"By the Heart, what?" exclaimed Isile, awkwardly following her. "What do you mean by 'necromancer'?"

She used another entrance onto the patio to reenter the house, then carefully made her way toward the back door into the small stables area. Apparently knowing better than to make a ruckus, Isile followed without making a sound.

"He kills people, then brings them back to life using their bones," Azul said once they were by the outer door separating them from the street.

"Such a thing exists?" Isile asked, shocked.

Azul wished Isile could be shocked while helping her with the heavy door, instead of standing uselessly by her side. She managed to pull it open enough to nudge her shoulder in and push in earnest. A pair of hands helped push from the street side. Her shadow, she recognized with relief. He tipped his hat after she thanked him.

Isile slipped out after her. "What you say isn't possible."

"And yet," she told him grimly, "you're about to experience it."

Two figures approached from the main entrance.

"Sister, I do not wish to harm you," said the footman. He carried no weapons, but the man by his side held a sword.

Isile stepped back toward the door they had just opened, his gaze darting from the footman's face to his companion's sword to Azul's shadow. "Surely there is no need for violence?"

In answer, Azul took out Nereida's long dagger. By her side, Azul's shadow covered her back, his rapier in hand.

"No serious harm," the footman warned. His companion moved toward Azul.

His aim was obvious—with no vital parts available for him to hit, arms and legs were his only options—and Azul deflected his lunge with ease, then blocked his swinging punch. She scraped her dagger up his blade to the guard, then pushed it to the side. She grabbed his wrist with her free hand but found gloves instead of skin.

His body shifted. Her knee came up into his groin before he could grab her, forcing him to bend. She pressed her hand against his face and watched his eyes bulge, his skin recede, his blade fall to the flag-stone with a clatter before his body followed.

A new pair of arms went around her from behind, pinning her own arms to her sides. The footman. Azul struggled. By the house, Isile watched it all, wide-eyed and gulping like a fish. Ramming her booted heel into the footman's foot earned a small break in his hold. She wrenched free and spun, but he held her wrist so she couldn't touch his face. His other fist delivered a heavy blow into her side. She doubled over, grunting.

Then her shadow was there, digging his dagger into the footman's neck.

"Not enough," Azul bit out between needles of pain.

Her shadow kicked the footman's knee, the crack like thunder in her ears, and the man buckled to the ground. Azul yanked her arm free and gave him a kick to the face.

"We must leave now." She bent with a grimace to touch the foot-man's forehead. Unlike the other bodies, it remained intact. A fresh corpse, she realized, her stomach turning. Maybe killed that very night.

She glanced at the looming house, which grew darker with each passing heartbeat. If she were to visit the servants' quarters, how many other living corpses would she find hiding away from her and the emissary? Her brother had suspected them to be the cause of Zenjiel's death from the start and had prepared accordingly.

This game, Virel Enjul and Sergado de Gracia had played with each other, with Azul none the wiser.

How smart she had felt sneaking around, so focused on Isadora she had missed how everyone around her was using her as card stock for their games. How shameful to see it so clearly now.

Straightening, she sheathed her dagger and began to walk away.

Azul's shadow fell into step by her side, and Isile recovered enough to follow them.

"You allowed me to slip away earlier," Azul said.

"Me?" asked Isile.

The shadow nodded.

"How did you know to return here?"

At the wry twist of his mouth, Azul understood. "You followed me with Enjul to the ossuary, waited while he went inside, then followed me back to Almanueva."

"What did you do to that man?" Isile asked. "His face . . . was it some kind of mask?"

"He had been dead for a while," Azul answered, distracted.

"You were serious about De Gracia?"

Isile's tone was more contemplative than shocked, but Azul didn't quite notice. She touched her shadow's sleeve. A knot in her throat made the next words hard to voice: "Enjul . . . The emissary is dead. You are no longer employed and are free to go."

The man flinched, his steps slowing down to a standstill. He glanced at her form, found the bloody smears on the front of her breeches, her dirty fingers.

"It's true. My brother killed him—"

"De Gracia?" asked Isile, sounding quite incredulous now.

"—so you are no longer required to look after me."

With a slight shake of his head, he took her by the elbow and urged her forward.

"You are not jesting?" Isile said, keeping up on her other side.

"I am not," Azul told him, reassured by the grim expression on her shadow's face. He believed her and still kept by her side. "You should go."

"I can help," Isile argued.

"Do you know where my brother could be, or where he might keep a set of private rooms? A studio of sorts?"

"No . . ."

"Then you can't help." Addressing her shadow, she asked, "Did Enjul mention such a place?"

He shook his head.

Azul thought for a few moments. "I know of someone who might be able to help with that, a woman Enjul met for business on at least one occasion. But I'm not sure I can find her house at nighttime."

"Then wait until daytime?" Isile suggested as if she had lost her intelligence somewhere back in the fight.

"The longer I wait, the higher the chance my brother might disappear." Disappear with all his treasure, with all the hopes for Isadora's bones. With no repercussions for the things he had done.

They stopped at an intersection, the crowd pushing them together, the warmth of the torches and lamps mixing with the summer heat. "This is where we go our separate ways," she said, looking at Isile.

"I can help you track whoever this is," Isile said. "I know Cienpé quite well."

"So does he," Azul retorted, pointing at her shadow.

"But what if you encounter more of your brother's men?"

"And you were such a help at Almanueva."

His cheeks darkened. "I was recovering from the shock! I vow that you will not find me quite so useless again."

"You are in danger, as much as I am," Azul said. "You know my brother's secret. Who is to say he might not kill you and take control of your body? No, Sirese Manzar, go home, gather your belongings, hide for a while. This is not your battle."

"But I wish it to be."

Azul and her shadow shared a long look. "I can't stop you, then."

"Indeed. Now, tell me of this person's place."

Azul described some of the more memorable alleys and riverbanks she had seen through the mouse. Her shadow nodded or shook his head at Isile's suggestions, eventually growing tired of the discussion and simply stalking away.

Following him through the carousing crowd, Azul and Isile remained side by side.

"Why are you so interested in helping us?" she asked, stepping aside to avoid a man in a hurry. "Sergado is your friend, why help me against him?"

Isile waved that aside. "He is not *that* much of a friend."

"Friend enough for you to wait in his house late at night. Friend enough to gift him a masterpiece for his rooms. Friend enough for you to make sketch after sketch of nothing but human body parts."

Isile fell silent until they arrived at an alley so low the river's water spilled over the edge. It smelled of dampness and rot, weeds sprouting everywhere. Azul recognized this from the mouse's travels. Conjuring more of the memory, she chose one direction, and they continued their trek through Cienpuentes's alleyways and narrow paths, stopping here and there while she tried to reconcile the mouse's viewpoint and how things looked to the human sight.

"I cannot condone it, if he's truly killing people," Isile said.

"Why did you think he asked for so many sketches?"

"Curiosity? Studies?"

"Like Sirese Norel at the mortuary?"

Isile brightened. "Indeed! Just like him. Why should I arrive to some bizarre conclusion? It's not unheard of, these tendencies to investigate human nature. What do you think he's trying to accomplish, making those fingers? Controlling those men?"

"I don't know. At first, we—I—thought maybe he meant to spy on the court," Azul said, worried. "But you don't need knowledge of the human body for that, and he's already a marquess."

"Might that be it?" Isile asked thoughtfully. "That he means to create a body?"

Azul stared at him, aghast.

Isile shrugged. "Why else practice making fingers—out of love for doll-making?"

"But a body needs blood and flesh."

"As you say," was Isile's noncommittal answer. He said no more, but became thoughtful, paying no attention to their surroundings until Azul found their destination—a two-story building of gray stone and dark brick squeezed between an overhead bridge and a more elegant house.

They pounded on the door to no avail, then settled on finding somewhere to rest nearby and trying again at dawn. There would be no point, Azul supposed, to breaking into an empty house when the owner was all they needed.

Luckily, it didn't take them long to find someone willing to rent out a room for the night. They were lent a small storage space, dusty and empty with some rags thrown into a corner. A second, smaller room was adjacent, not unlike Sergado's rooms.

Isile walked inside, surveying it with distaste. "I suppose this one is mine, yes?"

Azul and her shadow exchanged looks again. Isile snickered. "You don't think me smart enough to know you mean me to remain locked up for the remainder of the night?" He offered up his wrists. "I am your brother's friend, after all."

Azul's shadow grabbed and tested one of the rags. Approaching Isile, he motioned for him to turn around.

With a groan, Isile complied. "This will make sleeping quite difficult. Have you no pity?"

Her shadow didn't, apparently, since he deftly brought Isile's wrists behind his back and tied them tightly.

Azul watched this with relief. She hadn't wanted to hurt Isile—he was curious, yes, too curious, and had surprisingly taken everything in stride—but she couldn't risk him having a change of heart and running off to tell her brother of her plans. Shock had made her tongue too fluent. She had said too much; she had shown him too much. At the time, it hadn't mattered.

But now her tired limbs begged for mercy, and the throb in her side reminded her of the damage a fist could do to a body. Now the woman the emissary had contacted was gone, or dead asleep, or dead.

Now Azul only wanted the nightmare to end.

Her shadow closed the door between the rooms. It had no lock, but he didn't seem bothered by that. He gave his half cape to Azul and pointed toward the floor. She thanked him, made a roll out of it for her head, and lay on the thick coating of dust. Her shadow had closed the shutters in the other room, but he kept these partly open, and Azul could hear some distant shouting and singing, could see a slice of the dark green sky.

Her shadow sat across from her, back against the connecting door, rapier close at hand. Ah yes. Azul took out the dagger she had pilfered from Nereida's room and put it under the roll.

"You still won't tell me your name?" she asked.

Her shadow simply lowered his hat until all that was visible was a half smile.

"Sombra, then," she couldn't help but say. When the smile widened, she reckoned he didn't mind. "I shouldn't trust you. Everyone else has stabbed me in the back, so why should you be any different?"

His answer was to close his eyes, settling in for what was left of the night.

✳ ✳ ✳

Isile was gone by the time they awoke. The shutters in his room were open and the rag was cut through, discarded on the floor. Sombra had searched him for weapons earlier, and yet, not well enough. Isile Manzar had turned out to be craftier than he appeared, but then, with Sergado as his friend, one had to be.

Azul refused to waste any time figuring this out. Dawn had pushed Noche Verde away, Luck and Wonder long gone. She and Sombra returned to the woman's door. More knocking, and still, no response.

But the upper shutters were now open.

Azul pointed at the corner where the building met one of the upper bridges. A series of lovers' footholds had been carved into the brick and mortar, and with Sombra's help, she climbed to the second story, then slipped inside the nearest window.

The woman who had met with Enjul slept on a narrow bed. Azul made sure no one else was in the room, then shook the woman's arm.

She woke with a start. "Who are you?" she demanded, scooting back until she was against the wall. Her eyes flickered over the room, trying to ascertain how many intruders had invaded her quarters.

Azul towered over her. "The Valanjian Virel Enjul sends me. I need whatever information about the Marquess de Gracia he had you search for him."

The woman swallowed, appeared meek. "You lie. He already knows everything."

"And now I need to know it," Azul said, lunging for the pillow and taking hold of the dagger hidden there. In the next breath, she tossed it out the window.

"Hey!" the woman exclaimed.

"I need the information. Enjul is gone, he can pay you no more."

"And you can in his stead?"

"I can."

"Now?"

"After I know the information to be truthful."

"Then you are of no interest to me."

Azul knelt on the mattress and pressed Nereida's second dagger to the woman's throat. "And now?"

The woman huffed. "You won't kill me. You're not the type."

She had a point. And dead people could give no information, so Azul straightened and spun the dagger, offering the hilt. "A good quality blade, sharp, with a beautiful hilt. It will fetch plenty."

The woman studied the dagger with a critical eye. A curt nod of agreement before she went to take it from Azul's hand.

Azul moved it out of her reach. "De Gracia. You were hired to investigate him. Did you find any gossip? Any secret lodgings bought under someone else's name?"

"He has property in the countryside, and investments in several ventures."

"In Cienpuentes?"

"There's a small house. Been in the family for years. Meant for lovers, but he hasn't had any reside there."

Could it be so straightforward? Azul wondered. Or was her brother smarter than to use his own building and had bought another property to use as his studio through one of his puppets?

But then, why go through the bother? Nobody would ever suspect him of being a necromancer, so why should anyone be curious about what he did on his own property?

After paying with the dagger, Azul and Sombra made their way to the address provided by the woman. Azul's muscles ached, and her head hurt from the lack of proper sleep, and there was not a damn horse or empty cart to be found to ease their trip. It was a long walk, and the house at the end of it bigger than Azul had expected. The higher echelons of Cienpuentes aimed to keep themselves in their lovers' good graces by giving them plenty of beautiful space, apparently.

The structure was made of even white stone, with glass windows on the second floor and a lovely layer of gables covering its roof. A tiny spread of bushes around a central tree adorned the plaza it bordered. Beautiful, soothing, far enough from the busier center of Cienpuentes to ensure a certain level of quiet.

Perfect for lovers' meetings. Perfect for secret studies.

After checking the building for any other accessible openings, Sombra worked on the front lock while Azul kept an eye out for anyone who might call the blue tabards on them. The neighboring houses were similar in style and wealth, some with glass-paneled windows, others with simple shutters. Luckily, no one was peeking out at them, as far as she could tell.

The door finally opened, and they found themselves in a deep, wide hall. A staircase rose from the back and forked into narrower steps leading up the sides. Second-floor windows focused all the light onto the steps, inviting guests to investigate the upstairs. A hearth opened on one side, tapestries and paintings adorning the half-timbered walls. Two doors led to what must be the kitchen area and the servants' rooms.

The moment Azul and her shadow walked farther into the hall, a handful of men and women—living corpses—poured out of the doors to block their exit. Some wore tabards of different colors and different insignias, some stood in simple shirtsleeves, one wore an apron, as if they had all been plucked while in the middle of conducting various duties. They were all armed.

Another four men trotted down the stairs, effectively closing the trap.

Sombra immediately faced the threats behind them.

Azul wished she could face the truth in front of her.

She was too horrified. It truly cost Sergado nothing to bring people back to life. He endured no pain, sacrificed no part of his soul: the proof surrounded her. Otherwise, wouldn't he have no soul left? No soul to carry his thoughts, and no soul to share with those he raised from the dead? It took him nothing, *nothing*, to maintain these many bodies.

How could this be?

"Thank you for visiting, Sister," came her brother's voice from above. He went down the steps of the staircase slowly, savoring his grand entrance. "But you really should have waited at home."

XXXIV

THE COUNT, ALWAYS

A YEAR AND A HALF EARLIER

"Congratulations on the promotion, Your Honor."

De Anví turned to face Nereida de Guzmán. She wore a short blue jacket, tight around her torso, and a set of lighter blue skirts flaring below her waist. Combs dripping with pearls kept her artfully arranged black strands away from her face. The only sign of mourning was the dark red ribbon braided with a lock of hair, pinned to her shoulder by a brooch sporting her family's coat of arms—a rose and a feather.

Nereida's direct gaze met his, but he could not read it. Once he thought he might be able to, but the knowledge had been taken away from him after she had become one of the queen's lovers. He hadn't been able to regain it after the affair had ended, and the dark circles under her eyes and tightness of her mouth told him he wouldn't for some time to come—he would not intrude while she mourned a sister on top of her queen.

"They are not needed, Sirese De Guzmán," he said. "I am not interested in the position, and shall refuse it." His duty to the royals was finished. All he wanted was solitude and the freedom to eventually pursue the woman in front of him, not the inconveniences that came with being second-in-command to the Golden Dogs. De Losa was supposed to reap the rewards, not him. So where was she?

"I believe the regent was firm about his choice. He won't take no for an answer," Nereida said with some mockery, and in the time it took him to inhale the soft floral scent wafting from her, he could almost believe they were back in the Cienpuentes of a year ago, trading wit and honest thoughts about the world surrounding them as they whirled around glittering ballrooms. Then the moment ended, and she was back to her usual demeanor these days—wariness bordering on anger.

He mourned the loss of her once-joyful spirit, and he wondered how to coax it forth again. "De Fernán is firm about many things, and then he forgets them in a week."

A flicker of a smile was his reward. "This is true. You do not wish to lead, then?"

"Lead my own life, yes. Lead others in theirs, not so much."

"Ah," exclaimed someone from afar, "just the two I hoped to meet!"

De Anví turned to see Sío de Guzmán advance through the small crowd gathered at De Nolo's house. Members of the court were not allowed grand entertainments during royal mourning, so instead, they held these small gatherings of fifty-some people. Sometimes a hundred. Sometimes with music. For art's sake, of course, not entertainment. And if someone then decided to dance, well, that couldn't be helped, could it?

"Sío," Nereida said, hands held tightly in front of her waist, knuckles white.

"Nereida, dearest, how lucky to find you here! But truly, not lucky at all," Sío said with a wink, "since I specifically looked for you."

De Anví frowned. He had met with Sío de Guzmán a couple of times in the past, but other than the panic he had shown on the night of his sister's death, he had been of a reserved countenance, someone who would never act so carefree while mourning.

"Are you drunk?" Nereida asked in a tight voice. Her eyes sparkled with ire, but also with something akin to fear. She was coiled so tightly, De Anví moved to block them from the sight of the others in case she struck her sibling.

"Now, you know I don't partake, dear." Then, addressing De Anví, Sío added, "And you, De Anví, are you ready to accept the regent's offer yet? Time is running out, you know. He will not wait forever. Do not make all my work go to naught. He was quite insistent on De Losa, I'll have you know."

Nereida looked sick. She withdrew a step, and De Anví put a hand against her lower back, worried she might actually faint.

"Nereida?" he asked in a low voice. He tasted her name like the delicacy it was—one he could not often partake of outside his private thoughts.

Her gaze wouldn't leave her brother's face, the rakish disheveled hair, the delicate lace mask covering the upper half of his face.

"Who are you?" she asked in a shaky voice.

Sío smiled wide. "Ah, I've been caught. I am the Conjurer of Dreams, my lovely. We've met before, you know, but never quite so officially. Isn't this body great?" He twirled in front of their stares. "So beautiful, so vital! I do not think I shall grow tired of it."

De Anví sucked in a breath. "Witch."

"Get out of him," Nereida demanded. "Leave him be!"

"Why?" the Witch asked. "So he can dwell on your sister's death? Or do you think he might appear as if nothing is amiss, showing himself to these gatherings as you do?" She made a sound of disapproval. "What would your parents think? Even your older sister refuses to show herself!"

"Rot in the Void," Nereida told him, livid. "Get out of him this instant."

"Ah, but he signed a contract willingly. Who are you to tell him what to do with his life?"

Nereida's left hand went to her hip, where her rapier usually hung. But there were no rapiers in a gathering such as this. Her hands balled into fists.

De Anví stepped forward, preventing any strike. "You can't," he told her in a harsh, hurried whisper. "Not while she's taken over Sío."

Any harm done to the body would be Sío de Guzmán's to bear, not the Witch's. Any injury, any illness. Death.

Nereida inhaled sharply, understanding his meaning. A look of shock and impotence crossed her furious eyes as she realized how neatly the Witch had played her.

But Nereida de Guzmán would not give up so easily.

"I will find out what you did to fool him into this mockery." She spat on the floor by the Witch's boots. "I won't let him become one of your toys."

She turned and charged across the room, narrowly avoiding some courtiers and shouldering aside those she didn't.

"Make sure to visit me later," the Witch called after her, another big grin on her face. "I can help you forget."

De Anví grabbed the Witch's arm. "What are you playing at, Witch?"

Her eyes brimmed with mischief. "Nothing of importance, De Anví. Now, say, when will you accept De Fernán's offer? The fun we had investigating the king's foiled kidnapping! The fun we shall have guarding him from now on! I will be very disappointed if you're thinking of refusing the post, you know. Who knows what it will take to convince others to allow me to stick around? I fear this body will wear down from all the effort. And it would be such a shame for the De Guzmáns to lose another sibling so soon after losing the youngest. But with you by my side? Why, I see nothing but health and success in all our fates."

De Anví stared in disbelief. "You truly have no shame."

"That might be so, but trust me, it will be for the best. Who else but you could help keep an eye on the Heart and the king?"

Anyone else, De Anví thought. Anyone in the continents but him. Yet looking at Sío de Guzmán's body in front of him and looking at the door Nereida had gone through, he understood with grim acceptance that it would have to be him. He would have to stay and watch over Sío's body, for he didn't think Nereida could make herself look at him. Not as long as the Witch wore him like a costume. And if Nereida did not look at the Witch, if De Anví turned down the post and left, what extremes would the Witch go to in order to be seen? De Anví would not be the reason for another dead sibling in Nereida's family tree.

Emiré de Anví fought the urge to reach up and touch his neck— the collar of everything he didn't want had been snapped closed, and it was tight indeed.

THE PRESENT

De Anví and Nereida stepped out of the room, leaving Sío de Guzmán's remains behind. They took a hallway, then a staircase, and joined the crowds on the street. The nearness of Nereida's body prickled his skin, and the bloody bundle she carried somewhere under her waist-coat was nothing he wanted to dwell on.

But it was hard not to.

"It's killing you, isn't it?" Nereida said, as if she read his thoughts. And perhaps she could—it wasn't as if he were being coy in the way his gaze kept returning to her waist, where her purse and pockets ought to be. "You were always too polite to ask, too reserved. You never asked how Edine died, even though everyone else did. You simply gave me your condolences."

"I asked Esparza."

A giggle escaped her. De Anví's steps faltered at the unfamiliar sound.

"He was drunk for three months straight afterward. He couldn't have told you his name." The strange hilarity in her voice subsided as she continued, "No, I cannot answer yet. You must continue extending this unfounded trust of yours."

"Where shall we go, then?"

"To the woman I brought to Cienpé: Azul del Arroyo. Have you met her yet?"

"I haven't had the pleasure, no. You sneaked in without my knowledge, how could I have known who you returned with?"

Nereida frowned slightly. "My apologies. I spoke without thought."

"And where is she?"

"Esparza was to bring her to Casa Rojita after conducting some business."

Ah, De Anví realized, the mysterious second arrangement Esparza had mentioned but withheld from him. Picking their way through the crowd, they continued in silence, Nereida likely putting the final pieces of her plan into place. De Anví simply relished the joy of walking close by her side. The Witch's revenge would be harsh and cruel—of this, he had no doubt—so he might as well enjoy the moment while it lasted, minus thoughts of bloody fingers.

Casa Rojita was unsurprisingly full of people, and a few extra tables and stools and benches had been dragged outside. Merriment was in the air, in the food, in the drinks. It filled their senses as they made their way to the guest rooms on the second and third floors.

The room Nereida opened was small, with a simple bed, a stool, and a narrow window. No Esparza, no woman.

"You must have paid well," De Anví commented, "to ensure this room's availability during Noche Verde." Another cursory survey of the room. "Not that it can fit many."

At the lack of response, he looked at Nereida and found her gaze fixed on him.

"Save your looks of worry, De Guzmán," he told her. "I am not yet keeling over. Doubt it not, the Witch will take her time."

Nereida looked torn at his words, then determined.

"No, don't look like that either," he said with a grim smile. "It was my choice. Don't take it upon yourself to help me. You owe me no debt."

Nereida offered no reply, just stood by his side and gazed out the window. But as time went by, she grew restless once again. What a shock this night had been for De Anví. What a myriad of expressions he had gotten out of her. He had known them to be there, hidden by what she wished others to see, and he welcomed seeing them in the flesh.

"Do you think my brother was speaking the truth?" Nereida asked in a quiet voice, rubbing her pouch beneath her waistcoat.

"About his hand in your sister's death?"

"Yes."

De Anví pondered this for a few seconds. "Perhaps. The approach of death brings forth all the regrets, all the truths." He should know—he carried his own regrets about that night like a heavy cloak that refused to be put away in the winter trunk.

"I cannot make myself believe it," she said, her voice cracking. De Anví fisted his hands so he wouldn't reach out to comfort her. Nereida was too proud for such a gesture unless she invited it. And Nereida was far from inviting. "Si-so was always there, our pillar. Always dependable. How could this happen? He said . . . he said there was a witness to Edine's killing, that nothing could've been done. He never mentioned he was close by."

"It might not be the truth of what happened, but what he feels is the truth. Perhaps the passage of time and guilt has warped his memories of the event." He watched Nereida's expression become cold again, composed. "Whatever happened, he was not by your sister's side. He could not stop the blade that killed her. It was not guided by his hand."

Nereida said nothing, and they fell into silence until she began to pace the small room.

"They're taking too long," she said.

"Could this Del Arroyo have gone ahead with the next part of the plan?"

Nereida shook her head. "No. Something must have gone wrong."

"Where would the next logical place be, for her to go to?"

"De Gracia."

"Is that where you've been hiding?"

"Yes." She strode for the door.

De Anví hurried to follow.

"Does it have something to do with the marquess's murder and the attempted kidnapping of his daughter?"

Nereida gave him a sharp look. "No."

She hadn't known about the kidnapping attempt, De Anví guessed. And while he didn't have reason to believe Nereida was lying to him so far, what were the chances these happenings were unconnected?

It took them too long to reach the Marquess de Gracia's house, and once they were there, they found only a worried brother.

"Ah, Count de Anví," he greeted in a distracted tone before focusing on Nereida. "Azul is missing. I lost track of her when we went to Karia's ball, and she hasn't made an appearance at the other houses we were to attend."

"And Sirese Enjul?" Nereida asked.

"He left before Azul disappeared. I don't think they are together."

"You are worried because of the kidnapping attempt," De Anví said, earning De Gracia's surprised attention.

"Yes," he agreed. "I thought I put the matter to rest, but what if they've tried again?"

"Then there is nothing to do but wait."

"Can't you find anything?" De Gracia pleaded. "If you know about the kidnapping, you must be able to figure out who might have taken her."

"I can make inquiries. You will wait here for the result?"

De Gracia agreed.

"Then I shall take my leave. And my suggestion is for De Guzmán to check the other balls you were meant to attend, in case your sister did, indeed, arrive at them, albeit late."

Nereida agreed to this, so they took their leave and left the house in separate directions, only to arrive within minutes of each other back at the tavern.

De Anví was first. The room was still devoid of occupants, the window open, the stool standing by its side. A bloodied cloth lay on top, carrying the dark crimson smears of someone wiping a bloody blade.

"Esparza must have waited until we left to leave us this," he told Nereida when she burst into the room. He waved the cloth like a flag, and she snatched it out of his grip to inspect it in the lamp's light.

"Why?" she asked. "A warning? Something must've gone wrong."

"What, exactly, was this task you paid him to do?"

"He was to sneak Del Arroyo into the ossuary and help her find her sister's bones."

De Anví's gaze went to her pouch.

"Yes," Nereida said dryly. "I shall explain in time."

"I believe the time has come," he told her.

The bloodied cloth reclaimed Nereida's attention, and for a heart-beat, he thought she might tell him. But the moment—like so many others between them—passed.

"Let us go back to De Gracia," she said. "Del Arroyo might return, or if she was truly kidnapped, we might be able to interrogate who-ever comes to ask for ransom."

They made their way back to Almanueva, this time waiting outside.

"It worries me," Nereida whispered, "that Enjul is gone too. He must be with Del Arroyo. He might have stopped Esparza from tak-ing her to the ossuary."

"Who is this Enjul?" De Anví asked.

"An Emissary of the Lord Death."

"An emissary?" Hard not to be shocked at the idea. "What is he doing here?"

"Stopping Del Arroyo from getting to her sister's bones."

"Hence Esparza?"

"Hence Esparza."

"Why not just take her away?"

Nereida didn't answer. Her hand drifted to the bump under her waistcoat on her left side. Her favorite sword, Sangrienta, hung at her right. He touched the hilt of his own Valiente. As the second-in-command of the Royal Guard, he was expected to carry it with him at all times—during court sessions, during formal meetings, during dances and gatherings. But what good did a rapier do against secret scheming, faceless witches, and his own ignorance?

"This is related to the things you're keeping from me, isn't it?" he asked.

"I am sorry, De Anví."

It was on the tip of his tongue to ask her to call him by his first name and finally get his wish, but he thought better of it. This sudden camaraderie was born of necessity, not a true willingness to become closer to him. His name on her lips would have to wait.

"Who is that?" Nereida asked, now alert.

A man was approaching the house. He knocked on the door, and light poured out when it opened, illuminating his profile.

"Isile Manzar," De Anví said. "One of De Gracia's friends."

Sometime after Isile's arrival, the entrance doors opened again, revealing De Gracia and two armed men.

"De Gracia's personal guard? Where is he going?" asked Nereida.

"It would seem either he no longer worries about Del Arroyo's fate," De Anví said, "or . . ."

Nereida smiled. "Or he's about to take us to her. The man dotes on her."

De Gracia led them across town to a house in a quiet neighborhood by the edge of the delta. Four more people joined De Gracia's group, some wearing different symbols on their cloaks and tabards, some wearing none at all.

"This doesn't bode well," Nereida said, watching them enter the building. "He's gathering a small army inside." She turned to De Anví. "We're going to need men of our own, in case we need to fight."

De Anví understood what she wanted from him, but he was loath to leave her behind. "Come with me," he urged.

"Someone must stay in case he decides to move."

"Tonio can." De Anví made a signal with his hand, and his personal guard stepped out from the shadows an alleyway behind.

Nereida startled. De Anví snorted. "You think me so careless as to travel without him during Noche Verde? He will keep watch, and he knows how to contact me if De Gracia's small army decides to make a move before we're back." To Tonio, he added, "Follow if he leaves, but do not interfere."

Nereida weighed her options in the light of the approaching dawn, then touched the bundle hidden under her waistcoat. "Very well. I shall trust you."

De Anví put a hand to his chest. "By the Blessed Heart, I won't let you down."

XXXV

MISTRESS OF BONES

Well, Azul thought to herself, *that was a foolish thing to do.* Barging in, too focused on finding more bones to wonder if Sergado might already be there, waiting for her.

"Why didn't you stay at home, as I asked you to?" said her brother.

"I was on my way to Almanueva."

The men blocking the way between Azul and Sergado waited silent and still for their orders. Such control her brother had over these bodies, it was still hard to comprehend. "I'm not interested in you, Brother. Only in my sister's bones."

"Why not simply ask me?"

At the reminder of his deceit, fury and shame rose within Azul. "I *did* ask you, remember? I won't ask again. You'll either string me along or lie to me, or both, as you've done so far. And if instead you decide to be truthful, the price you'll ask of me won't be something I'd be willing to pay, will it?"

"So, you'll simply take?"

Azul waved at the contingent of living corpses surrounding her and Sombra. "Isn't that what you do? It must run in our blood."

Sergado tilted his head, a satisfied edge to his smile. "Yes, you are very much like me, aren't you?"

Virel Enjul had been wrong, she realized. Her brother had known she was to blame for the demise of his men, and had guessed how she did it, judging by his victims' gloves and long sleeves.

"So let us talk, Sister," Sergado continued. "I will not harm you—you have my word."

Azul dug under her waistcoat and brought out her bone-hilted dagger. "No."

Sergado ignored her rejection. "I knew from the first time we met, when you were nothing but a child—how stubborn you were then, how stubborn you are now. I should have dragged you back home, as was my right and duty as your older brother. I was too busy with my own self, and I must ask forgiveness for that. But I won't fail you again. We will talk, and we will see about your sister, since you wish it so much. That sort of urge, I can understand. Are we not alike in every other way?"

One of Sergado's men advanced on her. Azul slapped his hand away and crossed his chest with her dagger, forcing him back. "No."

She heard swords clanking behind her. Sergado wouldn't be concerned with Sombra's well-being, but she couldn't afford to check.

Azul grabbed the man in front of her by his shirt and pivoted her body to send him stumbling to the wall. She was on him the next instant, pushing him to the floor and thrusting Nereida's dagger deep into his gut. It wasn't enough to stop him—back in the ossuary, she had seen how mortal wounds mattered little to these living corpses—and the man's strong hands clamped on her forearms. She pushed the blade deeper until the hilt reached the skin, slipped her fingers through the tear in the shirt, and touched flesh.

The stench of putrefaction filled her nostrils, invaded her throat. A shout came from the stairs. A body thudded against the floor by her side. Sombra, giving her more time.

Azul tightened her hold on the bone hilt and opened the Eye of Death.

Power coursed eagerly along her arm all the way to the dagger. It sucked greedily at the bone, drank from the man slumped against the wall, and demanded its cut of Azul's soul, which she gave up willingly.

The bone reshaped itself, and then demanded more, going after the wooden column behind the man. The house groaned; the plaster and paint on the wall crumbled.

Muscle re-formed in the blink of an eye. Azul snatched her hands back and scrambled to her feet as fur crept over flesh and a gray catlike creature stood as tall as her chest. Fangs protruded from its mouth, big black eyes opened, and muscles strained under its hide, ready to strike.

She let it go.

The beast ripped into the living corpses, shredding their limbs to butchers' meat. Sombra handed her a new dagger. She plunged it into the back of a man about to stab the big cat. The man's body jerked, his weapon still firmly in hand. Azul felt for the neckline of his shirt and touched his neck with her knuckles. The man dropped instantly.

The huge cat sank its teeth into someone else. Azul kept her back against the creature's side, protecting its flank. She saw a man with a raised pistol, waiting.

Her brother was shouting something. Was it "Enough, enough"? Sergado's eyes were wide, his cheeks flushed. "Enough! Or it's his death."

Her brother's words finally made it through the maelstrom of her thoughts. Panting, Azul glanced at the corpses surrounding them to find Sombra with a dagger to his neck. Azul's stomach clenched. Even with his life in danger, Sombra's countenance remained unperturbed, as if he were enjoying the situation. The beast stopped attacking Sergado's men and backed against Azul, warm and alive and growling.

Why hadn't her brother left? Did he have so much faith in his men? More than half littered the floor. If he tried to keep her and Sombra here, the rest would soon join them.

But Sergado knew her well, hadn't he said so? And she would not risk a friend's life. But then . . . would it really be such a risk when she could just touch one of Sombra's bones after she was done felling everyone else?

The big cat shifted suddenly, but the warning came too late. A powerful hand gripped her arm and spun her around. Azul cried out in pain, barely keeping the cat from mauling the new threat.

Because Virel Enjul stood in front of her.

The world went still.

You survived! she wanted to say, but her voice failed her. Those harsh features, the wide violet rings, the golden irises, the unfocused black pupils. He *had* survived. The Lord Death's touch had reached Cienpuentes, after all. He had struck some kind of deal with Sergado.

A loud growl broke through the sudden silence, not from the animal, but from Sombra. He didn't strain against his captors, but his mouth had twisted into a feral snarl. Over Enjul's strange change of heart?

No, she realized in horror. Of course not.

"Why?" she cried out, despair filling her as she admitted what stood in front of her: the skin, lacking the life it ought to have; the eyes, flat like simple round stones. "Why him?"

One of her brother's dolls.

Sergado's heels echoed against the steps as he descended the staircase and stopped well outside the cat's reach. "*Azul,*" he gushed, motioning to the creature. "Sister! This is beyond any of my dreams! Why did you not tell me you had this gift?"

"Why him?" she shouted.

"Why not? An Emissary of the Lord Death will be useful. He'll open so many doors. He can demand access to any ossuary, any crypt. Just imagine the things we can create, between your gift and mine. The bodies! We can pick and choose among the best, make a god of our own with nobody to stop us. *We* can become gods."

The speech washed over Azul like background rain. She only saw Enjul's face, remembered how it had twisted with horror in his last moments, how he pleaded to remain with his god.

"Don't bring me back. I want to stay with him."

She longed to touch her forehead to Enjul's chin, end this torment in her gut, in her thoughts, in her guilty conscience. But even if she did, even if her touch stopped her brother's gift, Enjul's body would not decompose. His death was too recent. Sergado could raise him again. Over and over again.

"Don't bring me back. I want to stay with him."

His face, his horror. His last wishes.

Azul could not abandon him to this. She must find a way to destroy his body—burn it beyond use, turn it into another animal, another being.

"We, the emissaries, were born with the blessing of the god inside us."

The god is here?

"He has no body, but we carry him inside us."

The cat twisted its head, sank one of its long fangs into Enjul's forearm. Tendons snapped, muscles tore. His grip loosened, and Azul broke free. She slammed her hand against his neck.

Sergado's laugh was immediate. "I admire your stubbornness, but this is a waste of time. Stop now, Sister, or risk the lives of your man and your new pet."

What did it matter? Azul thought as Enjul's body folded over hers. Their lives were forfeit anyway—Sergado would kill them once he had her safely in his grasp and tucked away.

She allowed the body to drop and followed it down to the floor. Her hand never leaving his neck, she straddled him.

"Azul," Sergado said. "Must you keep up this foolishness? Even if you do something to him, I'll simply reclaim the body later. You know this."

Her gift searched and searched. Desperation clawed at her. The large bones of the huge feline came into sharp relief, as well as the bones of those lying around her, of those still standing by her brother and keeping Sombra in check. The bones of those sleeping in the other houses, the bones of those farther away. A forest of bones, indistinguishable from one another.

She tried to bring back the focus she had gained in the ossuary. From flesh to muscle to bone, she searched and searched. Azul squeezed her eyes shut, willing her gift to work faster, better. There was nothing. Nothing there other than Virel Enjul. Had she been wrong?

But no. There it was.

So tiny. So small.

Enough.

A piece of the Lord Death.

Since Sergado de Gracia loved death so much, she would give it to him.

Leaning down, she placed her lips against Virel Enjul's, Emissary of the Lord Death, for this was the last time they would ever meet, and there was no shame in saying goodbye to him the way she now realized she wanted to say hello.

The Eye of Death opened in her palm, flush against Enjul's cool neck. The cat coiled closer around her, ready to strike. Her brother shouted something. His guards stepped away, allowing him a better view. There was nothing to see—her gift rushed into Enjul, made its own network of bridges over his bones to reach that other presence inside him. And once they connected, the god demanded flesh. It demanded power. It demanded her essence. It demanded everything.

Her soul was severed suddenly, torn apart by invisible teeth. Azul cried out in pain. She dropped on her side, curling into herself. It had taken so much—too much. A gaping hole had been carved out of her, and she feared she would never have enough soul to bring anything else to life again. That Isadora was truly lost to her because she had chosen someone else. Some*thing* else.

Enjul's eyes snapped open. He rose, pushing Azul's leg off his midriff. She tried to focus and tell the cat not to attack him, to stay out of his way. When Enjul got to his feet, he looked around, taking stock of the room.

On the stair landing, her brother gaped, stumbling as he took a step back. Enjul spared him a glance, then focused on his own hands, flexing them as if he were trying them out for the first time.

"Hmm," he said. "It'll do."

All of Sergado's men dropped to the floor.

"What?" Sergado cried in shock.

He said something else, but Azul was doubled over again, a new wave of pain rippling through her. Tears raced down her face. She panted against the floor, the room coming in and out of focus. Enjul—no, not Enjul, the Lord Death—knelt by her side to look at her. His eyes were wide with equal parts surprise and curiosity. Something crashed in the distance and shouting followed. The pounding of boots shook the tile beneath her cheek. More of Sergado's guards? How would she face them?

That was her last coherent thought.

XXXVI

WHAT REMAINS

A YEAR AND A HALF EARLIER

E dine de Guzmán knew she was in over her head, like the time
Si-so threw her into the deep part of the lake and she had stared
right into Lord Death's eyes. But she survived the lake, and she
would survive this.

She had begged Si-so to come help, just as she begged him at the
lake, but this time he refused. This time it was all on her.

After all, hadn't she come to Cienpuentes to make her fortune?
Si-so and Nida and Iriana had all done it before her, so perhaps this
was the Lady Dream's way of telling her that some things must be
faced alone, that the fortune she had begged for in the shrine back
home as she tied her wish to the goddess's leg could only be earned
on one's own.

She crept along the narrow passageway between two of Cienpuentes's stone buildings. It was late at night, and this part of the city
lay quiet and sleepy and dark. So dark she could barely see her hand
in front of her eyes, Luck and Wonder's shine hidden behind a mass
of clouds.

A few days earlier, she'd slipped into an old servants' corridor,
forgotten after some renovations in Iriana's house. The De Guzmáns'
oldest sister had never liked secret passageways in her home, not after

Edine and Si-so played so many tricks on her at their family's estate, but whomever she had contracted to close this one up had done the shoddiest job.

The door at the end of that corridor had been nailed shut, and wallpaper was all that hid it from view on the other side. Voices drifted clearly through the cracks between the frame and the uneven edges of the door. Edine hadn't intended to spy on Iriana, but working for her sister as a messenger had piqued her curiosity: the sealed messages she delivered, the constant reminders not to call attention to herself; the flickering of the recipients' eyes when she handed them the letters, as if they were checking who might be watching the exchange.

Cienpuentes was a city full of schemers, as Si-so had reminded her when she went to him with her worries, but something about this hadn't felt right. Perhaps it was the worry lines marring Iriana's face, perhaps the tightening of her mouth after certain friends paid her a visit.

So, Edine had listened in on these visits, and when they yielded nothing beyond vague mentions of the Heart and Anchor and the regent and the king, she stole a missive before her sister threw it into the fire. It contained a place and a date.

The place and date being here and now, in a small square walled by buildings. Edine had assumed the people in attendance would check the alleyways before conducting their business, so she had waited before slipping in. Catching half a conversation was better than being discovered and catching nothing.

Carefully, she peeked into the square. Three caped figures stood in close formation, their voices only murmurs. Edine strained to catch the words.

". . . Witch . . . ," accompanied by spitting.

". . . De Guzmán . . . ," followed by a shake of the head.

". . . must kill her . . . ," in a female tone she recognized as one of Iriana's friends.

Edine's blood ran cold. Assassinations had become less common over the years, and Edine could not believe her sister would be involved in such a thing. Oh, if only Si-so were here to burst into the square and demand an explanation! If Edine did that, who would listen to her? The only one who ever did was Miguel, and she couldn't tell him. Not when family was involved.

For all that she feared she might love the man, she loved her siblings a lot more.

"Can't," a voice snapped. "If she has the goddess inside . . ."

At this, Edine scowled. She? The goddess inside? Did they mean the Witch? She had heard rumors about some woman who dealt in people's dreams. But Edine came from a place where such things were common tales with no grounding in reality, so she hadn't thought much of it.

"Then we'll end this before it starts," the woman said, anger coloring her voice. Edine wondered where her sister was and why she wasn't here to end this strange argument.

Edine had come here to unravel plots about palace insurrections, not listen to folktales about gods and creatures.

"The Lady Dream would never betray us," one of the others insisted. "Watch your tongue, Dela."

"Why shouldn't she?" Dela answered, acerbic and sour, and Edine could imagine the lines on her forehead deepening as her lips pursed. "What have we done to ingratiate us with her? With the Blessed Heart? All that work to put the Anchor ban in place and now—gone with the queen!"

One of the figures shushed her.

But Dela wasn't done. "If we eliminate the hosts before the gods come, we'll have nothing to worry about."

Edine reeled back, shocked. Hosts? For . . . for the gods? What did that mean? Her heel slipped backward, connecting with a rodent. Its squeak filled the air, and the three figures snapped their attention to her.

"Who's there?" one of them asked, reaching for his rapier.

Edine swallowed a curse and retreated through the alleyway. Loudly. Too loudly.

She had taken not two steps into the wider street when someone slammed into her. She went sprawling to the ground with a grunt, then rolled and got to her feet, hand immediately going to her rapier.

"Where were you?" came the harsh demand from the alleyway.

The three figures spilled out to join the one who had knocked her down.

"Doing a perimeter walk," the newcomer answered. A female voice. "Like you asked me to. This one"—she gestured toward Edine with the dagger in her hand—"slipped past me."

Edine shuffled backward, but the woman waved her dagger. "Not so fast."

"How long were you listening?" Iriana's friend asked.

"I listened none," Edine answered. She looked for an escape route, but they had her surrounded.

Four versus one. Well, she had faced those odds before, against bullies back home, hadn't she?

But those had been kids, and these were adults armed with rapiers and daggers, and Edine had never been quite so good with her sword as Nereida. Her sword! She hadn't even named it yet.

Oh, how she wished Sío were here.

"She's here. That's enough," one of the men said. "Get rid of her."

Edine swallowed but raised her rapier.

She had come alone to find her fortune, and it appeared that alone she would find it.

THE PRESENT

Azul lay on a narrow bed in a small room. A window graced one wall, its shutters open to the late morning sun. The sheets were clean, the white walls high and bare, and someone had put her into a thin nightgown.

Sombra sat on a stool by an old trunk, legs stretched in front of him, back relaxed against the wall, and arms crossed over his chest. He wore the same clothes as before, but his hair had been brushed and fell loose around his shoulders.

"You're alive," Azul said, then winced, the void inside of her trying to feed off her guts. But innards could not feed the soul. Nothing could. It would either grow back, or stay as it was. And what if she were stuck this way for the rest of her life? Tears started to form but she blinked them away.

Sombra nodded. His face showed some bruising, but their adventures had not marked him otherwise, except for the dirt on his clothes and the occasional rip in his sleeves.

"En . . ." Azul swallowed hard. She could not breathe. "The emissary? D-Death?"

He stood, pointing at the door.

"Are we at Almanueva?"

A shake of his head.

Not at her brother's mercy then.

Air finally made it into her lungs. It helped with the gnawing hole at her core. It helped calm her heart.

"Where are you going?" she asked, sitting up and gathering the sheet against her waist. Belatedly, she noticed a hulking mass of fur lying at the bed's end—the large gray feline she'd brought back to life. It opened one eye to look at her, huffed, and went back to its rest.

Sombra retrieved his hat from the top of the trunk, bowed deeply, and stepped outside. Somewhat rude, and definitely not helpful, but Azul found a strange sort of comfort in Sombra's familiar actions.

"We are in Valanje's local house," said the Lord Death from the doorway.

He strolled into the room and took the stool her shadow had vacated. The seat was too low for him, and he leaned forward to prop his elbows on his knees. He wore no emissary mask—she supposed there was no need for one anymore, but she missed the sight of it—and unlike Sombra, he had changed into clean clothes. His hair was tucked into a braid at the nape of his neck; his violet-gold eyes gave nothing away.

This man, who had intruded into her life, into her thoughts, into her heart, was nothing but a shell now. A suit of clothing worn by someone else.

How could she ever reconcile the sight of him with the knowledge of what had been lost? Of what could have been?

Azul breathed deep and tried not to drown. "My brother?"

"It has been strongly suggested that he not leave his house while the investigation into the bodies found at his property runs its course."

"He'll be gone within the week," she said grimly. Along with any bones he had left over, for whatever he planned to do with them. Become a god, supposedly. "What are they going to accuse him of? There are no witnesses except for me and Sirese Sombra. And how are we to prove that he kept the corpses alive? No, this will come to naught. He's the Marquess de Gracia; I'm simply the half sibling." Her gaze meandered toward the window, then back to him. "Will you take me back to Valanje now?"

A cruel smile curved his mouth. But perhaps he simply wasn't used to human reactions, because there was no bite to his words: "There is no need."

Azul swallowed. "Even though I'm a necromancer?"

Death chuckled. "You might be the Mistress of Bones, but you are no necromancer."

Stunned, she could only stare. "Then what am I?"

"Is it not obvious?"

Azul didn't need to tell him no; her shocked expression spoke for her.

His eyes brightened with mischief. "You are a child of the Lord Life. You do not—cannot—control death. You can only create life."

"I don't understand," she whispered. "Enjul said—"

"Virel Enjul was a good emissary, but he allowed his fears to twist his understanding of my wishes."

"Is . . . is he really gone?"

"Yes." The word carried as much finality as death itself.

Azul squeezed her eyes shut.

Ah, what could have been.

"Why did you not revive him as you did in Diel?"

"Death eventually touches all of us." A crooked smile appeared on his face as he looked her up and down. "Almost. I retain all my emissary's memories, Azul del Arroyo. You seek your sister's bones."

"Yes." Warily, she scooted closer to the end of the bed until she was sitting across from him. She would eagerly bear all the sacrifices, have all the deaths on her conscience, if it meant she hadn't failed her search.

"Seek no more. They are gone."

Azul reeled back, his words, sharp and sure, incomprehensible to her.

He pressed on: "There is no way for you to bring your sister back to life. You may search to the ends of the continents, go through Sergado de Gracia's collection—or any other cache of bones in existence— and this fact will not change. It is beyond your capacity, for nothing of her remains."

The room blurred. An unendurable bleakness began to weigh down her limbs, her heart, what was left of her soul.

"But I can," he said.

Her gaze snapped to his.

"I can pluck her essence from the Void," Death continued. "For I *am* the Lord Death and it is within my power to do so."

A pause. Too long a pause. Surely, Azul would die if he didn't speak soon.

"If you do as I say."

She gathered the folds of her nightgown in her hands and waited.

"It would seem," Death explained, "that my gifts in this form are somehow tied to you. I take from your essence, as I am sure you can tell by now, and I have no wish to leave this body quite yet. There are things I mean to do."

Unease churned Azul's stomach.

"You do not like this. You do not trust me," he continued. "Who would? Worry not, I am not lacking in feeling. Did I not, along with the others, sacrifice my body for the sake of life on these lands? Thus, you shall be rewarded for your help. Is it not worth your sister's life?"

Azul studied his face. His expression told her nothing, just as Virel Enjul's hadn't. Death retained his emissary's mannerisms as well as his memories. She recognized the small tics, the slight tilting of his head while he waited for a response, the stillness of his hands, the way he would not play coy but prey on everything he set his mind to. The strange pull she had once felt in his presence was still there, mingled with deep wariness and amplified a hundredfold.

"What are your plans?" she finally asked.

"I mean to find my brethren."

"The other gods?" Azul exclaimed. "They are around?"

"They will follow." He gifted her with a dazzling smile, which was as shocking as the knowledge he had shared with her.

"Why?"

The smile turned devious. "There is something we want back." Before she could ask anything else, he stood up and told her pleasantly, "Now, I have ordered for clothes to be brought to you. Another dagger, as well, since you are keen on them. I will not begrudge you your gift, as my emissary did.

"As long as you don't use it on my land without my permission, I will not step in the way. I have some affairs I must deal with in this city, so you may take a few days to organize your own before we leave."

Her acceptance was taken for granted, and Azul resented this deeply. Like Enjul, the god wasted no time waiting for answers when he already knew the outcome. The illusion of choice, though, would've been welcome. He might be a god—Death embodied, thanks to her—but she did not trust him.

"And my brother?" she asked. "Will you make sure he pays for his crimes?"

"What harm can he do? I can claim any bones he takes from death. Or do you wish me to kill him?"

That gave her pause. "Is there no way to simply restrain him?"

"Ah, Life, always seeking a way. How refreshing. It was his idea, you know, to raise the continents."

"Well?" she insisted, refusing to delve into theology. "Sergado will be free soon, and he'll seek to carry on his work elsewhere. He must be stopped or he'll continue killing."

"He is of no concern for now."

Of course the god would show no concern, Azul thought bitterly. What were a few human lives compared with his godly one? If he didn't need her, he would not have cared about hers either.

"Why not simply force me along?" she asked. "Why tempt me with Isadora when it was your fault her body crumbled on your shores? You are a god—you can do as you please."

"I am the Lord Death, not the Lord Control of Your Thoughts. Your willingness will save effort and time." His smile was a dazzling invitation, a dare. Mischief, promise, eagerness. Temptation.

"I shall go with you," Azul said, because it felt important that she make the choice even though none had been offered to her.

His smile changed, morphed into something that could either send a person down into the Void, or reform them into greatness. This was where Enjul's body ended and the god showed himself. For the first time, Azul saw the power behind this being—that this was a walking god, that the Temples weren't built in vain, the way Isadora and so many others believed. That once upon a time, he had cared enough for life to elevate the lands, but life itself held no sway over his whims.

It held no sway over any of the gods who, by his own words, would follow.

What did they want? Why take human form now?

Her blood chilled, Azul had one more thought:

That perhaps, for once, she shouldn't have fought for life.

XXXVII

THE WITCH WITH NO FACE

DAYS EARLIER

"I wonder what happens now," Nereida de Guzmán said. "Will you die along with your host, Witch?"

The Faceless Witch had no wish to find out.

Panic overtook her as she awoke in her own body. Painful gulps of air barely made it past her throat—the slits of her nose were of no use, darkness enveloped her for she had no eyes, claustrophobic silence formed an impenetrable wall around her thoughts for she had no ears. She only had that mouth, that toothless mouth, working to suck in more air, and her hands, wrinkled and attached to stick-thin arms, clawing at her throat as if they could force the air inside. This weak, sagging body that had begun its existence so many decades past. This hated bucket of flesh, good for nothing but burning with white-hot rage.

How dare De Guzmán? How dare De Anví? The rage spread through the tethers connecting her to so many of Cienpuentes's inhabitants, spreading from her consciousness like spiderwebs. A bounty of minds prime for her taking. Masks. Hah! Her power had nothing to do with masks, and everything to do with dreams.

To enter into a contract with the Faceless Witch was to ingest a dream. The mask was simply an added point of pride. She, who had no face, would hide the faces of those who granted her the use of their bodies.

But she did not need the mask.

Triumph surged in the dark, silent box of her mind when she found De Anví. She tasted revenge as clearly as the concoctions she was forced to drink to keep her body alive.

How sweet it would be to take control of him. To use his hands to squeeze the life out of his sweetheart, to see Nereida de Guzmán's face as the only person faithful to her committed the ultimate betrayal.

Shivers of anticipation racked the Witch's frail, old body.

And when De Guzmán lay dead in his hands, by his hands, then she'd allow her dreams to rot the count from the inside out. She'd allow him plenty of time to wish himself dead. Yes, this she would relish like nothing before.

But De Anví's mind wasn't so easy to overtake, even with the tether connecting them. While sliding into a willing host took no effort, trying to get into the count was like slamming into a brick wall. The Witch hadn't attempted the latter since she was a child and took her first body, and realized now it had been too long since De Anví last consumed one of her dreams. Punching into his mind was taking too much out of her—her eviction out of Sío de Guzmán had weakened her.

Later then, she decided, when she had recuperated some energy. Let them think they were free from retribution—their shock would make her revenge all the more delicious.

Instead, she searched for Isile Manzar. For there must be a reason Nereida de Guzmán had chosen this moment to kill her brother—if she'd wanted to, she could've slain him long ago—so something must have changed. She would pry the truth out of De Guzmán first. And since De Guzmán was staying at De Gracia's, and De Gracia himself had never partaken of her dreams, who better to gain access to the household than the marquess's dear artist friend?

Because the temptation to seek the Faceless Witch's dreams had proved too strong for him to resist. They all succumbed to it eventually— Sío de Guzmán, De Anví, Manzar.

Manzar put up a fight, much like De Anví had, but the remains of the Witch's dreams were too fresh, his mind too malleable. It was still a wall, but brittle. Breakable.

And then she was inside. Noises bloomed in her ears, smells filled her chest. She savored them, as she always did, before forcing the body's eyes open. Victory, so close to her fingers. They would pay. Oh, how they would pay.

The tethers snapped all at once.

The Witch stumbled. She reached for the tethers and found nothing.

The web of minds linked to hers—gone. The connection to her own body—gone. She was jostled to one side by the crowd, then to the other. She tried to find the connections again—nothing. Waves of dread rolled through her. She reached a wall and leaned against it, gasping.

Without tethers, how was she to go back to her body? To any other body? Even now, Isile Manzar's consciousness dug into the edge of her thoughts, trying to claw back into control. Sweat broke over her brow. This . . . this takeover was meant to be temporary.

Had her true body chosen this moment to die?

No, the Witch reasoned, pushing away from the wall and directing her steps toward De Gracia's house. This strange situation must be due to the energy she had spent trying to force her way into De Anví and then into Manzar. It did not mean the tethers were truly gone and she was stuck in this body forever. She only needed some rest. Simply that, rest.

She repeated this self-assurance with every step, as every sight, every sound, and even the taste of smoke intruded into her thoughts, her senses unnervingly unfiltered. There had always been a layer between her and the outside world, a screen filtering everything through her host's thoughts. That buffer was gone now. She had no way to know whether the objects around her evoked desire or hatred in her host, if the voices rising in the air were familiar or those of strangers. She had been walled off, Manzar's memories locked behind his stubborn mind.

The Witch was left clueless.

She didn't enjoy the feeling. She hated being disoriented as much as she hated her own body. Gods damn De Anví and De Guzmán. At least De Anví would pay no matter what—the poisoning had already been set in motion before she was locked away from her tethers. The Witch hoped that he still had some of her dreams at hand, for when the pain got too severe and he dipped into them as a means of escape, they would only feed the sickness and worsen his suffering.

The thought put a spring into her step. Soon she was knocking on De Gracia's front entrance and then was ushered into one of the parlors.

She hadn't been waiting for long—and that time had been well spent imagining all the ways she would torture the truth out of De Guzmán—when a commotion arose from the front entrance: a pounding against the door, the footman's feet, terse words she couldn't quite catch. Curiosity overwhelmed the simmering rage in her veins, and the Witch slipped out of the parlor in time to see Azul del Arroyo charging down the corridor toward the stairs. When the footman didn't follow, the Witch did.

Del Arroyo strode along the second-floor hallway, ignoring several doors and turning the corner. A door was open up ahead, and the Witch chanced a peek around the corner. Del Arroyo had entered one of the rooms, not bothering to close the door behind her. Soon, a ruckus followed. How intriguing. So late at night and Del Arroyo took no care to silence her actions, was unconcerned if servants became curious, lured by the noise.

Approaching the open door, the Witch could savor the mystery in every crash, every thud, every thump emanating from the room. Another door opened, slamming against the wall. Ah, definitely not her guest room, then, if there was a connecting room.

Yes, she thought once she had looked inside, this room was most definitely not Del Arroyo's—one did not need to lay waste to one's own property in the search for something. The girl had sought the key to the second room, the Witch assumed, glancing through the doorway. Paintings hung on the walls, and the furniture was beyond elegant. She waited for the tingle of recognition, but Manzar's thoughts remained closed to her. If he had ever set foot in this room, the Witch could not tell. And surely, this room must belong to De Gracia himself, so why had Del Arroyo wrecked it instead of simply asking to be shown in?

Hmm-hmm. How delicious, all these questions winding into a great knot for her to unravel. She stepped into the room and reached the second doorway.

Azul del Arroyo stood by a big desk, lost in thought as she glanced down at a series of finger-shaped things spread over a cloth.

Yes, how delicious.

"Breaking into your brother's rooms, Sirese Del Arroyo?" she asked. "How unsisterly."

Del Arroyo jumped and spun to face her. "What are you doing here?"

"What are those?" the Witch asked.

Del Arroyo's look dripped with disgust. "Fingers."

The Witch could wait no longer. She went to the desk and held one up. The surface was smooth and solid under pressure. "A sculpture? Painted clay?"

"Bone."

Gods. The Witch dropped the finger immediately. It thudded against the desk, then rolled away. She wiped her own digits on Isile's shirt and rushed to follow Del Arroyo out of De Gracia's room, around the corner, into another room. By the time the Witch caught up with her, Del Arroyo was kneeling by a trunk, searching its contents.

"It's not on me to judge De Gracia's interests," the Witch said, allowing the gathering shiver in her nape to run down between her shoulder blades, "but are you sure it's bone?"

"What are you doing here?" was the reply.

"Is this your room?" the Witch asked, then noticed dark smears on the girl's breeches and hands. "Have you been wounded? Your hands . . ."

Del Arroyo paused her search. "It's nothing."

Soon she had appropriated a dagger from whomever this room belonged to—De Guzmán, possibly, judging by the blue waistcoat now lying discarded beside the trunk—and returned to the hallway outside.

"I was waiting for De Gracia when I heard you come in," the Witch told her as they made their way back over to the stairs.

"Do you know where he is?"

The Witch laughed. "I wouldn't be waiting here if I knew where he was, yes?"

Down the stairs they went, trotting like eager children until the sight of two footmen stopped Del Arroyo in her tracks.

"Sireses, please come back to the parlor," one of them said. "The Marquess de Gracia will return shortly."

And so, into the parlor they went. The Witch reckoned Manzar must've visited a lot—the room was cozier than the one she and the count had occupied during their visit days ago. This parlor was for close friends and dear family, not annoying visitors.

"Sister, stay put until I return, I beg you." The footman's words took the Witch aback. "I will explain everything—you have nothing to fear. Isile, I will talk to you later as well."

Having said that, the man left, the *snick* of the door loud in the room.

"Did the footman lock us in? Why did he call you sister? Why would I want to talk to him?"

Del Arroyo appeared to find nothing strange in the situation. Instead, as if she were out for a stroll, she simply went for the window and opened it onto the patio.

"Have you no concern about all of this?" the Witch asked, going to her side.

"My brother is a necromancer," she said, and, truthfully, the Witch wasn't too aware of what happened next, other than she scrambled after Del Arroyo and asked her to explain herself.

"He kills people, then brings them back to life using their bones."

Euphoria exploded inside the Witch, so strong her fingers tingled with it.

As she watched Del Arroyo fight De Gracia's men, then accompanied her and her guard through Cienpé, the Witch's mind whirled and disentangled everything she had learned. Plans flowed, hopes swelled.

Getting out of the room Azul and the stranger had left her in for the night proved to be somewhat of a hurdle. She had no tethers, but concentrating hard, the Witch found she could reach those sleeping nearby. Not Del Arroyo or her guard, for they had never partaken of her dreams, but with some time and a lot of energy, she was able to slip into someone else.

The feeling was unendurable, like being in two places at the same time. Nausea rolled her stomachs, the link so weak both bodies soaked in shivers and cold sweat. If the connection were to snap, like the tether to her body had, would her consciousness die along with it, adrift like the understars in the Void? One body heaved, the other retched. The pressure was insurmountable, Manzar's mind using the opportunity to attempt to reclaim its territory.

The Witch wouldn't let it. Manzar's closeness to De Gracia was too convenient to lose. She fought back, and the connection between the bodies weakened further. Like a children's tug-of-war, the Witch managed to bring one body to her room while she wavered in and out of the other's mind. Drunkards' dreams were so much easier to control.

The window was opened carefully, if in small jerks rather than the smooth motion she'd have preferred, then the Witch forced Manzar's body to stand. She sent the drunken gent to pass out a street over and retreated fully into Manzar.

The trembling of her limbs abated, the racing pulse calmed. She felt Manzar hide in a corner and lick his wounds. *And stay there*, she added viciously, as if she could communicate with him. His body was young and strong, but so were any number of other bodies that had hosted her. His wasn't special—once her need was met, Manzar was welcome to have it back.

She ran through Cienpé back to De Gracia's residence. She wasn't sure how long it had been since Del Arroyo and her guard locked her in the small room, but a fast glance at the sky told her Luck and Wonder were well on their way down, dawn a couple of hours away.

De Gracia was home, seemingly worried and frantic, a calculating gleam in his eyes. The Witch recognized it easily. She'd have preferred him angry, for angry people made mistakes, but, alas, at least he was willing to talk.

She was ushered into the same parlor they had escaped from, the window still open, a slight nightly breeze rustling her hair.

De Gracia seated himself on the opposite settee.

"I have a proposal for you," the Witch wasted no time in telling him. "I know what you are, and I know who you want. You raise corpses; you are attempting to make your own body." She watched carefully for his reaction, but it was as if he were a corpse himself. "I would like a body of my own too." Giving voice to the hope that had carried her the whole night was like eating the most decadent dessert. She wanted more. "Raise a beautiful body for me, De Gracia." A body with no mind of its own to fight her off, young, powerful, completely hers—a rebirth. Shivers of pleasure ran along her back, and she closed her eyes briefly. "If you will do this for me, I will give you your sister's whereabouts."

"I don't haggle. I can find my sister on my own."

The Witch gave him a sardonic smile. "Ah, but it will take time, and she is intent on escaping you, isn't she? She's cunning, that young woman. She might give you a chase you could easily avoid."

De Gracia shrugged, unbothered. "That might be so, but in the end, I will still find her. Is that all?"

"Of course not. That was simply the initial lure. I feel we are similar, you and I, De Gracia."

"I doubt that."

"I'm willing to offer you something else in addition to Del Arroyo's whereabouts."

"And that would be?"

"It's obvious by now that Isile Manzar is not in command of this body. Give me another one, one that fits my wishes, and I will return this one to him. Otherwise, you will never speak to him again. And you hold him in great esteem, don't you?" the Witch added with a touch of malice.

"I hope you are bringing something else to the table, because that is no concern of mine."

The Witch fought the blink of shock and the floundering of her thoughts. Had the footman not appeared unsurprised at Manzar's appearance in the middle of the night? Had Manzar and De Gracia not been sitting so cozily when she and the count had visited? Were they not always together at gatherings? "You have no wish to see your darling free?"

De Gracia laughed, a surprisingly genuine sound. "Is that what you thought? That we are lovers?"

The Witch cursed herself. "I can see you are not, and that you hold no regard for your friends."

"Oh, I regard them well, and I shall miss his company and his words. But as I told you before, I do not haggle, whoever you are—and *who* are you?"

"You may know me as the Faceless Witch," she answered to earn herself some time, her thoughts chasing each other into never-ending loops as she tried to come up with a new plan.

"Ah yes, of course, the Conjurer of Dreams. I should have guessed," De Gracia said. "I'm sorry our meeting must be cut short, but I have other things to do."

"Wait," the Witch cried. "You want to make a body, don't you? Those fingers in your study are proof. But without a mind, it will simply be a puppet. What if I could help you give it thought? Dreams are made of thoughts, after all, and dreams are what I do best."

Or she hoped she still could. Was her gift of dreams dependent on her consciousness, her essence, or her body? If the latter, she was truly, royally screwed.

De Gracia snorted. "I don't want the body to *think*. I want it doing as I wish."

The Void take this man. What was it going to take to crack him? "Why not simply make a doll out of wood, then?" the Witch asked in irritation. "Why not keep using these bodies, like your footman?"

"Humans are inefficient, flawed. My aim is to construct the perfect conduit for my will. A body made from the best pieces of the best bones."

"Wouldn't that still make it a human—an inefficient—body?"

"Ah, but not all our bones are made of humanity."

The Witch leaned in, unable to hide her curiosity. "How so?"

De Gracia made a sweeping gesture. "Anchor seeps into the land, Conjurer of Dreams, and the land feeds us. We all carry vestiges of the gods within our bones—some more than others."

Sergado de Gracia wanted to make a god. The idea was too absurd. And yet, he must *know* it could be possible; otherwise, why continue with his plan? He must be able to sense which bones carried the gods' essences within. A new god, made from human bones. And what of the gods' powers? Would this new god have them too? Was that his true aim? To somehow become a god himself?

And why was he speaking so honestly about his plans?

It came to her notice, then, that two armed guards had slipped into the room behind her, and the answer to her last question became alarmingly obvious: She would not survive this meeting unless she thought fast. *Faster.*

"If this is your aim," she said, uncaring of the panic betrayed by her hurried words, "you should make sure it does have a mind you can take over, one that supersedes the gods' will, or they might decide to steal your body away from you. How else would you make sure it remains under your control?"

De Gracia frowned and the Witch thanked the gods, the moons, and every piece of Anchor she had ever seen at court.

"If we work together," she continued, "we could make these godly bodies—or simply the one, I do not care for godhood—and rid ourselves of our current shells. A body with the possibility of thought would be easy to claim for yourself, wouldn't it? Think of this, De Gracia. Think of the possibilities death and dreams could achieve if we work together." Offering her hand, she allowed a faint smile. "And I will even tell you where Azul del Arroyo has gone."

THE PRESENT

Two Blue Bastards waited outside Almanueva's main entrance, their shoulders leaning against their pikes in boredom. They barely paid the Witch any attention as she was ushered inside. De Gracia took his sweet time to receive her, and when he did, he simply asked if she had taken care of making the arrangements for their travel.

She had, the Witch assured him, somewhat peeved at De Gracia's lack of awe and gratitude that she had achieved so much in so little time. It had been two days since the marquess was escorted back to Almanueva and ordered to remain within. Didn't he realize how much effort went into arranging horses and carts with Manzar's thoughts hammering her mind the moment she stopped thinking for too long?

She had checked on her body, the pathetic carcass that used to host her mind. A body so useless the midwife would have thrown it into the river if not for her mother's pity. She had covered the remains with a sheet and paid her servants for months in advance, making sure they would not open the door if they wanted their blissful dreams to continue.

Now the Witch and De Gracia were ready to leave. De Gracia had told her they could not stay in Cienpuentes, not with Del Arroyo around, not until he found a way to nullify what she could do to his "studies." And while the Witch wasn't privy to what had transpired inside De Gracia's second house, she couldn't help but feel there had been more to the story than Del Arroyo and Virel Enjul calling the Blue Bastards on him.

But it didn't matter, did it? The Witch would figure it out. She would figure him out, same as she had figured out everyone else, and then she would know how to own him. The excitement and hope at the thought of a new body had faded into cautious optimism, but the curiosity—ah, that remained in full force.

Four horses were brought out—for her, De Gracia, his main

guard, and his treasure trove of bones—and then off they went, out in the streets and toward Bremón.

The blue tabards charged with keeping Sergado confined to Almanueva didn't blink when their four horses trotted out right under their noses. Didn't try to stop them, didn't even twitch.

The hairs at the back of her neck stood on end. Even Manzar faltered in his incessant hammering against her mind.

And then a new voice, a melody of a female voice that brought meadows and wildflowers and sunny skies and *gods* to mind, spoke within the Witch's head.

Well, well. What do we have here?

EPILOGUE

A FEW WEEKS EARLIER

"They've taken the younger Del Arroyo into custody," Ambassador Diagol de Mial, head of the Cienpuentes envoy from Sancia, announced in a somber voice.

Nereida wanted to snort—with the older sister gone, was the chit still *the younger*, or simply *the only remaining*?—but she couldn't forget the sight of Isadora del Arroyo crumbling into dirt right in front of her eyes.

A person—flesh and bone one moment, nothing but soil the next.

Impossible. And yet, Nereida had witnessed stranger things than this in Cienpuentes. She had witnessed her brother's voice speaking someone else's words. Someone who lived for the kind of scheming that only the Cienpuentes court could do justice to. Someone who thought of everyone else as puppets to play with.

Nereida went right to Sío's quarters after learning that the Witch had taken over his body, but he'd had the mask on. Sío wore the mask every time she'd tried to reach him. Nereida even tried to grab the thing more than once, and the Witch had laughed because the mask would not come off no matter how hard she pulled. She wrote letters and received no response. She went to the Temple and swore under the Lord Nightmare that she'd make the Witch's life a horrific dream unless she freed her brother. Yet how could she follow through when the Witch never left Sío alone?

"What will happen to Del Arroyo?" another member of their group asked with obvious concern.

"I don't know. It's customary for there to be an investigation in cases of strange deaths. They have called for an emissary."

The room gasped. Emissaries of the Lord Death—the god's will made human flesh, here to drag you from your hiding place to face death.

And the reason Nereida was here.

"I have a favor to ask," the Witch had said, and because Nereida knew first-hand that the Witch didn't believe in favors, it had taken all her composure not to laugh. It wouldn't do to laugh at the Witch. Not while she still wore Sío.

"I need you to go somewhere and look into something for me," the Witch continued.

"Go there yourself." Nereida had regretted the harsh words, but the Witch took them in stride.

"I would if I could. Alas! It needs to be you. You will go to Valanje with the court's ambassador."

"No."

The Witch's mouth—Sío's mouth—formed a mockery of a smile. "I thought you loved your brother, but if I was mistaken . . ."

And so here she was, supposed to investigate all matters of death. To somehow gain entry into the Order's archives and see what they knew, what the Lord Death had taught them. During the trip, Nereida had a lot of time to entertain theories about the Witch's sudden interest in death. Was she facing her own natural demise? After all, a witch who took over other people's bodies had to originate somewhere, didn't she? If Nereida took her sweet time in Valanje, might not the Witch save her the effort of forcing her out of Sío by dying herself?

But, no, what if by dying the Witch could never abandon her brother, taking his body forever? The thought was unendurable.

Then Isadora del Arroyo had crumbled to dust in front of her, and her sister had begged to go back to Sancia, back to Isadora's bones. The younger Del Arroyo had told Diagol that if he wanted to see Isadora again, he must help her get back to her bones.

Nereida had been raised in the northern countryside of Sancia, where strange tales abounded and superstition ran high. Put a piece of Anchor over your front door to stop ungodly things from entering your home. Spit three times near your well so it recognizes you and won't try to drag you into its depths. Place a doll of yourself under your bed so when the necromancer comes, he mistakes it for you.

The necromancer: a being who thrived on bones, who went from house to house, stealing them at night before they could be put to rest in the ossuaries. It was stuff of rumors, she'd thought, tales to make children behave.

Until Isadora had crumbled into dust and Azul del Arroyo had demanded to get to her bones.

All Nereida's resentment, all the impotence that came with being just another one of the Witch's tools, suddenly transformed into something new and bright and almost too powerful to hold in her heart: hope.

Hope that she might save her brother from the Witch's clutches, thwart the Witch's plans, and finally be able to sleep at night.

"I shall talk with Del Arroyo," she said, shocking the room even further, "and give her the news about the emissary."

And, Luck willing, Azul del Arroyo would be the answer to her hopes.

THE PRESENT

Azul dismounted the horse with the help of Sombra. He had ridden behind her, one arm around her waist the whole way since she was still so weak. Death had allowed her this personal time, as promised, but must not wish her to mysteriously disappear or fall off the horse and break her neck. Azul was glad Sombra had no trouble transferring his allegiances from Enjul to the Lord Death, and perhaps even to her. They had bonded, had they not, during that awful night—a faraway night that yet happened only a couple of days ago.

Nereida urged her, impatient, and Azul followed the woman over the slight rise of a hill until they were out of sight from her shadow and the horses. Here, about two hours away from Cienpuentes, the fields opened up, nearing harvest. Sancia, extending for leagues and leagues in front of them.

Azul knelt on a vibrant patch of tall grass and weeds, waiting expectantly.

But Nereida hesitated, unexpectedly reluctant. She stood, studying her boots intently. What a contrast with the person who had demanded to speak with Azul just an evening before.

It had been Nereida who led the blue tabards to her brother's house, refused to answer Azul's questions, and then tried to drag Azul out of her room. Death had forbidden it—as far as Nereida knew, he was still Emissary Enjul—because Azul needed to rest. His source of power needed to regain her strength, Azul amended wryly to herself. And so, two days of rest.

Now Nereida looked like she wished Azul had rested for weeks. Her hands roved her waist and hips, as if making sure she had gotten out of Cienpuentes with her pockets and purse safe.

Then, coming to a decision, Nereida sneaked a hand under her waistcoat and closed the distance between them to hand Azul a tiny bundle of cloth.

Azul took it from her shaking hands. "Are you certain?"

Nereida's eyes brightened, full of tears. "Yes." She inhaled deeply, closing her eyes to the morning sun. "Yes. The Lady Dream forgive me, but, yes, I am."

So much sorrow, so much despair, so much *hope* in those words. Azul swallowed thickly and averted her gaze, concentrating on opening the small packet of cloth. A baby tooth lay inside.

"You kept this?" she asked in wonder.

"A family tradition," Nereida said tersely.

Unease ran through Azul. "It's not . . . it's not yours, is it?"

"Gods, no!" exclaimed Nereida, taking a step back with disgust. "Ask no more. Do as you promised."

"As promised," Azul agreed. With the utmost care, she picked the tooth and pressed it into the ground. Allowing instinct to take over, she opened what she now knew was the Eye of Life, and life itself re-formed under her palm. Weeds shriveled around them; tall grass dried into drooping brown blades. Nereida took another step away. The ground beneath her gave up its life for the body emerging under Azul's care, and Azul was left with nothing but an ever-deepening ache that left no space for air or anything else. She barely felt the slicing in her soul, for the loss there was still so overwhelming, what was another chunk missing?

Then a young girl of about twelve lay naked on the ground, big green eyes blinking in confusion, long midnight black hair tangling on the dry dirt.

Nereida gasped and rushed forward, helped the girl sit up, and draped a cloak over her shoulders. The girl's hands fisted on Nereida's waistcoat, her mouth opening and closing a few times before words made it out of her throat: "Who— Nina?"

More tears welled in Nereida's eyes as she hugged the girl tightly. This time, they flowed down her cheeks.

"Edine."

CAST OF CHARACTERS

DEL ARROYO SIBLINGS

Azul: A young woman gifted with the ability to bring the dead back to life, constant companion of her eldest sister.

Isadora: Firstborn of Del Arroyo family, proud troublemaker and easy lover.

DE GUZMÁN SIBLINGS

Nereida: Will not start fights, but she will end them. The late queen's mistress at one point, she has amassed a reputation for being cool and aloof.

Sío: Only son in the family. Joined Cienpuentes's City Guard to make a name for himself apart from his sisters.

Edine: Youngest sibling, closest to Sío and on the lookout for her own fortune.

Iriana: Oldest sibling of the De Guzmán family and permanent resident in Cienpuentes.

VALANJE

Virel Enjul, Emissary of the Lord Death: Drafted into the Order at a young age, he has complete faith in his god and will stop at nothing to serve his will.

CIENPUENTES COURT (CAPITAL OF SANCIA)

Emiré, the Count de Anví: Second-in-command of the Royal Guard. Would rather be anywhere else.

Sergado, the Marquess de Gracia: Advanced into the title after the death of his sire. He's among a wave of believers in science over faith.

Regent de Fernán: Regent for the child king after the queen's untimely—and very coincidental, some might say—death.

Lendra, the Countess de Losa: A power player in the court of Cienpuentes, she's continuously searching for ways to curry favor.

Dío, the Marquess de Mavén: Head of the City Guard, natural enemies of the Royal Guard.

CIENPUENTES CITIZENS (CAPITAL OF SANCIA)

Miguel Esparza: Flirt, rogue, and lowly member of the City Guard. Unlikely friends with the Count de Anví.

The Faceless Witch: Can turn pieces of Anchor into dream pills. If you're desperate for an escape from your life, she has a proposition for you.

Isile Manzar: Artist and close friend of the Marquess de Gracia.

Sombra: Hired guard whose actions speak more than words.

ACKNOWLEDGMENTS

A book is not just a book but a compilation of everything that came before it—every finished story and every failed start, the inspirations and the dashed dreams, the successes and the dark times, and all the people who left a mark one way or another.

I'd like to thank my agent, Dorian Maffei, for always believing in me and my stories and answering my panicked emails without fail, my editors, Mara Delgado-Sánchez, for giving me a chance, and Vanessa Aguirre, for bringing my vision to the next level—I will never be thankful enough for your guidance. I also couldn't have done this without Rae Castor, Olivia Hofer, and Kathryn Ann Kingsley, who kept me going through the lowest of the lows. Your friendship means more than you'll ever know!

I would also like to thank Rati Mehrotra, Sophie Clark, and Keshe Chow for their wonderful support and advice; Lisa, Krista, and Trudie for always being there for me; Jasmine Skye, Genoveva Dimova, Emily Thiede, and Andrea Tang, for giving me such lovely blurbs; Dae, who gave me my first fan art ever; the 2025 debut group, for its invaluable support; 100, for being the best FC, but especially Fae, Simi, and Liren, the best talls one could ever game with; Cabin81, who were invaluable at the start of my writing career; Kerri Resnick and Kelly Chong, for the most amazing cover; Mom, for letting me read Dragonlance as a kid, and mi Abuelita Rosa, for watching *Star Trek* with me and introducing me to *Jane Eyre* and Victoria Holt.

Finally, I'd like to thank the Wednesday team for bringing my story to life in such an amazing manner—you all made my dream reality, and I couldn't appreciate you enough: Sara Goodman, Eileen Rothschild, Devan Norman, Merilee Croft, Cassie Gutman, Lena Shekhter, Brant Janeway, Alyssa Gammello, Alexis Neuville, and Esther de Araujo.

And thank you, dear reader, for welcoming this book into your life!